Scotth Hill
JessicA
Boat Building school
D0327203

TRUST FUND BOYS

BOOKS BY ROB BYRNES

The Night We Met
Trust Fund Boys

Published by Kensington

A Novel

ROB BYRNES

KENSINGTON BOOKS
www.kensingtonbooks.com

KENSINGTON BOOKS are published by

Kensington Publishing Corp.
850 Third Avenue
New York, NY 10022

Copyright © 2004 Rob Byrnes

All rights reserved. No part of this book may be reproduced in any form or by any means without the prior written consent of the publisher, excepting brief quotes used in reviews.

All Kensington titles, imprints, and distributed lines are available at special quantity discounts for bulk purchases for sales promotions, premiums, fund-raising, educational, or institutional use.

Special book excerpts or customized printings can also be created to fit specific needs. For details, write or phone the office of the Kensington special sales manager: Kensington Publishing Corp., 850 Third Avenue, New York, NY 10022, attn: Special Sales Department; phone 1-800-221-2647.

Kensington and the K logo are Reg. U.S. Pat. & TM Off.

Library of Congress Control Number: 2003112545

ISBN 0-7582-0544-9

First printing: June 2004

10 9 8 7 6 5 4 3 2 1

Printed in the United States of America

TRUST FUND BOYS

Brett Revere's Theory of Life, Part One:
The Sun Won't Necessarily Come Out Tomorrow

I never used to think of myself as the sort of man who takes life too seriously. After all, I'm an actor, which means that I have to face rejection and poverty every day, and you can't face rejection and poverty every day without an optimistic disposition and a healthy respect for macaroni and cheese. Four nights a week.

And I'm a New Yorker. Out of necessity, I have learned to thrive on chaos and to ad-lib my way through life, reasoning that when you have to take the N train to travel between home and civilization, you can't afford to be a creature of habit.

And I'm a gay man walking the tightrope of the aging process. The New York State Department of Motor Vehicles says I'm thirty-nine, but that's between me and the DMV. Not that I lie about my age as a rule; I just keep my mouth shut when people peg me for thirty-one. I have found that this works best, not only with ageist casting directors but also with ageist young gay men, and I'll ride it as long as I can keep this full head of blond hair. And *technically* I'm not lying; I'm just not indulging in full disclosure.

I may not make a practice of overtly lying, but the one thing I lie about—and consistently, at that—is my name. I doubt you'll be surprised to hear I wasn't christened "Brett Revere." I do have a real name, but if I liked it enough to tell you what it is, you wouldn't now know me as Brett Revere. And that's the way things are going to stay.

So there you have it: Brett Revere has created a lifestyle centered around survival, flexibility, and hopefulness.

Until one bad period, that is, when a depression slowly settled over me, despite an adulthood of resilience and optimism. Here's why.

It was early June and I still hadn't earned enough to qualify for health insurance through the Screen Actors Guild. Not that I was particularly concerned about health insurance, but there did seem to be an inordinately large number of struggling actors being run over by tour buses that year.

And I was living in a far-too-small converted one-bedroom apartment in Queens with a roommate whose very presence unsettled me.

And although I may not have *technically* lied about my age, I was coming to the realization that this career experiment might be drawing to a close. I had long ago accepted the fact that I'd never become the next Brad Pitt, but I was starting to imagine that I'll never even be the next Wilford Brimley. In fact, I saw my career trajectory running from stardom in a high school drama club production of *The Music Man* to extra work in *Cocoon XVII*.

Not to mention the fact that I hadn't had a date in four months. Let alone sleazy anonymous sex, which would have contented me in the meantime.

So there it was. I was just another supposedly indomitable New Yorker having a sudden crisis of confidence in my early middle age.

I should have been sitting on a therapist's couch, but I couldn't afford it, and in any event, I'd never been sold on the concept. Instead I was sitting in my talent manager's office, all vinyl and tile and stripped of anything resembling character. My manager is Alan Donovan, whom you might have heard of if you're in the business. Donovan Management mostly handles juvenile actors, but—as Alan has told me—few actors are more juvenile than me. And no, he doesn't mean that in a nice way; he means that in that catty way that only people who share both a personal and professional relationship can get away with.

Alan Donovan was not only my manager, he was a close friend. He had managed to create two different versions of himself, both residing in the same body but adhering to strict schedules. Sort of like a personality time-share.

The Alan who existed between 10:00 A.M. and 6:00 P.M. was all business, juggling phones, barking orders, and generally doing whatever he had to do to land work for his clients and, not incidentally, commissions for himself. The Alan who existed between 6:00 P.M. and 10:00 A.M. was a hard-partying, vodka-swilling lecher who may have been the funniest person I knew. I preferred Night Alan to Day Alan, although Night Alan would admittedly have been pretty useless as a manager. In fact, I doubt Night Alan could have earned a living wage, unless Absolut had openings for tasters. Fortunately, Night Alan had Day Alan to live off of.

I had stopped by his office to see if he had any work for me. As usual, he said he didn't.

But Emily, his ever-smiling assistant, piped up and said, "What about that show Walter Pomeroy is putting together? Wouldn't Brett be good in that?"

Alan pivoted in his chair and glowered at her. Emily shrunk back into her seat, not quite knowing what she had done wrong, but knowing that she *had* done wrong. That's usually the thing about the ever-smiling: they can smile twenty-four hours a day because the thought process seldom interferes.

"What's the job?" I asked.

Alan sighed. "If you're just looking for a survival job"—his way of telling me that his lead could help pay the rent, but that he wanted nothing to do with it—"I know a guy who's putting something together. Actually, I shouldn't even call it a survival job . . . it's more like a subway token job."

"I might be interested."

"It's non-Equity," he cautioned, shooting yet another nasty look at Emily, who, I feared, was not long for Donovan Management. "And if you decide to do it, I don't want to know about it."

"Fair enough."

He told me that his acquaintance was casting for roles in a new, gay version of the maudlin Broadway musical *Annie.* It was called *Andy,* and—as you might suspect—it was supposed to be hilariously campy . . . "supposed to" being the operative phrase. Even without Alan's prompting, I was certain it would also be in complete violation of all applicable U.S. and foreign copyright laws. If I knew my fly-by-night Off-Off-Off-Broadway theater, I would bet that the writer and producer—one and the same, no doubt—was planning on running the play to sell-out audiences in some West Village church basement for as long as possible until the *Annie* folks heard about it. At which point, he would begin preproduction on his gender-bending version of *Evita.*

"*Andy*?" I was not happy. Yes, I wanted work. But not *this* work. "Don't you have any television work? Industrials? Anything? Can't you get *Law and Order* to cast me as a dead body again?"

"This is the only thing I know about that's right for you. If you don't want to go, don't go. It doesn't matter to me. But if you want to work . . ."

"What's it pay?"

"I don't know, but I'd bet it pays virtually nothing." He paused and ran one hand over his quickly vanishing hairline. "Now, in fairness to you, I should point out that *Andy* could be a cult hit. Maybe then it'll go legit. Who knows? It could be great exposure. But until then, well . . . I'm not going to ruin my name by sending clients to non-Equity auditions, so let's just keep this discussion here in the office. Okay? Remember: I know nothing about it, and I don't want to know about it." He glanced at his watch. "I've got to make a few calls. Call me later and tell me how the audition went."

"So you *do* want to know . . ."

"As a friend, Brett. Not as your manager." He leaned forward, stretching his arms across his desk. "Listen, Brett, can I level with you?"

"As friend or manager?"

"Both." He drew a deep breath. "Brett, a few years ago you were a hot property. I had no problem getting you work. But things are different these days. I don't get many calls for fortyish white males."

"I can still play younger."

"Yeah, for maybe fifteen more minutes. Listen, I really want things to work out for you, but I think you might want to start reevaluating your career." I started to protest, but he raised a hand to silence me. "I'm only thinking of you. Hey, it doesn't cost me anything to keep your eight-by-tens on file, so this isn't a matter of my own self-interest."

With that, Day Alan picked up the phone and swiveled away from me. I was dismissed. Maybe I'd call Night Alan later, to remind myself why I enjoyed his company.

The auditions were being held in the back room of a bar just off Christopher Street. I was early, so I sat on a stool in the front section, nursing a club soda while I waited. A handful of other *Andy* hopefuls sat on nearby stools with their own club sodas. We all avoided eye contact.

Well . . . all except for one man, who, after throwing the front door open and washing the dusty room with fading afternoon sunlight, announced, "You might as well go home, 'cause Joey Takashimi is in the house and none of you tired old things stand a chance. I *am* Andy!"

The rest of us silently looked at him as he sashayed into the room, sweeping the door closed behind him. He was tall—well over six feet in height—but unmistakably of Japanese origin, despite the platinum blonde hair. And as if the contrasts between skin tone, hair color, height, and facial features weren't enough, he managed to find himself an outfit that almost diverted attention from them: a sparkling orange-and-yellow jumpsuit, with a single beaded white lapel along the left neckline.

"Didn't you hear me? I said you can all go home. Unless you're just looking to be an orphan." He spotted one of the hopefuls leaning against a wall and homed in on his fading hairline. "Or my Daddy Warbucks."

Joey Takashimi made a move to stroke Daddy Warbucks's wide forehead, but his hand was brushed away.

"Sorrrrry!" he mock-pouted. "But you're *way* too old to be an orphan, honey."

I was quite confident that every other man in that room was gay, and that all of us were well-versed in the art of Urban Gay Verbal Warfare, but, collectively, we all looked away. Even Daddy Warbucks averted his gaze from the new arrival. Sometimes it's just not worth it.

For his part, Joey Takashimi grabbed one of the giveaway nightlife magazines from a pile near the door and stretched out at a table, apparently realizing that he would not be able to provoke any preaudition cat fights. Once again, the room fell into a gloomy silence.

I looked at the half-dozen waiting men and, with the exception of Joey Takashimi, saw my face in theirs. We were a roomful of actors sitting precariously on the edge of total failure, scraping by as busboys and temps and living paycheck to paycheck while we watched the clock tick away on our dreams. No one comes to New York City hoping and dreaming one day to star in a rogue gay parody of *Annie*, but there we were.

Once upon a time, some twenty years earlier, I had been filled with hope. Starring roles in high school productions, good reviews in community theater, an encouraging acting coach who had once had a prominent supporting role on a television series before retiring to Albany to raise her family . . . all of this, and still not twenty.

So, with heady dreams, I packed my bags, hopped a train, and moved to New York. Back then, I knew exactly how my life would turn out: acting lessons; some commercial work; industrials; Off-Broadway. Along the way, I'd meet someone who would serve as my mentor. I'd make friends who would encourage me as their careers began to gain steam. Eventually, with some hard work, luck, and help from my friends, I'd make it. Broadway. Television. Major motion pictures.

I knew it wouldn't be easy. I just didn't know it would be quite this hard. And I didn't know that I would end up twenty years later waiting to audition for *Andy*. On that, I think I could speak for the entire room, with the possible exception of Joey Takashimi.

Maybe Alan Donovan was right. Maybe it was time to start re-evaluating things.

The door to the back room opened, and a tired-looking man—probably no older than me, but looking decades worse for the wear—stepped out.

"You're all here for the *Andy* auditions?" he asked. We nodded.

"You brought your resumes and eight-by-tens?" We nodded.

"Then follow me." He walked into the back room, and we followed in a depressed, resigned silence.

I was the second-to-last person to enter the room. Behind me, Joey Takashimi whispered in my ear. "It's all over, blondie. You might as well go home." Again, I ignored him.

The tired-looking man introduced himself. "I'm Walter Pomeroy, and I'm the hyphenate of the show."

"The what?" asked one hopeful.

"The hyphenate. I'm the writer-producer-director of *Andy*. Oh, and I'm also the accompanist." We laughed on cue. "Let me give you a little background about the play before I audition you. How many of you are familiar with the musical *Annie*?" All hands went up. "Okay, then, I don't have to review the plot. *Andy* is a gay parody of that show. It's a little raunchy . . . a little risqué . . . but I think it will be a lot of fun. Before we start, is anyone uncomfortable with the premise?"

We were all silent, not expressing that, yes, we *were* uncomfortable, dammit! Our acting careers were supposed to amount to so much more than this!

Walter continued. "Here's the concept: instead of orphans in an orphanage, Andy and his pals are young street hustlers working for a pimp named Hannigan. Daddy Warbucks is now called 'Sugar Daddy Warbucks,' and he picks Andy up one night. Andy thinks everything's gonna be cool with his life, but Hannigan gets wind of his situation and decides to scam Sugar Daddy by having his brother and his brother's drag queen boyfriend pretend to be Andy's parents. You follow?"

We all nodded. We would have to be brain-dead not to follow this idiotic reworking of the story.

"Good. Now, before I hear you sing, there are a few more things you should know. First, this is a non-Equity production." Duh. "Second, it doesn't pay much—in fact, it pays less than not much—but I think it'll draw huge crowds and offer those of you with talent some exposure."

We collectively murmured an agreement of mutually acknowledged defeat. What he was saying was: if you're lucky, you'll make twenty bucks a week and maybe get noticed by some other hopeful actors who will forever use you as a yardstick to measure how their careers don't suck, by comparison.

"So now, if you're ready, let's start. Hand your head shots and resumes forward, please." A shuffling filled the quiet room as the photos were handed forward, and when we were finished he asked, "Does everyone know the song, 'Tomorrow'?"

We nodded in unison.

Walter sat at the battered upright.

"Okay, then." He glanced at the pile of resumes. "Rick Atkins?"

Daddy Warbucks stepped forward. "That's me."

"Ready?" The actor nodded, and Walter began to play.

In a shaky baritone, he began to sing: "The sun'll come out tomorrow, bet your bottom dollar that tomorrow, there'll be sun. . . ."

And so it went. Five up, five down, and nothing to write *Star Search* about. Then it was my turn, which was also nothing to write *Star Search* about, although—unlike some of the other hopefuls—I managed to hold the tune.

"Joey Takashimi?"

He bounced up to the front of the room and announced, "Your Andy has arrived!"

Walter looked him over. "Hmm. Alternative casting. I like the concept."

Joey Takashimi nodded smugly. "Ready when you are, Walter."

The accompaniment began and Joey Takashimi threw himself into the song. In this smallish room, there was no balcony or back row to play to, so he had apparently decided to play to the folks out on Christopher Street. Taking his diva turn, he attacked the song and made it his own, forcing Walter—a functional and unexceptional pianist—to struggle behind him as he drew out the well-worn lyrics and found new octaves to showcase his voice.

Now, I most certainly did not want to be cast as Andy. In fact, I was deeply ambivalent about even being in this dingy back room auditioning for this low-rent production. But as it became apparent that Joey Takashimi *would* be cast as Andy and that the show would then become all about Joey Takashimi, I dearly hoped that Walter Pomeroy would forget he had ever heard my name. Alan Donovan could drop me as a client; I could live with that. I could live with the knowledge that I'd be temping for the rest of my life. Anything, I prayed, but being trapped in a show with Joey Takashimi as he sucked the life out of everything around him.

". . . You're always a daaaaaaaaaaaaay . . . aaaaaaaa-waaaaaaaaaaaaay!"

Then the song was mercifully over, and Walter clapped delightedly as Joey Takashimi grinned smugly. I stole glances to my right and left, and saw that my fellow hopefuls were obviously sharing my thoughts.

"Thank you," said Walter, speaking to Joey but meaning to include the rest of us. "You'll be hearing from me."

And so we did. The next day, Walter left a message on my answering machine. I was cast as an orphan-cum-hustler, if I wanted it. Alan made some discreet inquiries and learned, as I expected, that Joey Takashimi would play Andy. Oh, and Daddy Warbucks—er, Rick Atkins—was cast as "Sugar Daddy Warbucks." Sometimes the acting career works that way, and it's all about your hairline.

I was told to report back to the bar between three and four that afternoon to pick up a copy of the script. There, I ran into Rick Atkins.

"Congratulations," I told him.

"You, too."

"Oh, I'm just playing a hustler. With Joey around, no one's even going to notice me."

"How do you think *I* feel?" he asked. "I have to pretend I *like* that asshole. I have to pretend that I want to be his sugar daddy. And all I really want to do is snap his neck." He sighed. "I never dreamed my career would come to this."

There you have it. We were all in the same hopeless boat together—the SS *Takashimi*—getting seasick as we prepared to watch our careers sail off the edge of the Earth.

Soon Walter arrived and began distributing the scripts.

"You'll notice that there's not a lot of dialogue," he announced. "This production is all about the songs. It's all about the spectacle! Remember that, boys."

I leafed through the pages, glancing at the reworked lyrics sitting bare on the page, without their music. It was just as well, I thought. I was hardly a prodigy, but after listening to my fellow cast members audition I was quite certain that none of them could read music.

"Oh, this is just in *such* bad taste," muttered Rick, who was standing next to me. "I mean, I never dreamed someone could make me long for the original *Annie,* but . . ."

I closed my script and said, "I don't think I can read this in public. I feel dirty."

"The things we'll do for a few bucks and an audience, huh?"

"We have sunk to new lows."

Script in hand, I ran into Joey Takashimi on my way out of the bar. He was wearing something approximating a kimono flecked with blue rhinestones over a T-shirt and jeans.

"Leaving so soon?" he asked.

I paused in the doorway, considering an appropriate response.

"Congratulations," I finally said. "I think you've got the showcase you deserve."

* * *

Despite my better judgment, I scanned the script as a subway train carried me slowly toward midtown, where I was to meet up with Night Alan at Bar 51, our regular haunt on West Fifty-first Street in Hell's Kitchen. That's why I had a full head of steam when I finally made my entrance into the bar.

"I think I'm going to kill myself," I said, cornering Alan at the end of the bar.

"Have a drink first." He called out to the bartender. "Jason, Brett needs his medication." That accomplished, he turned back to me. "Okay, so why are you going to kill yourself? And should I care? Am I in your will?"

As Alan watched, I leafed through the script until I found an especially egregious song lyric. "Do they really expect me to sing a song called 'It's a Hard Cock Life'?"

"Let me see that." He took the script from my hand and set it on the bar, using a candle to help illuminate the words on the page. "Well . . . hmm . . . Okay, it's not Shakespeare, but it's a job."

"A humiliating job."

"You're an actor. Get used to it."

I thought about that for a moment. "Maybe this is God's way of saying that I shouldn't be an actor."

Alan turned and looked me squarely in the eye. "Brett, as I told you before, you've got some thinking to do. You know I like you. You're a good friend. But you're not generating any income for either of us. I'm telling you this as a manager *and* a friend: make a plan. If you want to be an actor, then buckle down and work at it. Fight the odds. Fight for those handful of calls I get for nonethnic male actors of a certain age. Get a manicure and become a hand model. Be creative." He paused. "But if you don't think you can cut it, then tuck and roll. Find something else to pay the bills."

"You must have something else you can send me on . . ."

"You want to hand out fliers in Times Square for the Big Apple Circus? I can get you that."

"I meant acting jobs."

"Nothing." Bartender Jason handed me my drink as Alan took a sip of his own before continuing. "You need a plan, Brett. Again, I'm telling you this as a friend. You need to figure out what you're going to do with the rest of your life. So far, you've managed to eke out a living between the acting jobs and the temp jobs, but you're not getting any younger."

"I can play late twenties," I said. "I'm still marketable."

He rolled his eyes. "Late twenties?"

"Thirtyish."

"With an emphasis on the 'ish.'" Day Alan—he had not quite morphed into Night Alan—took another sip, ignoring my reddening face. "Brett, make a plan."

"All right," I said, feeling a bit surly. "I'll think about it."

We sat quietly for a few more minutes, checking out the crowd, until he suddenly brightened and turned to me. "I almost forgot! I have a check for you."

"Excellent. And here you're telling me I don't generate any income."

He handed me the envelope. "It's for eighty-two dollars. Don't spend it all in one place."

I pocketed the check, my first in two months. Residuals from a long-forgotten and little-seen commercial I had filmed for a Toyota dealership in Nassau County years earlier that every now and then was recycled. Yes, indeed, things were looking up. Only a thousand more checks like this in a single calendar year and I could call myself a success.

Yeah, I needed a plan.

I returned home several hours later, feeling no happier despite several drinks and my eighty-two dollar check, which I had deposited at an ATM before catching the N train to Astoria, Queens. Clutching the *Andy* script in my hand, I uneasily climbed up the rickety stairs to the fourth floor, then let myself into the apartment.

The living room was dark, and I breathed a sigh of relief. That meant that Quentin King, my roommate, was either already in bed or spending the night at his girlfriend's apartment.

Like most roommates, everywhere in the world, Quentin King was a necessary evil; necessary because I needed him to help pay the rent, evil because, well, there was just something very wrong about him. He wasn't merely irritating, the way many roommates can be. There was something . . . creepy about him, something unsettling about the way he silently lurked around the apartment. And for a straight guy, he seemed to have an inordinate interest in my sex life, although I hadn't had much to tell him about in recent months. Still, if I didn't like discussing the intimate details, when they happened, with Alan, I *certainly* didn't like being subjected to an in-depth interrogation from Quentin.

But he paid the rent on time, and, in a close call, I decided that I needed that more than I wanted him out of my life.

I walked across the warped, squeaking, battered floorboards as quietly as possible—if Quentin was home, I didn't want to wake him—and settled onto the lumpy couch, flicking on a lamp on the end table. Then, starting on the first page, I began to read through the script for *Andy*.

I had hoped that "It's a Hard Cock Life" was as bad as things were going to get, but my hope was misplaced. Each page revealed fresh horrors, appalling new lows in the history of bad theater. I tried, but I couldn't manage to find anything amusing about it. And what made my reading experience even worse was the knowledge that, in four short weeks, a bunch of drunken gay men would be hooting and hollering over the same material I found so repulsive, in the process making Joey Takashimi a minor celebrity. I could only hope that the *Annie* people found out about Walter Pomeroy's bootleg bastardization and shut it down real quick.

A plan. I needed a plan. I shut off the light and lay on the couch, listening to the elevated subway train clattering down its tracks a few blocks away as I gathered my thoughts. I was loathe to admit to myself that my acting career had never taken off and never would, but, well . . . I had a lot to loathe these days.

I awoke, still on the couch, to the sounds of Quentin banging around in the kitchen. I spotted his gangly, pale body out of the corner of my eye and briefly considered feigning sleep until he was gone, but the couch was getting uncomfortable, I had to empty my bladder, and I knew I couldn't avoid him forever.

"You were out late," he said, holding a cereal bowl as he walked into the living room the moment he saw me stirring. "Get laid?"

"No. I just went out for drinks. What time is it?"

"Six-forty-five. So if you didn't get laid, are you gonna masturbate today?"

"I don't see how that's any of your business." I stiffly lifted my upper body into a seated position. "And how do you know that I haven't taken a vow of chastity?"

"You don't seem like the chaste type," he said. "Well . . . not on purpose, at least." He held his bowl out to me. "Froot Loops?"

Oh, sure, like I was going to eat out of his bowl, let alone off of his spoon. I wiped sleep from my eyes and said, "No, thanks."

"Suit yourself." He swallowed a spoonful of cereal then said, "I read your script. Very funny stuff."

"You what?" I looked around and didn't see the script.

"I read that script. It was laying on the floor next to you, and you were sleeping, so I figured you wouldn't mind."

"Where is it now?"

"In my bedroom. I woke up about three and couldn't get back to sleep, so I decided to do some reading. Anyway, like I said, it was wicked funny."

If anything validated my feelings about *Andy*, it was *that* comment. I got to my feet and was about to set off for his bedroom when he added:

"It made me want to jerk off."

I stopped and turned to face him. I hoped the disgust I felt showed on my face.

"Would you mind getting it for me?"

"Help yourself, dude. You know where my room is."

"Quentin . . ."

He set the bowl down on a bookshelf, where I knew it would remain until I picked it up, and, with a sigh, walked to his bedroom. A few seconds later, he returned, holding the script. When he handed it to me, I inspected it and was elated to discover that my worst fears had not been realized.

"So what part are you playing? Andy? Man, you'd be great as Andy!"

"No, I'm an orphan. Er . . . a hustler. Whatever."

"Hey, it's a role, right? You don't get many of them lately." For a brief moment, he sounded frighteningly like Alan Donovan.

"Yeah," I agreed somberly. "It's a role."

"Hey, are you the hustler that gets humped by Sandy?"

Ugh. I was *so* over this conversation. "No, Quentin. I escaped that fate. Now, if you don't mind, I want to jump in the shower. I'm temping at Citigroup Center today."

"You got it."

I went to my room, finally stripping off the previous day's clothes. I felt my thickening stomach and realized that I hadn't been to a gym in months, which was a situation I would have to correct as soon as I made some money. Not that that was a sure thing.

Wrapping a towel around my waist, I walked to the bathroom, which—between me and my roommate—was overrun with every conceivable toiletry product. I closed the door firmly behind me, taking care to make sure the often faulty latch caught, turned on the water, and stepped into the shower.

As the hot water cascaded over my body—the body which was beginning to betray me, going soft as my thirties drew to an end—my thoughts again returned to formulating a plan. I even began thinking of it not as "a plan," but The Plan. Anyone could have a plan; I'd probably had hundreds myself at various points of my life. The Plan, however, was a life-changing course of action. It was the personal Big Bang, the reinvention of self.

And as each minute passed, it became more imperative that I escape plays like *Andy,* abject poverty, and Quentin. In my head, I calculated how much money I would have to earn to lead a roommate-free, somewhat tolerable life. More than eighty-two dollars, certainly. Not that the calculation was worth much without a way to earn it, but, well . . . The Plan could be built around the bottom line.

Seven minutes later I turned the water off, stepped from the shower, and dried myself off. The mirror above the sink was steamed over, and I wiped a crescent-shaped patch clear with my towel. I was reaching for my hair gel when I thought I caught a flicker of movement in the hazy reflection.

I turned and saw that the bathroom door was ajar.

"Quentin," I called out, wrapping the towel tightly around my waist. "Did you need the bathroom?"

His face appeared too quickly at the door. "No, dude. Why?" He looked at the door, then said, "Oh, you know this door. Sometimes it swings open."

"Yeah, I know."

"I'll close it for you. Give you some privacy." With that, he closed the door until I heard the latch catch. Of course, I had heard the latch catch when I came in.

I finished my bathroom routine, then returned to my tiny bedroom and dressed. Realizing that I had my first rehearsal that evening—and therefore a late night ahead of me—I also took the time to pick out clothes for the following day, gently laying them across the bed to minimize the wrinkling. I was proud of myself; it wasn't quite the creation of The Plan, but, by thinking ahead, I was already starting to break my routine.

It was only then, when I was not only ready to face the outside world but also to do so the following day, I emerged to find Quentin sprawled on the couch, rereading the *Andy* script and laughing out loud at the inanity.

"This is a howl," he said when he saw me. "I can't wait to see it."

"You're going to have to be patient," I said, taking the script from his hands. "It won't open for four weeks."

"Dude, I don't know if I can wait four weeks to see Sandy humping that hustler." He doubled over with laughter. "You gay boys know how to put on a show!"

"I'm glad one of us is enjoying this." I checked myself out in the mirror and adjusted my collar. "Okay, then, I'm off to work."

"No problemo. And in case you're wondering, I'm staying in tonight. Joanne's got her period."

More information I really didn't need.

"Uh, okay. Anyway, I have a rehearsal after work, so don't wait up."

"Hey, I don't mind waiting up."

I smiled weakly. "Well, okay, then. I'll probably see you tonight. I suppose."

I couldn't devise The Plan fast enough.

I thought about The Plan on the N train to Manhattan, throughout my day of mundane filing, and on the 6 train to the East Village after work. Then I thought about it some more on my fifteen-minute walk across town to the West Village. Now, I'm a realist, and I know that there are many people in the world whose lives are a lot tougher than mine. But still, everywhere I looked were signs of affluence. Expensive townhouses, exclusive clubs, four-star restaurants, limousines, passersby decked out in thousands of dollars' worth of Prada and Armani—while I was making do with faded, fraying Banana Republic. There was so much money in this city, and none of it was mine. I was a Have Not, and I was beginning to resent that. I wanted to be a Have.

And dammit, I had paid my dues. I didn't move to New York two decades earlier thinking that the world owed me. I worked. I did trade shows and industrials and Toyota commercials and modeling and voice-overs and five-and-unders, and when I wasn't trying to build an acting career, I was temping. Was it too much to ask that all that hard work and years of scraping by would culminate in more than a role as a singing hustler in a completely illegitimate backroom production of *Andy*?

By the time I reached the entrance to the bar, I had completely tortured myself with feelings of hopelessness and worthlessness. And those feelings only deepened when I opened the door and was face-to-face with Joey Takashimi and a huge drag queen.

"So you didn't back out," Joey said, sneering. "I had you pegged as one of those guys who never comes back."

"I'm a working actor," I replied, with a bit of exaggeration. "I don't walk out on a job."

"This," he said, motioning to the drag queen, "is the divine Miss Iris Whiskey. She's going to be playing Rooster Hannigan's boyfriend." When I didn't reply, instead merely standing there in disbelief, he added, "Rooster's drag queen boyfriend, who pretends to be Andy's mother to scam Sugar Daddy Warbucks."

"I know, I know," I heard myself say. But I wasn't focused on what I was saying; I was focused on figuring out how the hell I was going to get myself out of the cast without burning any bridges.

Joey continued. "I think we've lost him, Iris. Anyway, his name is Brent something."

"No, it's *Brett* something," I said, trying to snap out of my funk. "Brett Revere."

"Of course," said Joey, and, dropping his voice an octave, hammily intoned, "Brett Revere. An actorly name for an actorly actor."

"Pleased to make your acquaintance," said Miss Iris Whiskey, extending a gloved hand to me.

"My . . . uh . . . my pleasure," I stammered.

I felt the stale air move as the door opened behind me. Joey looked over my shoulder and said, "And this is Ron something."

"Rick," said the actor who would soon be transformed into Sugar Daddy Warbucks.

"Right. Rick. Rick, this is Miss Iris Whiskey. She's playing Rooster's boyfriend. Iris, I bet you can't guess who Rick will be playing." With that, he exaggeratedly rubbed his hair.

The drag queen clapped her hands together with delight. "Sugar Daddy! Come to mama!" she shouted, crushing him in her flabby arms as she pulled him into her ample bosom. Rick looked to me, silently pleading for help before she squeezed all the oxygen out of his body.

Fortunately, I didn't have to react. Miss Iris let him out of her grasp before he turned blue, and, with the shortest of good-bye waves, Rick grabbed my arm and hustled me away from them.

"Every time you think it can't get any worse . . ." he said.

"I know. I'm really, really scared about what comes next."

And I should have been, because what came next was this: we ran through a few of the songs—including the dreaded "It's a Hard Cock Life"—and then Walter clapped his hands to get everyone's attention.

"Wonderful, people! Simply wonderful! This show is going to be *fabulous*! For the next scene, though, I need a volunteer from the hustlers."

No one volunteered. In fact, we all cast our eyes to the floor and tried to disappear.

Then I heard Joey Takashimi pipe up. "What about"—and here he again dropped his voice an octave—"Brett Revere?"

"Excellent choice," said Walter, before scanning the row of hustlers and saying, "Er . . . which one of you is Brett Revere?"

Resigned, I took a step forward.

"Of course," said Walter. "Yes! Brett! Of course!" He strode up to me and, placing one hand on each of my shoulders, said, "I have a featured role for you that will bring down the house!"

I remained silent.

"You, Brett, will be the hustler who gets humped by . . ."

I didn't even stay for the end of the sentence.

* * *

Okay. I still needed The Plan. Yes, it was a good plan to not get humped by Sandy, but it still wasn't The Plan. And as I stood at the Astor Place station waiting for a 6 train to take me to an N train to take me home, I realized that walking out on *Andy* wasn't going to help my career.

I thought. How do people make money? They make money by utilizing their talents. What are Brett Revere's talents? Acting. Well, acting is *allegedly* one of my talents.

And filing is the other.

I had every right to feel hopeless. More so when I considered that I was about to take a 6 to an N to spend an evening at home with creepy Quentin King, who no doubt had a day's worth of masturbation and menstruation stories saved up for me.

"I saw the actor who's playing Sandy. You should have let him hump you."

I turned and saw Rick Atkins standing next to me, smiling slyly.

"What are you doing here?" I asked, shocked out of my introspective sulk.

"Going home. Walter canceled rehearsal after you flounced out of there. Joey volunteered to get humped, and that was that."

"Joey *is* a hump."

"No argument from me." He paused, then, seeing the unhappiness on my face, asked, "Is everything all right?"

"If you're wondering about the play, don't. I'm glad to be out of there. But it's just sort of been a bad couple of months."

"Boyfriend problems?"

"No boyfriend, no problems."

"Sorry. I shouldn't ask."

"No, that's all right. It's a bit of a career crisis, a bit of a cash flow crisis. You know, the age-old worries of the struggling artist."

"Oh, yeah," he said. "I know."

We stopped talking as a train rattled into the station, its brakes squealing their eardrum-piercing screech. When the doors whooshed open, we boarded.

"So where are you heading?" he asked, as the train pulled away from the station.

"Fifty-ninth, to grab a train to Queens. You?"

"Fifty-ninth, to go home."

"Oh," I said, "you're an east side boy. And here I thought you were another impoverished actor. It must be nice to be rich."

He smiled. "Far from rich. But my lover, well, that's another story. And I'm happy to enjoy it while he's got it and is willing to share."

"Good philosophy."

We rode a few more stops in silence, until he said, "I think I'm going out for a drink. Care to join me?"

"This isn't a proposition, is it?" I only half-joked. Rick Atkins really wasn't my type, but, well . . . it *had* been four months.

He smiled. "Hey, remember, I've got a rich boyfriend. I wouldn't risk throwing that away on a destitute actor who won't even let a dog hump him."

I laughed, and laughed again when I noticed the couple across the aisle from us unconvincingly pretending not to hear us discussing what could easily be interpreted as bestiality.

"I don't know about a drink," I said finally. "I mean, yes, I could use one. But I've had such a long day and I really should get home." As soon as those words came out of my mouth, I remembered what awaited me at home, and I scrambled to take them back. "On the other hand, maybe I *should* go out for a few."

"Great. How does the Penthouse sound?"

I recoiled.

"The Penthouse? Isn't that a bar for old guys?"

"No," he insisted. "I mean, yeah, the crowd's a bit older, but they get a lot of cute guys. Young professional types."

"Yeah. Hustlers looking for old guys."

"No. Guys like me. Except with hair. The Penthouse can really be a lot of fun. I think you'd like it."

"I don't know," I said, still unconvinced. "I've always heard that it was like a private club for old gay guys with money, and the only people there under forty are auditioning for the role of kept boy. I'm not sure someone like me would fit in."

He mulled that over for a moment before saying, "Well, you're an actor, right?"

"Yeah."

"Then act. Make yourself fit in." He paused, mentally fleshing out his thoughts before continuing. "Look at it this way: until half an hour ago, you were playing the role of a street hustler. Now you're going to be playing a different role. Tonight you're not Brett Revere, struggling artist; tonight you're Brett Revere, trust fund baby! You've already got the name for it, so run with it for a night. What can you lose?"

He was right. There was nothing to lose. I had just walked out of the cast of a bad play, creepy Quentin was waiting at home, and I had forty dollars in my pocket and another eighty-two dollars waiting to clear at the bank.

And until I formulated The Plan, I was a free man.

"Am I dressed all right?" I asked, glancing down at my slightly shabby clothing. "This is a suit-and-tie crowd, right?"

"Mostly. But you're dressed fine. Very preppy. They like that there."

"Okay, then," I said, as the train approached the Fifty-ninth Street station. "Let's go."

Brett Revere's Theory of Life, Part Two:
Plans Are Good . . . Trust Funds Are Better

The Penthouse was located in the low East Sixties, a few buildings off Second Avenue. I followed Rick through the front door of what I first thought was a residential brownstone until he opened the interior door and the commingled conversation and laughter of a hundred male voices spilled out into the vestibule.

And that's how, minutes after nine o'clock on a warm Thursday evening in June, Brett Revere, Trust Fund Baby, made his debut at the Penthouse, following Rick Atkins dutifully as he snaked his way through the crowd to a long, polished bar.

I took a look around the room while Rick ordered drinks. The rumors were true: the patrons *were* on the older side, and many of them were still in suits, not yet having had quite enough cocktails to steel them for home. However, as Rick had promised, there were enough young men not readily identifiable as prostitutes to give the place a bit of variety.

And older or younger, this was a crowd that drank . . . and appeared to drink from the top shelf. There were no empty glasses in those manicured hands. Better yet, I saw no evidence of that bane of my existence, the plastic water bottles so prevalent among the Chelsea set that advertised, on a case-by-case basis, either the health-consciousness or intended drug-indulgence of their bearers. Although neither the health obsession nor the Ecstasy addiction interested me all that much, those damned water bottles still had a way of making me feel guilty on those seven-martini nights when all I wanted to do was enjoy my clear liquids out of stemware, and with the additive of alcohol, thank you. Not to mention that bar owners aren't stupid: the prevalence of the water drinkers meant that fewer people bought cocktails, which meant that the price of cocktails—and, for that matter, bottled water—grew correspondingly. Sometimes a cover charge was abruptly tossed into the mix, adding insult to injury.

But not here at the Penthouse. This was a bar where men drank grown-up beverages and water was a mixer—and a mixer for wimps who couldn't drink their scotch like a proper gentleman, at that.

While waiting for Rick, I gave the room a once-over. I don't really know what I had been expecting, but the feel of the bar came as a pleasant surprise. The lighting was low and subtle, and the furnishings and paintings hanging throughout the room were tasteful, in an Anglophilic sort of way. The room was redolent of the same sort of money I had envied only a few hours earlier during my self-pitying walk between the East Village and the West Village, but now—as the Penthouse's newest patron—I felt part of it, not separate from it.

This wasn't the new money of the loud downtown clubs, where trend-setting Beautiful People engaged in fashion wars as they sipped the latest craze in flavored martinis or—*shudder*—drank their bottled water. This was old money. Comfortable money. Money that drank *real* martinis with only the slightest trace of vermouth. Money that wore Brooks Brothers and Burberry. Money that summered in Palm Beach and the Hamptons before the Hamptons were . . . *common.*

And for this brief moment in time, Brett Revere, Trust Fund Baby, was part of it.

I felt dozens of eyes on me and remembered that, whatever the setting, a gay bar is a gay bar, and a good-looking man is going to attract attention. Especially if he's the fresh meat. In fact, I was bound to attract even more attention than usual at the Penthouse, given my comparative youth contrasted with the regular clientele. So I stood aloofly, waiting for my drink, and allowed myself to enjoy it. After all, it was just another acting job, albeit an unpaid one, and Rick was right: I *did* have an appropriate name to pull it off.

When he returned with our drinks, we pushed our way to the back of the lounge where a wide spiral staircase led to an upper floor. As I climbed the carpeted stairs, I heard the unmistakable noise of boisterous off-key singing and realized that we were heading to a piano bar.

"See?" Rick asked, when we reached the top of the staircase. "It's not so bad, is it?"

"No." I raised my voice slightly to be heard over a seventy-something man singing "The Surrey With the Fringe On Top." "Not bad at all. Do you come here often?"

"Once a week or so. We live nearby, and Bill likes it."

"Bill?"

"My lover. My significant other. My husband. Or whatever terminology you prefer." Rick craned his neck. "I sort of thought he'd be here, but maybe he's running late." He tapped his watch. "Wait here for a second, okay? I want to call his cell."

"No problem. I know how to take care of myself in a bar."

He smiled. "I thought so." And then he disappeared into the crowd.

Again I felt eyes on me, but I simply tossed my hair and remembered that I was playing a role and belonged here. For tonight, at least.

"Can I buy you a drink?!"

Startled, I turned to see an older man, his mouth just millimeters from my ear. He had recently dyed his hair an unnatural shade of black, and if I wasn't mistaken in the discreet lighting he was also wearing an application of make-up over his pale cheeks, giving them an unearthly rosy glow.

I held up my almost-empty glass.

"Thanks, but I'm still working on this one."

"That's almost gone. C'mon, let me buy you a drink."

"Thanks, but I'm set."

I smiled politely and turned away, but he struck again.

"What's your name?"

I sighed. "Brett."

"Brett? I'm George. Nice to meet you." He stuck out his hand, forcing me to cordially shake it.

"And it's nice to meet you, too." Again, I turned away, and this time he caught my shoulder before I completed the pivot.

"I've never seen you here before."

"That's because I've never been here before."

"Are you a tourist?"

"No."

"Then why don't you come here?"

I impatiently stole a glance at my watch. When was Rick going to return and rescue me from Mr. Twenty Questions?

"I asked you . . ."

"Yeah, yeah, I heard you. I just . . . don't come here. I go to other places."

"Where?"

Another glance at my watch. "Here and there."

"Here and there where?"

"Listen," I said, turning to face him. "You seem like a nice guy, George. But I'm here with someone."

Something dark and unpleasant appeared in his face, just below the surface of those frighteningly rosy cheeks.

"All I did was offer to buy you a drink," he said, a bit too aggressively.

"And I appreciate that."

"I was being friendly. Do you have a problem with that?"

Fortunately, I didn't have a chance to answer that, in his case, yes, I *did* have a problem with that, because Rick was suddenly next to me.

"Oh," said the man, sizing Rick up.

"How's it going, George?" Rick said, but the old man just turned and skulked away.

"Who was that?" I asked.

"His name is George, but we call him the Evil Mime. He's, like, eighty years old, and once upon a time he even worked with Marcel Marceau. He actually made a career out of being a mime, if you can believe that. If you give him five minutes, he'll tell you all about it." Rick paused, then added, "The key is not to give him those five minutes."

"Why do you call him the Evil Mime?"

"George is very old school. He comes from an era when men were men and women were invisible. I had it out with him last year when I brought a woman here and he told her that she didn't belong in a bar for gay men." Rick took a sip of his drink, then added, "Plus, he's really, really obnoxious."

"He told her to leave?"

"Yeah. He wasn't even subtle about it. Unfortunately, it's not an uncommon attitude in this place. But at least most of the old boys have enough discretion to keep their mouths shut." His head turned slowly, taking in the room. "Lots of successful white men, who don't know how to interact with anyone except other successful white men."

He was right. As I scanned the patrons, I saw only two or three black or brown faces, and no women. Just a sea of white, capped by a lot of gray.

"But," he continued, with a smile, "I like it here. Not very PC, am I?"

I decided to change the subject. "So where's your boyfriend?"

"Well . . ." He shrugged. "Bad news. I'm afraid I brought you here under what have become false pretenses. I forgot that it was Thursday, and Thursday is our 'quiet night at home' night."

"So you have to take off?"

"Yeah. I mean, I can stay for another drink, if you'd like. I don't want to just abandon you here."

I smiled. "Rick, I'm thirty- . . . thirty-two. I'm old enough to take care of myself."

"But you've never been here before. I shouldn't just leave you."

"Leave," I insisted. "Go take care of your boyfriend, before he tosses you out and you end up sharing my apartment." I took another long look around the room. "This isn't anything like I was expecting. I'm very comfortable here."

"You're sure?"

"I'm sure."

While Rick finished his drink, we quickly exchanged phone numbers on stray pieces of paper; an ATM receipt for him, a grocery receipt for me. Then, reaching across the men lined two-deep at the bar, he set his empty glass down and ordered me another drink.

"You didn't have to do that," I said, when he handed me my vodka and soda.

"Let me do it," he said. "I feel guilty about running out on you."

"Okay. I'll take the drink. But don't feel guilty."

"*Now* I won't." He hugged me goodbye. "Have a good night."

"Good luck, Sugar Daddy," I said.

"Ugh." He shook his head. "Don't remind me."

With that, he turned and vanished down the spiral staircase. And I was left on my own in the second-floor piano bar of the Penthouse.

But not for long.

Only minutes after Rick left me, a distinguished-looking man was close at my side. Out of the corner of my eye, I sized him up: sixtyish; a slight paunch; a full head of silver hair; slightly tipsy; expensively dressed. Best of all, he had no obvious traces of makeup. Since there was nothing to set my internal alarm off, I decided to hold my ground and see if he would try to start a conversation.

He did.

"Nice night tonight," he said out of the corner of his mouth, not really looking at me. Originality, it seemed, was not one of his strong points.

"Very nice. Good crowd, too."

"Uh-huh."

Then there was silence for a minute, maybe longer, until he followed up his banal observation with the equally banal: "Come here often?" Again, he didn't look at me.

"Every now and then," I said vaguely, not willing to become the focus of an Evil Mime-type interrogation on my nightlife patterns.

Another minute came and went. Finally, he sighed deeply and said, "You could be a model."

"I've modeled." Which was true enough, although most of my modeling career consisted of wearing cheap suits in newspaper ads for discount clothiers, which didn't exactly put me in the social circles of Mark Vanderloo and Marcus Schenkenberg.

The cone of silence fell again, but since I didn't feel annoyed or harassed by this man—in fact, I felt somewhat sorry for his conversational ineptness—I decided to take matters into my own hands. That second drink was helping, of course. They always do.

I turned to face him, forcing him to look me in the eye.

"I'm Brett," I said, but what I was thinking was 'I'm Brett Revere, Trust Fund Baby.' I was totally in character, ready to ad lib my dialogue. It had to be better than *Andy*, after all.

"I'm Jeffrey," he said, his smile slightly askew as he offered me his hand.

I shook it and held the eye contact, noting as I did that what initially seemed to be social ineptness was, in reality, most likely the result of a few too many Johnnie Blacks. That, and someone who apparently was holding his attention near the piano, although for the life of me I couldn't tell who it was.

"Nice to meet you, Jeffrey," I said, raising my glass slightly.

He looked down and mirrored my motion, then quickly looked back to the piano. I followed his gaze, and saw a quartet of wolfishly smiling men—older men, of course, none probably younger than fifty-five—break away and stride toward us. I realized then that I was the treasure in their treasure hunt, and dear old drunk Jeffrey had won the prize.

"So," said the first to reach us, who was wearing an ascot—an *ascot*—and a blue blazer. "You met the cute boy, you old fox." And there was my validation.

"This is Brett," Jeffrey slurred, smiling at his friends with self-satisfaction.

Ascot Man looked me over. "You should be a model."

"And you," I said, forcing a smile, "should learn some new lines." As the words burst out of my mouth, I wished them back. Yes, these guys were walking clichés, but I didn't want to offend them. I need not have been worried; Jeffrey and his friends didn't seem to offend easily. In fact, they burst into laughter at my comment.

After we introduced ourselves—a pointless introduction, for my part, since I immediately forgot their names—Ascot Man went off to buy a round of drinks, taking care to include me in the round. That's when Jeffrey leaned over and asked:

"Do you ever go to the Hamptons?"

For the first time that night the Trust Fund Baby faltered, and I remembered that I was merely Brett Revere, failed actor and competent filer. Not only did I not summer in the Hamptons—the string of eastern Long Island towns that serve as the epicenter of Manhattan social life during the months when Manhattan is too damned sweltering to be tolerable—but I had never even been out there. The Hamptons were only one hundred miles away, but for me they may as well have been in Europe. Or on Jupiter.

I didn't even know how to fake my way through it, so I decided to answer honestly. Well . . . *semi*-honestly.

"I haven't been out this year, but I've been following the scene in *Haute Manhattan* magazine, so I don't feel as if I've missed anything." All of which was technically true—yes, here we go with the "technically true" thing again—down to my subscription to *Haute Manhattan*.

Jeffrey smiled broadly, first at his companions, then me. "You read *Haute Manhattan*?"

"Religiously. It's my secular Bible."

"Really." He paused, then went for the kill. "Well, I'm glad to hear that. I'm the publisher of *Haute Manhattan*!"

I congratulated him on producing such an excellent magazine, made small talk, tried to make my speech patterns sound just a bit more affected and, well . . . I did what Brett Revere, Trust Fund Baby, told Brett Revere, actor/filer, to do. The specifics of what happened after Jeffrey Ryan, publisher of *Haute Manhattan*, introduced himself to me don't really matter, though.

What matters is that a cartoon light bulb suddenly was illuminated over my head, and I finally had . . .

The Plan.

In those first few seconds after Jeffrey Ryan, drunk lecher, revealed himself to be Jeffrey Ryan, publishing magnate and member of the social elite, my thoughts began to fall into place. I was a pretty-boy, a preppy WASP of the sort in demand at the Penthouse. And as a pretty, preppy WASP I could befriend not only Jeffrey Ryan but all his kinsmen, all those faded, graying drunken lechers packing the bar.

No one needed to know that ninety minutes earlier I had walked out of *Andy*. No one needed to know that I mostly temped for a living. No one needed to know that I shared a fourth-floor walk-up in Astoria with Creepy Quentin King. Those things were merely matters of reality, of no real importance. The only thing that mattered was that the Brett Revere they were going to come to know was a charming, pretty, witty WASP, and he belonged in their crowd.

I mentally ticked off the negatives and found them wanting. The threat of exposure as a fraud was almost nonexistent, since no one knew me and I seriously doubted I was worth the investigative effort should someone be so inclined. Sure, one of them might try to get me into bed, but I was confident in my ability to disarm them without offending. And that, well . . . that was about it on the negative side of the ledger.

The positives, though—I could sense that a whole new world was about to open up for me. All I had to do was be chummy with this slightly older crowd and I would enter their Old Boy network, a network that was all about money and success. I would no longer be the down-at-the-heels actor enviously eyeing their homes and restaurants and limousines, let alone reading about their Southampton mansions and East Hampton parties in *Haute Manhattan*. I'd be on the inside . . . and *not* catering, either.

Logic dictated that it would be only a matter of time—and, I was confident, a short time at that—before one of the Old Boys decided I'd be perfect for some irrelevant yet overpaid job. Of course, as one of their crowd, I'd have to mull it over. Work wouldn't be what I was bred to do. But in the end I'd come to the rescue of Jeffrey or Ascot Man or one of the others and accept their offer.

Then it would be goodbye, Joey Takashimi! Goodbye, Quentin King! Goodbye, N train!

With a start, I realized I was getting too far ahead of myself. Worse, I was missing the conversation around me, and if I was going to fit in, I would have to pay careful attention. I would have to observe and learn. I would have to be a Method social climber.

"I asked you if you were interested in going out to Southampton this weekend," Jeffrey repeated to me when he noticed my blank gaze.

Too soon, I thought. The real Brett Revere needed a few days to wrap his head around The Plan.

"Can I take a rain check?" I asked.

"Certainly," he said graciously. "I'm out there almost every weekend. In season, of course."

"Of course," I said, and joined in his laughter. As *if* I'd think he'd go to the East End off-season!

Someone handed me another drink and I gratefully accepted, vaguely promising that the next round would be on me, which I knew wouldn't happen because I didn't have the cash. That's when a mop of dark brown hair swept in among the gray.

"Hey, Jeffrey," said the new arrival, kissing the publisher on the cheek, then making the rounds of the others. He was much younger than them—maybe even younger than me—although his slightly weathered, overly tanned face aged him slightly, the way that so many children of leisure seem older than they really are. All that sun, sand, and surf are a bitch.

"Are you going to East Hampton this weekend, Jamie?" Ascot Man asked the new arrival.

"Yeah, but I have to take the Jitney." He made a face. "You?"

"Not this weekend. I'll hold everyone's place here at the bar, if I don't drive upstate to visit folks."

Jamie nodded absently, then spotted me. "Hi," he said, pushing through the circle of men, forcing them to take a step back. "I'm Jamie."

"Brett," I said, offering him my hand. "Nice to meet you."

He took my hand and I felt an involuntary jolt race through my body.

My first impulse was to pull away. I didn't need the complication of impulsive attraction when I was on the threshold of making the first completely cynical career move of my life. But I didn't. I held the grasp until his hand slackened, then dropped it. He had a slight, sly smile on his lips, and I realized that he had felt the jolt, too.

"Have I seen you before?" he asked. "I think I would have remembered."

"No. I'm a first-timer."

He raised an eyebrow and grinned broadly. "A virgin?"

Ascot Man interrupted. "Now you're going too far, Jamie. Do you have to swoop down and steal everyone from us?"

"Who says I'm stealable?" I asked.

Jamie, the smile off his face, aimed a smoldering stare at me. "If I say you're stealable, you're stealable."

He was trying for "seductive," but missed his mark. The knot of older men erupted in laughter, and, intrigued though I was by the new arrival, I couldn't help but join them. Even Jamie, after affecting a brief pout, smiled at his fumble.

"Okay, now," slurred Jeffrey. "We've established that Brett cannot be stolen, no matter how hard Jamie tries. And he doesn't look like the sort who can be bought." He raised his glass and tipped it toward me. "Wonderful to make your acquaintance, Brett. Based on first impressions, I think you'll fit in with our little Penthouse family."

I clinked my glass against his and said, "So I'm part of the family now? That makes you all my . . . what? Uncles?"

"Older brothers," said Ascot Man, and I finally detected the vestiges of a Southern accent in his voice. "*Slightly* older brothers."

"With one exception," added Jamie.

"Yes, of course," said Ascot Man. "Most of us are your *slightly* older brothers, and Jamie is your strange half-cousin from the side of the family no one really wants to talk about."

Again there was laughter, although I thought I saw some confusion on Jamie's face before he joined in. Cute, apparently rich, somewhat young by the standards of The Penthouse . . . but, I was beginning to think, not the sharpest knife in the cutlery rack.

Did it matter though? No. Because I felt that jolt when he took my hand. I know that the "electricity" thing between two people upon first meeting is a cliché, but . . . I felt it.

As the others gossiped about almost everyone in the room—apparently there were two prominent and married philanthropists, a major book publisher, a social columnist, and a former congressman within sight—I watched Jamie scan the crowd. His eyes betrayed none of his secrets, if he had any. He seemed to be completely self-possessed, assessing waiters and CEOs alike with an insouciant eye, a half-smile always on his lips. It was the same look he gave me, on the half-dozen occasions our eyes met.

I felt a twinge of envy. I was pretending to be a Jamie type, even before he arrived and I saw what a Jamie type was really like. But he did it so much better. I was doing Improv 101, and he was poised, collected, completely comfortable.

That's when it finally occurred to me that I was in the presence of a *real* trust fund baby. This Jamie was everything I was pretending to be: affluent, confident, wealthy—all wrapped up in a nice package, albeit one weathered by too many days in South Beach or Malibu or wherever young gay men with money took their sun.

I looked over and caught him looking at me, those lips just slightly smiling. It had the same effect as when he took my hand.

He took a few steps forward, brushing wordlessly—almost unseeingly—past Jeffrey, Ascot Man, and the others while they were distracted by something—or someone—new, and said, "Want to grab a bite to eat?"

"Um . . ." I thought about the handful of small bills stuffed in my pocket, and how he'd expose me as a fraud before I was able to put my fledgling thoughts into action if I pulled them out, crumpled five by crumpled five, still coming up far too short to cover my half of a restaurant check. Reluctantly, I said, "I think I'll have to pass."

He paused for a moment. "In that case, let me buy you another drink."

I looked at my glass, and was surprised to see that my third drink—the one Ascot Man had just handed me—was almost gone.

"I shouldn't," I said.

"Come on. Have a drink with me." He looked around. "If you're worried about what these old queens will say . . ."

"No," I lied. "Not at all."

"Good. Don't. It's ten o'clock—almost their bedtime anyway." He fixed me hard in the eye and purred, "We have a lot of catching up to do."

I started to feel very, very stealable

The next morning, as I laid in bed with my eyes closed and head humming, these were the memories that ran through my head as my brain worked to recapture the rest of Thursday night's festivities:

Jamie and I had a few more drinks. Jeffrey Ryan and company departed, and we promised to see each other again at the Penthouse the following week. The Evil Mime made another pass at me, telling me about how he had attended acting school with Jayne Mansfield, before Jamie chased him away. Jamie and I laughed a lot.

At some point, Jamie told me his last name, which I no longer remembered. We exchanged phone numbers. Something happened . . . not clear about that, but maybe a kiss. Whatever it was, it was charged.

We walked up Second Avenue. No, we walked up Second Avenue hand in hand. I remembered thinking, at the time, that it was incredibly romantic, walking with our hands clasped—and, at one point, our arms around each other—without caring about the passersby. If they couldn't handle it, well . . . fuck'em. I think we might have even said that to each other.

I remembered that I said something about going to catch the N train, but Jamie suggested something so I didn't catch the N and that meant . . .

. . . that meant I wasn't in Queens.

My eyes popped open.

I didn't recognize the room.

I closed my eyes and tried to fill in a few more of the previous night's missing hours.

More details struggled to the surface. I was in Jamie's twenty-second-floor apartment on Second Avenue, somewhere around East Seventieth Street. Maybe East Seventy-first. We slipped in quietly the night before, so that we would not wake up his roommate, and went straight to his room, undressed, and . . . yes, it certainly felt like four months of self-deprivation had been lifted from me. Although most of the specific details had evaporated with the vodka, those I still remembered were fantastic.

I rolled slightly, first to the right, then to the left. Jamie wasn't in the bed with me.

I reached over the side of the bed and felt around for my clothes, retrieving my pair of white DKNY boxer briefs from the crumpled pile on the floor. I slipped them on, then crawled out of the tangled sheets and began collecting the rest of my clothing.

"Good morning." I looked up, expecting to see Jamie . . . but this wasn't Jamie. In the doorway stood a rotund older man, balancing himself on a wooden cane. Instinctively, I held my wrinkled khakis in front of my almost-naked body and croaked, "Good morning."

"Did you sleep well?"

"Uh . . . Yes. Uh . . . I'm . . . I'm Brett. A friend of Jamie's."

He didn't say anything—didn't scowl, didn't smile, didn't do *anything*—for several long moments, until I had almost forgotten what I had said when he interjected, "So I assumed."

"A *new* friend of Jamie's," I sputtered, as if the situation needed further clarification.

"So I assumed."

There was another long gap in the conversation.

"Do you know where he is?" I asked finally, still holding the khakis protectively in front of me, approximately where they would be if I was actually wearing them.

"Showering."

"I see . . ." My conversational skills were failing quickly, and the man with the cane didn't seem in any great hurry to help me out.

"I'm Benjamin Grover," he said finally. "This is my home."

"Oh, I'm . . ." I passed off the khakis from my right hand to left, then awkwardly offered him the right. "I'm Brett Revere."

He shook it and said, "Very nice to meet you."

After the handshake, we again stood in silence.

"So Jamie seems like a nice guy," I said.

"Jamie is entertaining. He can be a darling."

"And how long has he lived here?"

He looked confused. Finally, he replied, "How long has he told you he's lived here?"

I was starting to get the picture. Jamie had a good arrangement in a great apartment on the twenty-second floor, with a view that could have included Astoria had not other high-rises been built on the east side of Second Avenue to block it. But just as I had a roommate problem, so did Jamie. His was just a bit older and more doddering, although probably more grounded, than mine.

I wanted to get dressed, and my personal code of modesty insisted that I do so alone. But Benjamin Grover seemed to be content to stand in the doorway, leaning on his cane. I spoke to him slowly and notched up the volume a bit.

"It. Was. Very. Nice. Meeting. You. Sir. Now. I. Would. Like. To. Get. Dressed."

He shook his head. "I'm not deaf, young man." And with that, he was gone.

Okay. Apparently I hadn't scored any points with the old guy. Whatever.

As I pulled on my pants, Jamie—covered only by a towel wrapped snugly around his waist—walked into the room. I gave him the standard morning-after size-up to see if the man standing in front of me in the light of day and under sober conditions was the same man I went home with the night before, and, except for noticing again that he had spent too much time in the sun, was relieved to see that he looked exactly as I remembered.

"Good morning," I said. "I met your roommate."

"Benjamin? He's a good guy. He's really watched out for me."

"I think I offended him."

Jamie looked at me, uncomprehending. "Ben likes *everyone*. That's his problem. He used to let Andrew Dice Clay hang out here after he performed in the city. I mean, *Andrew Dice Clay*. If you like Andrew Dice Clay, I think that you must like everybody."

I found my shirt. The sleeves had been pulled inside-out, and as I started pulling them back through their holes I said, "Maybe I read him wrong."

"The one thing you don't want to do," he said, turning his back to me and dropping the wet towel from his waist to the floor, giving me a nice view of his ass, "is treat him like an old man. That's the only thing that seems to piss him off. He likes to think he's still twenty-seven and discovering rock 'n' roll."

Jamie leaned over to climb into a pair of briefs, and I somehow managed to stop myself before grabbing a buttock.

"Maybe that's the problem," I said. "I thought he was losing it."

"Nah," he said, now facing me and pulling up a pair of tight jeans. "If he's slow, and if he sometimes looks a bit confused, it's probably a delayed reaction from the drugs he took in the '60s. He was real close to the Stones. Do you see my belt?"

I found it for him, then started to dress myself, saying, "Well, I hope he'll be okay with me. I just wanted some privacy while I dressed."

"I'll make everything better before we leave," he said through a yawn. "Speaking of which, what time is it?"

I glanced at my watch, which was still not quite strapped to my wrist. "Seven-thirty."

"In that case I'll make things better with Ben *after* the weekend. Right now, let's get moving. I have to catch the Jitney in, like, twenty minutes."

In a frenzy, he finished dressing and threw handful upon handful of clothes—dirty, clean, it didn't seem to matter—into a carryall.

"Here," he said, tossing me a baseball cap as he zipped his bag. "Hide the bed head."

I pulled the cap over my hair, which I knew from experience was sprouting in all directions, and then we were racing out of the apartment, both of us barely acknowledging Benjamin Grover, friend of Andrew Dice Clay and partyer with the Rolling Stones, in the rush. For his part, Benjamin told Jamie to have a nice weekend . . . and ignored me.

"What time is it?" Jamie asked again when we were out in the morning sunshine, power-walking down Second Avenue.

"Seven-forty-two," I said.

He yawned and stretched as he walked, turning west on East Sixty-ninth Street. "Lord, I wish I didn't have to go out to the Hamptons this weekend. It's just past Memorial Day and I am already *so* bored with those people." He slowed his pace a bit and glanced sideways at me. "And what are you doing for the weekend?"

"No plans."

He stopped and spun around to face me. "You know, maybe . . ."

"What?"

"Maybe . . ." He paused for what seemed an eternity, giving me a great opportunity to stare into his blue eyes. "Maybe I can arrange to have you come out over the weekend. Maybe you could take the Jitney out tomorrow morning . . ."

My thoughts echoed those of the previous night, when Jeffrey Ryan had issued a similar invitation. It was much too soon. If I was going to successfully carry out my freshly hatched plan to jump-start my bank account, I was going to have to train myself to at least *look* like I'd been to the Hamptons before. But . . . damn, I wanted to get on the Jitney with him.

"Call me," I said. "It could be tough, but call me."

A puzzled look crossed his face. "Do I have your number?"

A puzzled look crossed *my* face. "I . . . I don't know." I felt through my pockets for a business card or stray piece of paper, but came up with nothing. I was fairly certain we had exchanged numbers, but I wasn't absolutely certain . . . and Jamie's phone number was something I wanted to be absolutely certain I had. "Just in case we forgot that part, let's do it again."

He programmed my phone number directly into his cell phone; I took his on the same scrap of paper on which I had written Rick Atkins's phone number.

We began walking again toward Lexington Avenue, where Jamie had a Jitney to catch.

"I know I'll see you again," he said, grinning.

I played it coy. "Why is that?"

"Because you're a gentleman, and by the gentlemen's code of conduct you're obligated to return my hat."

I smiled back at him. Yeah, I knew that.

In the shadow of Hunter College on Lexington Avenue, we stopped walking. Standing in front of us were a dozen people, almost all black or Hispanic women.

"Looks like I'm traveling with the help this morning," he said. I cringed at his comment, but then remembered that not only did I like this guy, but I also had a larger project to consider. And achieving my goal—ingratiating myself with the whiter-than-white world of the Penthouse—would out of necessity require me to bite my tongue now and then. Every mercenary understands the concept.

Moments later, the bus pulled to the curb. As the Jitney driver began stowing bags, Jamie turned to me and slid his arms around my waist, swallowing a yawn in the process.

"Sorry," he said. "But you wore me out last night."

I smiled stupidly at him, staring into those blue eyes. "So when do you come back?"

"Probably Monday. Maybe Sunday night. I'll call you."

"Great," I started to say, until his mouth covered mine and he kissed hungrily.

You can get away with a lot of things in broad daylight on the streets of Manhattan, so we didn't even seem to raise an eyebrow as we kissed on the busy Lexington Avenue sidewalk. When he finally pulled away, I felt my head spin. And the stupid smile was back.

"Gotta run." He tossed the carryall over his shoulder and walked a few steps backward.

"See you," I said, trying my hardest to play it cool. He turned and darted for the bus, hopping up the stairs moments before the doors hissed closed.

I stood on the sidewalk and watched it as it began its slow rumble down Lexington Avenue and thought, he's just the sort of man I could fall in love with.

Maybe I *could* have it all—the money, the security, the wealthy friends, the photos on the PartyPix page in *Haute Manhattan*—and have it all in the handsome, sexy package of Jamie . . . Jamie . . . *whatever-his-last-name-was*. Jamie the Trust Fund Baby. Jamie the *real* Trust Fund Baby.

I walked on air all the way to the N train.

Brett Revere's Theory of Life, Part Three:
In a Pinch, the Waiter Is Expendable

"You look like *you're* in a good mood," said Quentin, when I opened the apartment door, and in fact I *had* been in a good mood until the moment I saw Quentin, sprawled across the couch wearing only a tattered pair of blue-and-white striped boxer shorts.

"It's a nice day," I said, hoping to avoid conversation.

"Get laid?" he asked, idly grabbing at his boxers to adjust himself. I looked away and sighed.

"None of your business, Quentin."

"You *did*, didn't you!"

"None of your business."

"Dude, did he have a big one?"

I tried to ignore him. My watch told me that it was already a few minutes after eight o'clock, and I'd have to move quickly if I wanted to avoid being late to my temp assignment for a law firm at the Citigroup Center. Without another word to Quentin, I raced to my bedroom, tore open the closet, and stared in confusion at the row of wrinkled clothing packed tightly together, hoping I'd spot something that was ready for wear. One of these days, I thought, I was going to have to start preparing in advance for my workdays.

That's when I remembered that I had done just that the day before. But my bed, where I clearly remembered laying out clothes for today, was empty.

"Quentin," I said, returning to the living room. "Do you know what happened to the clothes that were on my bed?"

"Clothes?"

"Pants and a shirt. I laid them out on the bed yesterday. But they're not there now."

One of his eyebrows arced and he puckered his mouth, as if he was trying to remember a thought that had just escaped him. But then he just shrugged and said, "Sorry, man. I don't know anything about it."

I shook my head in disbelief. The TV was still there, the VCR was still there, and the stereo was still there. Which meant that if Quentin hadn't moved my clothes, they must have been stolen by the most inept thief in the Borough of Queens.

"Oh, wait a minute," he said. "Maybe Boomer moved them."

"Boomer?"

"This dude I know. We call him Boomer. I think that's his last name. I don't know what his first name is. Anyway, he stopped over last night with this girl—I think it was his girlfriend, but I'm not really sure—and I let them use your room for a little privacy."

"What?" I asked, suddenly boiling. "What's wrong with *your* room?"

"Dude, have you seen the sheets on my bed? Even *I* don't want to lay down on them."

I was trying to remain calm—well, I was trying to appear calm, at least—so I sounded strangely muted as I forced my words out through a clenched jaw. "Let me get this straight. You let a guy whose name you don't know into this apartment with a girl who may or may not be his girlfriend, and you let them do—whatever—on my bed?"

He nodded. "Basically. Except I told you I know his name. Boomer. I just don't know if that's his first or last name."

"Let me help you on this. *Nobody's* last name is Boomer. And nobody's first name is Boomer, unless it's a dog or a quarterback. Boomer is not a name for a human being."

"Are you pissed off at me?"

I took a few deep breaths and tried to cool down. "All I want to know is where my clothes are."

"I don't think he would have stolen them."

Another couple of deep breaths. "That wasn't what I asked. I just want to know where they are."

He shrugged. "Sorry, man. You're just going to have to wear something else."

I realized there was no point in belaboring the conversation—if I spotted someone who looked like a Boomer wandering around in a yellow Ralph Lauren shirt and Gap khakis, I'd deal with it at that time. In the meantime, I had a job to get to, and I was losing precious minutes discussing the missing outfit with Creepy Quentin. I stormed off to my bedroom and dug the least wrinkled clothes I could find out of the closet, then carried them into the bathroom with me, hoping that I could steam out the worst of the creases.

I glanced at my watch as I closed the bathroom door, and my heart skipped a beat at the realization that I had to be at work in twenty-five minutes. I went into hyperspeed, showering quickly, shaving so quickly I nicked myself and missed a few spots, and doing little more than a quick once-over with my toothbrush. I looked at my watch again. I had sixteen minutes.

The steam had no discernible effect on the wrinkles, but, having no time to iron, I decided to make do. I raced back to my bedroom, threw on the clothes, slipped into loafers, and was back in the living room with nine minutes to make it from Astoria to East Midtown. There was no way I'd be on time, but if I wasn't too late maybe no one would notice.

"Your clothes are really wrinkled," said Quentin as I dashed for the front door.

I didn't answer him. I didn't have to. Because now I had The Plan—the true Plan, the happily-ever-after Plan—and Quentin King would soon be history. He could live on the streets for all I cared. Or room with Boomer.

And if for some reason things didn't work out with Jamie, well . . . I'd make things work. Some other way. The light bulb in my head didn't start with Jamie, and it wouldn't have to end with Jamie.

Jeffrey Ryan . . . Ascot Man . . . any of the others could very well be the means to my end. If necessary. There was no reason any of that had to change. True, with Jamie I would get the entire package—money, security, and, I hoped, love—but I already noted that I was flexible, and I could continue to be flexible. After all, in my current situation it wasn't hard to justify that one out of three ain't bad.

And I'd do anything but continue to live the way I was living.

As I rushed to the subway through an increasingly warm and humid Friday morning, though, my thoughts were focused on Jamie. Our casual, romantic, devil-may-care drunken saunter up Second Avenue . . . the passionate, albeit barely remembered, lovemaking . . . the way he dropped his towel when he was dressing . . .

And most of all, Jamie's kiss on Lexington Avenue just an hour or so earlier, before he boarded the Jitney. Passionate . . . so unconcerned about anyone but the two of us . . . the thought of it . . . Well, I felt that jolt again.

And I thought, Jamie might not be the means to my end, but I want him to be.

You probably already realize that, at that point in my life, I was pathetic enough. I had no money, I worked as a temp, I lived in a grubby little apartment with a creepy roommate, my acting career had tanked, and I was wearing a very wrinkled shirt and pants because someone named Boomer had walked off with my clothes. But things got more pathetic that morning.

This was roughly the time when all of the world, but especially New York City, was under a heightened terrorism alert. And at approximately the same moment I was racing for the N train, some moron forgot his briefcase on a bench two stops ahead at the Queensboro Plaza transit hub. Upon discovery of the briefcase, exactly forty-three seconds after my train left its station, the Metropolitan Transit Authority immediately stopped all N, R, and 7 train service. And service wasn't back up for fifty-two minutes, until the police determined that the briefcase—a cheap briefcase, at that—contained no explosives, only the sort of empty legal pads and Hostess snack products commonly found in the pretend business accessories of the average summer intern.

The long and short of it: for almost an hour, I stood in a sweltering, stalled subway car perched on elevated tracks over Astoria, as sweat permeated my shirt—not enough to get rid of the wrinkles, just enough to make me thoroughly disgusting—while I waited for the Bomb Squad to defuse junk food.

And then, because these delays have a ripple effect, everything ran so incredibly slow that I didn't make it to work until ten-thirty, meaning I was ninety minutes late. And rumpled. And sweaty. Which is *not* a good thing when one is a temp.

I wasn't surprised to see that my assignment had already been filled by another person from the agency—and she was a sweet girl I'd met before, so I couldn't blame her—but I was unhappy to then be summoned to the agency's headquarters. Especially because I didn't want them to know that until the brilliant intern left his Twinkies at

Queensboro Plaza, I had every intention of showing up for my assignment in clothes that looked as if I had slept in them.

But summoned I was. So a few minutes after eleven-thirty, I walked into the offices of MetroTemp, on the rundown eighth floor of a gritty building on Seventh Avenue. As usual, the receptionist's desk was empty—they probably couldn't find a MetroTemp temp who was willing to work for them.

Still, my manager, Cruella DeVil—born Mary Devlin; known to her family and friends, if any, as Mary Devlin; known to the IRS and SSA as Mary Devlin; but known to me and everyone else who had to deal with her as Cruella—was waiting.

"What happened today, Brett?" she asked, sizing up my decidedly unattractive physical appearance. As if on cue, one carefully gelled-and-styled forelock suddenly broke loose, cascading over my eye. I brushed it off my face, to what was certainly no better aesthetic effect.

"There was a bomb scare at Queensboro Plaza," I said. "They held the train for an hour."

"Why didn't you call?"

"My, uh . . . I canceled my cell phone." Which is sort of the same thing as admitting that my cell phone service had been cut off one month earlier for lack of payment, but not exactly.

"You placed this company in an awkward position. We're close to losing that account. And look at you!" She sniffed, no doubt noticing that I had been sweating for most of the past three hours, but passing on the comments. "Did you sleep in those clothes?"

I *knew* she was going to ask that. But I couldn't think of a way to blame Boomer. Not only would the explanation take too long, but she'd never believe me.

"No," I said defensively. "But when you're trapped on a train for an hour, you get wrinkled."

"I've been trapped on a train," she hissed. "We live in New York at the beginning of the twenty-first century. We *all* get trapped on trains. That's what happens here. But we don't end up looking like we're coming home from a three-day bender."

In all honesty, I thought I looked more like I was coming home from a *six*-day bender. With blender drinks. But I figured it was best to keep that to myself.

"Are you on drugs?" she asked suddenly, throwing me off guard. "Because if you are, there are places that can help you. Not here, of course. But I can refer you to AA or NA or something like that."

Stunned, I couldn't immediately reply.

"Here," she said, grabbing a piece of paper and furiously jotting down numbers. "These people can help you."

I finally managed to squeak, "But . . ."

She handed me the paper. "When you're . . . what do they say? Oh yes . . . When you're clean and sober, come back and we'll see if I have any work for you."

Okay, so my typing skills weren't the best. But I was a good filer. A damned good filer. And I wasn't on drugs. And I deserved better than the slip of paper Cruella handed me.

I walked up Seventh Avenue, past clusters of tourists and office workers, to which group I no longer belonged, and realized that if I ever had any second thoughts about charming my way into the gay upper class, it was time to put them aside. The acting thing had died the night before, and the temp thing was now on hold until I checked myself into rehab, so, frightening as it was, I had to buck it up and stroll confidently into either Jamie's arms or the Penthouse every night for the foreseeable future until things clicked.

I thought, how hard can it be? Oh, difficult, yes, but many others had done it. I was quick with a line and a story, and—once I got myself into Trust Fund Baby mode—I was confident with my act. I'd be fine.

In time.

I just had to make sure I could pull it off in the next three weeks, because that's when this particular Trust Fund Baby had to come up with his July rent. And between *Andy* and Cruella's referral to various support groups ending in "Anonymous," things weren't looking very good for the July rent.

I was close to Alan's office, so I decided to stop in. That wasn't something he encouraged, but at least he tolerated it. And maybe he had finally come across that made-for-TV movie that would launch the acting career that I still had distantly hoped for.

"Where's Emily?" I asked, when I found Alan alone in his office.

He shook his head. "She wasn't working out. And speaking of things not working out, what are you doing here?"

"Who's your favorite client?"

"Corey Carthew. And since you're not him, what are you doing here?" Day Alan was apparently present in full force.

I didn't care. "I was in the neighborhood, and wanted to see if anything new came in."

He wasn't amused. "If you can play a twelve-year-old black kid, I can send you out for a Fox sitcom next week. Otherwise, the answer—as always—is no." He must have sensed a bit of desperation in me, because his features suddenly softened. "Okay, what's wrong?"

"I just lost the temp job," I said. "They think I'm on drugs."

"Are you?"

"No!"

"Well, I mean . . . look at you. You're a mess."

"I was trapped on the N for an hour. Bomb scare."

"Honey, you don't look like you spent an hour on the train. You look like you spent thirty-six hours sleeping in those clothes!"

"Okay," I said, putting my hand up in the universal gesture meaning "stop making fun of me." "I'm a little wrinkled, but I can explain. Boomer stole my clothes."

"What's Boomer? A dog?"

I wanted to explain, but, resigned, said simply, "Yeah. A dog. Anyway, I had to make a quick change and didn't have a chance to iron, which is why I look like this. Although my train *was* delayed for an hour. And it's unfair that they've suspended me."

"MetroTemp suspended you?"

"Basically." I pulled Cruella's phone numbers from my pocket. "I can come back when I have a clean bill of health."

"You don't do drugs."

"I know!"

"You drink, but . . ." He paused. "Let me see your eyes."

"Why?"

"Just show me."

I widened my eyes, and Alan took a long look. Finally, he said, "I don't think you need AA."

"I *know* I don't need AA! What was that about?"

"Trust me, I know actors. I've seen plenty of alcoholic actors. I'm good at weeding them out."

"You don't need to weed me out for drinking. You've already done it based on my age."

"*And* talent." He grinned smugly at his remark, but quickly added, "Okay. Cheap shot. I'll apologize now before you get all whiny on me." He paused. "So tell me about *Andy*."

I raised an eyebrow, uncertain of what he already knew. "What about *Andy*?"

"How about the part where you're not in the cast anymore."

"I thought you didn't want to know anything about that show."

"I didn't. But since Walter Pomeroy is a friend of mine, and my day started with his phone call bitching about your lack of professionalism, I thought I'd hear your side, too."

I sighed. "I couldn't do it, Alan. They wanted me to get humped by a dog."

"Boomer?"

I shook my head. "No, Boomer is a . . . never mind. Anyway, I couldn't take it anymore. It was just too tacky. So I bolted."

"So . . . no *Andy*, no temp job, and I don't have anything for you. What are you going to do?"

I thought for a moment. "Well," I said, "I have an idea. Sort of."

"Sort of? Is it acting?"

I smiled. "Yeah. It's the biggest acting job of my life. And I think I can make it pay off." He didn't say anything, just looked at me expectantly, so I began to explain. "I went to the Penthouse last night."

"*The Penthouse*!" Alan's upper lip curled. "What were you doing *there*?"

"I went with one of the other actors from *Andy*. Anyway, I think I figured out a way to survive. I met this group of older guys who seemed to be quite taken with me."

"Honey, you're too old to be a kept boy. And as for hustling, well, *you'd* have to pay your clients."

"You've got a real age obsession when it comes to me, don't you? Now, listen for a minute. Here's my plan: I'm going to impress the Old Boys' Network—infiltrate it—and land a decent-paying job through my new connections. It's . . . it's . . . it's not a whole lot different than simple networking. Except for a little . . ."

He shook his head. "Um . . . I don't know how to tell you this, Brett, but you're an unemployed actor-slash-temp."

"No I'm not," I said. "I'm a trust fund baby."

"What?"

"I sort of led them to believe that I'm a trust fund baby. Well, I never actually said that, but I just acted like I belonged there, so I think they made the assumption."

He shook his head again. "This is just wrong."

"You don't think I can pull it off?"

"No," he replied curtly. "You'll find some way to fuck it up, and I'll have to pick up the pieces. Not to mention the fact that you'll probably end up sleeping on the couch in my office after you lose your apartment."

"Alan," I said, "I really think I can do this. I mean, these guys *loved* me. And you have to admit I can be charming."

"Well . . . yes."

"And urbane."

"Now you're pushing it."

I continued: "Trust me on this. And if you don't believe me, come with me to the Penthouse and see for yourself."

"Ugh," he moaned. "I wouldn't set a foot in that place. It's a gay WASP's wet dream."

"So? I'm a gay WASP."

"Maybe. I really wouldn't know, since you've never told me your birth name."

I ignored him, continuing to bask in my successful debut the night before. "It was great, Alan. I met the publisher of *Haute Manhattan*, who seemed to really like me. And I also met another trust funder . . ."

"You didn't meet *another* trust funder," he said. "Because you are *not*—let me repeat that, Mister Delusional—*not* a trust funder. You're a temp. Correction: you're a *former* temp. A *suspended* temp. Which has probably never happened before in the world of temps, so I hope you feel special."

"Whatever. Anyway, this guy I met is about my age."

"Whatever that means. Are you still claiming you're thirty-two?"

Again, I ignored him. "He's about my age, he's cute. You know, if I play my cards right maybe I can land a *real* trust fund baby and live happily ever after."

Alan looked at me, skepticism etched on his face. "I don't see this working, Brett."

"It can. It will." I didn't verbalize my afterthought: "It has to." "This guy Jamie, well . . . He's already talking about bringing me out to the Hamptons with him."

He paused for several long moments before saying, "I wish you well. Because if this doesn't work . . ."

"I know," I said. "Goodbye, New York."

"Right. And hello, wherever-you-came-from. Which, come to think about it, is another thing I don't know about you."

"And another thing you'll *never* know about me."

He picked up an actor's headshot from his desk and, flipping it over, idly scanned the vital statistics on the back, as he said, "You vastly overrate the interest I have in your real name and hometown."

"Albany. All right? Now you know."

"Albany, New York? You come from Albany, New York?"

"Yes," I confirmed. "Now you know one of my deep, dark secrets."

"I got arrested in Albany once."

"Really?"

"And that's all *I'm* prepared to share."

I leaned against his desk. "Come with me to the Penthouse tonight."

"Not my crowd," he said, setting the photo back on his desk.

"Come on. Watch me in action, Alan. You'll see that this can work."

"I'm going to Bar 51. Doug's on tonight, which means free drinks." When I started to protest, he added, "And while I wish you the best, I can't see how this suck-up-to-the-rich-guys plan you have factors into my professional life in the slightest way."

"And hanging out at Bar 51 helps you professionally?"

"No. But it's close to the office."

When I returned home to Astoria, Quentin was still splayed on the couch in those frayed blue-and-white striped boxers. It was early-edging-into-mid-afternoon.

"What's up, dude?" he said as I walked through the front door and greeted him with a sneer of contempt. "They have half-days on Fridays?"

"No," I said. "I was suspended."

"Suspended?!" He seemed genuinely surprised. "Why?"

I was in a guilt-inducing mode, so I lied. "Because I was wearing wrinkled clothes. Which I was wearing because your buddy Boomer took my ironed clothes."

There was no contrition, though. Not even an acknowledgment that his friend Boomer walked off with my clothes. Instead, he muttered, "Bummer," and went back to reading the club listings from a three-week-old edition of the *Village Voice*.

I walked into my bedroom and hit the power button on my elderly computer. There was a flash on the monitor, which then faded to black for a moment before slowly flickering back to life. While it completed the process—which, through experience, I knew could take several minutes or even several reboots—I began changing into more casual, and less wrinkled, clothing.

I finished my change into shorts and a polo shirt at the same time the computer came to life, and logged into my e-mail account. Methodically I deleted a slew of spam based on the subject line alone—"Add 3 Inches to Your Penis," "WHY R U AVOIDING ME," "Farm Girls and Their Favorite Animals"—before I came across a subject that intrigued me.

"Web Access Terminated"

I was fully convinced that it was just another junk e-mail, but, well . . . my interest was piqued. So I clicked and opened it.

Your access to this web site has been terminated due to your failure to abide by the terms of service you agreed to upon joining the live chat rooms at www.teentalk-n-hangout.net. Be advised that this notice is issued pursuant to the complaints of no less than five (5) members. Complaints associated with attempts to access these chat rooms through another ISP or screen name will be immediately investigated and referred for prosecution, if applicable.

Since I had no recall of visiting www.teentalk-n-hangout.net, and in fact couldn't begin to imagine why I would ever lurk at the site, let alone inspire a termination, I entered the URL in my browser. I hadn't even typed the second "e" before the web address appeared in the box . . . so *someone* had been there. And I was quite certain it wasn't me.

A message flashed on the screen: ACCESS DENIED FOR PREVIOUS VIOLATION(S).

"Quentin?!"

"What?!" he yelled back from the living room.

"Come here for a minute."

He shuffled in, still wearing only his boxers. Still adjusting himself.

"Do you have any idea why I'm in trouble with a web site called teentalk-n-hangout.net?"

"*Excellent* web site!"

"Okay," I said dryly. "I guess that answers *that* question. Now, would you like to elaborate?"

"Nothing to say."

"Have you been using my computer when I'm not at home?"

"No." I swiveled in the chair in front of the computer and looked him in the eye . . . and he looked away. "Dude, that's *your* computer. When I surf, I go to the library."

I didn't play along with him. "So what did you do to inspire multiple complaints and get me kicked out of a web site I've never even heard of?"

"Nothing," he said, doing his best to look clueless, which didn't take a lot of work. "I don't know anything about this."

A thought suddenly occurred to me. "How do you know the password to my account?"

"Oh. No. You've got me all wrong. I don't use your computer."

"Maybe Boomer did?"

He thought a minute. "Maybe."

That was it. That was so totally *it.* Maybe I wouldn't find true love with Jamie Whatsisname, and maybe The Plan wouldn't work, and maybe I'd die in a cardboard box in an Amtrak tunnel, but Creepy Quentin King was leaving this decrepit apartment in Astoria. He could do it voluntarily, or he could do it in a body bag, but he was leaving.

"I want you out of here by the end of the month," I told him.

"Dude, if this is about your clothes . . ."

"It's about everything," I said. "I want you gone."

So of course I had to have a drink. And I knew where to find Alan Donovan: Bar 51.

It occurred to me as the N train made its lazy way through Queens that I now had an even greater incentive to make my social ascent work, because once Quentin was out of the apartment I was going to have to come up with the entire $1200 monthly rent myself, which—with no income—wouldn't be easy. But it would be worth it to no longer see him, hear him, be thrown off of web sites I had never heard of, or have Boomer steal my clothes.

When I reached Manhattan, I stopped at an ATM and was relieved to see that the eighty-two dollar check had already cleared. I quickly withdrew eighty of it.

Alan was sitting at the bar when I finally arrived.

"You're not at the Penthouse?" he asked. "What happened to your road to riches?"

"Maybe later," I said.

"And your trust fund baby? The *real* one? Did you hear from him?"

I shook my head no. "I will, though." Changing the subject, I said, "I told Quentin to be out by the end of the month."

"Probably not a bad thing," he said, raising his voice a bit commensurate with the increased volume on the CD player. "But how are you going to pay for that apartment?"

"I'll find a way."

"I knew it. You're gonna end up on my couch."

"Not if I can help it." It was Friday, so Bartender Doug was on duty. I waved him over and said, "Your finest white wine."

"We don't have 'finest,' " he said. "We have wretched and less wretched."

"Then I'll take less wretched."

He bowed slightly, saying, "Excellent choice, sir," before leaving to get my drink.

Alan looked me in the eye. "Are you focused on what you're doing?"

"I think so," I said. "I'm pretty enthusiastic about this . . . this . . . plan of mine. I think I can pull it off."

"And live happily ever after in the Hamptons?"

"Just during the summer months." I thought for a moment. "You know, just calling something this massive 'The Plan' makes it sound so mundane. Like it's a diet or something."

He rolled his eyes. "Now you're going to retitle this little misadventure of yours?"

"It's only a misadventure if it fails," I observed. "And I don't intend to fail."

"Pulling it off and living with it are two totally different things."

"I know, I know. But it just makes so much sense." Again, there was a lull in the conversation, until I blurted out, "Operation Hamptons!"

"What?"

"That's what I'm calling this. This is Operation Hamptons. What do you think?"

"I think you've lost your mind."

"No, seriously."

"I seriously think you've lost your mind. I mean, you're making a cynical stab at meeting rich people sound like some sort of covert CIA operation!"

"Remember," I said, "I tried it the other way for decades, with all the hard work and pulling myself up by the bootstraps and suffering for my art. And what do I have to show for it? *Andy* and a referral to AA. So now that I've done my part to prove that life's not fair, what's the problem with using Operation Hamptons to reinvent myself."

"You're really proud of that name, aren't you," he said, downing the last of a vodka-and-seven as Bartender Doug set a full wineglass in front of me. "I don't know, Brett. Maybe it all makes sense. Maybe you *will* find a rich husband in New York and have your fairy tale ending. I just need a little more convincing."

"It's not your life," I reminded him.

"Thank God." He paused, staring at a few ice cubes at the bottom of his glass. "I'm probably going to regret this, but let's go to the Penthouse. I think I need to see you in action before I'm convinced of the viability of this idea of yours."

"But I just got my drink!" I protested.

He sank back into the stool. "Okay. I'll have *one* more. Then we'll go to the Penthouse." He looked down the bar. "Doug! Pick me next!"

* * *

Three hours later we were practically holding each other up as we climbed the steps off the sidewalk into the Penthouse. It was still fairly early—maybe ten o'clock, maybe even earlier—but the bar was packed with the same well-manicured patrons I had seen on the previous evening.

"You really want to be part of this?" Alan asked as we picked our way through a very blue-blazered Friday night crowd.

I smiled. "Want and need . . . I no longer see the difference." I paused, spotting a familiar face in the crowd. "Look at that."

Alan strained. "Is he wearing makeup?"

"Yeah. They call him the Evil Mime."

"He looks like a mime. No, he looks scarier. Like some Raggedy Andy who's come to life and dyed his hair black."

"He studied acting with Jayne Mansfield."

"Then God took off the wrong head." He stopped, distracted, then pointed at someone I couldn't make out through the crowd. "Oh, look at *that* one!"

I asked, "Is that an expression of lust? Or mockery?"

"Shut up." With that, he disappeared from my side, which, I suppose, meant that it was lust.

I stood alone for a while, as Alan—the reluctant visitor to the Penthouse—went off to make a new friend. For someone who only came to this bar to see me in action, acting up a storm in my new role as a member of the idle rich, his attention level was quick to dissipate. Then again, that was the Night Alan I knew so well. I'd be lucky if I saw him again before the end of the evening.

In the meantime, I simply leaned against the rail across from the downstairs bar, playing my acting game and trying to avoid eye contact with anyone who appeared to be unworthy of my new persona. And even at the Penthouse, there were plenty of them.

Until I heard the softest trace of a Southern accent.

In my ear.

"Look who's here. How are you?"

I turned to the right, and Ascot Man—friend of the beautiful Jamie, not to mention publisher Jeffrey Ryan—was standing there.

"Hey," I said, greeting him with a smile. "How's it going?"

"Not bad. Not bad at all. Stuck in town this weekend?"

"Yeah." My actor's brain was already spinning a web of ad libs—well, some would call them lies—any of which could, I hoped, save me. "This weekend was bad for me. I have a wedding at the Waldorf, so I decided to stay put. And anyway, I just don't feel like dealing with the traffic."

"Not *your* wedding, I hope," he said with a crooked smile.

"No," I said. "If it was mine, you'd have read about it in the *Times* 'Vows' column." Then I gratuitously added, "And I'd be dressed by Vera Wang."

Ascot Man threw out a throaty roar of laughter . . . right up to the point where he started choking. For the briefest of moments I could do nothing but stare at him as his face reddened, and think, "well, this is a hell of a thing to happen just as I'm launching Operation Hamptons and about to break into his social group."

It finally occurred to me that I should do something, although I had no idea what that something should be. I took one step toward him and asked, "Do you need water?"

He nodded yes, and I signaled for a waiter.

"Maybe you should sit down," I suggested, but he shook his head no.

I took a step back and waited casually for the red-faced Ascot Man to catch his breath, all the while continuing to make sure that the bartenders and waiters were at the ready in case he turned blue and plunged to the floor in front of me. Finally, a dark-eyed, brown-skinned young waiter appeared balancing a glass of water on a tray, which he handed to Ascot Man.

"Thanks," I said, keeping one eye on Ascot Man as he downed the water.

"De nada," said the waiter, with a soft Spanish accent.

Ascot Man, his hue beginning to return to normal, finished the glass of water, then wordlessly and without so much as an acknowledgment handed it back to the waiter, dismissing him. Over his shoulder I saw the waiter, unfazed by his rudeness, shake his head, a discreet grin on his lips as he turned and vanished into the crowd.

"Whew! That was a rough one!"

"Are you okay?" I asked him.

"Something went down the wrong way, that's all."

"You probably should have thanked the waiter for the glass of water," I said gently, wary of pushing too hard.

"What, that little Puerto Rican boy? All he did was bring me water. It's not like he gave me the Heimlich."

I held my tongue, silently lecturing myself that I was playing this game for my own self-interest, not in the cause of social justice.

"Anyway," Ascot Man continued, "you seem to have captivated our Mr. Brock."

I did? Who the hell was Mr. Brock? Then it occurred to me that Mr. Brock must be Jamie. Yes, that was it.

Mental note to self: Jamie's last name is Brock. Remember that.

"He's a nice guy," I said. "I like him a lot."

Ascot Man leered. "Do tell! Were you two boys naughty last night?"

"A gentleman never tells," I said.

"Which means I'll have to get the scoop from Jamie when he gets back from the Hamptons. *He*'ll tell me. *He*'s no gentleman." He looked around, then caught the eye of another waiter—"Dewars and water, por favor"—before returning his attention to me. "Jamie's something, all right. A word of warning, though: he's a handful."

"You don't think I can handle him?" I asked playfully.

He leered at me again. "You look like you can handle almost anything. *Except* Jamie Brock."

"How well do you know him?"

His drink arrived before he had an opportunity to answer, so I waited while he paid the waiter, adding—I noted—an almost nonexistent tip. Between this paltry gratuity and his rudeness to the water waiter, it was clear that Ascot Man didn't care what the staff thought of him. That was one "observe and learn" lesson that I didn't think I'd be imitating.

Drink in hand, he returned to the subject of Jamie. "I suspect I'm about his best friend. I met him in L.A., before he moved here. That would have been . . . seven months ago or so."

That clarified a question that had been rattling around my brain without gaining focus. Until now.

"So he just moved here?"

"Recently."

"Okay," I said. "I was wondering why Jamie was living with that old guy. If he recently moved here, that explains it."

"Benjamin? He's a nice guy. He takes care of our Jamie." With that, dismissing talk of Benjamin Grover—friend of Andrew Dice Clay and the Stones—Ascot Man leaned close to me. Apparently, I was now his confidante, which made me all the more regretful that I hadn't bothered to learn his name the previous evening.

"You seem to like Jamie," he said, which his vague Southern accent rendered a harmless statement, rather than a potential minefield.

"He's kind of hot," I admitted.

"Jamie knows a lot of people, but he never really lets them get too close."

"I don't know about that." I said, grinning with what could have been a bit too much self-satisfaction. "He let *me* get pretty close."

"Well . . ." He looked at me skeptically. "Good luck to you, then. I will say that you make a cute couple."

I changed the topic from Jamie Brock, but I didn't stray from Ascot Man's side. My logic was structured like this: I saw Jamie as my ticket to having it all; Ascot Man described himself as the person closest to Jamie; therefore, by buddying up to Ascot Man, I would remain in Jamie's orbit. Which was no guarantee of success for Operation Hamptons, but went a hell of a way to advance my position.

The awkward side to all of this, of course, was the fact that I didn't know his name. And no one was giving me a clue. Fortunately, Alan finally found me, and I saw my opportunity.

"This is my friend Alan," I said.

"Hi, Alan," Ascot Man said, shaking his hand. "I'm Michael."

Mental note to self: Ascot Man's name is Michael. Remember that!

"And what do you do, Alan?" he asked. It occurred to me that I had yet to be asked that question. More evidence that my ruse was working: everyone just assumed that I did *nothing* for a living.

"I'm a talent manager."

"Really? And how do you know Brett?"

Alan looked at me, and we both realized that we hadn't come up with a cover story. So I fearlessly jumped in with, "I used to do some modeling, and Alan represented me." No need for Michael to know about my grungy failed acting career . . . especially the debacle that was *Andy.* An experiment in modeling seemed clean and prestigious, exactly the sort of thing a good-looking young man who didn't want to work too hard might indulge in.

"And what do you do?" Alan asked in return.

"A little of this, a little of that." A non-answer, which to my ears sounded like a reasonable explanation for what I envisioned Michael doing for a living. A little investing, a little sailing, a little traveling, a little art collecting, a little ascot-wearing . . . a lot of a little of everything.

After a few more minutes of small talk, Michael excused himself to go to the men's room. No sooner was he out of earshot than Alan grabbed my arm.

"Oh!" he gasped, pointing behind me. "There's one for you!"

I pivoted, and saw that Alan was gesturing to the Puerto Rican waiter who had brought Michael his water.

"Alan," I said. "I don't think so."

"Why not? He's very cute. And, honey, I know how you like that accent."

I smiled at him. "That's past. I'm not that person anymore. And . . . not for nothing, but he's just a waiter. How is he going to change my life?"

"Well, I'll say this for you," he said unhappily. "You've certainly got your eye on the prize. I hope this Jamie is all that you've made him out to be." He paused. "And I hope he feels the same way about you, because if he doesn't . . ."

"I think he does," I said. "But if he doesn't, I'll come up with another option. Or I'll *make* him fall in love with me."

The waiter passed me, offering me a shy smile as he brushed by. Alan was right—the waiter was cute and he was my type, and, yes, I loved that accent—but flirting had taken a new dimension in recent days. It was now more than recreation. It was business, too.

"No waiters," I said, although he had said nothing new to prompt my comment.

"Fine with me. Do what you have to do."

I returned home some time after midnight to find the apartment Quentin-free, which delighted me no end. I turned on the stereo and settled onto the couch, then saw I had a waiting message on the answering machine. I tapped the "play" button.

"Hey, baby." I recognized Jamie Brock's voice immediately and could tell he was calling from a cell phone. "I'm here and safe in the Hamptons. Just thought I'd give you a call, but I guess I missed you. I don't know if I'll have a chance tomorrow, but I'll definitely call you on Sunday night when I get back to New York. Later."

Operation Hamptons was going to work. Operation Hamptons had to work.

Brett Revere's Theory of Life, Part Four:
Don't Get Caught with Your Pants Down

I managed to keep myself occupied for the daylight hours the next day—a little of this, a little of that, as Michael might have said—but kept in earshot of the phone. When it didn't ring and I realized that Saturday night had passed the nine o'clock point, I decided to once again visit the Penthouse. Just because Jamie and most of the ring of older guys I had met were in the East End didn't mean I couldn't continue to make progress on Operation Hamptons. And if things worked out with Jamie, which I certainly hoped they would, well . . . I could just consider this night's visit as a supplemental activity.

The N Train eventually reached the Lexington Avenue stop in Manhattan, where I took a few flights of stairs to street level, emerging just across the street from Bloomingdale's. I couldn't help but say under my breath, "I'll be shopping with you soon enough," to the unexceptional block-long building, passing it as I headed north on Lex. It was an optimistic mutter, given the fact that Bloomie's had cut off my credit the year before, but I was suddenly feeling very optimistic.

When I reached the Penthouse, the first thing I noticed was a sea change in the clientele. The genteel, graying crowd from Thursday night—which was admittedly diluted upon my return visit Friday night—had almost wholly turned into what looked to me like a typical Bridge and Tunnel crowd. And as a B-and-T-er of long-standing, I could pick out my fellow non-Manhattanites a mile away.

First, I noticed that the men—again, it was an all-male enclave—were younger than the Penthouse patrons on the other two nights. There were also a few more nonwhite faces who were not serving cocktails. But mostly what I noticed was the way people were dressed. They weren't casual as in the casual of the wealthy—Ralph Lauren, nice khakis from Barneys, expensive loafers. No, they were casual in the casual of, well, Gap and Banana Republic and, yes, Levi's.

And then there was what they were drinking. The top shelf must have been collecting dust that night, because there were a whole lot of beer bottles being handed over the bar. I didn't even think the Penthouse *served* beer until I saw that. When I saw a small group of men holding their plastic bottles of water, though, I think I audibly gasped.

Over the course of three evenings I had not only laid claim to the Penthouse, but I had also apparently adopted its attitude. And now I felt as if these Philistines were defiling *my* temple.

I was glad Alan wasn't with me, to witness what had become of me.

At last a familiar face appeared near the stairs to the piano bar. It was Ascot Man—I remembered that his name was Michael just in time—and he was waving me over.

"You escaped from your wedding at the Waldorf already?" he asked, when I reached his perch against the staircase railing.

It took me a moment to remember why he asked me that, until I recalled my excuse for staying in town over the weekend.

"Yeah," I said. "Afternoon wedding. Very nice." I trailed off, not wishing to get into more detail than I had to. Especially since, like the Hamptons, I had never been to the Waldorf-Astoria.

He nodded absently and scanned the crowd.

"Can you believe this place?" he said finally. "It's B-and-T Night here tonight."

It was as if he had read my mind. I silently congratulated myself on mastering the Penthouse attitude so quickly.

"*Very* B-and-T," I echoed, shaking my head in a sadness that was almost sincere.

"I don't think there's a 212 area code in the entire room except you and me," he added, and I started to agree until I remembered that my area code was not 212, which was all of Manhattan and *only* Manhattan, except some of the arrivistes who were saddled with a 646, so I just kept silent. "It's like an invasion from Queens." Again, I kept my mouth shut. "Or worse, Staten Island."

I decided it was in my best interest to change the subject.

"I heard from Jamie last night. He left me a message."

"Yeah, I talked to him this afternoon." Damn! One-upped! "He sounded bored out there. It's those people he's staying with. Nouveau riche white trash."

"Who is it he's staying with?"

"This crass couple from somewhere like West Virginia who hit the Powerball lottery and decided to buy their way into society. First thing they do is build one of those ugly McMansions out in East Hampton for eight million dollars, throw money at every charity they can find, and push their fat bellies into every social event from Westhampton to Montauk. And of course *no one* will tell them to get lost, because everyone wants some of that Powerball money. Not me, though. No thank you."

"What's Jamie doing hanging out with people like *that*?" I asked, as I wondered if Jamie would introduce me to Mr. and Mrs. Powerball at the appropriate point.

"I love Jamie," Michael said with a smile and a nod of his head, "but that boy's always working some angle."

I must have shown a bit of surprise, because Michael immediately corrected himself.

"Now I'm not saying that Jamie Brock is a player. He's a real hard worker. But he's always looking for connections for his decorating business, and he thinks those lottery hogs are going to make that happen for him." He paused, then added, "I don't think that's gonna happen. I think they're just using him."

"Using him? How?"

"Building *their* connections on *his* connections. I know he's young, Brett, but Jamie's been around, and he knows a lot of people. It's almost as if he collects them. Other decorators, artists . . . not anyone you'd necessarily know, but people very prominent behind the scenes." He took a sip of his drink then lifted one eyebrow in my direction. "You'll have to accept my apologies."

"Why?"

"For what I just said. Sometimes I am such a snob."

"I still don't . . ."

"When I indicated that you wouldn't know the people Jamie knows. That was a presumptuous thing for me to say. You're obviously a young man who knows his way around, and I shouldn't start assuming whom you do and don't know just because the Penthouse hasn't been your regular bar until the past few days. We probably know a lot of the same people."

"Oh, that. Uh . . . don't worry about it. I could have said the same thing myself." Which I *couldn't* have said, of course, but that was of no matter to me. I was suddenly more intrigued that Jamie was a decorator. There seemed to be a disconnection between the thrown-together clutter of his clothes-strewn bedroom and his career. So I asked.

"Oh, yeah," said Michael. "Jamie was one of the top decorators in L.A. before he moved here. He's still trying to establish himself in New York, but it won't be long before he's big here. As big as he was on the West Coast. I've seen his work, and he's very good."

Don't get me wrong: I was suitably impressed. Still, I was having a hard time reconciling *my* Jamie—the imaginary trust funder I had expected him to be—with the real Jamie that Michael was now presenting me with. I mean, I hadn't expected to learn that Jamie *worked* for a living. But since I was sort of pretending to be a trust funder and I also expected to be working soon—in a field yet to be determined, provided by some rich gay man yet to be determined—I shook off this slight change in images. It really didn't matter, and it gave me a better insight into what Jamie Brock was all about.

Speaking of which . . .

"So, you heard from him today," I said. "What did he have to say?"

"Mostly, he's bored out there. And those lottery hogs are making him crazy. But I must say . . . well, maybe I must *not* say, but I'm going to, anyway. He was talking an awful lot about you."

"Me?" I felt my heart flutter and face redden.

"You. I don't know what it is with the two of you, but you both seem to have made a real connection."

I did the best I could to play it cool, but I wanted to know all the details. "Why? What exactly did he say?"

Michael turned to me and gave me only the most barely noticeable of smiles. "I consider myself a gentleman, and a gentleman doesn't share the intimate details of a phone conversation with a friend. Much as I think you'd like to hear all the dirty details, and you *would*, you're just going to have to be content for now knowing that he was very complimentary."

"You're gonna leave me hanging?"

"Ask him yourself," he said, his smile now brighter. "He'll be back on Monday."

"Monday?" I was momentarily crestfallen. "But his message said he was aiming for tomorrow night." Yes, I know he said he *might* be back Monday, but I wanted to feel that electricity again on Sunday. Which was all that mattered.

Michael sneered. "The white trash family is having a barbecue on Sunday, and for some reason half of the crowd is going. Hell, even Jeffrey Ryan says he's going to be there and write it up for *Haute Manhattan*, with a bunch of photos by Patrick McMullan." He took a sip of his drink, emptying it. "Good thing those piglets are too huge to fit in a frame, so we won't have to see them on the PartyPix page."

"So Jamie is hanging around for the party?"

Michael set his empty glass on the tray of a passing waiter. I noticed it was the Puerto Rican boy who brought him water when he was choking the night before. Michael didn't.

"One thing you'll come to learn about Jamie is that if there's a party, he's there. And if there's a party where you could reasonably expect to see Calvin, Donna, Ralph, Puffy, Alec, half of Wall Street, and all of publishing, he's *really* there. That's not a bad thing—I'm sure you know a lot of people just like that—but that's Jamie."

Okay, so I had my brief moment of disappointment, which was tempered by the knowledge that my Jamie—the man who on such short acquaintance was stealing my heart and, it appeared if one read between the lines of Michael's cryptic comments, vice versa—was going to spend the day rubbing elbows with the Hamptons elite. Which meant that not only did I see more clearly than ever the potential of a future with Jamie, but it could be a future filled with Jamie's friends and acquaintances. Unlike Michael, I was fairly certain that I could abide the Powerball family enough to make that work.

But now I had a free Sunday ahead of me. And Michael—boycotting the East End and the "lottery hogs"—also had Sunday free. Thinking clearly for once in my life, I said:

"So, if Jamie's out there for the party tomorrow, I guess I have a free Sunday."

He took the bait. "If you're interested, I'm driving up to Scarsdale to visit with the cutest couple. You could come with me."

"Me?" Very realistic feigned surprise, if I say so myself. "Are you sure I wouldn't be in the way?"

"Not at all," he said, waving to a waiter—a *different* waiter—for another drink. "I think you'd like them. They're a couple of fun kids."

"Then I'm there."

"Good. I was thinking of driving up around one in the afternoon. Is that okay?"

"I can do that."

"Give me your phone number, and I'll call you around noon."

"No problem." I was carrying a pen and picked up a pack of matches from the bar, ready to pass along my number. I reached the point when I was just about to write the seven of my 718 area code when I stopped.

Seven-one-eight. A dead giveaway to my Bridge and Tunnel status. A dead giveaway that I was a fraud. And yes, Jamie had my phone number with that area code, and don't think I didn't suddenly panic about *that*, too.

So I wrote down the phone number for Donovan Talent Management. And silently hoped that I'd find a way to get into Alan's midtown office by noon on a Sunday.

Michael handed me an elegant business card that had nothing on it except "Michael DeVries" and his phone number, which, of course, had a 212 area code. Then again, when your occupation is "a little of this, a little of that," what else would you put on a business card?

We parted a short time later, and I went off to hunt down Alan. When I found him, he was—not unexpectedly—at Bar 51. And he wasn't happy with my proposal.

"This was *just* what I was expecting, Brett!"

"Alan, this isn't *anything* like what you were expecting. I'm just asking for one night."

"One night sleeping in my office. Next thing I know you'll be measuring for curtains."

"But I needed a 212 area code."

"Most people, if they need it that badly, move to Manhattan and hope they don't get a 646. I'd ask you to explain this to me, but I've already heard your explanation six or seven times and it *still* doesn't make sense. So you don't have to waste your breath again."

"Thank you."

He flagged over Bartender Micah, ordered a drink, then dropped his voice. "Okay, I'll give you my keys. You know the routine: sign in with security, and if they question you, have them call me on my cell. But I swear to God, that place had better be immaculate when I walk in there Monday morning. I want to see no evidence that you were ever there. No soap scum in the shower, no toothpaste in the sink, no cigarette butts in the toilet . . ."

"I don't smoke."

"The way things are going, I no longer know what you do anymore. Which reminds me: no syringes!"

"I don't . . ."

"I'm the one doing you a favor, so listen to my rules. One night only. No guests. I swear to God if I find a cum stain on that couch . . ."

"Alan!"

". . . I'll be so pissed off that I'll *personally* call Walter Pomeroy and beg for you to be recast in *Andy*. Do I make myself clear?"

"Yes."

Bartender Micah put Alan's drink in front of him. Alan sipped, then looked me squarely in the eye.

"You think this is right? You think this is a good thing? An appropriate way to live your life?"

"It's working so far."

"So far." He sipped again. "I have to admit that I have no clue whatsoever how you can pull off your Hamptons Offensive . . ."

"Operation Hamptons."

"Whatever. I have no clue how this is going to work. I hope you do."

I told him that I thought I did. And I hoped I knew what I was talking about.

I reached Alan's building just after 2:00 A.M., waving the key at the security guard in the lobby to authenticate the fact that I belonged there. He didn't look twice at me as he pushed a smudged register across his desk for me to sign in. That accomplished, I took the rickety elevator up to Alan's seventh-floor office and let myself in. There, I stripped to my underwear—my clothes would be needed in somewhat fresh condition the next day—and found a thin, old blanket in a closet, which I wrapped around my body before I lowered myself onto the plastic couch in the reception area.

Ten seconds later, I was sliding off the couch.

I readjusted a few times, and each time I began sliding almost immediately, so, resigned and still wrapped in the blanket, I gathered a few small throw rugs together into something approaching bedding and settled down on the linoleum.

In the almost four decades of my life, I had slept in some uncomfortable places: a tent in the woods, leaking in a thunderstorm when it wasn't swarming with mosquitoes; more than a few sleazy motels on thin, stained mattresses; a Greyhound bus wedged between an icy cold window and an obese, phlegmatic, and unhygienic man who, I suspected, was masturbating under the blanket covering his lap . . .

But none of those experiences quite compared with spending a Saturday night in the office of Donovan Talent Management, high above Seventh Avenue in midtown Manhattan . . . but not so high that the traffic didn't seem to be blasting its horns in my ears.

Oh yes: although it was very early on a Sunday morning in June, the air-conditioning kept the office bone-chillingly cold. But when I opened the window, hoping to catch a warm breeze, the noise from the street below almost made my ears bleed. Damned if I did and damned if I didn't, I decided to bundle up and remind myself that I had been through worse, even if "worse" meant Februarys in Albany some two decades earlier.

"This is not going to work," I muttered to myself. I stood up and took a walk to the window, hoping to spot an all-night diner where I could hole up for the night, before I thought things through and determined that pulling an all-nighter before meeting the cutest couple in Westchester County would not be one of my better ideas.

So I turned to Plan B. If I slept in my clothes, I would be warmer. Yes, they would wrinkle a bit, but I could always steam some of the wrinkles out while I showered. And in the meantime, I'd be less likely to freeze to death.

The decision was made. I dressed again, then wrapped the blanket around my shoulders and settled back into my makeshift bedding, where I continued to shiver, willing to no avail for the drinks I had consumed at Bar 51 to put me quickly to sleep.

* * *

I must have drifted off at some point, because I did eventually awaken, but, as I stretched, I realized that any sleep I had managed had been far short of a healthy amount. I did, after all, see the sun rise through the grimy window of Alan's office.

Slowly and painfully I stood, and unpleasant spasms rippled through my back. What a beautiful start to a Sunday morning.

All in all, my shirt and pants weren't in that bad a state, and I was confident that I could look presentable by the time I had to meet Michael. Which reminded me. . . .

I found my watch under the couch and looked at it. Then I looked again, much more carefully, because my eyes were obviously still too blurry from sleep to have possibly read what I read . . . except when I reread the time, I realized I was right the first time, and it really *was* a few minutes after noon.

And as if to mock my sudden panic, the phone rang at that precise moment.

I reached the phone on the third ring and gasped, "Hello."

"Happy Sunday," said Michael, his voice cheerful. "Are you dressed and ready to go?"

"Yes," I lied. Well, I *was* dressed, at least.

"Good. It's a beautiful day, and I want to get an early start. Meet me at Tenth and Fifty-seventh in an hour."

"Tenth and Fifty-seventh?"

"That's where I garage my car."

"Ah."

I hung up and looked again at my watch. I had just enough time to shower and get over to Tenth Avenue, but I had to make tracks.

I quickly stripped off my clothes, then, wearing only my jockey shorts, looked for a coat hanger. The closet in the waiting room was empty, so I charged into Alan's inner sanctum and made a beeline for his personal closet.

It was locked.

I muttered an epithet under my breath and walked back into the waiting room . . . just as the door to the hallway opened, and I was suddenly face-to-face with a uniformed security guard. Startled, I screeched something unintelligible and leapt back.

"Stop right there," he snapped, apparently confusing himself with a television cop, as he warded me off with a heavy flashlight.

"Christ, you scared me," I said, as I tried to calm myself down. "I'm . . . I'm . . . it's okay. I'm allowed to be here."

"You work here?"

"No. I'm a client."

He looked me over warily, a hard expression on his young face.

"Okay," I continued. "I know it seems unusual to find an undressed guy in the office on a Sunday afternoon."

"Never seen it before."

"I don't doubt it. But I'm a client of Alan Donovan, and he said I could sleep on his couch last night."

"Why's that?"

"Because I needed a 212."

"What?"

"Because I . . . had too much to drink last night, and couldn't make it back to Queens."

He remained unsatisfied.

"Look," I said, pointing to the clothes I had left on the couch. "Those are my clothes. I was just going to take a shower."

The security guard took a look at the clothes, and another look at me.

"Building management rules: no sleeping overnight in the offices."

"Well . . . I didn't know that."

"I'm gonna have to report this."

"Yeah, yeah, okay. Report it. I just want to take a shower and get out of here."

He shook his head. "Not so fast. How do I know you didn't break in?"

"I told you . . ."

He reached for the radio clipped to his belt. "I have to call my supervisor."

"While you do that, can I shower?"

"You're staying right here." Into the radio, he said, "This is Brian. I'm in 705, and I found a naked man who says he stayed here overnight with the permission of Alan Donegan."

"Donovan."

He ignored me. I heard a tinny voice respond, "I'll be there in five."

"Ten-four." The guard clipped his mic back to his belt and resumed his flashlight-warding.

"Listen," I said. "I do apologize for all this. But if I don't take a shower while we're waiting, I'm going to be late." No reaction. "Can't we just call the guy whose office this is? I have his cell phone number." No reaction. "Can I at least put my clothes on? Or can you close the door to the hall? I feel . . . exposed."

"You stay the way I found you." It wasn't what I wanted to hear, but at least he was finally communicating.

Soon enough, his supervisor appeared, along with the building superintendent. Apparently, finding a man wearing only his briefs was a big draw on a slow Sunday afternoon in this building.

"Let me see some ID," said the supervisor, a man who wore with sourness his decades-long career in private security.

I took my wallet out of my pants and handed over my driver's license.

"Mr. Revere?"

"Yes."

"That your real name?"

I didn't answer, except to say, "I'm an actor."

"Uh-huh. Well, Mr. Revere, why don't you tell me what you're doing running around this office in your underwear."

"As I told this guy, I'm a client of Donovan Talent Management. Last night, I had a little bit too much to drink and couldn't make it home, so Alan Donovan—he's the boss here—Alan told me I could sleep it off in his office."

The building super, a short, bald man who was taking great delight in all this activity, especially since it required nothing of him but to observe, piped up. "No sleeping overnight in this building."

"I know that now. But I didn't then. It won't happen again."

The security supervisor turned to the young guard. "You found him like this?"

"I was checking doors down the hall, and heard someone answer a phone. Went to check it out and found him running around naked."

"I'm not . . . Okay, I'm mostly naked, yes, but I was going to take a shower. Can we call Alan Donovan? I'm sure he can resolve this."

The supervisor turned to the building super. "You have an emergency contact number for this place?"

"In my office."

"I have it," I said, and rattled off Alan's phone number from memory. In response, the three men just looked at me. "That's it! That's his number! Call him!"

The security supervisor shook his head. "With all due respect, Mr. Revere, I think we'd better handle this with our own contact information. We don't want to learn we've called a friend of yours, instead of the tenant." He nodded to the building super, who went off in search of Alan's phone number.

While we waited for him to return, I picked up my watch from the desk to check the time. It was already twelve-twenty.

"Put the watch down," said the supervisor, when he caught me holding it.

"But this is my watch . . ."

"I don't know that yet. Until I can ascertain its proper ownership, please return the valuables to the desk."

It took the building super another ten minutes to return, and then the security chief picked up Alan's phone and dialed, looking perplexed for a moment until I said, "You have to dial 9 for an outside line."

"Thanks," he muttered, and punched in the numbers. After a short wait, he said, "Is this Mr. Alan Donovan, of Donovan Talent Management? . . . Yes, sir, this is Don Crary. I'm the security supervisor at your building. Anyway . . . Well, yes, sir. That's exactly why I'm calling. One of my guards found Mr. Revere running around your office naked . . ."

"I'm wearing underwear!" I hoped Alan had heard me.

". . . And he says that he's allowed to be here. Is that true?" The supervisor listened to Alan for a few beats, then turned to me. "He wants to talk to you."

"Alan?" I said, taking the phone. "I am *not* naked."

"I *knew* something was going to happen," he said. "I just *knew* it. Do you want to tell me how you managed to get busted by building security? Not to mention, why you're naked?"

"I'm not naked. I'm wearing underwear."

"Brett . . ."

"The security guard heard me answer the phone, so he came

down the hall to check it out, and then . . . well, I was getting ready to shower, so I was in my underwear . . ."

"Get to the point."

"Right. Anyway, when he saw me, he called his supervisor to verify it was all right for me to be here, and then, well . . . that's why they called you."

"Right about now, I feel like having you arrested for trespassing. Just for fun. I swear to God . . ." He sighed, then said, "Put Crary back on the line."

I handed the phone back to the security supervisor, who listened for a moment, nodding in agreement, before ending the call. As he cradled the phone, he said, "Mr. Donovan backs up your story."

"Thanks," I said. "See? I told you I was telling the truth."

The three men filed out with no further acknowledgment of me, except the building superintendent, who once again stated that overnight sleeping wasn't allowed in the building.

Now that I was allowed to pick up my own watch again, I checked the time. It was twelve-forty, and I was seriously behind schedule.

But I felt I now deserved that shower. It was the last thing I would have voluntarily given up at that point.

Michael was waiting when I reached our designated corner in a BMW that had seen better days, and he didn't seem happy about it.

"You're late," he said, without a smile, as I approached the car.

"Yeah, but in a few years, it will make for an amusing story."

I walked past his window and around the front of the car, opening the passenger door.

"Well, aren't you a sight," he said, as I climbed in the car. "Aren't those the same clothes you were wearing last night? And your hair is still wet."

I looked down and inspected my clothes.

"Uh . . . no, I think last night I was wearing a different-colored shirt. And khakis are khakis."

"Maybe . . ."

"As for my hair, it will dry on the trip up there."

Without responding, he pulled away from the curb and into light traffic, then made a few turns until we entered the highway.

As the elderly BMW started its trip up the West Side Highway, or the Joe DiMaggio Highway, or the Henry Hudson Parkway, or whatever we were supposed to be calling it those days, I felt a weight lift off my shoulders. The last few months had been tough on my soul, and part of the problem, I was beginning to suspect, was that I hadn't been out of New York City in close to a year. And the beginning of my day had been nothing short of a debacle. Now, though, I was on my way to meet the cutest couple in Scarsdale. I was going to be spending an elegant Sunday in the khakified rolling greenery of Westchester County, far from the cacophony of car horns that had become the natural background noise of my life.

"So tell me about these folks," I said, as we passed the exit for the George Washington Bridge. Michael weaved through traffic as the traffic signs pointed us north to Westchester.

"They're just the cutest couple," he said, his mood sunny once again as we put most of Manhattan behind us. "Blake and Winston Culver-Benchley. Don't you just love their names? Well, they're just as adorable as their names are." I thought that no matter how cute Blake and Winston were, they would have a hard time living up to their advance publicity. "You are going to love them. *Love* them."

I was quite sure I would indeed love them. Brett Revere, Trust Fund Boy, couldn't help but immediately become fast friends with people like Blake and Winston. And they would love me, too. I was feeling especially charming that afternoon as we now sped through the Bronx, and it was totally in keeping with the spirit of Operation Hamptons that I should immediately become fast friends with a cute, WASPy, rich couple of Westchester dwellers with a hyphenated last name. These were the type of people that Brett Revere should be close to; the type of upwardly mobile gay couple who had their commitment ceremonies profiled in the pages of *The New York Times*.

The groom is a Harvard lawyer whose father ran a bank and whose mother founded a cultural institution; the other groom is a prominent architect whose late father was president of an exclusive private club and whose mother is chair of the Newport Ladies Yachting Society. They met at a party thrown by George Plimpton to celebrate the publication of the hot literary sensation of the season, and have been together ever since.

They will live in their homes in Scarsdale, Manhattan, Aspen, Southampton, Belize, and Switzerland . . .

Michael's voice brought me out of the daydream.

"And let me tell you, Brett, we're talking money here. More money than you or I will probably ever see . . ." He trailed off, quickly adding, "Oh, there I go again. Acting as if I know everything about you."

I leaned back in the padded seat and smiled. "In time, Michael. In time."

Soon we were racing through Westchester County, our trip largely undertaken in silence. I had no idea what was going on in the mind of Michael DeVries, but I was feeling incredibly relaxed and happy to be out of the city.

After a while, Michael slowed the BMW and we turned onto a tree-canopied lane, then drove up a brief rise in the road past a stone fence.

"Here they are," he said, pointing at the fence. When it ended, he turned into the gravel driveway.

"Nice," I said, almost to myself, as I surveyed the grounds. No house was yet in sight; just a panorama of green lawn under a heavy cover of trees, with a few carefully landscaped boulders to break things up. A tenth of a mile or so down the driveway a gazebo appeared on the grounds, the sun flashing off its conical whitewashed roof.

We drove up another short incline and the house finally came into view. Given the amount of land, the house seemed smaller than I had expected, a modest two-story structure painted a slightly faded white, surrounded by beds of colorful flowers. An open porch wrapped around the front of the house and disappeared down each side.

Michael pulled to a slow stop in front of the house, and the gravel crunched beneath the tires.

"Here we are," he said, adding, "Now be on your best behavior."

I was a bit taken aback. "I'm always on my best behavior."

"I know, I know," he said, patting my leg. "But out here, be on your *extra*-best behavior. Do you know what I mean?"

"Uh . . . I think so."

He shook his head. "Just follow my lead, and you'll be fine."

Okay. Extra-best behavior it was. At the same time, we opened our doors and got out of the car, and were immediately greeted by a voice from the porch.

"About time you got out of that city, Michael DeVries!" said the man's voice. I squinted to find the source from the shadows of the porch, finally spotting a heavyset older man holding a drinking glass, half-hidden behind an overgrown rose bush.

"Blake, you old dog," said Michael, taking the lead down the stone path leading from the driveway to the house. It seemed that his ordinarily soft Southern accent had grown noticeably thicker. "You'd see a lot more of me if you'd get on that phone and invite me up here more often."

Wait a minute . . . *that* was Blake Culver-Benchley? No, no, that was not Blake Culver-Benchley. Blake Culver-Benchley was cute and young, and there was not only nothing cute or young about this man, there hadn't been since the Eisenhower Administration. He was seventyish, maybe older, and looked every bit of it, and when he rose to greet Michael I saw that his stomach extended a full twelve inches in front of him, straining at his golf shirt. No, no . . . *cute* Blake Culver-Benchley was a younger, leaner . . . well, *cuter* version of this man. This was Blake's father . . . Blake, Sr. . . . the parent who ran my imaginary bank.

But, no . . . Michael didn't ask if Blake, Jr. could come out to play. By his actions, it was clear that this was, in fact, one-half of the cutest couple in Westchester. I could only imagine what his boyfriend Winston looked like.

Michael introduced us, and Blake invited us to sit down.

"You must need a Bloody Mary after that ride," he said.

"Well . . ." Michael hesitated, and although I would have loved a Bloody Mary, I was going to follow his lead, as instructed.

"I'm afraid I have to insist, Michael." The old man raised his glass and said, "I refuse to drink alone."

Michael smiled. "What about Winston?"

Blake cleared his throat and said, "I believe that Winston is drinking in the kitchen. That's not the same as sharing a Bloody Mary with me out here in all this beautiful nature."

"Maybe just one. I have to drive home later, remember, so I can't overdo it."

"And you, young man?" Blake asked me.

"Yes, please."

"*Winston!*" he suddenly bellowed. "*Better bring out that pitcher, honey!*"

The moment of truth was about to arrive. I would get to see the man who completed the pair that Michael thought of as "cute."

The screen door snapped open and . . .

. . . Winston was a woman.

A painfully thin woman, every bit as old as Blake, maybe older. She was overdressed for the setting, and shakily carried a pitcher of Bloody Marys.

"Well, darling, don't you look cute this afternoon," drawled Michael. "Can I give you a hand?" Cute. Yes, of course.

"No, thank you, Michael," she said. As she neared the table, Michael rose. Again, I followed his lead, vaguely remembering that that was something gentlemen did. She set the pitcher down, splashing some Bloody Mary on the table, and Michael gave her the lightest peck on the cheek.

"Winston," he said, "This is my good friend, Brett Revere."

I extended my hand, and she wrapped both her bony hands around it and smiled, or approximated a smile to the best of her ability, given what looked like more than her share of face-lifts.

"Very nice to meet you, Brett. Michael has told us quite a bit about you."

I arched an eyebrow. "Really?"

"Oh yes, dear. He told us . . . now, what was it that he told us again?" Confusion washed over her face for a split second, then that taut smile returned. "Oh, yes. You're descended from Paul Revere, aren't you?"

"Uh . . ." I mean, yes, friends had made that joke over my two decades of living under an assumed name, but I had never heard someone state it seriously. I shot Michael a look.

But he merely smiled and shook his head. "He doesn't like to brag about that, Winnie."

Reluctantly, I found myself playing along. "That's right. It's just a name, after all."

"A very distinguished name," she said, delicately taking a seat, and thereby allowing Michael and I to sit. "You must be quite proud of your ancestry."

"Well, I didn't exactly do anything to become a Revere. I was just . . . *born*."

"As I was born an Adams," she said. "We share a proud Revolutionary heritage. But remember, Brett: those of us who are privileged to be born to a special lineage have an obligation to preserve that heritage."

I caught myself wondering if she was preserving her Adams ancestry as aggressively as she was attempting to preserve her face, but forced the thought from my head. Instead, I nodded and muttered an indistinct agreement, and then, fortunately, we were on to the next topic.

"Winnie and I thought lunch at the club might be nice today," drawled Blake, swishing his Bloody Mary in the air. I watched the celery stalk slide around the rim of the glass.

"That sounds like fun," Michael gushed.

Winnie Culver-Benchley turned to me and asked, "Have you ever been to Sterling Hills, Brett?"

"I don't think so. That's . . . a country club?"

She laughed. "It's not *a* country club, dear. It's *the* country club." She turned to her husband and asked, "Darling, how long has Sterling Hills been in existence?"

"Eighteen ninety-four. And membership has been restricted since World War II."

I felt the hair on the back of my neck bristle and, to Michael's obvious discomfort, I had to ask. "Restricted?"

"Yes," said Blake, but a thought crossed his mind before he had an opportunity to continue. "Oh, no, no, no. I'm sorry, son, when I say 'restricted,' I mean that the number of members is limited. I don't mean that it's all white or no Jews are allowed."

Winnie cackled and placed a grandmotherly hand on my wrist. "Goodness no, Brett. Why, one of our favorite members is a perfectly nice doctor, and he's black!"

Michael forced a laugh, although I sensed his discomfort. "I'm sure Brett didn't think you'd belong to a segregated club."

Winnie shook her head. "It would be close to impossible to have a decent country club in Westchester County with a segregated membership . . ."

"See, Brett?"

". . . Especially when half the people here are Jews."

A throat full of Bloody Mary almost came up, but I held it back.

"And a lot of the Jews are lawyers, so you can be sure we'd be facing a new lawsuit each week. Easier to just let them in and be over it. The Jews and the blacks, both." With that comment, she returned her attention to her Bloody Mary.

I must have looked a bit stunned, because Michael kicked me under the table.

"Ah, well . . ." mumbled Blake, sipping on his drink distractedly. "Things change, don't they, dear?"

"They do," she said.

"In the Governor's day, well . . . I don't know if things were better than they are today, but they were certainly different."

"The Governor?" I asked.

Winnie again took my wrist, and her bony fingers gripped tightly. "Blake's father, Judge Culver-Benchley, was known as 'The Governor.' "

I looked at Blake. "Your father was a governor? That's interesting."

He stared thoughtfully out at the lawn. "He wasn't actually a governor. My father was a lot of things—a judge, of course, and also a businessman, a Wall Street lawyer, an ambassador—but he was never governor. That was the one thing he wanted that he couldn't get. People just started to call him that one day to give him a hard time, and the name stuck." He leaned close to me. "When the *Times* ran his obituary, they even put it in the headline. How do you like that? *'Blake Culver, Civic Leader, Known as The Governor.'* I think Judge Culver got as big a kick out of being called 'The Governor' than he would have had holding the office and dealing with all those damn tax-raising liberals in Albany."

Now Blake was getting Winnie's wrist-holding attention, as she cooed, "Now, dear, don't get yourself so worked up."

"You're right, Blake," said Michael, piping in. "New York State is becoming positively socialist."

"Bah. It's been socialist for quite some time. Started before Rockefeller, if you ask me. I used to tell Nelson that he was part of the problem, not the solution. And now it's out of control."

"Oh, dear." Winston Culver-Benchley forced a smile through her thin lips that seemed to pull at her forehead. "Let's not talk about politics, gentlemen. It's too nice of a day."

"These drinks need more vodka," Blake announced, setting his glass roughly on the table. "Less celery, and more vodka."

"You can have more vodka at the club. And you should eat your celery, dear. It's good for you."

Blake pushed himself away from the table and stood uncertainly. I was getting the impression that he had no need for any more vodka.

"You're right, my dear," he said, smiling crookedly after consulting his watch. "Let's go to the club. We should get there before the restaurant fills up."

Michael's survival instincts kicked in, and he said, "I'll drive."

While the cute couple freshened up, Michael and I sat in silence in the shade of the porch, finishing our drinks.

"So what do you think?" he asked finally. "Aren't they cute? The way they squabble and all that, it's just . . . cute."

What I thought, of course, is that this had the potential to be one of the longest afternoons of my life, as I tried to be a good boy while listening to bickering, alcoholic relics prattle on about socialists in Albany and Jews in their country club. But I couldn't say that—not just yet—so I tried to avoid looking at Michael, in case my eyes betrayed me. "They definitely are cute. Very cute." Lie over, I faced him. "And how long have you known them?"

"I met Winnie through friends of friends." Of course. The relationship equivalent of "a little of this, a little of that." Michael was clearly not going to share their history with me, and I was fine with that.

Several lazy minutes later Blake and Winston were back on the porch, locking the door behind them, and a few minutes after that—minutes in which Blake almost tumbled off the porch into a rose bush and Winston couldn't find her keys at the bottom of her purse—we were in the Culver-Benchley SUV, with Michael at the wheel. He rolled the vehicle slowly along the driveway, getting used to its feel, until he reached the main road. Blake, sitting next to him in the passenger seat, pointed in the direction of the club, and Michael punched the accelerator.

"That's the Corcoran place," said Winston, seated next to me in the back and pointing a long, lacquered fingernail at a large home gone to seed. "Blake and I were thinking of buying it so that no undesirables moved in, but the asking price was just too much." She paused while she rummaged through her purse, finally pulling out a cigarette case and lighter. "So we're taking our chances."

"Hmm," I replied, noncommittally.

"Hopefully, the asking price will serve as a deterrent. But my cousin in Greenwich thought the exact same thing about a parcel near her home, and the next thing you know, an Arab bought it and painted it the most garish colors."

"Hmm."

"Of course, these days . . . oh, listen to me babble!" She shifted in her seat and again grabbed my wrist with those bony, bony hands. "Enough with all that. You'd think civilization itself was coming to an end, the way Blake and I go on and on."

"Speak for yourself," Blake growled from the front seat, as he gestured to Michael to make the next left turn.

"So tell me about yourself, Brett," she continued. "What do you do for a living?"

The words "I'm an actor" almost spilled from my lips, but I caught myself at the last possible moment.

"I'm not doing much of anything right now," I said, which was, after all, more or less the truth. "I'm just enjoying my summer. Relaxing."

"Where do you summer?" she asked. "The Hamptons? Or . . . uh . . ." She turned red and glanced away.

I didn't understand the blush and stammer, so I chose to ignore it. "Actually, I'm spending the summer in New York. I'll probably get out of town on random weekends, but I like the city when no one else is around."

"That's so true," said Winston. She leaned close to me, beckoning my ear, and whispered. "I apologize if I'm getting too personal. I'm afraid those Bloody Marys . . ."

"Oh, but you weren't."

"I mean, I know that some young men of Michael's acquaintance have . . . *other* summer destinations."

Aha! That was it! Winston Culver-Benchley had picked up a *ping* from her very own "gaydar," and thought I might "summer" on Fire Island.

"Don't think twice about it," I said, which I hoped would provide a sufficient degree of vagueness to bring the discussion to an end without the need for me to explain further. Which it did. That, or she forgot what she was talking about, because soon her concentration was exclusively dedicated to lighting her cigarette.

Before long, a discreet sign posted several yards off the roadway announced the entrance to the Sterling Hills Country Club. Michael turned right through a stone gate and onto a paved private road that snaked between two rolling hills, which served as a natural buffer between the club and the unwashed masses outside the gate. We drove on, passing a scenic pond, then several greens, where old white men and old white women in new white electric golf carts waved at the familiar SUV as Blake and Winnie waved back. Out of the need for something to do, I found myself giving these strangers a friendly nod as we passed.

Finally we reached the parking lot. Michael pulled close to the front door and said, "Brett, why don't you escort Winston inside, and Blake and I will join you in a moment."

She absently stubbed out her cigarette in the ashtray, sending ashes flying into the air, and sat back in her seat, waiting for me to walk around and open the door for her. I got the hint, and did what I was supposed to do as a proper gentleman.

"Thank you, dear," she said, steadying herself on my arm as she climbed out of the backseat. "Blake would have let me sit there all day and roast in the heat."

"It would be worth it for the peace and quiet," he sniped from the front seat through her open door. I smiled as if I found his comment humorous and closed the door, and Michael steered the SUV away.

"Let's hurry," said Winnie, dragging me across the asphalt with renewed energy. "If we get right inside, we can get in a quick drink before they're back from parking."

I obediently followed her up the front steps and into the club, where she was greeted by the two doormen with a chipper "Hello, Mrs. Culver-Benchley" and I was given an indulgent nod after they quickly determined that I was her escort. Her heels clicked as she maneuvered quickly down the hardwood floor of a hallway, past sepia-toned photographs of the club's long-dead past presidents, and into a dark bar decorated in oak and hunter green.

"Marcel," she said, waving to the bartender before we were through the arched doorway.

"Good afternoon, Mrs. Culver-Benchley. The usual?"

"Yes, dear," she confirmed, taking a seat at the empty bar.

"And for you, sir?"

"Um . . . a glass of white wine."

"Chardonnay?"

"Yes, please." I sat down in the stool next to Winston, who was rummaging in the purse again for her cigarette case. As she lit a fresh cigarette, I felt compelled to make conversation, so I said, "So . . . this is Sterling Hills."

Her cigarette lit, Winston looked dreamily around the room. "I *love* this club, Brett. I adore it. Blake and I have belonged to other clubs, but Sterling Hills is special." She leaned closer, taking her drink from the bartender's hand without a glance in his direction. "And do you know what makes it so special, Brett? *The people.*"

"It sounds like . . ."

She talked right over me, which was fine. "The people here are just wonderful. Sometimes I honestly think I could live here."

"It's good to have a place to go that you enjoy."

"Oh, indeed." She patted my hand once then sat upright on her stool. "I need to ask you a question. I hope you don't mind."

"Me, too." I smiled, as if we were gossiping coconspirators, but her expression was dead serious.

"It's about Michael."

"Oh?" I took a sip from my wineglass.

"Is he happy?"

"I . . . I . . . Well, why wouldn't he be happy?" I didn't think I liked the direction the conversation was taking.

"Living in that city, all alone. Michael DeVries is well into his fifties now, and he really should settle down."

"He's got a lot of friends. He's very socially active. Maybe he's not the type to settle down." I *really* wished I knew what Winston knew about Michael's life. I didn't want to be responsible for outing him in the bar of the Sterling Hills Country Club, if at all possible.

"Oh, I know Michael is a social animal. I've seen that firsthand, and on numerous occasions. But that doesn't mean . . . *Hush.* Michael and Blake are coming into the bar. Not a word of this."

"Not a word," I agreed, and said a little prayer for their perfect timing.

"Thought I'd find you in here," said Blake. He was wheezing from the exertion of the walk from the parking lot.

"Brett and I were just having a quick drink before lunch," she said.

"That sounds like a good idea. Marcel, let me have one of your famous Bloody Marys, except hold the celery. And the Bloody Mary mix."

"Coming right up, sir."

As Marcel mixed—or, rather, didn't mix—Blake dropped his considerable weight onto the stool on the other side of his wife. Michael hovered behind us, but centered himself at Winston's back.

"I was just telling Brett how much we enjoy the club," Winston said, catching the others up on our mundane conversation.

"Hell of a place," said Blake. "The Governor was club president from '52 to '55. He's the one who was responsible for adding the driving range."

"I thought that was Schuyler Hunt," said Winston.

Blake was clearly annoyed with his wife. "It was The Governor."

"Are you sure?" She paused, lost in thought.

"Quite. Schuyler Hunt was the one who embezzled from the club treasury in the seventies."

"Oh, yes. I remember now."

"You had a club scandal?" I asked, for some reason intrigued. Maybe it was because it seemed incongruous to hear of rich people engaged in such petty thievery. "Did this Hunt guy end up going to jail?"

"No," said Blake. "We keep things to ourselves here. Schuyler Hunt was thrown out of the club and, well . . . basically, he was ostracized."

"No one had anything to do with him again," added Winston. "And four months later, he killed himself."

"Whoa," I said, genuinely shocked. "He killed himself because no one would talk to him?"

"Yes," said Winston. "Membership here is considered just that important."

"Enough about that," said Blake, with a finality that let us know that was enough about that. He turned to his wife and said, "Michael was telling me out in the parking lot that he's arranging a luncheon for you, sweetheart."

She smiled and craned her neck to catch a glimpse of Michael. "Oh, really?"

"I was trying to keep it a secret," Michael said, "but now that things are pretty much arranged, I figured I'd better tell you, so you can make sure to keep that busy calendar of yours free. How does two weeks from Thursday sound?" As Michael asked the question, I saw Blake nodding approvingly. "I know I have to schedule you *far* in advance . . . We'll all meet at Swifty's at 1:00 and make an afternoon of it."

"That would be marvelous," she said, reaching back in her purse for her calendar, and in the process, I noted, letting her cigarette slip off the ashtray. I leaned over and grabbed it, setting it back in the ashtray.

Winston Culver-Benchley never even noticed my gallant gesture. Instead, as she drew her calendar from her purse, she asked Michael, "Who are you inviting?"

"Now, dear, I have to keep *some* secrets from you, don't I?" Behind her back, he nodded to me, and I soon understood why. "But Brett and I will keep you and the ladies entertained all afternoon."

I would?

While I let that information filter through, I glanced over at Winston's calendar. It was full of penciled-in appointments—luncheons and shopping and, frighteningly enough, I think I saw a Brazilian bikini wax scheduled—and I began to understand why she had to be booked weeks in advance.

"Oh, no!" she gasped. "I can't have lunch two weeks from Thursday! That's the day before Independence Day weekend!"

Michael seemed, for a moment, to be speechless, but Blake swept in to fill the void.

"That's perfect, Winnie! I'm supposed to be in Manhattan for a meeting that day that should last until late afternoon. Maybe four or five. I can pick you up after lunch and we can drive out to the Hamptons together."

She sprung back to life.

"In that case, Michael, a lunch date sounds wonderful," she said. "A day in the city would be divine."

Several minutes later, Blake announced that he was hungry, and without argument we gathered our drinks and left the bar. I followed the three of them back down the halls, Winston's heels clicking away, until we reached the club restaurant. It was a wide, low room, bright from the afternoon sun spilling through full-length windows overlooking the pool and part of the golf course. A number of tables covered with white linens were interspersed throughout the restaurant, with the smaller ones—those seating four—closer to the windows. After a brief greeting, a hostess led us to one of those tables. As we sat, I was pleasantly surprised to find that a light breeze was blowing through the open window.

"I really enjoy this room on a nice day like this," said Winston, verbalizing what I was thinking. We all mumbled our agreement.

As the small talk resumed, I found myself growing more and more distracted. I didn't really like Blake all that much, and Winston's prattling grew quickly boring. And they were definitely not a "cute couple." While Michael kept up with the conversation, I spent more of my time half-listening, while I eyeballed the handful of younger club members, wondering what life was like to be that young and that wealthy. Was it preordained that some day you would become a Blake or a Winston? Or could you break free?

We ate—well, the men ate, while Winston picked at her salad, drank Bloody Marys, and excused herself more times than I could count to go out for a cigarette—and then, just when I thought we were finally going to get out of there, Blake suggested a tour of the grounds. Mercifully, between Blake's obesity and Winston's drunkenness, the walk was a short one. I was forced to endure one more drink in the bar before we were finally back in the SUV, heading back to the Culver-Benchley estate.

"Over there," said Winston, once again next to me in the backseat. I followed her finger to a familiar sight. "That's the old Corcoran place. Blake and I were going to buy it . . ."

Oh, dear God.

"Wasn't that fun?" asked Michael, as we whizzed south through Westchester County, quickly putting distance between us and the relatively loathsome Culver-Benchleys.

I grunted what I hoped sounded like a qualified agreement.

"What's the matter?" he asked. "You've been quiet all afternoon."

"Just tired I guess."

"I just love them," he said, more to himself than to me.

For my part, I watched the road signs, silently rejoicing as they announced we were entering the Bronx, then Manhattan, then West Fifty-seventh Street. I got out when Michael pulled the BMW to the entrance of his garage.

"They really liked you," he said. "I could tell. I knew it wasn't going to be a mistake bringing you with me."

"It was my pleasure," I said, as I closed the car door.

Standing alone on the sidewalk, I allowed myself a smile, and remembered that my eye had to stay on the prize. Being like them and being liked *by* them were two very different things.

And I had just aced an important entry test on my journey into high society . . . a journey I knew as Operation Hamptons.

Brett Revere's Theory of Life, Part Five:

Always Take Credit Where Credit Is Due . . . Especially at a Low, Low APR

If my disappointment with Michael's cute couple in Westchester was complete, and I was still a bit rattled by the whole naked-in-Alan's-office incident, and I generally felt as if my Sunday had been a miserable exercise in the misuse of time, despite proving to myself that I could wow the rich old-money set, you can only imagine how I felt as I approached my apartment and glanced up at the window, only to see a light on.

It meant that Creepy Quentin King was at home.

I trudged up the stairs, dreading the sight of him, probably sprawled on the couch in three-day-old boxer shorts eating peanut butter out of the jar with his finger. It would not be a relaxing way to unwind after a tense day at Donovan Talent Management and the Sterling Hills Country Club.

I turned the key in the lock, opened the door, and was heartened to see that the couch was free of both peanut butter and Quentin. It was the smallest of victories, but I welcomed it. Glancing around, I saw a light on under his bedroom door. Fine. Stay in there.

Unfortunately, he didn't. Moments later his door swung open, and there he was in all his boxer-shorted glory, holding a bag of Doritos in one hand and a bottle of beer in the other.

"I found a place," he said.

"Good." I turned my back to him and walked to the kitchen.

"That's it, dude? Just 'good.' "

I sighed. "What do you want from me, Quentin? Okay, that's *great* news. I am *so happy* for you. Is that better?"

He followed me to the kitchen doorway. "Listen, this isn't very easy for me. It's sort of abrupt, you know?"

I spun around. "It's not easy for me, either, and I'm not thrilled that I'll have to pay the entire rent bill. Twelve hundred dollars is a lot of money for an unemployed person. But you didn't give me much choice. You've been screwing around with my computer, and my clothes have been disappearing, and your friends are all over the place when I'm not here, and . . . and . . . and . . . I don't have to justify this, Quentin! Anyone else would have tossed you out a long time ago."

"You don't have to get personal," he said, leaning against the doorframe. "I'll be out by tomorrow." He paused. "And there's a benefit to you, too, dude. I've already paid for June, so I'm leaving you with, like, half a month's rent."

"I'll try to pay you back. It may take me some time, but . . ."

"Don't worry about it. Keep it."

What was he trying to do? Make me feel guilty? Well, it was starting to work. I focused my concentration on the annoyances—the missing clothes, the computer abuse, the general *ickiness* of sharing an apartment with Quentin—and that temporary sensation of guilt faded.

"I'm sorry it had to come to this," I said. "But . . . it did."

"Whatever." With a toss of his head, he walked back to his room and slammed the door behind him.

I don't happen to like confrontations very much, but I felt this one was worth it, because I would only have to wait twenty-four hours to have Quentin out of my life. Yes, it was definitely worth it.

In my bedroom, I changed out of the clothes I'd been wearing for two days and threw on a T-shirt and shorts, then returned to the living room. There were no messages on the answering machine. No Jamie. Damn.

Behind me, I heard Quentin's door open again, and I felt my back tense up.

"Dude," he said.

"What?"

"Forgot to tell you that a friend of yours called earlier."

My heart started racing. Jamie *had* called . . .

"Some guy named Alan. Something about his office."

"Oh." Well, *that* certainly slowed my racing heart. "Thanks."

"Also somebody named Jim."

"Jim?" I thought for a second. "*Jamie*, maybe?"

"That's it. Jamie."

Damn, but wasn't there a part of me that almost wanted to hug

Quentin at that very moment? I resisted the urge, of course, but I was markedly more civil to him when I thanked him.

When Quentin was back behind his closed door I grabbed the telephone and punched out the numbers to Jamie Brock's cell phone. It rang twice, and then his voice was on the line.

"Jamie, it's Brett."

"Hold on a second," he said. "I can't hear you that well. Let me try to get a better connection." I heard some sounds—doors opening and closing, perhaps, and now the sound of traffic in the distant background. "That's better. So how has your weekend been?"

"Uh . . . interesting. I went up to Scarsdale to meet some friends of Michael."

"Winnie and Blake?"

"Yeah."

"I love them. How are they? Did they ask about me?"

"Sorry, no. I didn't realize you've met them."

"I really don't know him very well, but I've had lunch and dinner several times with her. She's a doll."

"Uh-huh. Anyway, how has *your* weekend been?"

"Wait a minute," he said. "Let me get a little bit away from the house. . . . Okay, that's better. My weekend has been fine. Nothing exciting. A few dinner parties and that's about it." He paused, and I wondered if I had lost the connection until he added, "I've missed you, though."

"I've missed you, too," I said, through a broad smile. "When will you be back in New York?"

"Tomorrow afternoon. I'm not sure what time yet—hold on." I heard him shout something to someone, and then he was back. "Sorry. I've got to go. Look for me on either the one-thirty or two-thirty Jitney. You know where they drop off on Third Avenue?"

"Yeah. Is that your way of telling me that you want me to meet you?"

"That's exactly what I mean."

My head was spinning, and I actually heard myself giggle as I said, "Then I'll be there."

"Good. See you tomorrow, baby." With that, he broke the connection.

* * *

When I woke up the next morning my first thought was that Jamie was coming home. I was going to see Jamie again. And we could finish what we had started a few nights earlier.

I showered, shaved, dressed, and rushed to the N train in record time, which was somewhat negated by the train's leisurely pace as it rolled to Manhattan. I couldn't stop myself from repeatedly checking my watch until it reached the Lexington Avenue stop, where I began my speeded-up version of time again, bounding up the stairs three at a time until I reached ground level. On the sidewalk, I nodded my respect to Bloomingdale's and walked swiftly up Lex into the upper sixties, before veering right and cutting over to Third Avenue.

I reached the Jitney stop on Third Avenue just moments before the bus pulled to the curb. Expectantly, I monitored the departing passengers . . . but Jamie was not among them.

Seconds before the driver closed the doors, I called out to him.

"When does the next Jitney arrive?" I asked.

"There's another in an hour."

I thanked him, then—my anticipation dashed—sullenly walked away.

Okay, though, it was only an hour. I had survived the previous three days without him, and I could survive another hour. Sixty minutes. Piece of cake. I could do it in my sleep.

Ninety, though. . . .

I wandered around the Upper East Side, once again feeling diminished by its affluence and craving membership in its vaguely defined private club. I could walk the streets where the affluent lived, and I could go to the bars where they drank, but I still wasn't allowed membership in its club. It was attainable, though, if I could only make Operation Hamptons work.

And so far, Operation Hamptons was working. Odious as they were, Blake and Winston Culver-Benchley had fully accepted me. I had bluffed my way into their club, and had an open invitation to become a tangential part of their lives. The Penthouse regulars had also started to embrace me. The fast friendship offered by Michael DeVries, who did nothing but a little of this and a little of that for a living, was evidence of that, as was my . . . whatever it was . . . with Jamie. Yes, I thought, things were definitely looking up. And if I kept at it, I *would* have it all.

New York, New York . . . the city where people go to reinvent themselves. And I was poised to be the latest Jay Gatsby in the city where the Gatsbys were celebrated.

The hour flew by, and soon I was standing on the Third Avenue sidewalk as another Jitney pulled to the curb. This time, Jamie stepped off the bus. When he saw me, he flashed a sparkling smile.

"Hey, baby," he said, dropping his bag on the sidewalk and kissing me. "I missed you."

"You have no idea," I said.

He smiled. "Let's go back to my place."

As we briskly walked to Second Avenue, he filled me in on a few of the weekend's highlights, including that big party thrown by the people known only to me as the Lottery Hogs. It sounded fun and elegant, an upscale but casual event. And I couldn't wait until Operation Hamptons took off and I would be a formal part of the festivities.

Within minutes we were at Jamie's apartment building. I followed closely as he entered the lobby.

"Hey, Gary," he greeted the doorman as we passed the front desk. "Has Mr. Grover been behaving himself while I've been gone?"

The doorman laughed. "Yes, sir, he's been very well-behaved."

"And how's your wife doing?"

"Good, thanks, Mr. Brock. Seven months along and big as a house, but we're both loving every minute of it."

"At least it's not her first one, so you both know enough to keep her out of this heat."

"True. Thanks for asking, and have a good afternoon."

We walked into the elevator, and when the doors closed, I said, "You charmer, you."

He smiled and leaned in to kiss me. "It's all about paying attention, baby."

We took the elevator to the twenty-second floor and entered Jamie's apartment.

"Ben, I'm home!" Jamie called out from the foyer.

"I hear you, I hear you." We turned and saw him sitting on the living room couch. When the old man saw me, his lip curled.

Oblivious to that, Jamie walked into the living room, and I had no real option but to follow him.

"Nico sends his love."

"How is that old gangster?"

"Christ, Ben, you think every Russian is a gangster."

"Not every Russian. Nicholas Golodnya, yes, but not every Russian."

Jamie laughed off his comment, then nodded in my direction. "You remember Brett, don't you? From the other night."

"Yes," he said, managing to make a three-letter, one-syllable word as clipped as possible.

Jamie continued, still apparently oblivious. So much for paying attention.

"Anyway, I'm going to change my clothes, and get out and enjoy the day. What are you up to this afternoon?"

"I was thinking hip replacement surgery." Benjamin Grover aimed that comment at me, underscoring it by staring humorlessly into my eyes. Again, Jamie laughed and seemed oblivious, leading me by the hand to his bedroom.

"He hates me," I said, when his door was closed.

"He'll get over it," Jamie replied, emptying the contents of his bag across the floor. "And don't take things too personally. I *told* you that Ben likes *everyone*. He acts like he hates Nicholas Golodnya, too, but Nico is one of his best friends. Let's face it: if he's calling one of his closest friends a gangster, why do you think he's going to give you a big hug whenever he sees you?"

"I know that name, Golodnya. Who is he?"

"Nico has been around forever. Ever hear of GolodnyaTech?"

"I don't think so."

"His firm designs computer systems. He has a *huge* contract from the Pentagon. So let's just say that life is good and your bank account is healthy when you're Nico Golodnya."

"And that's the sort of person who you hang out with in the Hamptons? Rich defense contractors and the Lottery Hogs?"

Jamie shook his head and sighed. "You *have* been spending some time with Michael DeVries, haven't you. He really has it in for Clara and Burt, that's for sure." He paused, then nudged me to the bed. "Relax while I change."

I lay on my back and watched him for a moment as he sorted through the clothes strewn across the floor.

"Clara and Burt? They're the Lottery Hogs?"

"Please don't call them that. That's just Michael being crude. They are . . . okay, they're sort of nouveau riche-y, but they mean well. They're trying. Maybe they're a bit ambitious, but I don't think it's fair for Michael to act like such a snob."

"Did they really win the lottery?"

"True fact. They won the lottery, moved to East Hampton, and started spreading that money around." He turned from me and started to pull his shirt off, while I tried not to stare too intently.

"Okay," I said, to distract myself as much as to converse, "so you're hanging out in the Hamptons with rich defense contractors and lottery winners and . . . who else? Alec Baldwin?"

"You probably think you're joking," he said, as he started to pull his pants off. I felt myself begin to stiffen and rolled onto my stomach to hide the evidence. "But I was at a party with him the other night."

"Alec Baldwin? Really? And did you try to seduce him with those bedroom eyes of yours?" I had no idea where I was going with that comment, but watching Jamie—now clad only in white briefs—strut around his bedroom, absent-mindedly looking for something he had buried under something else, put seduction prominently in my head.

"No, baby, I didn't try to seduce Alec Baldwin. Two reasons. First, he's just not my type. Too hairy. Less important . . ." He stopped and picked up his wallet, which had apparently been the missing item, from the floor. "Less important is that he's straight."

"Straight, and therefore immune from your powers of seduction?"

"If I want to seduce someone," he said, crawling onto the bed next to me, "he's going to get seduced."

Jamie didn't need to prove the truth behind those words, but I was grateful that he did, climbing onto the bed and slowly covering me with his all-but-naked body as he caressed my back with kisses, starting at my neck and working his way down. When he reached my lower back, he pulled up my shirt and began again in the opposite direction, and this time I felt his lips directly on my flesh.

When he was back at my neck, he kissed me deeply for quite a while . . . until I could no longer stand to be a passive participant.

"Let me roll over," I whispered.

"Not yet," he said, and I felt him reach under me to unclasp my belt.

"What are you doing?"

"Shh." His hands reached for the top button of my pants. "Just stay quiet and don't move."

"Jamie . . ."

"Don't worry," he said. "I'm not going to do anything bad."

"But what . . . ?"

"Shh."

I felt him pull my pants down below my buttocks, and had a sudden body-image crisis. I hadn't been to the gym in months, and despite the amount of walking I did, that lack of treadmill time had to show in my glutes. When we slept together a few days earlier, it had been dark and we had been drinking, but now he was going to see my ass in the daylight, while sober. And . . . and . . . my mind ticked through any number of imagined problems, from cellulite to ingrown hair to pimples.

But whatever the problems—if there *were* problems—they didn't seem to pose an obstacle to him. Instead, I felt his tongue tenderly lick my flesh, gentle strokes against smooth skin. Slowly, almost imperceptibly, he grew more intense, until he had a mouthful of flesh and muscle—and fat, but maybe that was just my body-image problem again—in his mouth, and . . .

"*Ow*!"

I cried out as I felt his teeth grab the skin, and tried to squirm out from under him. In response, he bore down, biting hard, gnawing. . . .

"*Ow*! Jamie! What are you doing?!"

He let go, and, above me, I heard him laugh as he rolled off of me.

"That hurt," I said, rubbing the bite mark.

He dropped to the bed next to me, rolling me over until our faces were inches apart. He was still laughing.

"What was *that* all about?"

"I was marking my territory," he said. "Now you've got an official Jamie Brock tattoo. Well . . . for a few days, at least."

"At least it will fade," I said.

He poked my nose with his finger, saying, "When it does, I'll just have to give you another one."

"Oh yeah?"

"Yeah."

Without warning I leapt on top of him, and had his briefs pulled down before he had a chance to react.

An hour or so later, as we lay intertwined and sweaty, despite the air-conditioning, he stroked my hair and said, "I really missed you this weekend."

"I missed you, too."

"Maybe . . . maybe you could come out there with me sometime. Meet the crew."

"Russian mobsters and lottery hogs? Hmmm . . . I'll have to think about it."

He laughed. "Well, we'll see how the summer shapes up. It would be nice. I could meet your friends, you could meet my friends . . ."

I turned to look at him. "You want to meet *my* friends?"

He looked confused. "Doesn't your crowd summer in the Hamptons?"

"Uh . . . no."

"Well, where . . . Fire Island? The Jersey shore?"

"No, Jamie. My crowd doesn't really . . . *summer.*"

It was as if I had just told him that my crowd summered on Saturn. He couldn't even grasp the meaning of my words.

I lifted myself to one shoulder.

"Jamie, I want to be perfectly honest here, okay?" He nodded. "I think something pretty fantastic is happening between us, and I don't want there to be any misimpressions."

"Okay," he said, and it was apparent I was doing nothing to clear his confusion.

I froze, unsure how much I wanted to tell him.

"You wanted to say something?"

I nodded. "Yeah. Like I was saying, I know that we've only known each other for a few days, but it's been . . . *fantastic.*"

He smiled. "I agree."

"And I want to start things off honestly."

"Of course."

"So I need to tell you . . ."

He put a finger to my lips. "Hold that thought, baby. I need to go to the bathroom." With that, he bounded off the bed, wrapped his naked body in a towel, and left the room.

Which gave me a chance to think about what I almost said, and why I felt so compelled to tell Jamie the truth.

I was largely comfortable in my new acting assignment. I had no problems putting on airs to cultivate the moneyed men of the Penthouse, or to charm the wealthy members of the Sterling Hills Country Club. My performances were dead-on, and I was waltzing through their rarified world without detection.

But with Jamie, the line had been crossed . . . the fourth wall had been breached. With Jamie, I wasn't performing. I might be using Michael DeVries and the others for their connections in order to secure my financial future, but that wasn't the case with Jamie. He was a man I could fall in love with—and, I thought, probably *was* falling in love with—for richer or poorer. And I could sense in the way he held me . . . and stroked my hair . . . and made love to me . . . and called me 'baby' . . . that he felt the same way.

When he returned to the bedroom he dropped his towel casually on the floor and crawled back into bed, nestling his body next to mine.

"So," he said, "you wanted to tell me something."

"Yeah." I closed my eyes and settled next to him, relaxing in the touch of his warm skin and the certainty that I was about to do the right thing. "I'm not like most of the people who hang out at the Penthouse. I'm not like *you*. The reason that I don't summer, and my friends don't summer, is because we're poor."

I felt him stir next to me. "Poor?"

"Poor. I mean, not poor like 'living on the street begging for quarters' poor, but poor enough. I'm an actor, Jamie . . . an unemployed actor. And I moonlight as an unemployed temp. I started to hang out at the Penthouse to meet people . . . make some connections . . ." I stopped and touched my fingers to his face. "I didn't go there to meet anyone as fantastic as you, but I'm glad I did."

I opened my eyes and looked at him. He was staring back, uncomprehending, so I felt compelled to continue.

"I, uh . . . I guess some people assumed that I was 'to the manor born,' but I'm just a working boy. Well . . . when I'm working, that is."

A slight smile finally crossed his lips. "So you're not just . . . I don't know . . . living off a trust fund or something?"

"No. I'm living off, well . . . pretty much nothing these days. In fact, it could be less than nothing, because I just kicked my roommate out of my apartment, and now I have to pick up one hundred percent of the rent."

"Wait." He moved a few inches away from me. "Let me get this straight. You're unemployed and you can afford to pay rent on a Manhattan apartment?"

"I live in Astoria." No reaction. "It's a neighborhood in Queens."

I wouldn't have believed it if I hadn't seen it with my own two eyes, but Jamie actually gasped and recoiled.

"It's not that bad," I said, trying not to sound too defensive. "It's only a few subway stops from here. And anyway, you already knew that I have a 718 area code."

"That's Queens? I thought it was another Manhattan area code. Like 646 or something."

"It's Queens and the other outer boroughs."

He shook his head. "Does Michael know that?"

I sighed. "Well . . . Michael sort of tipped his hand that he considered 718 to be inferior, so I borrowed a 212 when I knew he was going to call."

"That was smart," he said, sitting upright in bed and gathering the sheets around him. "Let me think about this for a minute."

"Jamie, it's no big deal. I want you to know that I like you for *you*, not because you have a successful career. I'm not a gold digger. I'm just trying to make some connections and get a leg up."

His brow furrowed. "You have got to keep this between us. Don't tell anyone."

"About what?" I asked. "Not having money? Living in Queens? What?"

"All of it."

"Well, I'm trying to be discreet," I said. "But it's not as if I'm ashamed of my background."

"And you shouldn't be. I'm sure you have a fine background, full of . . . full of . . . lots of proud things. But these people we're surrounded by *do* care about it." I started to protest, but he cut me off. "I know, I know . . . they shouldn't. But for them, it's all about the pretense. Michael, for instance. Michael's such a snob that I can pretty much guarantee he'd have no use for you if he knew the truth."

"That doesn't surprise me about Michael. But you're telling me that everyone else feels the same way?"

He ticked off names on his fingers. "Michael . . . Jeffrey Ryan . . . Ben . . . Shit, even Clara and Burt Matthews."

"The Lottery Hogs are snobs?"

"After the first ten million dollars, *everyone* is a snob."

I slumped back on the bed. "So, I'm supposed to do *what*? Lie?"

"Is not telling the truth the same as lying?" I nodded. "In that case, lie." He moved slightly closer to me and placed a reassuring hand on my shoulder. "It's not that big of a deal, Brett. Is it? I mean, has anyone even asked you what you do for a living?"

"No . . ."

"See? No one cares, as long as they *think* you belong. Just play it cool. If the subject of work comes up, change the subject. If money comes up, change the subject."

"And if the subject of where I live comes up?"

"Deny! Deny! Deny!" He laughed, and I couldn't help but join in.

Jamie hopped off the bed and again began sifting through his clothes, looking for something clean to wear. I took that as a signal that I should get dressed myself.

"You know, Queens really isn't all that bad," I said, as I pulled on my underwear.

"I have to take your word for it," he said. "I've never been."

"Never?"

"Well . . . I've been to LaGuardia. And I must drive through Queens on my way to the Hamptons. Does that count?"

"Not really."

He was dressed before I was and waited patiently for me to finish. As I buttoned my shirt, he said, "It's a beautiful Monday afternoon and we don't have anything to do. So what should we do?"

I shrugged.

"I was thinking that maybe we could go to Queens."

I turned to him, surprised. "Seriously?"

"Why not? It will be an adventure." He smiled. "Plus, you owe me a hat."

* * *

The ride on the N train was not quite the exotic excursion Jamie was expecting, although, in fairness to myself, I should point out that I explained to him several times that a subway ride is a subway ride is a subway ride. The elevated tracks in Astoria were unusual by the standards of anyone who never left Manhattan, but nothing that hadn't been seen by anyone with an Amtrak, Metro-North, or Long Island Rail Road ticket in their past.

"This is cute," he said as we walked from the train to my apartment, and, in fact, cute was not a bad word to describe Astoria. It was certainly slower-paced than even the quieter neighborhoods of Manhattan, and built much closer to the ground.

When we turned the corner, he found one building much less impressive.

"What an ugly building," he said.

"Sorry you feel that way, 'cause that's where we're going."

"You live *there*? Oh, Brett, baby, we've *got* to get you a job!"

I unlocked the front door and let us into the vestibule, then grabbed a few pieces of mail from the box before unlocking a second door, leading to the stairs, and motioning him in.

He looked around the cramped entry. "Where's the elevator?"

"You're standing on them."

"Shit. What floor do you live on?"

"The fourth." He frowned. "Come on, baby, you can do this."

As we mounted the steps, I said, "I have to warn you that I have no idea what this place is going to look like. Hopefully, my roommate has moved out by now, but God knows what kind of mess he's left behind."

When we finally reached the fourth floor landing, we both took a moment to catch our breath. Then I pulled my keys out of my pocket, unlocked the apartment door, and . . .

And . . . *shit!*

We were *not* confronted with the mess I had expected and feared. Quite the opposite, as a matter of fact.

Quentin had found his own way to recoup the weeks of rent I owed him.

The television—*my* television—was missing from its stand.

There was an empty space where a stereo—*my* stereo—used to be. There was . . . too much to take in.

"*Fuck*!" I said. "*Quentin*!"

"Who's Quentin?" asked Jamie.

I didn't answer him, but walked aimlessly into the living room. I couldn't even begin to comprehend that this had happened to me.

"It looks like Boomer came back for the things he forgot," I muttered to myself, shaking my head.

"Who's Boomer? A dog?"

"No, he's . . . Never mind." Jamie looked confused, so I explained the situation to the best of my ability, realizing that, as a first-time visitor to my apartment, he would have no idea of the scope of what had happened. "It looks like he decided to get revenge. I've been cleaned out."

"That's Quentin? Your ex-roommate?"

"That's Quentin." I tossed the mail on the coffee table and took a mental inventory of missing items. The television: gone. VCR: gone. Stereo: gone. He had left the answering machine, but that was about it.

"This is bad. He took everything that had any value."

"Do you have insurance?"

"I used to, but when money started getting tight, I let it lapse."

"That's not a good idea."

"I wish you had told me that last week." I looked over to the kitchen. "Fuck! He even took the microwave."

Jamie followed me as I surveyed the rest of the apartment, walking room to room and compiling a mental list of missing items. Not surprisingly, Quentin's bedroom was cleaned out. Surprisingly, he had left behind my ancient computer, but other things had vanished from my bedroom. I immediately noticed that there were a number of empty hangers in my closet, and a small jewelry box in which I kept some relatively inexpensive cufflinks was missing from the top of my dresser. He had even stolen my coin jar, which had a net value of maybe forty dollars. For some reason, the less expensive items stolen from my bedroom had more of an impact on me than the expensive electronics missing from the living room. They made this theft much more personal.

"Here," I said, grabbing Jamie's cap off the closet doorknob and tossing it to him. "Quentin must not have wanted it."

"Thanks. Any chance that a real burglar did this?"

"No. Not really. This was all Quentin." I paused for a moment, collecting myself, then grabbed the phone and dialed 911.

"Here goes an exercise in futility," I said.

"What do you mean?"

"I have no idea where he is. I might as well have been robbed by a stranger, because the police . . ." The voice of an operator was on the line. "Yes, hi, I'd like to report a burglary . . ."

The 911 operator took my address and advised me to wait at the apartment, adding that I should be patient. It wasn't hard to read between those lines: I was a low priority call, and I shouldn't expect to see the police for quite some time. They probably had another Twinkie to defuse. In the meantime, I again walked through the apartment, to see if other items had disappeared.

"He took the vacuum," I muttered, looking in the hall closet. "He stole the fucking vacuum cleaner."

"What's that?" asked Jamie from the kitchen.

"Nothing." I closed the closet door and walked back to the kitchen, saying, "I'm sorry you have to witness this on your first real visit to Queens. You know, I've lived in New York for more than twenty years, and nothing like this has ever happened to me. I was never even mugged before." When I entered the kitchen, Jamie was sifting through my mail. "What are you doing?"

"What am I supposed to do? Watch television? Anyway, maybe there's something good here."

I reached for the envelopes in his hands. "No offense, Jamie, but I've just been violated, and I'm feeling very defensive about my personal items right now." Mail in hand, I leafed through it. "Just bills anyway." I came across an envelope addressed to Quentin. "And I guess we won't be needing *this* anymore." I dropped the envelope into the trash, where it landed with a click.

"There was something in there," said Jamie.

"It was from a bank. Probably just a statement. Hopefully it was a bill, and he won't get it because I've thrown it out, and they'll ruin his credit."

"Revenge fantasies," said Jamie, as I walked out of the kitchen holding the remaining mail. "Gotta love 'em."

In the time it took me to drop the mail on the top of my dresser and return to the kitchen, Jamie had fished Quentin's mail out of the trash.

"Come on," I said, when I saw him holding the envelope.

"I told you there was something in here. It feels like a credit card."

"All the more reason to trash it. That bastard doesn't deserve credit."

"You're not getting what I'm trying to say," he said, slitting the envelope with his index finger. "I'm trying to say that you should take this credit card . . ."

"Stop," I said. "I may be broke, but there are still a few things I won't do."

"Brett, be reasonable." He now had the card out of the envelope and was holding it in front of me enticingly. "You deserve this."

"Two things are wrong here, Jamie," I said. "First, this is not my card. It's Quentin's. Second, it's illegal. And I've just thought of a third thing: knowing Quentin, there's not a high enough line of credit to make it worth my while. This is a triathlon of wrong."

Jamie looked at the notice enclosed with the card, then said, "Fifteen thousand dollars isn't worth your while?"

"What? Let me see that."

I read the notice, and it was true. Creepy Quentin King had somehow managed to get a card in his own name with a fifteen thousand dollar line of credit. I could only imagine the amount of fraudulent information he must have provided to con the bank.

Shaking my head, I tossed the notice into the trash then plucked the credit card from Jamie's hand. "That's just one more very wrong thing about this," I said. "You're trying to turn a triathlon of wrong into a quadrathlon of wrong."

"Is that even a word?"

"No offense, baby, but shut up." He looked wounded, so I tried a softer approach. "You're suggesting fraud upon fraud upon fraud, and I don't do that. I have no idea how many lies Quentin told to get this card, but it doesn't belong in circulation." With that, I tossed the card in the trash basket, where it landed quietly in the folds of the bank notice.

The police actually arrived fairly quickly and took a report. They were deeply sympathetic, but basically advised me that unless Quentin voluntarily popped back into my life and confessed, it was unlikely I'd ever see my television, VCR, stereo, microwave, clothes, cufflinks, change, or vacuum cleaner again. One officer even chided me for not returning the last weeks of Quentin's June rent, as if, by not doing so, I was asking to be robbed. I did not appreciate her advice.

After they left, I noticed that the blender was missing, too, but decided it wasn't worth reporting. Quentin had effectively stripped my apartment, and one more item wasn't going to have much impact on my life.

"You look like someone who could use a relaxing dinner," said Jamie, wrapping an arm around my waist.

"What I could use are some drinks. About thirty-two of them."

"Dinner *and* drinks, then. What do you say?"

"I don't know," I confessed. "I'm not sure I'd be very good company."

He pulled my face close to his and kissed me. "You're always good company, baby. Come on. Let me buy you dinner. *And* drinks. Thirty-two of them. Let's see if I can put a smile back on that handsome face."

A few hours later, we found ourselves outside La Goulue, a restaurant on Madison Avenue.

"It's really good," said Jamie, before we walked through the door. "A big Upper East Side social scene. Michael got me hooked on the place."

"It's a little pricey, though, isn't it?"

"I already told you that I'm buying, so why don't you just relax and enjoy yourself." He patted my back and said, "After a day like today, you deserve it."

We had hoped to get an outside table, but the small amount of space available for sidewalk dining and the lengthy waiting list led us to accept fate and take a table indoors. I settled into my chair carefully, still feeling the bite mark on my ass.

Drinks were ordered, and soon dinner was served, and through the entire meal we talked about everything, especially my recent robbery. The one subject we didn't broach, though, was what was happening between us.

Over coffee, I decided that the time felt right to take on the subject.

"Today has been horrible," I said. "And I don't think I would have made it through the day if you hadn't been with me."

A smile crept across his face. "I'm sorry that had to happen to you, baby. But since it did, if things were better 'cause I was there, well . . . I'm glad." He reached across the table and took one of my hands in his.

"Jamie . . . I . . . I . . ." I wanted to say something deeper, more profound, but I was stuck. And in any event, his eyes were piercing mine, leaving me at a complete loss for words. I gripped his hand, lost in his blue eyes, and that electricity jolted us again.

Which is when Jamie abruptly dropped my hand and sat back in his chair, dropping his arms from the table.

"What's wrong?" I asked.

"I can't . . ."

"But . . ."

"I like you, Brett," he said. "I really do. But . . . we hardly know each other. And I think we're moving too fast."

I thought for a moment. "This isn't because of what I told you before, is it? About how I don't have much money?"

"No. Of course not." He said the words, but I couldn't help notice that he wouldn't meet my eyes. "I'm just . . . I'm just a little hesitant to get involved in anything too serious right now."

"I understand," I said, although I wasn't quite sure that was the truth. To cut through my disappointment, I tried to remind myself that nothing he said precluded a serious relationship in the very near future.

The waiter interrupted us with pleasantries and the check. Jamie handed him his credit card and, after he departed, turned to me.

"Any thoughts about where your roommate might be?"

"None. And I really don't want to talk about it anymore. What's done is done. I'll just have to start over."

"How can you afford to buy replacements?"

"The same way I bought the originals. One at a time, over a long,

long time . . ." I brightened. "Of course, maybe I'll meet my future employer at the Penthouse, and the process will be expedited."

"I'd use that credit card."

"I know you would. But I won't. It's just that simple."

He smiled. "You're an honest man, Brett Revere."

"I try."

Fortunately, that was when the waiter returned to our table with Jamie's credit card.

"Will there be anything else?" he asked.

"No," we said in unison.

"In that case," he said, primarily addressing Jamie, "Thank you, Mr. King."

Mr. King?!

When the waiter walked away, I lunged for the credit card, but Jamie quickly pocketed it.

"Let me see that," I said.

He tossed me a crooked smile. "Let's get out of here. You've had a long day."

"I want to see that credit card."

"Outside."

In less than a minute, we were on the sidewalk outside of La Goulue, as the northbound traffic on Madison Avenue rumbled past.

"Jamie, you can't do that! That's not your credit card! It's not even *my* credit card! It's . . . it's . . . that credit card is totally illegitimate. Not even Quentin has any right to use it. That card is one big felony."

"Keep your voice down," he hissed. After looking around to see who might be eavesdropping, he said, "He cleaned you out, Brett. He owes you this. You deserve this."

"No. It's wrong. It's illegal!"

"Then just use it to replace what he stole. The cops said you were never getting your stuff back . . ."

"No," I said again. "They said I *probably* wasn't getting my stuff back. But maybe . . ."

"Whatever," he said, pressing the card into my palm. "You know as well as I do that you're never going to see Quentin again. *I* think you should use the card to get your stuff back, but you make up your own mind. All I know is that if *I* was poor, and if *I* didn't have a job, I'd think about it a lot more carefully."

I felt dazed. For some reason that I now couldn't put into words, until this moment I would not have thought of Jamie in this light. I had only known him for a few days, but I had idealized him, and now . . . now he was acting like a common thief. I could understand his reticence about entering into a relationship with me after just a few days, even if I didn't want to hear those words, but *this* was beyond my comprehension.

I had had a real eye-opener over the past few days about how, as Fitzgerald famously wrote, the rich are different from you and me. The casual racism and anti-Semitism, the disregard for the feelings of others . . . and now this. Now, the man I thought I was falling in love with was advocating that I get ahead in the world through what amounted to credit card fraud.

I dropped the card to the ground.

"Jamie, if anything is going to happen between us . . ." I quickly corrected myself. "Maybe not now, but in the future . . ."

"Stop, Brett," he said. "Please stop."

"Did I say something wrong?"

He turned away from me and said, "Nothing is going to happen between us. Okay? We've already been through this. What has already happened was fun, but it was only fun. Don't think of it as something it isn't."

"But Jamie . . ." I felt something pierce my heart.

"Brett, please." He turned back to face me, looking me squarely in the eye. "I like you, Brett, but I just don't feel what you do. I want to be your friend, not your boyfriend. Do you understand that?"

For the second time in less than a minute, I was dazed. It showed in my rambling response.

"But, Jamie, I just assumed . . . I mean, we . . . this afternoon, we were together and, well, I thought I meant something to . . . and you called me from the Hamptons and . . ."

Jamie mercifully put me out of my verbal misery.

"I'm sorry, baby. I *do* like you a lot, but I just can't see it happening." When I didn't reply, he added, "And I *am* sorry, because you're a great guy. Someday, though, you'll meet the right man." Another uncomfortable pause. "I just don't think I'm that man."

Dammit, I was afraid I was going to cry. I bit my lip and looked away.

"I think I'd better leave," he said softly, placing a hand gently on my shoulder. "I'll give you a call, okay?"

"Okay," I said, my husky voice barely audible. When I turned back, he was already crossing Madison Avenue.

Well *that* had been a reality check. It was just my luck to finally meet someone and come damn close to falling in love—for the first time in a long time, at that—only to realize that my dream man had his own deep flaws. For all that trust fund money and upper class mien and weekends in the Hamptons, he had an amoral dark side.

But maybe none of that would have mattered if he hadn't just told me that he didn't love me.

I looked down and stared at the credit card laying on the curb, and thought that maybe it was better to know the real Jamie Brock now, before he had completely stolen my heart.

Or maybe it wasn't.

Brett Revere's Theory of Life, Part Six:
Sometimes Your Hallucinations Are Real

As the sun rose, I was still staring at that damn credit card. No, I was no longer standing at the curb on the Upper East Side; now I was at my stripped-down apartment in Astoria. The card had come home with me for safekeeping, until I could figure out what to do with it.

Return it to Quentin. That's what I had to do, loath as I was to admit it. Find Quentin, return the credit card, and reimburse him for a far too expensive dinner for two at La Goulue.

And maybe he'd see that as such a kindly gesture that he'd reimburse me my stereo, my VCR, my television, my vacuum . . .

Yeah, right. Maybe he'd even reimburse me on a two-for-one basis.

Having no idea what to do about the credit card, I decided to try to work on the other problem bedeviling me that morning: Jamie Brock. I dialed his home phone number and waited until the call was answered.

Unfortunately, it was answered by Benjamin Grover.

"Uh . . ." Part of me wanted to hang up, but the better part of me decided to tough it out. "Hi, Ben, it's Brett. Brett Revere. Jamie's friend. Remember me?"

"Well, now . . . let me see. Brett Revere? No, sorry, I can't say I remember you. I don't remember much, with this Alzheimer's."

Oh, shit. He was never going to let that die, was he?

"Haha," I said, hoping that if I played it lightly, he'd go easy on me. "I was wondering if Jamie was home."

"No."

Okay . . . *that* was abrupt.

"Could I leave a message?"

"I'll tell him you called." With that, Benjamin Grover hung up on me. And I seriously doubted that there was any message-taking going on.

The next few days passed without a word from Jamie. More convinced than ever that Benjamin had not passed on my message, I considered calling back, but . . . no. Jamie knew how to get in touch with me.

It was that damn credit card. I *had* to fight with Jamie over using the card, didn't I?

The card was still sitting on top of my dresser, both shaming and angering me every time I passed it. Part of me wanted to cut it up, another part wanted to track down Quentin and return it, and a third part wanted to follow Jamie's advice and use it to replace the things that had been stolen. That third part also considered the dinner at La Goulue to be just compensation for my inconvenience.

Twice I had thrown the credit card in the trash, and twice I had almost immediately retrieved it. I knew it wasn't mine, but I still couldn't bring myself to dispose of it. It was as if I felt that by possessing it, both Jamie and my missing electronics would be drawn back into my life.

But they weren't, of course. And in the meantime, I spent long day after long day staring at the walls of my apartment.

I finally reached the point where I realized that I had to get out of the apartment and move forward with Operation Hamptons, Jamie or no Jamie. Things had been so promising just days earlier, before I saw the petty venality of Michael's world and the casual lawlessness of Jamie's.

Still, there was no reason I had to become them. They couldn't all be like that, could they? I remained convinced that I could still play the role of Brett Revere, Trust Fund Baby, without losing my soul. I could charm my new wealthy acquaintances and move ahead, and I could keep my dignity while doing it.

At least, that's what I wanted to believe.

In any event, Jamie wasn't going to return my call. Between the credit card incident and our disagreement over the potential for a future together, I suppose that shouldn't have been a surprise.

I briefly considered calling Michael, but I wasn't quite sure I was ready to face him after our Sunday in Scarsdale. To say I was disappointed in the quickness with which he embraced the bigotry of the Culver-Benchleys was an understatement. It was bad enough that I was committed to a luncheon for Winston, which I knew in advance would be dreadful.

But I was bored in the confines of my apartment, especially since it was stereo- and television-less. I had read everything there was to read, which left . . . nothing to distract me. If I stayed home another night, I would be reduced to reading instruction manuals for appliances spirited away by Quentin.

No, I had to get out of the apartment. And I wanted to go to Manhattan.

So I called Alan Donovan.

"I'm game," he said, when I asked him if he wanted to join me for a few drinks. "I just have a few things to finish up here, and I can meet you. Where do you want to go?"

I knew Alan, which meant I knew I should suggest Bar 51.

"We could meet there," he said. "Or . . . do you want to go to the Penthouse?"

"I thought you hated it there."

"Yeah, well . . . maybe I should give it another chance. The last time I was there I met someone, remember? I'm sort of hoping . . ."

"Aha. So you're using me to set up a date. I should have known something was up when you suggested the Penthouse." Actually, I was more than a bit intrigued. I knew the type of man Alan was attracted to, and he wasn't of the Penthouse variety. He liked his men darker—preferably Latino or African-American—and if they looked especially rough it added a lot of bonus points. Since neither of those looks were sported very often in the Penthouse, I decided that Alan must have met his mystery man on one of the nights the Penthouse was dominated by the Bridge and Tunnel crowd . . .

. . . and I immediately mentally kicked myself for thinking that. Was I really falling into the mentality I loathed—the Penthouse mentality—so quickly and easily?

I agreed to meet him at seven o'clock.

The Penthouse was a sea of strange faces that evening. There was no Jeffrey Ryan . . . no Michael DeVries . . . and, especially, no Jamie Brock. And for the longest time, there was also no Alan Donovan, until he came strolling in around 7:30, unapologetic, despite having left me waiting for half an hour.

Alan's prey, he informed me, frequented the second-floor piano bar. We climbed the circular staircase and were greeted with a serenade of "All of Me," sung with enthusiasm by a tall black man standing next to the piano. I suspected immediately that we had found the object of Alan's affections.

"That's him," he said, pointing, as I knew he would, to the singer.

"So I figured."

I followed him as he crossed to the piano. When the song ended, we clapped appreciatively.

"Thank you," the man mumbled humbly. He spotted Alan and, approaching us, added, "And especially thank *you*."

"Ty," he said, "this is my friend Brett. Brett, Ty." We shook hands as Alan explained, "Ty is on Broadway."

"*Was* on Broadway. But I shall return."

I felt my back tense up, my normal reaction upon meeting a fellow actor. After twenty years, I recognized the sensation as a survival instinct: if you were another actor, we would have an instant camaraderie, but I also might have to cut your throat tomorrow to win a role. You were my soulmate, but you were also my competition.

But then I remembered I was no longer Brett Revere, actor. I was a trust fund boy, and Ty's Broadway credits no longer threatened me. The tension eased.

We traded a few pleasantries, until it became apparent that I was a third wheel. When Alan and Ty decided to find space at the bar, it seemed to be a good idea to entertain myself elsewhere. That, or suffer the humiliation of being ignored, which I didn't think my fragile ego could take.

I was going to return to the bar downstairs but, from the top of the stairs, I saw the Evil Mime holding court below, at which point it seemed preferable to stay where I was and listen to show tunes and standards belted out with mediocrity by the piano player and patrons.

Fortunately, I wasn't alone for long.

"Been humped by a dog lately?"

I turned, and *Andy*'s own Sugar Daddy Warbucks—Rick Atkins—was standing next to me. Great . . . *another* actor.

"Hey, stranger," I said. "How's life on the small stage?"

"Oh, the fame, the glory . . ." He smiled. "Only three more weeks and the public will finally have its first opportunity to see me embarrass myself."

"Fortunately, no one will notice you with Joey Takashimi on the stage."

"So true," he said. "The cast has given him a new nickname: 'Upstage.' You could stick a dozen naked porn stars on the stage and he'd *still* find a way to command everyone's attention."

We laughed, and I said, "So nothing's changed . . ."

"Nothing's changed at all. My life is *so* incredibly wonderful." He paused. "Actually, I have to hand it to Walter Pomeroy. I mean, yes, the show sucks, but he's managed to land advance write-ups in all the bar rags. There's actually a buzz about *Andy*."

I shook my head and said, "God bless you all."

"Where did Bill go?" he asked himself. He swiveled a bit, and for the first time I noticed the sixty-something gray-haired man standing behind him.

"Right here," said the man.

"Hey, honey." Rick turned back to me and said, "This is my husband, Bill. Bill, this is Brett. He's the guy I told you about. The one who walked out on the show."

Bill offered me his hand and said, "Ah! *You're* the one with good taste. Nice to meet you, Brett."

"My pleasure." I quickly gave Bill the once over, and made a guess that Rick Atkins had married for the money. Bill was probably a decent enough looking man decades earlier, but that was then, and this was now.

"Rick told me how you stormed out," Bill continued. "When I read the script, I told him he should have followed you."

"I would have," said Rick. "But they didn't threaten to have me humped by Sandy."

Bill shook his head indulgently. "The things you'll do for an acting job."

"It's work," said Rick, with a shrug.

Bill excused himself to go to the bar, giving me the opportunity to stick my foot immediately in my mouth.

"So that's the lover," I said, as soon as Bill was out of earshot. I gave Rick a wink and added, "It must be nice to be supported by a patron of the arts."

"Excuse me?"

"He's a doctor, right?" I said, pushing that foot just a bit deeper into my throat. "Nice catch. He must be worth some major bucks."

The instant the words were out of my mouth and I saw the expression on Rick's face, I realized that I had gone *far* too far.

Rick fixed me with a cold stare. "Is it that hard to believe that I could love an older man on the merits?"

I felt my face redden. "Sorry, I just . . ."

"I know, I know," he said. "Maybe I shouldn't get so pissed off when people jump to conclusions, but I do. I love Bill for who he is, and I get a little tired of people always assuming that I love him for the summer house and the Porsche. Yeah, he's a little older than me, but I love Bill for all those extra years he's lived a lot more than for the material things."

"I'm sorry," I stammered again. "I shouldn't have said . . ."

"Don't worry about it," said Rick. "It's not just you." He took a sip from his drink, then added, "We gay men are ridiculous, aren't we?"

"We are," I agreed, "But in which context do you mean?"

"It's all about youth . . . flesh . . . pretty faces . . . gym bodies . . . Prada . . . big dicks. I mean, when was the last time you heard someone described as 'hot' because they were intelligent, polite, and considerate?"

I nodded a silent agreement.

"The sad thing is that we worship these . . . these . . . these fashion-conscious beefcake idols at all costs, and offer up an impossible standard for anyone to meet."

"The fashion-conscious beefcake idols meet the standard," I observed.

"For a few years, if they're lucky. And then what? One day they look in the mirror and realize they're forty-eight-years old, their faces and bodies are sagging, and no one is looking at them anymore. They've been reduced to the status of a mere human, and the so-called 'hot' men don't want them anymore. It would be funny if not for the fact that the average guys out there—the ones who were never fashion-conscious beefcake models to begin with—continue to pray at the altar of the new hot boys. Collectively, we just don't seem to get it, do we?"

I tried to playfully tease him out of his tirade. "This is your indictment of the superficiality of gay male culture, I take it?"

"I can go on for hours," he replied. "Long screed short, though: if you want to know why I love Bill, it's because he deserves it, and I realize that someday I'm going to be older. And at that time, *I* hope to deserve love, too."

"Your point is well taken," I said. "Even if I can be *more* than a bit superficial. I'm really sorry about what I said."

"Don't worry about it," he said, waving away my apology. "What I said was the truth . . . *my* truth. I love Bill, and he loves me, and he's the best thing that's ever happened to me." He took a sip of his drink, then added, with a grin, "And the summer house and the Porsche, well . . . they ain't bad, either."

We laughed. The awkward situation had been defused, and I was suddenly overwhelmed with gratitude for Rick Atkins's good humor.

"Thank God I'm not the only one here who likes beautiful things," I said.

He smiled. "You're not the only one, Brett. For example, despite everything I've just ranted about, I do appreciate the beauty of youth. For instance, there's this cute, cute, *cute* waiter who keeps cruising you, and I totally approve. In fact, I'm a little jealous."

"Where?"

Rick motioned with his shoulder, and I caught a glimpse of the Puerto Rican waiter taking a drink order nearby.

"He's been cruising *me*?" I asked.

"Big time."

I smiled. "We've exchanged a few glances recently. But . . . I don't even know his name."

"Angel," said Rick. "Angel Maldonado. And he's a real sweetheart."

"You know him?"

"Sure. Remember, I've been coming here for years, and he's worked here for . . . oh, I'd say he's been here for two years. You can't help getting to know the staff a little bit."

"True," I said, recalling that Alan and I knew more about the staff of Bar 51 than we'd ever care to admit, although unlike Alan—Night

Alan, that is—I had never taken one of them home at the end of his shift.

"What did I miss?" asked Bill, returning with a drink.

"Angel is cruising Brett," said Rick.

"Really! That Angel is a cute kid."

Rick turned to me and asked, "So do you want an introduction?"

I blushed. "That's okay. I'm . . . I'm sort of seeing someone."

"Really? I didn't know that. Give up the details."

I brushed his question off, because I really didn't know why I was saying what I was saying. For some reason, my vocal chords had spontaneously decided that I was dating Jamie Brock and I just blurted that out. Apparently, my brain had not shared the news that Jamie just wanted to be friends. If that.

"Come on, Brett," Rick persisted. "What's his name?"

"I'm . . . It's just that we've dated a few times, but I'm not sure if it's serious or not, so I really don't think I should talk about it too much. I've probably already said more than I should have."

"Well if you're just dating, I can still introduce you to Angel . . ."

I laughed. "You don't give up, do you? Are you playing matchmaker?"

"For that, I think I'll wait until Walter Pomeroy rewrites *Hello, Dolly!*" He paused for a moment, then smiled broadly. "And can you imagine the songs he could write?"

"Oh, please, no," I protested. "One Walter Pomeroy musical is enough."

Nevertheless, Rick, Bill, and I played around with the Walter Pomeroy/*Hello, Dolly!* songbook for a while. It was too good a concept to leave alone.

Eventually, Alan joined us, with Ty close behind. He looked at Rick and Bill and said, "You I don't know."

"My friend Rick, and his lover, Bill," I said, making introductions. "And this is Alan and Ty. Alan is my manager, and I met Rick in *Andy*."

Alan put his hand to his mouth. "You're in *Andy*?" When Rick nodded, Alan added, "Poor thing."

"Uh-oh," muttered Rick, nudging my arm. "Here we go again. Cruising in progress."

I followed his gaze and saw that the waiter—Angel—was brushing past a group of drinkers, walking in our direction.

"Go for it," said Bill.

"I can't stand the suspense, Brett," added Rick.

I shook my head. "You guys are shameless, aren't you? I told you that I'm seeing someone."

Alan looked at me, confused. "Who's that?"

"Well . . . Jamie and I . . ."

"Oh, please," he said. "Jamie? The trust fund boy I've never seen? I think you're hallucinating him. And every time we come here, that little cutie waiter boy is cruising you."

I leaned close to Alan and hoped the others wouldn't hear. "I told you, I can't date the Penthouse wait staff."

He rolled his eyes and said, "And I told you you're a dumbass. But, okay, don't date him. Just *talk* to him."

I sighed. There was no hope of dodging the unanimous consensus of my drinking partners. So although I still had half a drink in my glass, I motioned for the waiter, trying my best to smile flirtatiously as I did. It must have worked on *some* level, because he smiled back.

"I think I'll have another," I said, when he reached me.

"Vodka and soda, right?"

"You have a good memory."

His smile broadened. "I've been watching."

One minute later he was back with my drink, ignoring other thirsty patrons as he made a beeline to me.

"Here you go," he said, handing me my drink. "Seven dollars."

I gave him a ten. "Keep it."

"Gracias."

"De nada."

And then . . . he didn't move. So breaking every Operation Hamptons commandment, I decided to engage him in conversation.

"So . . . um . . . nice place."

He smiled and looked around the room. "Thanks, but it's not mine."

"I'm sorry," I said. "I know that was really lame. I just . . . wanted to say something, and drew a blank."

"You could have asked me if I come here often."

"Or . . . I could have asked you what your sign is."

"Sagittarius," he said, laughing, and there was something about hearing that word pronounced in his lilting accent that went straight to my heart to the extent that, for a brief moment, I forgot that I had ever even heard of Jamie Brock.

"I've seen you here a lot lately," he said, continuing the conversation when he realized that I was again drawing verbal blanks.

"Lately," I agreed. "A new set of friends."

We spotted Michael DeVries moving through the crowd toward us—no, toward *me*, of course—at the same time. An evident frown spread across Angel's face.

"One of your new friends?" he asked.

"More like an acquaintance."

He shrugged. "Your call." With that, he turned and began to part the crowd, heading back to the bar.

Wait a minute, I started to say. *I want to get to know you*. But then Michael was there, and my impulse to shout it out went away.

"Absolut and . . ." Michael began, but Angel pivoted and deftly disappeared between two patrons, pretending not to hear him as he vanished.

"Well, doesn't that just beat all," sniffed Michael. "Maybe it's about time this place had a little shake-up in its staff."

"I'm sure he didn't mean to avoid you," I lied. "It's loud in here. He probably didn't hear you."

He didn't answer, but flagged over another waiter and ordered his drink. I looked around, but the couples—Alan and Ty; Rick and Bill—had melted into the crowd, no doubt to give me privacy with Angel. I would have to find them later.

"So did you enjoy your visit to Scarsdale?" he asked, when the waiter left.

"It was . . . it was quite interesting," I said. Realizing that a little more gushing might be in order, I added, "I had a great time. The country club was unbelievable."

"Blake and Winston were quite taken with you. They said I could invite you up there any time."

"Well they are a . . . they're . . . they're a *cute* couple." Of course.

"Aren't they? They sure are. And you'd never believe how much money they're worth."

True enough, I thought. The Culver-Benchleys had to be worth tens of millions of dollars. But proper people didn't talk about such subjects. And that was just as well, because if a couple of reprehensible fossils like them rubbed my nose in the fact that they had money and I did not, I didn't think that I could bear to live.

"And remember," he continued, "we're taking Winston to Swifty's for lunch in a few weeks."

"Gee, Michael, thanks again."

"Just try to fit it in, okay, Brett? I've got all these cute ladies as my luncheon dates, and, as the other man at the table, you have an important role to play in keeping things hopping."

Good lord. If the cute ladies were anything like Winston Culver-Benchley, we would need the fire department and the Betty Ford Clinic standing by during lunch.

I smiled weakly and said, "I'll do my best, Michael." A thought occurred to me. "Why don't you ask Jamie to join us for lunch? Wouldn't another man at the table . . ."

"Not a good idea. Jamie is . . . Jamie is a nice young man, but he is not the type of person who fits well with this crowd. Do you know what I mean?" I looked at him blankly, because, as a matter of fact, I didn't have a clue what he meant. "What I'm trying to say is that these ladies know interior designers, okay? They all have their own designers, and, well . . . they know what designers are like."

"What they're like?"

"Yes, what they're like. And their designers are all, well . . ." He flounced his wrist around for a split second.

"Ah! I get it. You think that Jamie is . . . uh . . . too *gay* for the ladies."

"Of course, I like the kid, but you have to respect their sensitivities."

"But Michael, they know that *you're* gay, don't they?"

"We never discuss it. Let's just say that I doubt their husbands would let them have lunch with me if they didn't have their suspicions."

"And me? I'm . . . what? Not as gay as Jamie?"

He cleared his throat. "Well, it helps that you're not an interior designer, because that's just a big red light to them that spells out G-A-Y. Beyond that, I figure that they just don't care a whole lot.

Winston and Blake probably figure you're just like me, and I suspect that's what the rest of the ladies will think. We're sort of sex-neutral. We don't make them feel as if they're having lunch with their hairdresser, we're safe enough to put their husbands at ease, and we're masculine enough to provide them with just the slightest bit of titillation."

"I see. I'm a desirable luncheon companion because I'm a neuter."

"Well, yes, when it all comes down to it."

"But Winston knows I'm gay."

His face went white. "She does?"

"She said something to me on our drive to Sterling Hills. I mean, maybe she isn't sure, but it was apparent to me that she suspects something."

"Well . . ." The color slowly began to return to his face. "Maybe she was just fishing. I'll tell you, that girl is always curious about something. She probably just saw a movie or something, and it put the thought in her mind."

"She asked about you, too."

The color again drained from his face. "She did?"

"Not if you were gay, really, but, well . . . she's concerned that you're alone."

"I have a lot of friends."

"That's what I told her."

It was clear that Michael was unsettled by Winston Culver-Benchley's curiosity, which made me wonder how good friends they could have possibly been. He leaned against the bar and mulled over this new information.

"It's not that bad, Michael," I said, hoping to reassure him, although I wasn't quite sure why I wanted to do that. "And you know Winnie. She probably forgot the question halfway through the answer."

"Yeah . . . well . . ." He brightened. "That's right. Just make sure at the luncheon to keep personal lives very discreet. Yours *and* mine."

Oh, yeah . . . the luncheon, again. It was time to change subjects until I had a chance to think of an excuse to get out of lunch with Winnie Culver-Benchley and company. So I went directly to the main thing on my mind, which, in a sense, we had almost been discussing.

"Have you seen Jamie lately?" I asked him.

"I haven't seen him, but we've had a few nice phone conversations."

"Well is he all right? Because I left a message for him the other day and I haven't heard from him."

He put a hand on my shoulder and looked into my eyes. "Brett, I said this to you once before, but I think it bears repeating. Jamie is a sweetheart, but he's not the type to be tied down. Ever."

I nodded my head. "He told you about the other night?"

"He did. And he said some very nice things about you, too. You know, he told me that if he was going to settle down with anyone, it would be someone like you." I felt my heart race until Michael added, "The important word there is 'if,' Brett. *If* he was going to settle down. And, again, I wouldn't count on that happening."

"Well . . ." I struggled for something to say that would save face, until I decided that repeating Michael's words would be most appropriate. "I'm not counting on that. I don't count on anything."

He smiled. People really *do* like hearing their advice repeated.

"I knew you were a smart boy, Brett," he said. "Now if you'll excuse me, I'm going to visit some people."

"No problem," I said. "I'll catch you later."

"And remember," he added, as he started to walk away. "We have that luncheon for Winston."

He wasn't going to let me forget, was he?

I found Alan and Ty near the piano. Ty was on deck to entertain the crowd, having had tritely selected "Somewhere Over the Rainbow" as his song, because there was an outside chance that no one else had sung it within the past hour. Yeah, right.

"Where are Rick and Bill?" I asked.

"Bedtime. Being old and married will do that to you."

I laughed. "Watch it with the cracks about age in this place. I almost got in a lot of trouble with Rick when I said something about Bill's . . . uh . . . *advanced years.*"

"Really," said Alan. "That's not even a May/December relationship. It's more like a May/December-of-the-following-year relationship."

"I am *so* not hanging out with you anymore," I said through my laughter. "You're going to get us in trouble."

"Do you want to hear my theory about why the air conditioning is set so high in this place?"

"No. But tell me."

"To keep the patrons from decomposing." When I laughed again, despite my better instincts, he said, "Thanks, folks, I'll be here all week!"

Yes, Night Alan was most definitely in the house.

Ty sang, and while he wasn't the knockout I expected from a Broadway veteran, he was by far the most impressive singer we had heard all evening. Sometime after that, we decided to get away from an ear-piercing rendition of "All That Jazz"—compliments of the Evil Mime, at that—and seek relative peace and quiet at the bar downstairs. Alan and Ty led the way, and I was about to make my descent down the staircase when a hand reached out from the crowd and grabbed my arm. I turned and was face to face with Angel.

"Are you leaving?" he asked.

"No," I said. "Just going downstairs."

"Maybe I'll see you down there. But just in case I don't, we forgot to do something before."

Oh, no, I thought. Please don't suggest a kiss. Not here, in front of everyone.

"Names," he said, and I sighed with relief. "I'm Angel."

"I know." He hiked an eyebrow. "Don't worry. I'm not stalking you. My friends Rick and Bill told me your name."

"Rick and Bill?"

"A couple. Older man, younger man?"

" 'Cause you *never* see that combination at the Penthouse."

Okay, so Angel had a sense of humor. That was a good thing.

"The guys I was talk . . ."

He interrupted me and laughed. "I know who you mean. I was just teasing you."

I blushed for perhaps the tenth time that night. Cute, a sense of humor, a nice deadpan delivery, and . . . *that accent.* If there had never been an Operation Hamptons . . .

But there was. I snapped back to reality.

"Anyway," I said, gripping the handrail at the top of the stairs, "it was nice to finally get a chance to talk to you, Angel." I took one step down, and again he grabbed my arm.

"You're still forgetting something."

"What?"

"I assume *you* have a name?"

I laughed. "Oh, yeah, sorry. It's Brett."

His smile was so adorable that I almost did kiss him, despite myself.

"Come back soon, Brett."

Oh. Yeah.

I was only a minute or so behind them, but it had apparently been a dramatic minute or so for Alan and Ty. They had managed to find stools along the crowded bar, but they were clearly not speaking to each other.

"What's wrong?" I whispered to Alan, after ordering a drink.

He turned and directed his response to Ty. "*Someone* is a little touchy."

"Fuck you," said Ty, not looking at him.

"Listen, I'm sorry," said Alan. Once again I had been relegated to the role of Third Wheel. "I don't own this place, and I don't tell anyone what to think, and . . . and . . . and the only reason I came here tonight was to see you."

In response, Ty glowered at him, then returned his stare to his drink.

"Someone said something he thought was racist," Alan told me, making no effort to hide his comments from Ty. "And he got upset."

"Understandably," I said. "What did he say?"

Ty put himself back into the conversation.

"This guy told me that he had never heard a black guy sing 'Somewhere Over the Rainbow' like 'that' before, whatever 'that' meant."

Alan shrugged. "See? I didn't do a thing, but he's taking it out on me. And what that guy said didn't even make any sense."

Ty swiveled on his stool so that he faced Alan. "It's not *your* attitude," he said. "It's this place. This is . . . this is the whitest place on earth."

Alan asked, "So why do you keep hanging out here?"

"For the career." I could understand. "If you're an old, fat, gay, *white* person in show business casting or management—which most of them are—you're going to be in that piano bar at one point or another. I'm here to . . . well, to *showcase* myself." He indulged himself in a few more seconds of "simmer" before adding, "But the crap I have to put up with, sometimes . . ."

The three of us sat in silence for a while, listening to the piped-in music through a backdrop of jumbled conversation. There was nothing to say to make the situation better, and Alan and I knew enough not to question Ty's sentiments. There are claims that can be made that cheapen the label of "racism," but none of us had any doubt that what Ty often experienced in the Penthouse was exactly that.

We had just about reached the point where the period of silence would have to end, or else it would drag the entire evening into a dark, unhappy place, when I glanced up and saw Jamie confidently walk through the front door.

I leaned over to Alan and said, "You know how you think that Jamie is a hallucination?"

"Well . . . I know he's not *really* a hallucination. But why?"

"Pink Ralph Lauren shirt and cargo shorts. Right by the front door."

Indiscreetly, he turned and looked, then turned back to me.

"That's him?"

"That's him."

He turned again.

"How old is he?"

"I don't know," I said. "I think he's a few years younger than me."

"Whatever *that* means."

"Hush. Anyway, what does it matter?"

"It doesn't. It's just that . . . it's strange. I mean, I've been a talent manager forever, and I can usually peg ages. He looks . . ."

"I think I know what you mean," I said, deciding on the spot to put Alan out of his confusion. "He's a bit weathered . . ."

"That's it!" he said, far too loudly, drawing Ty out of his funk.

"That's *what*?" asked Ty.

"Brett's imaginary boyfriend. He's got the Robert Redford syndrome going on."

I shushed Alan as Jamie wandered up to me . . .

. . . and past me.

"Jamie!" I shouted, and he turned, offering a weak smile and a weaker greeting.

"Oh . . . hi."

Yeah, it was just that weak.

"What's up?" I asked, trying to pretend I hadn't heard the lack of enthusiasm in his voice.

"Just out with some friends from L.A.," he said, and for the first time I noticed that he wasn't traveling alone, but had a crew of three other men—all dressed somewhat the same—accompanying him. They looked at me with the boredom I had encountered at the one circuit party I had bothered to attend a decade earlier, their eyes saying, *"You aren't nearly fabulous enough to talk to me."*

"Oh . . . well . . . enjoy your evening."

One of his friends asked when they were going to the hot new bar downtown as they walked away. Jamie didn't answer him.

"Maybe he *was* a hallucination," said Alan, but for once he wasn't joking. Day Alan had poked his head out of the shell he wore for the evening.

"Maybe he was . . ."

I watched Jamie shepherd his friends from L.A. up the stairs. He was midway to the upper level when he paused and looked at me, smiling sadly, before he disappeared.

Or was that a hallucination, too?

Brett Revere's Thoery of Life, Part Seven:
When Necessary, a Polo Pony Can Be Substituted for a Heart

Because I had nothing better to do, the next morning I paid an office visit to Donovan Talent Management. Since I was again dealing with Day Alan, he made me wait.

"Did Ty calm down?" I asked, when I finally had my audience after twenty minutes of thumbing through outdated issues of *Backstage*.

"Ugh," he said. "I mean, I know what he means, but he keeps putting himself in that situation by going to the Penthouse, so what does he expect?"

I shrugged. "To be treated like a human being?"

He waved a hand at me. "Brett Revere, *faux* trust fund boy, you are absolutely the *last* person I'm going to listen to about that."

"Well, the attitude sucks."

"That's the attitude you aspire to . . ." Seeing the look on my face, he changed course. "So now I've finally seen your Jamie . . ."

"Everything is wrong. Jamie is *not* into me. Not like I'm into him, that is."

"Maybe in time . . ."

"No." I sat silently for a moment, then added, "I think you were right, Alan. I think Operation Hamptons is a waste."

"I'm not going to say I told you so."

"Thank you." I took a deep breath.

"But still . . . you're basing this on . . . *what*? That Jamie doesn't like you?"

"He likes me."

"In his own way. Which isn't *your* way."

"Whatever. I've met a few people, but . . . it hasn't moved the way I thought it would. And almost everyone I meet is looking out for themselves, not me. Plus, I'm spending an awful lot of money I don't have, which is exactly the opposite of what you should be doing when you're unemployed and the rent is due and your former roommate has just stolen a few thousand dollars' worth of things from your apartment."

He gasped. "Quentin *stole* from you?"

"Quentin cleaned me out. Quentin left, like, a half-full box of Rice Chex, and that was about it."

"I'm sorry to hear that. Really. Did you call the police?"

I shrugged. "For all the good it will do." I really didn't want to talk about *that* bad aspect of my life anymore—it offered only depressing news on top of more depressing news—so I changed the subject without further comment. "But Operation Hamptons is . . . I don't know. It just doesn't seem to be working. The people I'm meeting are . . . well, they're sort of *vile.* And I'm not making the progress I was expecting."

He shook his head. "What *were* you expecting?"

"I was expecting things to go the way I'd envisioned. Meet people, move up . . . I didn't mind spending the money at first, because, well . . . you have to spend money to make money, right? And when I met Jamie, I really saw it all coming together. But now it's falling apart."

"It's only been . . ." He stopped and glanced at his desk calendar. "Christ, Brett, you've only been at it for a week or so. I mean, the *earth* was barely created in that time period!"

"No," I said. "I know when something is working, and when it's not, and . . ."

He leaned forward, anchoring his elbows to his desk. "Are you telling me that Operation Hamptons is a bust? Or is this all about Jamie?"

"Yes."

"You know I think this whole thing is a nitwit idea. Don't you?"

"Yes."

"Well, since I'm already on the record, let me add something. If you want this to succeed, you can't let a single Jamie be the measuring tape. Okay, I know that you really like him and want to have his babies, but . . . face it, Brett; at the end of the day, he's just a man, and all men are pieces of shit, and it doesn't matter if the piece of shit is a cute rich boy or some hustler from the piers, because you can't measure yourself or your goals by what one of those pieces of shit thinks, says, or does. Am I making myself clear?"

"Sort of."

"No," he said, settling back in his chair. "I'm making myself *very* clear. If you want this stupid Operation Hamptons of yours to work, you can't judge it based on whether or not you end up happily ever after with Jamie, because it was never about Jamie to begin with. So get back on your horse, ride it back into the Penthouse, and work the room, Brett. Because if this plan of yours has any chance to succeed—which I doubt—you've got to work for it."

His combination pep rally and tongue-lashing concluded, Alan rose to dismiss me. I followed suit. As he showed me to the door, he said, "I hate myself for asking this, but do you need cash?"

I did, but wouldn't admit it.

"If things get that bad, call me." He opened the door and gave me the briefest of hugs. "And . . . good luck."

"Thanks."

I waited until I was in the elevator before I braved the contents of my pants pocket. Six dollars and change. No money in my checking account. Broke. Not even enough left to buy a drink at the Penthouse, which suddenly sounded like a very appealing idea.

Broke and going nowhere. Michael and Jamie could survive on trust funds and wealthy patrons, and still they had no hesitation to cut ethical corners to add to their edges. Me, though? No. I had to be the lone beacon of morality, a man who couldn't even follow through on a cynical plan to charm my way to a brighter future. And because I was the beacon of morality, I was falling further and further behind.

Six dollars and change, without even a television to entertain me. This was not the way my plan was supposed to work.

I got on the N train and rode a few stops, staring longingly out the window when the doors opened at the Lexington Avenue stop . . . just blocks from the Penthouse. Then the doors closed, and the train descended under the East River for the trip to Queens.

Somehow I decided that a large part of the blame for my predicament fell squarely on the shoulders of Quentin King. If Quentin hadn't used my computer, I never would have gotten so angry that I threw him out of the apartment, and therefore I wouldn't have to shoulder the entire upcoming rent bill. And if Quentin hadn't subsequently stolen almost everything of value that I owned, I'd at least be able to watch television tonight. And, well . . . none of this would have happened if Quentin hadn't been such a frightening creep. Even my disagreement with Jamie would have possibly been surmountable if Quentin's credit card hadn't intruded.

Quentin's credit card. With its fifteen thousand dollar line of credit, minus an expensive dinner at La Goulue.

Temptation flickered in my brain. I knew I shouldn't do it, and I doubted I *could* do it, but I couldn't stop thinking about it.

Which is why I ended up rummaging through the trash the instant I was back in my apartment, looking for the notice that came with the credit card, which I hoped included a PIN.

It did.

Thanks to an amazing line of credit most certainly obtained through fraudulent information, I had a new, fabulous-fitting wardrobe from Barneys New York when I walked through the Penthouse doors a week or so later.

And, at home, I had a new stereo, a new television . . . yes, even a new vacuum cleaner.

So sue me—not an altogether unrealistic option, I realized. I had no cash, rent was coming due, and Quentin had stolen everything of value from my apartment. A cash advance or two and an occasional charge on the Magic Credit Card solved a few problems, and I still planned on paying it back, so it was only dishonest in the most unforgiving and literal interpretation of the law.

I had a new plan. Call it Operation Hamptons: the Second Wind.

I felt thoroughly dishonest and thoroughly corrupt and thoroughly in sync with the Penthouse regulars, right down to the Ralph Lauren polo pony where my heart should have been.

I scanned the downstairs bar, looking for familiar faces but coming up empty, so I walked up the spiral staircase to the piano bar. A stooped, gaunt man was singing "I'm Still Here," and I wished someone was around so I could verbalize my observation, "Not for long." But, no, even the upstairs bar was devoid of anyone remotely familiar.

Well . . . there was one familiar face. Angel, the waiter, who happened to be working behind the bar that night.

"Remember me?" I asked with a smile, when I had his attention.

He smiled back. "Brett! How could I forget? Vodka-soda?"

I shook my head. "I think a change of pace is in order. Make it scotch. Dewars."

"And . . . soda?"

"No. Water. Let's make this a complete change."

He poured my drink, then traded it for my cash. Setting a few dollars on the bar in front of me, he said, "Here's your change. And speaking of change, what's the deal?"

"Haven't you ever wanted to change?" I asked. "Overhaul yourself?"

"Not especially. I've wanted *other* people to change, but I'm content enough."

"Well, you've changed a bit." When he didn't react, I added, "For once, you're behind the bar. That's change, right?"

He nodded. "A small change. Very small. I'm only covering until Paolo gets to work."

"Paolo?"

"Cute guy? Brazilian? Very funny?" I shrugged. "He's almost white, Brett. You should know who he is."

"That's not fair."

He smiled. "I know. Sorry . . . cheap shot. Anyway, back to what you were saying: I'm content to stay as I am."

I laughed. "That's admirable. I wish I could be like that, but, well . . . hanging around this place, I've started to feel more and more like I don't fit in."

"How's that?"

"I just felt I needed to class things up a bit."

He shook his head. "Whatever." After a quick glance down the bar, he added, "Excuse me. I have to take care of some customers."

Angel was gone for a long time, but he made it back to my corner of the bar before my glass was empty. After pouring another, he said, "So are you trying to turn yourself into one of . . . *them*?"

"Them?"

He motioned around the room. "These people." When I didn't respond, he added, "I don't think you want to be like most of them.

Trust me on this. Very unhappy people, who like to make other people unhappy. Phonies, fakes . . ."

I smiled, hoping to bring some lightness to his dark observations. "But they're successful."

"It depends on your definition of success." His tone was casual, although his words were anything but. "Money is a good thing, I suppose. But it's not everything. I'll bet anything that you or I enjoy life ten times more than most of these people with money."

"What makes you think that *I* don't have money?"

"Oh, come on . . ."

Despite the fact that Angel was the one who had seen through my lie, I found myself getting angry. "No, really. Why are you lumping *me* in with *you*?"

Shit. I think I knew the damage was done before he did.

Okay. The words were out of my mouth now, and I couldn't take them back. So I was going to make a joke, but it was, in fact, too late.

"I don't think you have to worry about fitting in with the regulars," he said, then he spun on his heels and marched to the other end of the bar, where he whispered something to another bartender, newly arrived, who I assumed was the previously discussed Paolo. They proceeded to exchange posts, although I knew that even the new bartender was going to give me the absolute minimum in service.

Which gave me time for an interior monologue/pep rally that went something like this:

> *Keep your eye on the prize. Waiters are expendable. I have spent thousands of ill-gotten dollars on clothes, and was prepared to spend more to entertain, and if Operation Hamptons was going to succeed, I couldn't get distracted by the hurt feelings of the servant class. There! I thought it! I thought of other people as being part of the servant class! Ha ha! I haven't even been at this for two weeks, and I'm already adopting the attitude. Ha! I have arrived! I am a real asshole!*

See? Even in an interior monologue/pep rally, I knew I was being an asshole.

But there were words of truth, too. If Operation Hamptons was going to succeed, I would need to stay focused. The wardrobe was a good start, and—even though I really didn't even *like* the taste of the scotch I was drinking—every element of everything I did in the bar was important.

And as if to prove my point, the next familiar face to walk in—Jamie—went straight to the superficial.

"Clothes don't make every man," he said, approaching me. "But they seem to make you."

"You didn't like my Banana Republic casual look?"

"It worked," he said. "But it was sort of common." I knew that for Jamie, "common" was the greatest insult. "So if you don't mind me asking . . ."

I shrugged. "People buy clothes, Jamie. Even poor people, like me."

He looked me over again. "You've got about two thousand dollars on your back. Well . . . counting the shoes. That's a lot for a poor person to spend on clothes."

"Outlet stores."

"I don't believe you." He thought things over for a moment, then asked, "Did Michael set you up with one of his old ladies?"

I brushed his comment off. "No way. And you know better than that."

He smiled. "Yeah, I do know better than that. But you're working some angle on something, and I'm trying to figure out what it is." He paused again, looking at me thoughtfully, then one eyebrow arched. His smile was devilish.

"You're using the credit card, aren't you?"

I kept my silence.

"Congratulations."

I sighed in defeat. He had me.

"Don't congratulate me. I don't feel good about it."

"I don't feel good about a lot of things," he said. "But that's the way the world works."

There was a pause, but that devilish smile was still on his lips.

"What?" I asked.

He shook his head. "Nothing."

That wasn't a good enough answer. But it was probably going to be the best I was going to get.

"Your friends from L.A. are gone?"

"Yeah," he said. "Some party they *had* to be seen at in Australia." He shook his head, and for a moment the brown mop of hair came alive. "I'm too old for that shit, though."

"I know what you mean. I won't even *go* to a city if I know there's a circuit party."

"Yeah, I . . ." He was certainly going to say something else, but stopped himself. Instead, he stared at me, still sporting that devilish grin.

"What?" I asked.

"I . . . can't remember what I was going to say." He laughed, but it was hollow, and the grin faded. "I'm just . . . I'm . . ." He stopped for a moment, and looked to the ceiling for either inspiration or delay. "Can I be honest with you?"

"Sure."

"I'm sort of in a very confused place in my life, Brett. Nothing personal, but you and I . . . I mean, I like you a lot, but . . . but . . ."

"But you want to," I thought, and knew it was the truth.

I decided I would have to help Jamie along. He didn't move away as I edged closer, which I took as a supportive sign.

And when our lips finally met, he kissed right along with me.

For several long minutes.

And when we finally came up for air, I wanted to tell the world about us.

"Come on," I said, grabbing his hand to lead him to the lower level, to the street, to an apartment where we could be alone, to another world where there would be nothing but Brett and Jamie.

We walked the first half-dozen steps together as a couple forever before he stopped so abruptly that I lost my grip on his hand.

"Brett, no," he said. His voice was gentle, but it was still a no.

"But . . ."

"I can't."

"But . . ."

"No."

On my way out of the bar, alone, Angel gave me a less than approving once-over.

This would have been what one might call "not a good night."

* * *

And yet, early the next evening, when the phone rang, Jamie's voice was on the line. I started to apologize, but the botched pass of the night before had already vanished into history. Now, he was concerned with something else. Something so dire he wouldn't even discuss it over the phone. He asked me to meet him at his Second Avenue apartment and, of course, I—forgetting or forgiving the pain and humiliation of the previous nights—agreed to meet him ninety minutes later.

I was six minutes late, but pleased to note that Benjamin Grover was out. If our paths crossed that evening, I was sure he'd tell me he was having prostate surgery or something similar to tweak me, and I really didn't want to deal with him.

We walked into Jamie's bedroom and he closed the door behind us. The room was, as always, a disaster area.

"I'm in trouble," he said. "You've got to help me."

"What trouble?"

He glanced back at the bedroom door. "Keep your voice down. Just in case Ben comes home. I don't want him to know." I nodded a silent agreement, and he continued. "You're the only one I can trust, Brett."

"Why me?"

"Because we're the same. Understand? The two of us are the same."

I shook my head, wanting to understand but not quite getting it. "I'm not following you . . ."

He put his hands on my shoulders and gazed forcefully into my eyes, swallowing before he continued. "The reason I ran from you is because I couldn't allow myself to have the feelings I felt for you."

"I'm still not following. If you have feelings for me, what's the problem?"

"The problem is that we're the same type of people. We wouldn't be right for each other."

"I thought that was the point of two people getting together. Because they shared a lot of the same . . ."

"Brett!" He dropped his hands from my shoulders and turned away. "You don't understand what I'm trying to say, do you?"

"No," I confessed. "Not at all."

"You know how you're trying to get out of Queens? How you want to network? Make connections? Use the Penthouse to advance your position in life?"

"Yeah."

"That's me."

I was still thoroughly confused. "I don't think we're as much alike as you seem to think. I mean, I know that you're always hustling for your decorating business, but that's not quite the same as what I'm doing. For me this is a matter of whether I'll be able to eat or not. What about that trust fund you're supposed to be living off?"

He turned and looked back at me. I noticed the slightest quiver in his lower lip. "When did you ever hear me say I was living off a trust fund?"

"But I . . . I'm sure you told me that."

He shook his head.

"Well someone did," I said finally.

"Then someone *assumed* I was living off a trust fund. Just like you *assumed* I was living off a trust fund." He paused. "Do you really think I'd be living with a brain-fried dinosaur like Benjamin Grover if I was a trust-funder? No, Brett, I'm just like you. And now I need help, and you're the only one I can trust."

This was too much information to process at one time. Jamie Brock was not—as I had assumed, or had I been told?—a trust fund baby. He was just trying to charm his way into their inner circles, to make it ahead in life.

Just as I was trying to do.

And now, in a revelation I almost found even more disturbing, Jamie was turning to *me* for help.

Shaking away the confusion, I asked, "So what do you want me to do?"

"Will you help me?"

"Probably. But I think you'd better tell me what's going on before I commit myself."

He sat on the bed, motioning for me to join him. Once I had settled onto the comforter, he asked, "Do you know who Nicholas Golodnya is?"

"Yeah," I replied. "I heard."

He was suddenly offended. "Who told you? I hate all that gossip!"

"Keep it down. Remember that Benjamin might come home, so chill. *You* were the one who told me about Golodnya. He's that defense contractor, right?"

"So you know that I dated Nico for a while . . ."

"Uh . . . no, I didn't know that."

"It was nothing serious, but I think he was into me more than I was into him. And, uh . . . he wasn't very happy when I broke it off."

"When was that?"

"A few days ago. He accused me of using him, of only dating him to get at his money." Some involuntary—or at least subconscious—twitch must have appeared on my face, because he grew defensive. "It wasn't like that, Brett. Okay, Nico isn't exactly the kind of guy you'd expect me to become involved with, but it had nothing to do with his money. I thought I liked him."

"But you didn't?"

"Not after a while. We dated for . . . I don't know, maybe a month. But I got to see another side of him, and he started to act very unpleasant around me. Controlling. That's when I called it quits."

They had been dating for a month . . . which meant that they had been dating when I met Jamie. I tried not to think about that.

"So what's the problem?" I asked. "It sounds like it's over and done, and you're a free man."

He leaned back on the bed and closed his eyes.

"There *is* a problem," he said, his voice a near whisper. "There's . . . Well, what happened is this: one night early on in our relationship, when everything was cool, we had too much to drink and got . . . um . . . we got a bit adventurous."

"Adventurous?"

"Nico had a digital camera and asked me to pose for him . . . and I did."

"That doesn't sound like the worst thing that could happen. It's not a crisis. Lots of people . . ."

"He says he's going to post the pictures on the Internet."

"*What?!*"

"Keep your voice down. Remember Benjamin. He could come home at any minute." After a brief pause, he continued. "Nico called my cell this morning and told me that unless I go back to him he's going to upload the photo to a gay porn site." Jamie looked at me, pleading with his eyes. "That could ruin my reputation forever, Brett. We've got to get that picture back."

"Jamie . . ." I cleared my throat. "Jamie, I'm hardly an expert, but there's a lot of porn out there. Even if he follows through on his threat, it would be hard for someone to find it. I don't think this is worth getting upset about."

"He'll tell people how to find it. He knows a lot of people, and he has tons of money. You can't underestimate what he'd be willing to do to get back at me, Brett. Nicholas Golodnya is a man who destroys competing businesses for sport. They say he's linked to the Russian mob. Destroying *me* would be . . . it would be *fun* for him."

"Wow," I said, shaking my head. "And how did you get involved with this charmer again?"

"It doesn't matter," he said, dismissing my question. Not that I had expected full disclosure. "So will you help me?"

"I'd like to, Jamie," I said, "but I don't know what I can do. I mean, I know how to use a computer, but that's about it. I can't hack into a porn site and destroy your picture."

"No, no. Nothing like that. We've got to do this in a low-tech way."

"What do you mean?"

"We've got to go out to Southampton and delete the photo from his computer."

I sat in silence, contemplating his plan. It sounded like the exact opposite of the sort of sensible thing we should be doing. Ignoring the threat and letting Jamie's photograph disappear into the ocean of Internet pornography seemed like a much more sensible approach.

"Jamie, I don't think . . ."

"We can catch an early Jitney and be out there before lunch. Then we can slip into his house, find the photo, and get back to New York. It's simple."

I sat on the bed, thinking it over. It sounded like an incredibly stupid idea . . . but it was Jamie, and he was obviously quite upset with the situation.

Still . . .

"I don't know, Jamie. So many things could go wrong. Maybe it would be best to let Golodnya do whatever he's going to do and ignore it. It's bound to pass quickly."

Jamie sighed theatrically and sank back onto the bed, his eyes staring blankly at the ceiling. He was silent for a while.

"Are you all right?" I asked finally.

He shut his eyes tightly and said, "I really need your help. You're the only one I can trust. I mean, I've never told anyone else the things I've told you, and now . . ."

"But it's just a picture. Even if people find out about it, you can say that it was Photoshopped or something . . ."

Jamie's eyes flashed open, and now his voice was angry.

"Don't you care about my *reputation?!*" he asked. "Don't you care about my *business?!*"

"Well, yes, but . . ."

"Brett, that's what he wants to destroy!" He stopped, and bit the knuckle of his thumb in frustration. It looked as if he was trying to hold back tears.

"Jamie . . ." I wrapped an arm around his shoulder and pulled him close to me. "Jamie, it will be all right . . ."

"Will you help me?" His voice was husky, and, as he burrowed his head into my neck, I felt the dampness of tears.

"Oh, no," I thought. *"Not tears. That wasn't playing fair."*

"I'll try to help you," I said, hoping I had left myself enough wiggle-room.

He rewarded me by pressing his lips against my shoulder.

"Thank you," he said softly, and his lips traveled to my neck. "This means so much to me, baby." The lips were now on my ear. "I don't know what I'd do without you."

Yes, I had my doubts about helping him. To me, a nude picture didn't seem like a reputation- and career-ending offense. But he was Jamie, and his lips were now on mine, and that overrode a lot of doubts . . .

. . . which disappeared altogether when, his lips still locked hungrily on mine, he started unbuttoning his shirt.

My thoughts were almost completely disrupted, replaced with that longing for Jamie that I had felt since the moment our hands first touched. The one consistent thought that remained was that, in his moment of need, I was the only person he could trust or turn to. I was the only person who could save him. I was the only person who loved him enough to sacrifice for him.

And, a few minutes later, I was the only person who was having sex with him.

It was simple, really.

Too simple.

Brett Revere's Theory of Life, Part Eight:

If a Picture Is Worth a Thousand Words, Then Dozens of Pictures Are Worth Much More

Even before I could recall the specifics, when I woke in the morning in Jamie's arms I knew I had made a questionable decision. It took half a minute for the details to surface in my memory, and the trip to the Hamptons to retrieve the nude photograph sounded even dumber by light of day.

But at least I was waking up next to Jamie. And that justified a lot of things. I would be his savior . . . his hero . . .

Yes, stealing a photograph from Nicholas Golodnya's home—most likely heavily guarded—in a town more than one hundred miles from Manhattan certainly qualified as lacking in judgment, by most measures.

And then there was the Russian mafia thing that Benjamin Grover had mentioned on an earlier occasion. Was that a joke, or was Jamie taking me along on a suicide mission?

But then I felt his body stir next to mine and I could no longer remember those rational thoughts. All I could think about was how I was going to rescue Jamie, and make him realize how much he needed me.

I felt the fresh bite mark on my ass and smiled.

"Good morning," he said groggily, his eyes still closed, as he curled closer to my body.

"Sleep well?" I asked.

"Mmmm . . . Of course, baby. How could I not sleep well, with you next to me?"

I kissed him lightly on the forehead. "When do you think we should get going?"

"Oh, right," he said, stretching. "We have to go to the Hamptons today. Shit . . . I don't know. We should probably try to go on the early side." He opened his eyes. "What time is it?"

I glanced at the alarm clock on his nightstand. "Seven-fifteen."

"I think there's a Jitney at eight-thirty. We can catch it, get out there, do what we have to do, and be back in the city by midafternoon."

"Sounds like a plan." I let my hand wander across his chest, lightly brushing the sparse hair, and wondered if mornings could get any better than this, waking up with Jamie.

"Hey, Brett," he said, concern in his voice. "The things I told you last night . . . you know, about not being a trust funder. You won't tell anyone, will you?"

"Of course not. That's our secret."

"It's just that, you know how those people can be."

"I know. I know."

"And I'll keep quiet about you."

"We'll have our own little conspiracy," I said, smiling. "We're the Trust Fund Boys, and no one else will be invited into our private club."

He laughed. "It's just the two of us, baby. You and me against the world."

At that moment, those words meant more to me than he would ever know. I leaned over and found his lips with mine, and, as I did, my left hand found his erection. I held him for a moment, until he broke away.

He laughed, squirming away from my grasp. "I like that, 'The Trust Fund Boys.' "

"Our own private club," I said, leaning over to kiss him, and feeling again for his erection under the sheets.

"Not now," he said, playfully slapping at my hand. "We've got a Jitney to catch."

Within the hour, we were on the Jitney to Southampton, and I reflected on the irony that my first actual trip to the Hamptons as part of Operation Hamptons would be to slip in and slip out undetected. That was not exactly the way the plan was supposed to unfold.

Jamie dozed in the seat next to me over the hours the bus rumbled out on the Long Island Expressway, his head rolling gently against my shoulder. When we reached Southampton, he called a car, instructing the driver to let us off not at an address, but at an intersection. He was doing whatever he could to cover our tracks.

After we were dropped off, we still had a seven-minute walk along the shoulder of the road, past hedgerows that towered above us. The road was nearly deserted; only a few slow-moving cars and bicycles passed.

"Here it is," he said, his voice almost a whisper, when we finally reached a gated driveway.

I looked at the entrance, and was stricken by doubt for the first time since I awoke and decided that saving Jamie was more important than common sense. "The gate . . ."

"It's all show," he said, and, to prove it, he shoved a shoulder against it. With a groan, the gate opened wide enough for us to crawl through.

When we were on the other side, standing on the Golodnya estate, he closed the open gate behind us and said, "And now for the moment of truth."

"What's that?"

"Just follow me."

I obediently trailed him on the grass along the side of the gravel driveway in silence, nervously surveying the area. Except for a few squirrels racing across the lawn, there was no sign of activity. That was a good sign.

A short distance away, up a slight hill, I could see the gabled roof of the house. From somewhere beyond it, I heard the waves of the Atlantic Ocean break along the beach, and the cry of seagulls circling in the sky.

We reached a crest in the driveway, and the front of the house came completely into view. Only then did Jamie break into a wide smile.

"No one's home," he said.

My jaw dropped. "You mean there was a chance someone could have been home?"

"Just a *small* chance. I wasn't too concerned. If Nico's not in the city right now, he's probably at his office. He's hardly ever home before late afternoon, even on the weekends."

As we quickened our pace toward the house, he said, "This is perfect. We can get the pictures without having to negotiate with him."

"And how were you planning to negotiate?" I asked, but he ignored me.

And then we were standing on a semicircular brick terrace, which fanned out before the solid front door. Each side of the door was bracketed by one long but narrow window.

Jamie cupped his hand to the glass, shielding his eyes from the sun's glare, and looked into the interior.

"Yeah," he said. "There's no one home." He turned to me. "Ready to get this over with?"

"Ready."

But suddenly I wasn't ready. There was something we weren't taking into consideration.

"Wait," I said, taking hold of his arm just inches from the door. "What about the alarm?"

He smiled. "I know the code."

Jamie flipped open a small box next to the door and deftly entered an alarm bypass code on the keypad, then slid his key into the lock. Moments later the door was open, and he pulled me into the foyer. The door closed quickly behind us.

"Nice," I said, catching my first view of Nicholas Golodnya's interior. "Did you do this?"

"Some of it," he replied distractedly, as he paced from one side of the door to the other, peering out the windows bracketing the door. "I did the master bedroom and the guest rooms, but I didn't get a chance to tackle the downstairs before Nico and I broke up." He took his attention away from the windows for a moment to quickly glance around the foyer and the sliver of living room in our range of vision. "Too bad, too. Nico's last decorator had horrible taste."

"So where's the computer?" I asked. "We should get this done and get out of here."

He was again looking out the window, and gestured blindly behind him into the foyer. "See those stairs to the left? The office is the first door to the right at the top of the stairs. That's where he keeps his computer."

"You're not going with me?"

"I'll be up in a minute. I just want to make sure no one saw us break in."

"Technically, we didn't break in," I pointed out.

"Technically, the police won't care a lot about the technicalities."

Point well taken. I found the stairs and took them two at a time to the second floor, where I quickly found the office and the computer.

Golodnya had left it on, and with a sweep of the mouse I made the screensaver disappear. That was the easy part. The hard part came when I was faced with a prompt asking for his password.

I typed in GOLODNYA. Too obvious. Access denied.

I tried GOLODNYATECH. Same result, and for the same reason.

On a hunch, I typed JAMIE. Access denied.

BROCK. Access denied.

JAMIEBROCK. Access denied.

MOTHERFUCKERGODDAMITLETMEIN. Too many characters for the 12-character field. Access denied.

I went back to the hall and shouted down the stairs. "Jamie! I need your help!"

In a flash he was at the bottom of the stairs, his eyes wide with panic. "Jesus Christ," he hissed. "What the fuck are you doing? We're not supposed to be here, remember? Keep it down!"

"Sorry," I said, muting my voice. "But I can't figure out how to get into his computer."

He rolled his eyes. "I thought you knew what you were doing."

"I do. But to do what I know how to do, I have to get into the damn thing. And I can't figure out his password."

He shrugged and shook his head unhappily. "I don't know it. Computers aren't my thing."

"Does he have any children? Pets?"

"No, and no. An ex-wife, but I can guarantee that he's not using *her* name." His attention went back to the front door and he stepped away from the stairs. "Figure something out."

"But . . ."

And I would have to figure something out on my own, because Jamie was back in the foyer. Resigned, I turned and walked back to the office.

Until I could get Jamie's attention, I was forced to improvise passwords on my own. HAMPTONS. ANDY. TAKASHIMI. ASTORIA. QUENTIN . . . I knew they had no chance of giving me access to Nicholas Golodnya's hard drive, but by typing them it felt like I was accomplishing more than merely scratching my head and trying to read the mind of a man I had never met.

BRETTLOVESJAMIE. No, far too personal. And too many characters. And even less likely to be the password than the name of Golodnya's ex-wife.

ILOVEJAMIE. No, because you never did, did you, Golodnya? No, you used him in pursuit of your deviant sexual appetite before casting him aside. You . . .

"What are you doing?"

With a start, I bolted upright in the chair.

"I . . . uh . . . I'm trying to come up with a password . . ." It was only when I finished stammering that I realized that I had no reason to be embarrassed, since the black dots on the screen did not reveal what I had typed. That knowledge did not make my face any less red, however.

"You've got to hurry. We've got to get that picture . . ."

"I know," I said, calming down. "But I can't get the picture until I get access to the computer." I typed a few random things—POOL, SWIM, MONTAUK, PENTHOUSE—and was not surprised when none of them paid off. "So I take it you're satisfied that no one saw us get into the house?"

"Yeah," he replied. "They would have been here by now."

"The police?"

"The police or the alarm company." I swiveled in the chair and gave him a look of surprise. "I was hoping Nico hadn't changed the code, but I wasn't really sure."

I turned back to the screen and grunted, "That's reassuring."

We were both silent for a few minutes as I typed random thoughts and very bad guesses while Jamie paced.

"Maybe," I finally said, "we should just take the computer."

"Take the whole thing?"

"Yeah. If we can't get into it, we're going to have to destroy it."

He let out a deep breath. "No. We can't do that. We'll be in big trouble if we steal the entire computer. I can't even begin to imagine what he's got on there . . . all his business records . . ."

"You," I reminded him. "Naked."

"Yeah, but . . . That's bad, all right? You know I feel that way, or else we wouldn't be here. But we shouldn't turn this into a major felony. If we can't delete the pictures, then I'll have to come up with another plan."

"Okay," I said with a sigh. "But I don't know how *I* feel about having . . ." I stopped. "Wait a minute. Did you say 'pictures'?"

"Yeah."

"Pictures? As in plural? As in more than one?"

He looked at the floor and mumbled, "There may be two or three."

"Shit, Jamie." I looked again at the unwelcoming screen. "Shit."

I felt his arm wrap around me from behind . . . felt his hair brush mine . . . and he whispered, "You've got to help me, Brett."

"I'm trying."

And that's when I saw it: a yellow Post-It almost hidden beneath the mouse pad. I slid it out and read the single word carefully printed with a ballpoint pen: NYSNICO1.

I instinctively knew that NYSNICO1 was his vanity license plate, or a variation on it. But that didn't mean it was his password. Still, it was worth a try. I held my breath and kept my expectations low—so low I didn't even dare mention it to Jamie—as I slowly typed N-Y-S-N-I-C-O-1 . . .

And the screen came to life: *Welcome! You have 9 unread messages!*

"We're in," I announced, exhaling with relief. He immediately let go of me.

Nicholas Golodnya was an organized man, if his computer files were any indication. It took me almost no time at all to find a file labeled PERSONAL, under which I found a file labeled PHOTOS. I opened it and immediately found what I was looking for.

And then some.

"Jamie? Exactly how many photos does he have of you?"

There was a pause before he replied. "A few."

I scanned the titles of dozens of images. JAMIE01.jpg . . . JAMIE06.jpg . . . JAMIE28.jpg . . . JAMIE36.jpg . . . In all, there were forty-nine Jamie photos on Golodnya's hard drive.

"A few," I repeated dryly. I double-clicked on JAMIE01 and the computer's photo editing program opened, quickly filling the screen with the image of my very own Jamie Brock, very much unclothed, reclined on an unmade bed, and smiling for the camera. I wondered if the bedroom he was posing in was one he had decorated.

"You really don't need to look at them, do you? They're sort of embarrassing."

"Just wanted to make sure I had the right pictures," I said, closing the photo editor then deleting the image from the file directory. I moved the cursor to JAMIE02 and deleted it as I asked, "So what are you doing by the time we get to the last picture?"

"Just . . . stuff. Nothing too bad."

"But I shouldn't look."

"You shouldn't look." He moved to my side as I deleted JAMIE03 and said, "But when we get back to New York I'll give you the show live and in person."

I felt my penis stir and tried to will it away as I deleted JAMIE04. "Not now," I said. "Let me finish this and let's get out of here."

I was deleting JAMIE25 when we both jumped with alarm at the dual sounds of crackling gravel and the purr of a car engine. Jamie raced across the room and peered through the curtain.

"Shit!"

"What is it?" I asked, knowing what it was.

"He's home. Turn off the—we've got to—we've got to get out of here . . ."

I closed the directory and prayed that the screensaver would start before Nicholas Golodnya decided to walk upstairs to check his e-mail, as Jamie busied himself with nothing much except for squelching his panic. When the sound of the car door slamming rose from the driveway, he almost shot through the ceiling.

"We've got to hide," he said in a forced whisper. We scanned the room, seeing few options besides one small closet, which seemed like too much of a cliché.

Of course, that's where I ended up. Jamie shoved me in among Nicholas Golodnya's fall outerwear, and then—since there was only room for one—latched the door with a barely audible, "I'll get you when the coast is clear."

Muffled in the closet, I couldn't hear a thing . . . until the sound of heavy footsteps was practically on top of me.

"Is someone in here?" His voice was deep, made distinct through a light Russian accent that had the effect of making him sound overly formal. "Show yourself, or I will call the police."

Nice. Because if Golodnya didn't find me, the police certainly would. My dreams of a cushy job and social standing seemed to shatter around me. I was going from failed actor and suspended temp to fake trust fund boy to common burglar with lightning speed.

"Show yourself," he said again, and I heard another set of footsteps enter the room. "What are you doing here?"

Now I heard Jamie's voice, and was grateful that he knew well enough to show himself before the Suffolk County Sheriff was called.

"You knew I'd come back, Nico. Didn't you?"

"I did not know."

"Well, I did . . ."

I held my breath to better hear them.

"So why have you come back here, Jamie?"

There was a long pause on the other side of the door. Far too long. Jamie was obviously drawing a mental blank, and I was totally unable to help him. Not that I had the first clue about what he should say.

In fact, Jamie never had to answer the question, because Golodnya followed it up with, "You know how I knew you were here in this house?"

"How?"

"The computer. No screensaver was on, meaning someone was just using it."

Another long pause. Then:

"That was me. I was using it while I waited for you."

"You were using it for what?"

Another long pause. This one was the longest by far.

"Your birthday," Jamie finally gushed. "I was on eBay shopping for your birthday gift."

"Very considerate," said Golodnya. "But my birthday is not until October."

Now Jamie seemed back in his element, and his comeback was smooth. "You think it's that easy making sure I have just the right gift for your birthday, Nico? It's not. You're a tough man to buy for. I can't very well just walk into Sears and buy Nico Golodnya the perfect birthday gift, can I?"

There was silence. I pressed my ear to the door to pick up any trace of noise, and was momentarily stunned to hear what sounded far too much like kissing to be to my taste. I listened more intently and . . . yes, that was kissing. My Jamie was engaged in a hot make-out session with Nicholas Golodnya, captain of industry and fledgling pornographer.

I was not a happy man, although I was not quite so unhappy that I was willing to leave the closet.

The kissing stopped and I heard Jamie's voice. "How about lunch? Can I take you somewhere nice?"

"*You* want to buy *me* lunch? That is something new."

I could hear Jamie's theatrical sigh through the outerwear. "I'm trying to be a new person, Nico. I know you think I was using you, but I'm trying to prove that that isn't the way I am. So . . . can I take you to lunch?"

The older man paused, then said, "Lunch would be good. First, though, dessert."

Oh no no no no no. Not at all what I wanted to hear.

I heard them leave the room. Moments later, Jamie cracked open the closet door.

"We've got about ten seconds," he whispered. "He's in the bathroom. Listen, I'm not going to do anything with him, okay? I'm just trying to get him out of the house. I'll let you know when we're about to leave, and you can finish erasing those pictures." Before I could respond, he shut the door in my face.

Mercifully, I couldn't hear anything from wherever they went for "dessert," although by not knowing what was happening, my mind was able to conjure up all sorts of worst-case imagery.

Half an hour later, the door cracked open again.

"My legs are cramping," I said.

"Sorry. But we're leaving for lunch in East Hampton in a few minutes. As soon as we're gone, delete those files and get the fuck out of here. If he catches you . . ."

"He's not going to catch me," I hissed. "I'll be out that door three seconds after the last file is deleted."

"Remember to shove the gate closed."

"I'll remember."

"And don't look at the pictures, okay? I'm embarrassed about them, and I don't want you to see them."

"I promise."

He started to close the door, then stopped. "One more thing. I need to borrow the credit card."

"What?!"

"Shh! The only way I can get him out of the house is if I buy him lunch, and I can't buy him lunch unless I have the credit card. C'mon, Brett. I need it. And it's the only way we're not going to get busted."

Not getting busted was a good idea right now. Reluctantly, I pulled out my wallet and handed Jamie the infamous Quentin King Credit Card.

"Thanks," he said, smiling as he pocketed it. "You're the best." Somehow he managed to kiss me though the small opening, although his kiss landed on my nose. And then he was gone.

Minutes later I emerged from the closet, stretching the aches out of my body before walking quietly but quickly to the window to make sure they were gone. There was no car in the driveway.

I typed NYSNICO1 and went to work, deleting files without succumbing to the temptation of peeking. As much as part of me wanted to see them, I knew that I really didn't want to see them. Hearing Jamie kiss Golodnya on the other side of the door, and imagining them carrying on in the bedroom, had cured me of that. Yes, I wanted to see Jamie in all those positions and contortions, but I wanted that private show. And I would get it soon enough.

In short order, the Jamie photos were off the computer's hard drive. I went into the recycling bin and deleted them again, to make them vanish for everyone except teenage hackers and the FBI. Mission accomplished, I closed the program and took my leave of Nicholas Golodnya's Southampton dream house.

It only occurred to me when I was outside, after making sure that the gate at the foot of the driveway was shut tight, that I was alone and had no idea how I was supposed to get back to Manhattan.

Or if I was supposed to wait for Jamie.

But waiting for Jamie meant . . . what?

So I walked efficiently down the side of the road, back past the hedgerows and the bicyclists and the slow-moving cars, retracing my steps and hoping I'd eventually run into a highway that would take me to a Jitney, and not particularly caring whether or not that walk was going to take me a long, long time.

Brett Revere's Theory of Life, Part Nine:
Treachery and Deception Trump Talent Every Time

I didn't hear from Jamie for a few days after that. Maybe both of us were afraid to talk to one another and confront the details of that afternoon in Southampton. Or maybe only I felt that way, and he merely saw me as a dispensable accessory, no longer of use to him now that the files were deleted.

It had not taken long for me to doubt that our private club—the Trust Fund Boys—was a long-term commitment. Now it seemed that our mutual secret, the fraudulence of our public faces, did not form as close a tie between us as I had hoped. Once again, it was every man for himself, and I felt as if I had been a fool for ever thinking otherwise.

Beyond that, I was starting to face some financial realities, and I didn't like what I saw. The week before, while I was rehabilitating my wardrobe, I had thought ahead and taken a thousand dollar cash advance on the credit card for spending money. But that had been trickling away at an alarming rate, paying for everything from drinks at the Penthouse to the Jitney tickets and cab we used to get to Nicholas Golodnya's Southampton estate.

With only $600 in my pocket, and nothing in my checking account, my ill-gotten cash advance was running thin. And as torn as I was about the morality of using the credit card to temporarily supplement my lifestyle, it, too, was out of my possession. Something was going to have to happen, and it was going to have to happen fast.

And then there was the impending luncheon for Winston Culver-Benchley.

I had conveniently put it out of my mind. Unfortunately, Michael remembered it quite clearly, and reminded me of my social obligation when I saw him at the Penthouse a few evenings after my porn-erasing adventure in the Hamptons.

"Michael," I said, "I really don't know if I can make it."

"You'll make it," he said firmly. "This is a great opportunity to meet some nice, nice ladies."

I surrendered, and resigned myself to another too-dull-to-be-believed afternoon with Winston Culver-Benchley. But I would be making it the last afternoon of its kind. That was for certain.

In any event, it was time to change the subject.

"Have you seen Jamie?" I asked.

"No. He's dropped off the face of the planet again. I heard he's back with Nicholas Golodnya, but I don't know for sure." He must have seen the crestfallen expression on my face, because he followed that up with, "Give him up, Brett. Jamie's a great guy, but you're worth more than that. And you can pursue him forever, but you're never going to get him."

"Maybe not," I said with a sigh.

"It seems to me that you're just too much alike."

"He said the same thing to me."

"Well, see? That's just how it is."

"Of course, we ended up sleeping together after he said that, so I don't know how he really felt about it." I noticed Michael shifting uncomfortably, so I got off that tangent. "Sorry. I'm sharing too much."

"That's okay. Why did he say you were too much alike?"

I shook my head. "Nothing, really. Our backgrounds . . . upbringing . . . that's all." The last thing I was going to do is tell Michael that Jamie Brock was just scraping by, that he wasn't really a golden boy, that he wasn't a trust fund boy. I didn't even want Michael to know that about myself.

Maybe I didn't have to say anything, because Michael just shook his head and quietly said, "My boys."

"Your boys?"

He smiled, but it was hollow. "You and Jamie. I think of you as my boys." He paused, then added, "Now more than ever."

I was going to ask him what he meant by that, but he suddenly grabbed my wrist, asking, "What time is it?" as he turned my watch toward him. "Almost ten. I think I'm out of here in a few minutes."

"I should go, too," I said.

"That's right. I want you to be well rested for Winnie's luncheon."

Ugh.

"And don't give me that face. You'll enjoy yourself." It was a command, not an expectation. I felt his hand on my collar and thought for a moment he was about to drag me off by the scruff of my neck, but he simply said, "Nice shirt."

I had no idea where that was coming from—the shirt was unexceptional, I thought—but still responded by rote. "Thanks."

We stood quietly, nursing our drinks and surveying the crowd, until he finally broke the silence.

"There's this cute, cute couple I want you to meet up in Connecticut next weekend."

I thought about it for maybe three milliseconds. "I don't know, Michael. The last cute couple you wanted me to meet was a pair of shriveled heterosexual alcoholics."

His smile was oily, without the slightest attempt to appear sincere. "I think you should go," he said. "You should meet more people like them."

"I'm sure they're very nice, but those just aren't the sort of people I enjoy spending time with."

His face was now inches from mine, and he took hold of my forearm, pulling me even closer. His voice dropped. "I understand you, Brett, for the same reason I understand Jamie. And that's why I think you should meet these people, and anyone else I *generously* invite you to meet."

I tried to appear amused, to hide my growing fear that somehow he was on to me. "You understand me?"

His hand closed over my watch. "I understand that this is a Seiko." His other hand flipped over the back of my shirt collar ever so slightly, and he added, "And I understand that your shirt is a Van Heusen."

I swallowed. "Your point is . . . ?"

"My point is that you aren't necessarily what you seem, are you?" When I didn't answer, he added, "That's okay, Brett. Most people aren't what they seem." He paused, then added, "But here, they don't flash their Seikos."

I'm sure he had more to say, but my reprieve came in the form of Alan and Ty, who were suddenly next to me.

"Alan, you've met Michael, right?"

"Good to see you again," said Alan, offering his hand to Michael, but withdrawing it when Michael kept his hand at his side. "And this is my friend, Ty."

Michael nodded, but didn't say anything in return. Instead, he turned to address me.

"I'll call you about the luncheon," he said. "I think I still have your phone number."

"Don't use that number. Let me give you a better number to reach me at." As long as my secret was out—the shame of Seiko and Van Heusen—I saw no further reason to pretend to have a 212 area code. Instead, I jotted my 718 number on a piece of paper and handed it to him.

"Seven-one-eight?" He shook his head. "Not the Bronx, I hope."

"Queens," I said quietly.

"Good lord . . ." He pocketed the number and said, "We'll talk about this later."

"Sweet," said Ty, sneering after Michael as he walked away. "What's wrong with the Bronx?"

I shrugged. "Michael is a Manhattan snob. What can I say?"

"And what was that business about not even saying hello to me?"

"I'm sure he didn't mean anything by that," I said, not quite sure why I was defending Michael.

"Easy for you to say. Typical Penthouse material, throwing his rich guy attitude at me." I opened my mouth again to protest, but Ty pointedly said, "Don't say you don't see it unless you're looking at it from my perspective."

"C'mon, guys," said Alan, acting the peacemaker. "Everybody chill." He poked Ty on the shoulder and said, "And anyway, I thought we were here so you could sing."

Ty smiled. "Any requests?"

"Yeah. 'You Made Me Love You.' And you'd better dedicate it to me."

Ty walked to the piano to put his name on the list of would-be singers, and Alan turned to me.

"I hate to say this, but Ty was right," he said. "That Michael *does* have a lousy attitude."

"I know."

"And you hang around with him . . . why?"

"I started hanging out with him because he's very close to Jamie. Now, well . . . Let's just say that Michael is the only one who's introducing me to people." Left unsaid was the fact that I didn't really like the people he was introducing me to.

Alan looked around the bar. "And where *is* your boyfriend Jamie tonight?"

"That, I *don't* know." I paused, then decided that Alan could be trusted with a censored version of the truth. "We actually hooked up the other day, but I don't know if it's going to work out. In fact, I heard that he might be back with his ex."

"Sorry," he said grimly. "That sucks."

"Yeah. It does."

Ty returned and greeted Alan with a kiss. I hoped that Ty hadn't noticed, but *I* noticed a few heads turn at the sight of an interracial couple touching lips.

The three of us exchanged small talk for a while, and then I caught sight of Angel as he zigzagged through the crowd. When he drew close to us, I called out his name. In response, he threw me a short wave, unaccompanied by a smile, and kept going.

"You'd better move quickly with that one," said Alan. "It looks like he's starting to lose interest in you."

"He caught me kissing Jamie the other night," I explained. "And I was sort of an asshole to him. But . . . but it really doesn't matter, because . . ."

Alan completed my thought. "Because he's a waiter."

"Right."

"Shit," said Ty. "You've been hanging around this bar too much. You're turning into one of *them*."

"Here we go again," muttered Alan, with a roll of his eyes.

"A nice guy like that is interested in you, but you won't ask him out because he's a *waiter*? That's fucked up."

"I'm sure he's very nice . . ." I began, but Ty cut me off.

"You won't meet a nicer guy than Angel."

"You know him?"

"Of course I know him. I've been hanging out in this bar for years." He paused, then added a not altogether unfair zinger. "It's only people with the Penthouse attitude that won't bother getting to know the people who serve them their drinks."

"Oh, shit," said Alan, as he put his arm around Ty's waist. "We're going to go. If I hear the 'Penthouse attitude' bit one more time, I'm going to lock the two of you in a closet, where you can bore Brett with that, and Brett can bore you with Operation Hamptons."

"I'm supposed to sing," Ty protested.

"You can sing in my shower later. Let's get out of here."

"Are you going home?" I asked.

"Not yet," said Alan. "Not until someone gets a few cocktails in him and relaxes."

"I'm relaxed," muttered a very unrelaxed Ty.

"I was talking about me."

We ended up at Bar 51, which was a mistake on two levels. First, both Ty and I were in sulky moods, and it was difficult even to discuss our problems, since they were essentially polar opposites. He was upset about the Penthouse attitude, and I was upset that I had more or less adopted that attitude, but it wasn't paying off.

The second reason it was a mistake was because none of us needed another cocktail.

Yet there we were, strung along three bar stools and continuing our night of excess. And, of course, rerunning the same conversation through a seemingly endless loop, because it was far too late for insight and revelation

"You're losing your soul," said Ty, for the umpteenth time.

To which I similarly responded, "No, I'm not. I am *not* turning into one of them. I'm . . . I'm *using* them."

"You don't think using people will cost you your soul?"

I sighed. "It's no different than what you do. Not really. You hate the place, but you go there to sing, because you're hoping one of those guys with the Penthouse attitude will want to hire you. We're engaged in the same pursuit."

"We're nothing alike," he said. "I'm using the place to show off my talent. *Real* talent. *God-given* talent . . ."

"I think you're going a bit far," Alan interjected.

"I didn't ask for your opinion."

"Okay. I'll go back to sleep now, 'cause no one could listen to the two of you and stay awake."

Ty ignored him and returned to me. "I'm using my *talent* to get ahead, but *you* are using treachery and deception."

My temper flashed. "*Treachery* and *deception*?"

He was unapologetic, and his voice rose as he continued hammering on me. "What else would you call it? You're pretending to adopt their mannerisms . . . their lifestyles . . . I mean, you're afraid to be seen *talking* to Angel! You're nothing but a big . . . a big *phony*, trying to bullshit those old white guys into thinking you're just like them. Where's the talent in that?!"

"It's not really like that . . ."

"*Where is the talent?!!*"

"Hey, guys, keep it down," cautioned Bartender Jason from the other side of the bar.

"Sorry." Turning to Ty, I said, "I think you have a totally . . ."

He interrupted. "You're just playing with them, and the scary thing is that you'll probably succeed. It'll cost you your soul, but what the hell do *you* care? White skin, blond hair . . . you'll fit right in. Oh, you'll never talk to Angel—you'll probably forget that you ever knew his name—but what the hell do *you* care?"

I turned away from him, and muttered, "I really don't want to talk about this anymore."

"Good idea," said Alan, with an exasperated sigh. "Why don't you both shut up. Not that anyone asked me, but I think you're *both* right."

"Sure," said Ty. "Take *his* side."

"I just said you were right, Ty. The only thing I agree with Brett on is that I think he has an outside chance to save his soul." He fixed me with a drunken stare and added, "And you'd *better* save your soul."

I didn't respond, except for staring back.

Alan crawled off his barstool and tapped Ty on the shoulder.

"Come on, sweetie. It's time for beddy-bye."

Ty obediently got off his stool, then, his passion apparently spent, offered me his hand.

"Sorry, man," he said. "I get worked up sometimes."

I took his hand in mine. "No problem. And I'll keep what you said in mind."

A few minutes later I was alone at the near-empty bar, drunkenly contemplating Ty's words. Deep down I knew he was wrong, but when I mulled over the shortcuts and compromises, the lies and misrepresentations . . . I was no longer quite so sure of myself.

I had, after all, taken pains to keep Angel at a distance.

Shit. Maybe Ty was right.

I flagged over Bartender Jason and ordered another glass of wine.

"You're sure?"

"One more. I'm not ready to go home yet."

He poured the wine and set it in front of me, and it took me all of three seconds to knock the glass over. It shattered against the bar surface and shards fell to the other side of the bar.

"Great," said Jason, looking down. "You got glass in the ice."

"Sorry," I said. "Maybe I should have my nightcap in a plastic cup."

He shook his head. "That's it for tonight, Brett. You've been getting loud and sloppy, and now . . ." He looked down at the ice again and crossed his arms in front of him. "I really don't need all this extra work at the end of my shift."

"So I'm cut off?"

"You're cut off." After another glance at the ice, he added, "In fact, I think it would be a good idea if you left the bar."

I stood in the darkness outside Bar 51 and reflected on the indignity of it all. Being asked to leave Bar 51 before closing was like being asked to leave a dive bar before all your teeth have fallen out.

Since the night was cool, and I wasn't ready to go home, I decided to take a walk through midtown to the east side, where I could catch a train back to Astoria. I needed to calm down, and I thought the walk might burn off some of the alcohol that had ceased doing me any favors.

I walked up Ninth Avenue, then turned east on Fifty-seventh Street, along surprisingly empty sidewalks. As I crossed Fifth Avenue, thereby officially entering the east side, a group of equally drunken girls shouted catcalls at me, which at least put a smile back on my face.

It had not been my intention to return to the Penthouse, but, as I walked, I realized that was exactly what I was going to do. I was going to find Jamie, and take him in my arms and promise to protect him . . . to never let him go . . . to . . .

The blare of a taxi horn stopped me seconds before I would have been run down, and I leapt back to the sidewalk. Besides saving my life, though, the shock of the horn had the benefit of clearing my head. I wanted Jamie to be part of my life, yes . . . but I also had something to clear up with Angel. I had to talk to him, and call him by name, and prove that I wasn't just another asshole at the Penthouse with a lot of money and no use for anyone not of his social status.

I needed to make sure I saved my soul.

I glanced at my watch—the Seiko—and realized that the 4:00 A.M. closing time was drawing near. I quickened my pace through the quiet streets, reaching the Penthouse just minutes before four.

Inside, the lights burned brightly. I was used to the soft, low lighting of normal business hours and felt disoriented seeing the bar illuminated. A handful of patrons were finishing their cocktails, their conversation drowned out by the sound of rushing water as the staff hurried to clean up and get home.

I spotted Jeffrey Ryan, quite drunk, weaving his way down the staircase from the piano bar. When he neared me, he registered a flicker of recognition.

"Jeffrey," I said. "Did you see Jamie here tonight?"

"Jamie who?" Yes, quite drunk.

"Jamie Brock." Jeffrey's eyes were glassy. "You know . . . younger . . . dark hair, blue eyes . . . medium height . . ."

"Oh," sniffed Jeffrey. "*Him.*"

Much as I wondered what the "him" was all about, I wondered more if Jamie had been at the Penthouse. "Yeah, that's the one."

"Haven't seen him all night. I think he's out in the Hamptons with Nico Golodnya. Where *I* should be . . . well, not with Nico, but . . ."

I sighed. "I had heard he might . . ."

He held a hand up to stop me. "I have to be sober enough to fly a Cessna to the Hamptons in the morning, so I hope you'll excuse me." With that, Jeffrey Ryan toddled out the front door.

I watched after him—and hoped the flight wasn't leaving too early—until the bouncer caught my eye.

"You've got to go, pal," he said, taking a confident step toward me.

"Yeah."

I turned to make one last scan of the bar's final dozen patrons, all slowly, reluctantly, shuffling toward the front door. Off to one side, I saw Angel picking up empty glasses from an end table. He looked up and our eyes met.

Twenty minutes later, I watched from the stoop of a brownstone across the street as the lights inside the Penthouse went out one by one. A few members of the bar staff left a few minutes later in a group; fortunately, when Angel left shortly after them, he was with only one other person. I stood when I saw him descend the stairs, and he saw me in the shadows.

"*Hola*," he said softly, crossing the street toward me, as I descended to the sidewalk. "I thought you might be here."

"Then you're a lot more confident than I was."

"This is Paolo," he said, indicating the other man. When I didn't react, he added, "The upstairs bartender. The Brazilian? We've discussed him. He's served you."

"Oh, right," I said. To Paolo, I said, "You'll have to excuse me, but when I'm in the bar, I only have eyes for Angel."

"Nice comeback," said Paolo, smiling. "Very nice." He turned to Angel and, giving him a quick kiss on the cheek, said, "Okay, I'm going home. Be careful, honey."

"Always," said Angel.

"Nice meeting you," Paolo said to me and, with that, he began walking into the shadows of the tree-lined side street, bound for First Avenue.

When Paolo was gone, I turned to Angel and asked, "Can I buy you a cup of coffee?"

He lit a cigarette before answering. "Sorry, I can't. I'm exhausted from working all night, and I have an early class tomorrow. But . . ." He patted his pants pockets. "I forgot my pen inside. Do you have one?"

I handed him my pen, and he scribbled something on the inside of a Penthouse matchbook before handing it to me. "My phone number. I was going to give it to you earlier, but . . . I wasn't sure you wanted it."

"*Of course* I want it, Angel."

"And I didn't know if that guy you were kissing the other day was your boyfriend." Ah . . . so *there* it was.

"No," I said. "We dated, but . . . he's not my boyfriend." *Damn*, those words were hard to say, despite being the truth. "He's just . . . part of the group I hang out with."

He nodded. "You always seem to be surrounded by a lot of people."

"That's me. I'm a popular guy."

"Well . . . I'm not exactly sure why you want to be popular with *those* people, but I guess that's your call."

"You don't like my friends?"

"I like the bald guy, and his boyfriend. The black guy who sings."

"Alan and Ty? Yeah, they're good people."

"And those guys Rick and Bill. They're nice. As for the rest . . ." He shrugged. "Maybe I'm just jaded because whenever I see them, I'm working."

"Could be."

"Or maybe they really *are* assholes."

I laughed. "That could be, too."

There was a pause in the conversation, which he filled with, "I'd better get home."

"Mind if I walk with you a bit?"

He pointed west. "Not at all. This way."

We began walking toward Third Avenue.

"So," he said. "Now that you've got my phone number, are you gonna call?"

He must have sensed my reticence. When he had given me the number, I wasn't quite sure *what* I was going to do with it. In my drunken state, I was anxious to prove to myself that I wasn't becoming the embodiment of the Penthouse attitude . . . but Jamie Brock was still the man I really wanted to call.

But I didn't say that, of course. Instead, I took the path of least resistance and, nodding my head, said, "Of course."

He gave me a wary once-over. "We'll see . . ."

When we reached the corner, he stopped. "There's my bus. So I'll be hearing from you, right?"

"I told you . . ."

"Just checking." He tossed me another smile and set off for his bus, leaving me on the corner, holding onto his phone number for dear life.

. . . and he smiled.

Brett Revere's Theory of Life, Part Ten: Everyone Should Collect Things for a Hobby

I didn't call Angel over the next few days, and I didn't call Jamie, either. I had other things on my mind.

As Michael reminded me when he lowered himself to calling me at my 718 telephone number, I had a luncheon to attend in honor of Winston Culver-Benchley.

Late Thursday morning, on the day of the luncheon, as I sat on my couch in sweltering weather, wearing nothing but a pair of boxer shorts, I seriously considered skipping it.

The weather had been oppressive for days, and I was getting very worried about my finances. More important, Jamie's MIA status for almost a week had left me in a deep funk. And beyond those mood-dampening factors was the simple fact that I did not want to spend time with Winston Culver-Benchley and whichever other "cute ladies" Michael had gathered for the afternoon.

I still had the $600—minus a few stray dollars for drinks at the Penthouse and takeout Chinese—but that was it. Unless a job miraculously fell into my lap, or Jamie returned the credit card, that was all the money I had. And July's rent was due.

Ironically, it was my dwindling financial situation that inspired me to get dressed and go to the luncheon. Skipping it would have led to a much more enjoyable afternoon, but it would have eliminated one more possibility for the success of Operation Hamptons. And *that* was what it was all about, after all.

So I dressed and caught the subway, and arrived at Swifty's shortly after one o'clock to find Michael and his ladies already seated.

"Sorry I'm late," I said, taking a seat between two elderly dowagers. "Traffic."

"Brett, dear," said Winston, attempting to force her facelift into a smile. "I'm delighted you could join us." She then introduced the other four women, none of them younger than seventy and none of whose names I remembered after the initial introduction.

The afternoon passed at a tedious pace, made only slightly more bearable by a few carefully paced glasses of champagne Michael ordered for the table. If I were interested in the gossip of the moneyed senior citizens of Palm Beach, Greenwich, Newport, and the Hamptons, I probably would have found the luncheon merely boring. But I wasn't, and there was nothing here for me but endless recitations of names I had never heard and places I had never been. Instead, my high point came every half-hour, when I let Winston pass so she could go to the sidewalk for a cigarette.

But I didn't yawn, and that was somewhat of an accomplishment. I was, as Michael had predicted, a perfect—if largely silent—luncheon companion.

It was almost three-thirty before the conversation began to wane, and Michael signaled to the waiter for our check.

"I hope you all had a nice afternoon," he said, smooth and polished—or was that *oiled*?—as he looked over the tab.

"I had a wonderful time," gushed Winston, and the other women clucked their concurrence.

"Why don't you let Brett and I pay for the meal," he said, and I heard myself audibly gasping. I faked a cough to cover the gaffe.

"Are you sure?" asked one of the women, the one whose husband had apparently died the year before, leaving her more money than I could expect to make in ten lifetimes.

"That's very generous," said another, who was married into deposed European royalty, which had nevertheless managed to smuggle a fortune in art out of their home country.

"Oh, Michael, don't be silly . . ." said Winston, feebly reaching to take the check from his hands.

"We insist," said Michael, shooing her away, and I suddenly realized that this was all an act. *Of course* they expected us to pay . . . because we were the *men*! Sure, they had more money than God, and therefore knew that they had to go through the motions, but they never had any intention of paying their share for lunch.

Michael knew that, too.

Apparently, only Brett Revere—unemployed actor-slash-temp—was not clued in to the way this world worked.

"Brett and I will split this fifty-fifty," Michael said.

Shit.

"Okay." I swallowed hard. "How much?"

"With tip . . . three should do it."

Three *hundred* dollars?

But of course all I really said was, "Oh . . . sure." And then I painfully peeled $300 from the bills in my pocket.

We walked the cute ladies outside. Blake Culver-Benchley's car was idling at the curb, and he waved to us as we emerged from the restaurant. Michael escorted Winston to the passenger side door, spoke briefly to her husband, and then returned to the curb, where we hailed cabs, one by one, for the rest of the luncheon party. When the last of the taxis pulled away from the curb I spun around and confronted Michael.

"What was that all about?" I asked. "That was a $300 lunch that I can't afford."

"I know you can't, Brett. I could tell by your watch."

I shook my head. "The point is to be able to tell time."

"No," he said. "The point is to be able to show off while you tell time. And when I took a look at your shirt label . . . Van Heusen? Now, Brett . . ."

I shrugged. "Whatever. That lunch cost a lot of money I don't have. That's the point here."

"These are the sorts of women it's in your best interests to woo."

I shook my head. "If you have to have another man at the table, why me? Why not Jamie?"

Michael placed a hand paternally on my shoulder. "We've discussed this, haven't we? I've taken Jamie to these luncheons before. He performed . . . all right. But his social graces are nothing like yours. I don't know if you come by them naturally or you were raised right, but you do a much smoother job interacting at this level of society. You were magnificent up in Scarsdale with Blake and Winston, and you were delightful again this afternoon."

"And Jamie isn't?"

"Jamie knows what to do. He was raised to be a proper little gentleman. But he's lazy, Brett. You're not." He paused for a moment. "By the way, I heard about your little adventure at Nico Golodnya's place."

"You did?"

"Uh-huh. Jamie filled me in. That was a stupid thing he did, but you were a good friend to help get him out of it."

"Well . . . I like Jamie. A lot."

"You'll get past that," he said. "The important thing is that you showed yourself to be a good and loyal friend, and we all need a few of those."

"Getting back to the central point," I said, "there's this whole thing with money. We spent, like, $100 per person for lunch."

"The champagne was expensive," he said, which was the closest he came to offering an explanation. "But these ladies have expectations."

"Let me make myself more clear, Michael. I cannot afford to take rich old women to expensive lunches. Ever again."

He shook his head, and let out a sigh heavy with disappointment. "I can't force you, Brett. But if you want to get ahead in this world . . ." He stopped and stared at something over my shoulder, then said, "What the hell . . . ?"

I turned, and saw the reason why Michael was shocked. It shocked me, too, and it was precisely the sort of thing that would *not* get me ahead in this world.

It was Joey Takashimi, two black bags from Barneys clutched in his hands, dressed in ripped jeans and a flowing lavender robe, and walking directly toward me. And to make matters worse, at his side—in full drag—was another *Andy* cast member: Miss Iris Whiskey.

"Brent!" he shouted from half a block away. "I *thought* that was you!"

"Who the hell are they?" sputtered Michael.

"They," I said, "are the Ghosts of Career Past."

"You know them?"

I nodded. "We were vaguely acquainted in another life."

"Don't let anyone ever know that," said Michael, seconds before Joey and Miss Iris were upon us.

"Brent, darling," said Joey, air-kissing in my general direction as Miss Iris waved a greeting. "How *are* you?"

"It's *Brett*," I said. "And I'm fine. How's the show?"

"Opening next week, thank God. I can't wait. Have you ordered your tickets yet?"

"Uh . . . no." I stole a glance at Michael, who was staring at the newcomers as if he had encountered some exotic and not particularly attractive species of insect. "Michael DeVries, Joey Takashimi and . . . Iris. Joey, Iris . . . Michael."

"That's *Miss* Iris," she said, taking Michael's hand. I could tell it took all Michael's will not to recoil.

"A pleasure," muttered Michael, clearly not meaning it.

"*Love* your ascot," said Joey, clearly being a bitch. He turned back to me and continued. "Anyway, based on advance sales, we're going to be packing the room every night through Labor Day. *Packing it!* There are hardly any tickets left. I expected to maybe make $50 a week off of *Andy*, and last weekend Walter handed me three bills."

"Three hundred dollars?" The amount struck a familiar and unpleasant chord.

"Well, remember: I'm the star. I don't know what he was handing the random orphan, but I'd guess it was a hundred or so. Not bad, considering we haven't even opened yet. But Walter believes in keeping the cast happy."

"I feel snubbed," said Miss Iris dramatically. "He only gave me two hundred, the cheap bastard."

"Walter's quite a guy," I said. In my head, I calculated what even an additional one hundred dollars a week would do for my standard of living. It wouldn't be enough to change my life, of course, but it would have been more than I'd earned through acting in several years. And unlike the cash advances from the credit card, it would have been earned honestly.

"You should talk to Walter," Joey added. "Maybe he'd take you back. There's always room for another orphan."

I shook my head. "I don't think so. My life as an orphan lasted less than one rehearsal, and I'm happy leaving it in the past."

Joey shrugged. "Whatever, dude. At least come to see the show, though. Catch it in the first weeks. *If* you can get tickets. Before the tourists find out about it." He turned to Michael. "You, too."

The face Michael made was . . . almost indescribable. Something between biting down on a lemon and biting down on one's tongue.

"Yes, well, I'll think about it."

"And when you're watching it," Joey continued, oblivious to Michael's antipathy, "just keep thinking about how much more interesting it would be if Brent . . ."

"*Brett.*"

". . . was the orphan who gets humped by Sandy!" He and Miss Iris burst into laughter.

"Thanks, Joey," I said. "That'll be all."

Joey glanced at his watch and announced, "We've got to go. We're meeting people at Serafina. Kiss kiss."

"Kiss kiss," echoed Miss Iris.

"Good seeing you," I replied, and Michael merely moved his lips, inaudibly wishing them goodbye. Probably death, too. With a flourish of the lavender robe and no further words, Joey spun around and dashed away, his Barneys bags swinging beside him. The oversized drag queen winked lewdly and threw us an air kiss before quickly following him.

Michael waited half a beat until they were barely out of earshot before he exclaimed, "Unbelievable!"

"That would be Joey and Miss Iris Whiskey."

"You know what I mean."

I felt I had to explain. "About the time I met you, I had just quit this show downtown. Joey was . . . *is* . . . the star, and Miss Iris is also in the cast. It's an all-gay send-up of *Annie*, called *Andy.*"

"It sounds dreadful."

"It *is* dreadful. And when you add Joey into the mix, it's . . . what's beyond dreadful?"

"Ghastly?"

"That's the word. Ghastly. Anyway, walking out of that rehearsal was the smartest thing I've ever done." As I said that, I thought about how nice it would be to have an extra hundred dollars in my pocket at that moment for nothing more than standing anonymously in the chorus. Just as quickly, I suppressed that thought. That was no longer who I was.

"I agree," said Michael crisply. "People like that"—his nose wrinkled—"are precisely the kind of people you should *not* be associated with. Just be glad it was me you were with when that purple fruitcake and that plus-sized drag queen popped up, and not someone else from our crowd. I can't even begin to tell you how quickly you'd be ostracized."

"Yeah, I'm lucky," I said. "I wouldn't have thought that I'd run into them uptown. They're so . . . *downtown.*"

"They're not even downtown," sniped Michael. "But just keep in mind that people can move around the city and appear where you least expect them. That's why it's important to always keep the right company."

"Got it."

He sighed, and stared at the corner where Joey and Miss Iris had disappeared. "That's it, Brett," he said. "Keep the right company. If you learn one thing from me, that's it."

The ringing telephone woke me up the next morning. It was Jamie.

"I'm out, Brett," he said. "I'm out."

"Out of what?"

"Out of Southampton, and, well . . . I'm out of Benjamin's, too. It's my own Independence Day! Yesterday I told Nico that it was over between us, packed my things, and got the hell out of his house. Of course, by the time I got back to Manhattan, Nico had called Benjamin and, well . . . let's just say that after I clear out my things I'm not welcome *here* anymore, either. But I'm a free man again. I don't know what I'm going to do, and I don't know where I'm going to live, but I'm free."

"And you're okay?"

"Never better." He paused, and somehow I just knew what he was about to say. "Can you do me a favor, though?"

"Ummm . . ."

"Two favors, actually. I need some help getting my clothes out of Ben's. Do you think you can help me out?"

"I guess. What's the second favor?"

"Can I crash at your place for a few days? Just until I find my own place? I have a few leads, but it may take me a few days to secure something."

Jamie Brock was going to be staying with me? Yes yes yes yes yes!

"Sure," I said calmly. "You can stay here until you find an apartment."

I agreed to meet him at Benjamin Grover's apartment in an hour. Not surprisingly, when I arrived it was apparent that he hadn't even started to *think* about packing, so I helped him cram whatever we could into his assorted luggage and load it on a cart, which had been courteously provided by the doorman with the pregnant wife. With most of Jamie's possessions ready to roll, we took the service elevator to the lobby, and minutes later we were in a cab en route to Astoria.

"You will never know how much I appreciate this," he said, as our taxi rolled over the Queensboro Bridge.

"No problem. Are you going to be able to find another place to live?"

"I'm not worried about that."

"Because you can stay with me as long as you'd like."

"I don't want to be an imposition," he said, placing his hand on my leg. "I mean, you're already doing so much for me."

I put *my* hand on *his* leg, mirroring him, and smiled. "It's not an imposition, Jamie. Not at all."

When we arrived in Astoria, I paid the driver while Jamie began unloading the trunk, and then we began the torturous process of dragging his bags up to the fourth floor. It took us each several trips, but it was finally over, and I reasoned that it counted as my week's exercise.

He started emptying the luggage, and soon the living room floor was covered with his clothing, an array not dissimilar to the way they were scattered all over his room on the Upper East Side. I was beginning to wonder if the Scattering of the Clothes was some sort of rite he practiced.

"Never again," said Jamie, taking a break and lounging on my sofa. "I am never letting myself get into a situation like that again."

I slid onto the sofa next to him, maybe a bit too close, and patted his thigh. "The important thing is you got out all right, and there was no permanent damage."

"Thanks to you," he said, smiling. "You've saved my ass so many times that I don't think I can ever repay you. I mean, you rescued me today, you've lent me money, you deleted those pictures from Nico's computer. . . . You're an amazing friend!"

"Hey, I'm sure you'd do the same thing for me."

"Not really. I'm a selfish bastard." He laughed, then added, "Of course I'd help you out. In fact, I've got this big decorating job coming up in Southampton . . . David Carlyle. Ever hear of him?"

"I don't think so."

"He's in publishing. Good person to know. Anyway, he's paying me a lot to redecorate his Hamptons house. I have no idea what he wants out there, though. He's also got this great place here in Manhattan, up on Fifth Avenue, and every year he has it completely redone in a new color scheme."

"Every year? It must be nice to have money."

"He's got it. *Believe me*, he's got it. This year the color is yellow, if you can believe it. Somehow, he carried it off, but, for his sake, I really hope he picks gray next year." He paused, lost briefly in thought. "Anyway, he's paying me a ton of money. When I get his check, I'll pay you back for everything."

"Don't worry about it. No rush."

Jamie fished around the clothes strewn on the floor until he came up with his wallet. "Which reminds me . . ." He pulled the credit card out of his wallet and set it on the end table.

"Thanks, I guess."

"And don't worry," he said. "I barely touched it." He looked around the room. "Where's your phone?"

I pointed to the end table. "Feel free."

"Thanks. I just want to call a few friends, to see if anyone knows of an available apartment."

"Well, like I said, you should feel free to stay as long as you want."

"And I appreciate that. You're the best." He picked up the phone and began dialing. "But this really shouldn't take me more than a few days." His attention was suddenly directed to the phone. "Jenny? Hi, it's Jamie Brock . . ."

He spent most of the rest of the afternoon on the phone, devoting more time to gossiping than apartment-hunting. But I was fine with that. I had meant what I said: Jamie could stay at my apartment as long as he wanted.

Early in the evening, I went to the liquor store a few blocks away and bought some provisions. When I returned to the apartment he was fresh from the shower, wearing nothing but a towel wrapped around his waist. And I felt a stirring that had nothing to do with mixed drinks.

"Vino?" I asked.

"Please."

I stowed the bottles in the kitchen, then uncorked a bottle of chardonnay, poured two glasses, and returned to the living room. He was back on the phone, sprawled on the couch and still wearing only the towel. I handed him his glass of wine then sat in a chair across from him, before realizing that, from that vantage point, I could see . . . everything the towel was supposed to cover.

So I crossed my legs and sipped my wine.

"Comfortable?" I asked, when he finally disconnected.

"Very. Thanks. And thanks for the wine. It's been a long week for me, and I need it."

He shifted, and I lost my view.

"So things were bad with Golodnya?" I asked.

"The worst. I was honestly afraid he was going to get physically abusive, Brett. And he was treating me like a houseboy."

"And, uh, the pictures. He doesn't know they've been deleted yet, does he?"

He shook his head. "I'm sure I would have heard about it if he had." He laughed and added, "That was quite an operation."

"I know. I can't believe he almost caught us."

"The important thing," he said, "is that he *didn't*."

Jamie set his glass on the coffee table and patted the couch next to him.

"Come here," he said.

He didn't have to say it twice. I crossed the room and sat on the couch.

"I want to tell you again how much you mean to me. The things you've done have been . . . well, let's just say that no one else would have done them for me."

"You're worth it," I said, placing a hand on his knee. "And, hey, we're the Trust Fund Boys, right? We have to watch each other's backs."

I closed my eyes and leaned in to kiss him . . . and he wasn't there.

"I'd better get dressed," he said, and I realized that he was now standing. "Things to do, people to see . . ."

I swallowed my disappointment.

"Are you going into Manhattan?" I asked.

"I want to look at an apartment," he said.

"Oh." So much for a quiet, romantic, passionate night at home. "Uh . . . are you going out later?"

"I might have dinner with the girl who has the apartment."

"I see."

Later in the evening, after a bottle of wine, which, in truly antisocial fashion, I drank alone, I managed to develop an edgy "I'll show you" attitude toward the absent Jamie.

I'm not good enough for you? My apartment's not good enough for you? My company's not good enough for you?

I'll show you, Jamie Brock. Yes, I'll show you.

And that's how I came to finally dial Angel's phone number. When the answering machine picked up, I said:

"Angel, hi, it's Brett Revere. Sorry it took me a few days to call, but I've . . . been busy. Anyway, I was wondering if you might want to have dinner or something next week. Or just get together for coffee . . . or . . . something. So call me when you get a chance." I recited my phone number and hung up.

And immediately regretted placing the call.

My relationship with Jamie wasn't a *normal* relationship, but there was still something there. And beyond that, even if it wasn't the sort of relationship I wanted, well . . . he was still *Jamie*. And Angel was . . .

Shit. Angel was a waiter.

That was it. Ty was right.

My soul was lost.

Jamie had this Independence Day weekend to celebrate his independence from Nicholas Golodnya, and I could celebrate my independence from my soul.

And at that point, all the fireworks in the world weren't going to brighten my spirits.

Jamie never did return home that evening, and—after keeping vigil until 2:00 A.M.—I finally surrendered to sleep. That's why I missed the calls placed by Michael DeVries at 7:30 and 8:15 before picking up the ringing telephone at 8:45.

"Did I wake you?" he asked.

"Hmmph."

"My apologies, then. But it's a beautiful day and I thought you might like to join me on a trip to Saddle Ridge."

"What's in Saddle Ridge?"

"The *cutest* couple you'd ever want to meet." I groaned, and he said, "That's not a very helpful attitude, Brett."

"I just don't think I'm up to visiting people today, Michael."

He took a long pause, then said, "You know, maybe I'll put off that visit. Instead, I think it might be a good idea for you and I to have a little talk."

And that's why I found myself at Michael's nineteenth-floor Upper East Side apartment a few hours later

On the surface he seemed friendly as could be as he ushered me into his apartment. But I could sense something a bit darker on a deeper level.

Michael got right down to business.

"You boys both have to rethink the way you're doing things," he said. "Especially you, Brett. You have a lot more promise than Jamie."

"What do you mean?" I asked.

"You're not making the connections you need to make if you're going to get out of Seiko and Van Heusen."

"But Jamie landed a job in the Hamptons," I protested. "And I . . . *might* have some leads."

Michael scoffed. "We'll see about your leads when they transpire. I just hope it's nothing that will ruin your manicure. As for Jamie, well . . . I heard about that, actually, and it's nice to land a job for David Carlyle, if you're the average worker, like a decorator or landscaper or something. But what is David Carlyle doing to get *his* hands dirty?"

I didn't get it. "Doesn't he work? I thought Jamie told me he's in publishing."

"That's not what I meant. David Carlyle is *rich*. Being rich is what he does for a living. And he goes down to his granddaddy's publishing house every now and then to be seen, but that's not work. Nobody is hiring David Carlyle to, oh . . . rip out linoleum or edge their lawn. Understand? It's the same thing with Nicholas Golodnya, and it would be the same with those lottery hogs, too, if they had an office to go to. Maybe they stop by their old still every now and then to see how the moonshine is selling."

"You're sort of obsessed with them, aren't you?"

"I'm contemptuous of them, if that's what you mean. They're trash. But at least they get it. They get that the way to be part of this scene is by staying above labor."

"Isn't taking old ladies to lunch labor?"

"I enjoy my girls," he said dryly. "And they remember me. But let's talk about you for a second. You don't even have an income. What are you going to do when you max out that credit card?"

My eyes fell to the floor and I silently cursed Jamie. "You know about that?"

"I do."

"I don't know what I'll do. Hopefully, it won't come to that."

"You don't know what you'll do. But every time I offer to introduce you to some nice people who might be able to help you out, who might enjoy your companionship, you call them dinosaurs."

"They *are* dinosaurs."

"You think I don't know that? They may be dinosaurs, but they're the dinosaurs who are in *Haute Manhattan*, *Avenue*, *Quest*, and *Town and Country* every month. They're the dinosaurs who are on the boards of the Met, MoMA, the Frick, and the Whitney. They're the dinosaurs who eat at Swifty's, Cipriani, and La Goulue." He paused and waved one hand around his apartment. "See this apartment? It's not huge, but it's all mine, and it has great views. And," he added pointedly, "the views may be of Queens, but the zip code isn't. Where do you think it came from?"

"I give."

"Mina Pfeffer gave it to me after her husband died. He used to use it to house out-of-town guests, although truth be told I'd bet he put up his mistresses here. Whatever. To her, it was surplus, and she gave it to me." He took me by the arm and gave me a gentle tug. "Come with me for a quick tour."

And so we toured Michael's apartment. Ordinarily, you wouldn't expect a tour of a one-bedroom apartment to last as long as this one, but, ordinarily, not every item of value is traced to its source.

Mina Pfeffer was not only the donor of the apartment, but also the couch, the diamond cufflinks, a leather overcoat, and an expensive camera, which she purchased for him when he escorted her on a trip to Greece and Italy. Needless to say, she also paid for the trip.

The Cartier watch was a gift from Helena Bourke. The Bulgari watch was a gift from Mariana Vanderbilt. The David Yurman watch was a gift from Betty Sorenson, who also provided the Steuben crystal, the Versace suit, and the cruise to Alaska.

Three pairs of John Lobb shoes were purchased by Lulu Benedict Rothenberg. Belinda Sweeney chipped in a Montblanc pen set. Rena Santiago thought the Paul & Shark yachting ensemble was "just perfect" for Michael . . .

. . . and on and on and on, to the point where my mind was growing numb from the catalog of names matched to expensive gifts.

"You see?" he said finally. "My girls take care of me."

"So you're a gigolo?"

Michael smiled, and I wondered which lady had paid for the teeth.

"I'm too old to be a gigolo. I've *always* been too old to be a gigolo. And I've always been too young to be a walker. I'm merely a companion, a luncheon date, a dependable ear . . . a reliable friend."

"But your girls," I said. "Aren't they . . . um . . . put off by your background? By the fact you don't have the same social standing as they do?"

"Who says I don't? One thing these women understand is how a well-bred son of the South can end up on the short end of the family fortune. I can't remember ever discussing my sexual orientation, but I suspect most of them know. And they put two and two together, figure out I was not bred for work, and therefore shouldn't be put to work, and they end up buying me nice things."

"I think I'm starting to understand."

"Do you? I've told you who I've befriended. Some of them, at least. And although Jamie's been dropping the ball a lot lately, he's managed to make some connections. Sleeping with Nicholas Golodnya wasn't smart, and I don't like it that he's actually performing physical labor for David Carlyle, but it's a solid start. But, Brett . . . what have you done to advance yourself? A few people like Jeffrey Ryan sort of know who you are, but mostly you're just 'that guy mooning over Jamie' to them."

"I'm that obvious?"

"And more. Both of you are just ridiculous, but at least Jamie has the good sense to avoid getting tangled up with you and focus on meeting people who can help him some day."

"You think Jamie likes me?"

"Oh, for Pete's sake. The last thing the two of you need to do is run off together. You'd end up as one of those disgusting couples cramped up in a studio apartment in the Bronx, living on Ripple and ramen noodles."

"Actually," I said, "we're rooming together now."

A look of concern crossed his face. "Rooming together?" Clearly, Jamie had shared a lot with Michael, but he hadn't shared *that* news.

"Don't worry. I'm just putting Jamie up until he finds an apartment. Benjamin asked him to leave after he broke things off with Golodnya."

"Well, now, that's . . . that's . . . that's good. I guess. It seems like the sort of thing he should have told me, but . . . that's good."

"It was sort of a snap decision," I said. "Jamie didn't have a lot of advance warning."

"I see." He scratched his chin thoughtfully. "Well . . . now, at least, you'll have a chance to experience how hopeless the two of you would be as a couple. Like I said, Ripple and ramen noodles. You'll be like . . . like . . . your bald friend and his black boyfriend are going to end up."

"What? That's not very . . ."

He waved me away. "Don't bother saying anything, because I'm not politically correct and never will be. I just call things as I see them from my perspective. But really, Brett, what's that all about? Look at the people you're associated with. You've got that interracial couple, that Japanese queen we ran into on the street, the one all in purple, and that big, fat drag queen . . . oh yeah, and that little Puerto Rican waiter you keep flirting with at the Penthouse. All of these people are either useless or count against you."

I was unsure how far I wanted to go to defend Joey Takashimi and Miss Iris Whiskey, but still. . . . "Well, that's *your* perspective."

"That," he said, "is the Penthouse perspective. Which is the only perspective that matters here. I know what you're trying to do, Brett, and I fully approve. The only way to get ahead in this world is to meet the right people. But you've got to make a commitment to the lifestyle and follow its code of conduct."

Michael left me alone to ponder his advice for a few minutes while he went to retrieve something from his bedroom. When he returned, he was carrying a small box.

"What's this?" I asked, when he handed it to me.

"This," he said, "is a gift from me."

I opened the box.

"A watch?"

"A *Cartier* watch. And I never want to see that damn Seiko again. Do you understand?"

I understood.

It was on the N train back to Astoria, as I discreetly studied the Cartier watch, that it occurred to me clearly for the first time that Michael and Jamie were more alike than I had initially thought. They were collectors.

They were collectors of people and shiny trinkets alike. Michael had his little old ladies, and Jamie had both his younger network of Hamptonites and older patrons like Benjamin Grover and Nicholas Golodnya, but they were still engaged in the same pastime. For them, it was all about accrual. More names with which to network . . . more presents from admirers . . . more people doing more things and bearing more gifts for them. It was all about getting more of everything.

And I was becoming one of them. I now had a Cartier watch, courtesy of Michael and, most certainly, originally courtesy of some random old woman who enjoyed his company.

I was on my way to becoming a collector.

I pocketed the watch and tried not to think about it.

Twenty minutes later, I was walking the streets of Astoria, en route to the apartment I had come to loathe. That loathing, though, was now tempered by the presence of Jamie . . . when he was there, that is.

My "I'll show you" attitude had vanished with my blood alcohol content, and I no longer felt taken advantage of. I didn't know how long I would have Jamie there, but I was trying to value every second.

He still wasn't home when I walked through the door. I called for him a few times, but when there was no answer, I sank onto the couch and, remote control in hand, clicked on the new television. I slowly scrolled through the channels . . . sports, bad made-for-TV movies, *Welcome Back, Kotter* reruns, more sports, scrambled premium channels, more sports . . . I finally found a documentary on the history of civil war in Somalia and, reconciled that that was as good as it was going to get, settled in.

I saw that there was a message on the answering machine and tapped the play button.

"It's Angel, returning your call. I was at work last night, but I'm home most of the day today if you want to call . . ."

There was no one else to blame. I had trapped myself into playing at least one more round of phone tag with Angel. Michael's advice would have to be deferred, but— in recognition of his efforts at guidance—I ceremonially slipped on the Cartier watch. I had to admit that it looked good on my wrist.

Jamie returned to the apartment within a half-hour, laden with two Prada bags.

"I needed shoes," he said, by way of greeting, as he walked through the door. "But while I was at Prada, I found the coolest outfit."

"Feeling rich?" I asked. "I can never bring myself to buy anything on Madison Avenue. It makes me too nervous."

"You've got to let go," he said, setting the bags down on the floor. "If you want to play the part, you've got to *feel* the part."

"Playing the part and feeling the part require a lot of cash," I said. "And my lack of cash is the part that makes me nervous." I looked again at the bags, then added, "Speaking of which, where did you get the money for a new outfit at Prada?"

He smiled. "I have my ways."

"No, seriously."

His smile flittered away. "Don't worry about it, Brett. I had a little money, and this is how I chose to spend it." My sober expression seemed to rattle him, and his façade cracked just a bit. "And . . . well, okay, I also ran into this guy I used to know."

"Not Golodnya."

"No. Another guy. Don't worry about it. Anyway, I had some

cash, and he had some cash, and . . . my cash plus his cash equaled just enough for a sharp new outfit from Prada. End of story."

I nodded. "I guess. So how are you going to pay him back?"

"I'll find a way. There's no rush."

"Uh-huh." Whatever the back story was, he wasn't going to share it. So I changed topics. "How was the apartment?"

"What apartment?"

"The apartment you went to look at last night?" He looked at me blankly. "You were meeting some girl . . . ?"

"Oh . . . yeah," he said haltingly. "It was . . . too small. So I passed on it."

"Where did you sleep last night?"

"At . . . the girl's apartment."

"At the *small* apartment?"

"Right."

There was something wrong with his story, as if he hadn't thought it out or was hiding details for some reason.

Sensing that he had somehow offended me, Jamie shifted gears and asked, "So what have you been up to today?"

"I was summoned to Michael's apartment for a heart-to-heart talk."

"Uh-oh. I don't like the sound of that. Was he giving you pointers?"

I shook my head. "Don't get me wrong, Jamie, but Michael makes me uncomfortable. There's something about the way he talks to me that sets me on edge."

"I think I know what you mean," he said. "He's a bit of a snob."

" 'Snob' doesn't begin to describe him. It's like . . . it's like he thinks he's my tutor in all things upper class."

Jamie laughed. "Oh, so you're getting the entire Michael DeVries seminar, are you? I know what you mean. Michael started in on me the minute my plane touched down at JFK. I know he can be a bit of a pain in the ass, but you should listen to him. He's like a lot of teachers: you can forget most of the specifics, but if you pay attention you can still get one hell of an education in life."

"In *his* life, maybe."

Jamie had started to rifle through his Prada bags, but when I said that, he looked up at me with surprise.

"Well, yes, in *his* life. But isn't *his* life what you're looking for?"

"No," I said, shaking my head. "No, it isn't."

"I'm confused," he said. "What *are* you looking for? Why have you been adopting the ways of the Penthouse?"

"I thought I had been clear about that. I want to make connections . . . get a decent job . . . make money . . ."

He picked right up on that. "Get out of Astoria . . . make wealthy friends . . . get invited to the right parties . . ."

"Well, yes . . ."

"Meet a rich boyfriend . . . never have to work a day again in your life . . ."

"Uh, no, Jamie. That's not what I'm after."

"Bullshit. That's what we're *all* after."

"Not me. I mean, yes, I want to get out of . . . *this*." I gestured around my apartment. "But I'm not on some cynical mission to become . . . well, to become *Michael*."

"You make it sound as if there's something wrong with living Michael's life," he said. "And I think you're trying very hard to convince yourself of that. But . . . there's nothing wrong with it. Nothing at all."

"Maybe not . . ." I replied, not wanting to pursue that conversation any further.

But it wasn't going to be that easy to drop the subject of Michael DeVries and the acquisition of goods and people, because that's when Jamie noticed the Cartier watch on my wrist.

"Nice watch. New?"

"Oh, this . . ." I looked down at Michael's gift. "Cartier. Think it suits me?"

"Cartier suits anyone. Where did you get it?"

"It was a gift from Michael."

Jamie took another look at the watch, and shook his head. "Can I see it?"

I slipped the watch off and handed it to him. As I did, I said, "This was my reward for listening to his lecture on everything you ever wanted to know about being a good little gentleman, but were afraid to ask. He wants to take me under his wing and teach me how to woo little old ladies."

"That's our Fagin."

I laughed. "Our Fagin?"

"Yeah," he said, with a smile. "Don't you see? We're in a demented version of *Oliver!*" I immediately thought of Walter Pomeroy, but kept my mouth shut. It would have required too much explanation. It was probably enough to consider that Jamie was utilizing musical theater, not Dickens, in his reference to *Oliver Twist.*

"Michael is Fagin," he continued, "and I'm the Artful Dodger, and you're Oliver, the relatively innocent one."

There I had it. I was probably never going to hear a clearer confession of character from Jamie. But the conversation seemed to be heading in a very dangerous direction, so I steered it back.

"I think I'll let Michael keep the old ladies for himself."

"Yeah," he agreed. "That's not what you want to do, is it?"

I shook my head. "Of course not. I want a decent income and a man to love. That's what it's all about . . . although I'll settle for the decent income." Part of me was tempted to impart Michael's observation that Jamie liked me, but I thought better of it. Instead, I returned to the subject of the watch and asked, "So what's the verdict?"

"Nice," he said, rolling it slowly through his fingers. "Just don't get it wet or drop it."

"Is it that fragile?"

"Yeah. But only because it's probably some five dollar knockoff, not the real thing."

"I assumed one of his ladies gave it to him."

Jamie raised a skeptical eyebrow. "Maybe." He paused, then added, "But did you think to ask yourself why Michael would give you a watch worth . . . well, for the sake of argument, let's say he didn't find it on Canal Street, and it's really worth thousands of dollars. Why would he hand it over to you?"

"Good question. I suppose if he has a few good watches and thought I needed one . . ."

"You're overestimating the generosity of Michael DeVries. If Michael thought he had too many Cartier watches, he'd want even more Cartier watches." He handed the watch back to me. "Still, on the outside chance it's real, congratulations."

"Well . . . it looks real." I strapped the watch around my wrist. It *did* look real. To me, at least.

"Yeah, it looks real." He let out a bitter laugh. "Story of our life, right?"

I ignored the comment, even though those might have been the most truthful words I had heard all day.

Brett Revere's Theory of LIfe, Part Eleven:

The Grass Is Always Greener on the Other Side of the Hedgerow

When I woke up the next morning and found Jamie watching the screen version of *Oliver!* on television, I didn't take that as a good sign.

For his part, Jamie was considering himself *quite* at home. Even Quentin couldn't have sprawled across the couch quite like he did, chatting on his cell phone while the musical played in the background, talking about nothing much at all. That sight, coupled with the mess he had made of my living room in less than forty-eight hours, made me once again question my judgment.

On the other hand, it was Jamie. And that made me forgive a lot of things.

I went to the kitchen and found that he had already brewed a pot of coffee. I felt a brief flash of annoyance at his presumptuousness—this was *my* home, after all, not his—but it was quickly dissipated by the realization that I could have coffee right away, without the bother of pouring and measuring and waiting.

By the time I returned to the living room, balancing my coffee cup as I weaved past mounds of clothes and discarded Prada shopping bags, Jamie was off the phone. The only sound in the apartment came from the television, where a group of juvenile delinquents sang and danced. There was yet another metaphor in there, but I didn't feel like pursuing it. Instead, I grabbed the remote and hit the mute button.

"Good news," he said. "I lined up another job."

"Great."

"Yeah. Another place in the Hamptons."

"When do you start?"

"Next week." He smiled. "See? I told you I'd be out of your hair soon."

Suddenly, I wanted nothing more than to wake up every morning to Jamie's clothes strewn across the floor and *Oliver*! blaring from the TV. But I couldn't tell him that, of course.

"No rush," I said, my concession to the truth.

"Thanks, baby. Hopefully, I'll get that check for the down payment from David Carlyle soon, and then I'll be able to give you some money."

"Uh . . . thanks. But . . . money for what?"

"Letting me stay here . . . paying for my Jitney ticket out to the Hamptons last week when we, uh, retrieved those photos . . . the lunch I bought Nico . . . stuff like that."

"Jamie," I said, "you really don't have to do that." Although it was nice to know that he hadn't forgotten.

"But I do," he insisted. "You've been great, Brett. I mean that. I don't know what I would have done without you."

"You would have survived."

"Don't be so sure. But . . . I . . . I . . ."

"What?"

"I need one more little favor."

I sighed. Of course he did. "What now?"

"Can I borrow the credit card?"

"Absolutely not."

"It's just that the new client wants me to go to East Hampton to take a look at the house, and I want to start working on the job for David Carlyle."

"Jamie," I said, "you know how I feel about that credit card. I mean . . . *yes*, I've used it. But I didn't feel good about it. And I can't help but think that every time I use it—or you use it—we're digging ourselves in a bit deeper. It's going to come back to bite us in the ass."

"It would just be for the Jitney."

Oh, shit. Was another couple of dollars really going to matter at this point, after a luncheon at Swifty's and dinner at La Goulue and a shopping spree at Barneys and whatever Jamie had used the card for in the week he had been back with Nicholas Golodnya? But . . . but . . . there was a principle involved here, too.

And as much as I loved him, I wasn't totally sure I could trust my Artful Dodger.

"I'll tell you what," I said finally. "I'll pay for your ticket and . . . How long will you be out there?"

"The client wants me out there tonight, if possible. And then I could get a few days in at David's . . . I don't know. Back Tuesday?"

"I'll do this. I'll buy your ticket and give you $100 spending money. But I can't give you the card. Deal?"

He thought for a moment, then shrugged. "That's more than fair, Brett. Deal. And thanks; you saved my life again." He got up off the couch and walked a few paces until he reached me, then delicately hugged me and kissed my cheek. "You're . . . the best. When I get this check . . ."

"Just use it to take care of yourself," I said.

"No, no . . . I want to give you half."

"That's generous, but . . . no. Get your own act together. If you feel strongly about giving me anything . . ."

"I do."

". . . pay me back for . . . the Jitney tickets and the $100 I'm giving you."

"I'm giving you half the check. And I'm not taking no for an answer."

I didn't really believe that I'd see half of his check from David Carlyle, but he oozed so much sincerity that I ended up giving him $200—as well as his bus ticket—after I took out a cash advance at the ATM. He blew me a kiss from the bus as it pulled away from the curb, and I went back into schoolgirl mode, mentally writing "Brett Revere loves Jamie Brock" on the inside cover of the notebook in my head, and imaging Brett and Jamie, sitting in a tree, K-I-S-S-I-N-G.

My thoughts became somewhat clearer as the N train rumbled back to Queens. *Damn, Brett, snap out of it!* Jamie was manipulative and a schemer and perhaps even more broke than I was. He was nothing like he presented himself to everyone else but me, and even I couldn't be sure what he was thinking, and . . .

. . . and I was totally in love with him.

I wondered if I should go back to see my old boss, Cruella DeVil, to find out if there were any "Anonymous" groups for hopeless romantics.

That's what I needed: an HRA twelve-step program. First, admit you have a problem . . .

* * *

I sat at home that evening amid the piles of Jamie's wardrobe and felt particularly unsettled. It wasn't just the separation from Jamie that gnawed on me. We had already spent quite a bit of time apart over the weeks of our indefinable relationship. No, it wasn't that.

It was Angel. I owed him a phone call, but I had no idea what I wanted to say to him.

Which is why I found myself doing solo line readings, trying to come up with the right words.

"I'm sorry, but I can't meet you for dinner after all. You see, I've met someone . . ."

No. "I'm being transferred out of town . . ."

Or, "I'm really straight . . ."

Or . . ."I can't meet you for dinner after all, because I've come to the realization that I'm just another Penthouse asshole who has no soul, so thanks anyway, and go get me my drink now."

Yeah. The truth is always the best option, isn't it?

I glanced at the clock and saw that it was almost 8:00. Whatever I ended up saying, I was going to have to do it now. I picked up the phone and dialed . . .

. . . and was momentarily relieved when his answering machine picked up.

Until I realized that I couldn't dump him with a taped message. This was just prolonging the agony.

"Angel, it's Brett," I said. "Sorry I missed you. I'll call again . . . tomorrow."

And I hoped that I would then have the courage to do it.

And the desire.

It didn't surprise me when Jamie called the next day and told me he was going to stay in the Hamptons for the week. That was just the way he seemed to operate. There were no apologies and no explanations; just a flat statement of a fait accompli.

What surprised me was that he invited me to join him later in the week. I would actually get a second trip to the Hamptons, and—in this particular case—I wouldn't have to sneak in and out through a security gate.

"I want you to come with me to a cocktail party Friday night," he said. "And maybe you could stay over 'til Saturday."

"You're inviting me to a party? Cool." With a tiny laugh, I added, "Will I be your date?"

"Of course." Well, *that* was a surprise. "David Carlyle is having one of his writers out for the weekend, and he's throwing a party in her honor. I guess there's some sort of big A-list dinner later, which I haven't been invited to." His voice betrayed his unhappiness with that fact. "But he's doing cocktails here first, and I'd really like to show you this place."

"Okay," I said. "I'll be happy to go."

"Fantastic. Everyone is anxious to meet you."

Another surprise. "You've been telling people about me?"

"Why wouldn't I tell people about you, baby? They're going to love you as much as *I* do."

Whether or not he realized it, Jamie was severely messing with my head. If we didn't talk about something else soon, I was afraid I would faint.

"Okay, okay . . . So how are you going to spend your week?"

"Getting David's house in order," he said. "I won't be able to finish the job by Friday, but I'll be able to take care of almost everything visible to the human eye."

Of course, there's always more going on than meets the eye. But I don't have to tell you that.

After I hung up with Jamie, I realized that there was another benefit to being out of town at the end of the week. *Andy* was opening Friday night, and I desperately wanted to be as far away from that catastrophe as possible. The other end of Long Island sounded like sufficient distance.

The next few days went quickly. Angel and I continued to play phone tag; it was almost as if he knew I had bad news to deliver, and avoided the phone when he recognized my ring. Finally, I had to leave him a lengthier message apologizing for our miscommunication, and informing him that I would be in the Hamptons, and therefore unreachable, for the next few days. It wasn't exactly resolution, but it bought me a few more days.

On Thursday, the day before the cocktail party, Michael called.

"I hear you're going to David Carlyle's party," he said. "Stepping out into high society?"

I forced a laugh. "I'm trying to practice what you preach."

"Good boy." He cleared his throat. "I'll be driving out, if you need a lift. I'm spending the weekend at Jeffrey Ryan's, so I don't know if I can bring you back, but you're industrious. You'll find a way home."

To which I thought, but, of course, didn't say, *"Yes, I know I can find my way home from the Hamptons."*

I really didn't care for Michael all that much at that point, but I cared less for the Jitney. So, after Michael had assured me that no one would mind if we arrived a bit early—that not being an uncommon practice among day-trippers trying to beat the traffic—we agreed to meet near his garage late the following morning to drive out together. I briefly considered trying to convince him to pick me up in Queens, but assumed—correctly, I was confident—that the only way he wanted to see the borough was at 60 miles per hour from the Grand Central Parkway.

The next morning, I was waiting at curbside, holding an overnight bag and wearing the Cartier watch, when Michael pulled the BMW out of his garage.

"Good morning," he said brightly, as I got in the car and put on my seat belt.

"Good morning."

And with those pleasantries exchanged, we were on our way to the Hamptons. To minimize conversation, I put on the radio, settling for a mellow station to which I assumed correctly Michael would not object.

Traffic was light, and we were making good time down the Long Island Expressway. Somewhere around the halfway point, he turned off the radio.

"This is your first cocktail party, isn't it?"

"Of course not," I said. "I've been to lots of cocktail parties."

"I'm sorry. I should have spoken more clearly. I meant, this is your first *Hamptons* cocktail party, right?"

"Right. Are you telling me there's a difference?"

"No. I'm just reminding you to be on your very best behavior. Your host and his guests are the cream of society, so act accordingly."

I sighed. To change the subject, I asked, "So what do you and Jeffrey have scheduled for the weekend?"

"Oh . . . a little of this, a little of that . . ."

Of course.

"Are you going to the dinner party after cocktails tonight?" I asked.

Michael stiffened. Without taking his eyes off the road, he asked, "There's a dinner party?"

"That's what Jamie tells me."

"Hmm." Still staring straight ahead, he said, "I wasn't aware of that. All I knew about was cocktails."

I shrugged. "Well, if it makes you feel any better, Jamie and I aren't invited, either."

"I don't care either way," he said, through a jaw clenched so tightly I half-expected to hear his teeth crack. "No, I don't care either way . . ."

I turned the radio back on, which also didn't please him. But he didn't say another word for the rest of the trip.

After another hour we were off the LIE, and, after darting down another series of highways, Michael pulled his car onto a crossroad and slowed measurably. The neighborhood looked familiar, and I couldn't put my finger on why until I realized I had walked these very streets on my way to and from Nicholas Golodnya's home a few weeks earlier. The thought unsettled me, and I had to keep reminding myself that Golodnya did not have the slightest idea I even existed on the planet.

"Here we are," said Michael, his first words in seventy-three minutes, as he pulled his BMW into a driveway almost hidden by the hedgerow on the slight curve of the road.

Jamie stood on the front lawn holding a plastic cup, almost as if he had been expecting us at that precise moment. Next to him was an older man, overweight and severely balding, with skin that was almost pink.

"Hey, baby!" yelled Jamie across the lawn, as I got out of the car. "You made it."

"I made it," I confirmed. "But where's *my* drink!"

"It's not worth getting excited about," he said. "Lemonade."

"Okay, then. I'll wait until the party."

I wasn't sure, but I thought I caught a glimpse of Michael frowning at me—at my perceived impertinence—out of the corner of my eye.

I also didn't care.

Michael greeted the other man, then Jamie, and then it was my turn to meet the other man to complete the circle of introductions.

"Hi," I said. "I'm Brett Revere."

"David Carlyle." He sized me up, seemingly with approval.

"Oh! Thank you so much for inviting me!"

"Think nothing of it."

I glanced around the grounds. "So this is your house! It looks fantastic."

He smiled warmly. "If you think *this* is nice, wait until you see the inside."

I put an arm around Jamie's waist and said, "Has my baby been knocking himself out on the interior?"

"His work, as always, is exquisite." I saw Jamie smile with self-satisfaction.

The relative tranquility was broken by the harsh shout of a woman's voice.

"David!"

I squinted but could barely make out the shape of her body behind the screen of the breezeway twenty yards away.

David Carlyle rolled his eyes and said, "Yes, Margaret?"

"You're out of bourbon."

He sighed in exasperation. "Would you excuse me, please? I know we're *not* out of bourbon, but my little diva needs attention."

After he returned to the house I asked, "Who does he have caged back there?"

Jamie laughed. "That's tonight's guest of honor. Margaret Campbell. She writes mysteries for David's publishing house." He leaned close to me and added, "Don't let her rattle you. She's really sweet. I think she just enjoys busting David's balls."

"Why is she in the breezeway? Is she being punished?"

He smiled. "That's the only place David will let her smoke. He doesn't like paying the gardener to pick butts up off the lawn."

"Let me ask you something," Michael said to Jamie, breaking into the conversation. "You know anything about a dinner party?"

Jamie nodded. "Her agent has a place in Amagansett, and she's hosting something after we have cocktails."

Relief washed over Michael's face. "Her *agent*? Oh . . . so that's what this is all about. I thought there was some sort of dinner party David was giving for the boys."

"Don't worry," said Jamie dryly, as he patted Michael on the shoulder. "You haven't been ostracized."

David Carlyle found more bourbon and, after personally delivering the entire bottle to his guest of honor, returned to the front lawn.

"I swear that woman will make me crazy one day," he muttered. "Positively insane." Then, turning to me, he said, "And Brett, I can't begin to tell you how pleased I am that you were able to join us."

"It's my pleasure," I said again. "Are you expecting many people this evening?"

He shook his head. "No, it's a rather intimate cocktail party. No more than forty people. But it's a nice, mixed crowd, including this very nice girl I've invited out from Manhattan in whom I've taken a paternal interest. And, oh, there may be a few others that aren't quite up to A-list caliber, but, well . . . they can be entertaining. I think having a mix of people makes for an interesting party, don't you?"

"I agree with you on that," noted Michael, who certainly did *not* agree with him on that.

Jamie cleared his throat. "But no Nico Golodnya, right?"

"No," said David, patting his hand reassuringly. "Fear not, young man. There will be no need for you to be on your guard." He looked at my overnight bag on the ground next to me. "I apologize for being such a poor host, Brett. We should get your things upstairs. Jamie, show Brett to the room."

I followed Jamie into the house and up a flight of stairs, then down a long hallway. When we reached the end, he opened a door.

"Voila," he said. "The bed."

The bedroom window faced out to the dunes and, beyond them, the Atlantic. I was going to like it here.

"Where's *your* room?" I asked.

"You're looking at it," he said. Then, with a laugh, he added, "You wouldn't think I've been sleeping here, would you? But David wanted all the clothes off the floor."

We were sharing a room? We were sharing a *bed*?

This was already shaping up to be one hell of a Friday.

Jamie showed me the grounds, and then we decided to take a long walk down the beach. He lent me an orange bathing suit that was a bit too snug around my waist, while he settled on a more discreet navy blue, and we left the house, following a wooden walkway through a break in the dunes until we were on unendangered sand.

It was a beautiful afternoon. The sky was cloudless, and a light breeze cooled the air as we trudged slowly down the beach, feeling the sand between our toes. After a while, tiring of fighting the dry, shifting sand, Jamie suggested we walk in the wet, more compact sand along the ocean's edge.

"I'm so glad I finally got you out here," he said. "Well . . . besides that other time. That really doesn't count."

"I was thinking the same thing. I needed a day out of the city."

He pointed at a roof beyond the dunes. "That's Nico's place. Want to stop by and say hi?"

"Uh . . . no."

He laughed, and I joined in.

We walked a little further, and soon the beach—which had been surprisingly quiet to begin with—was virtually empty.

As if he read my mind, he said, "I wonder where everyone is today. There must be some big barbeque I wasn't invited to."

I laughed . . . but stopped when I realized that he *wasn't* laughing.

"Is that what this place is like?" I asked, kicking at the sand. "Michael was enraged when he thought that David was hosting a dinner party tonight and hadn't invited him. Is everyone always looking over everyone else's shoulders to make sure that their neighbors aren't getting more invitations than they are?"

"Often enough," he said, with a shrug. However, whatever distress he felt about possibly being snubbed, but more likely just encountering a spontaneously light day on the beach, quickly disappeared, and he tugged on my arm. With a laugh, he ran toward the surf.

"What are you doing?" I asked, struggling to catch up to him.

"As long as the beach is empty, we should take advantage of it."

Jamie ran into the water and I followed, letting out a small shriek when I felt the cold water swirl around my calves. Without breaking my pace, though, I chased him until the water rose to my midthigh, and when he dove into a wave, I followed.

The cold ocean water shocked my body as I swam against the current, my eyes closed tight to protect them from the salt and sand. After swimming a few yards, I scrambled to gain my footing as the water rushed back out, pulling the sand out from under my feet, but stumbled and splashed back into the cold surf. From somewhere close behind me, I heard Jamie laugh.

"What's the matter, Brett? Can't get your balance?"

I was about to answer when another swell lifted my floating body up, the force of the water pulling my swimsuit down around my thighs and . . .

I realized with a start that the wave wasn't tugging at my suit. But Jamie was.

"What are you doing?" I screamed, flailing in the water as he pulled the suit down around my legs. "Jamie!"

As the surf rolled back out, I fell again. When I regained my balance he was waving the swimsuit triumphantly in the air, and I was naked in the Atlantic Ocean.

"See you back at the house," he yelled over the roar of the ocean, taking a few awkward steps through the water toward the beach. "Remember that cocktails are at six, so don't be late!"

Laughing, I started to follow him, but when I realized that an older couple was strolling along the beach just yards from us, I squatted in the water, trying to hide my nakedness. While the couple took their time passing, Jamie stood in ankle-deep water, tossing my suit from one hand to the other and cackling gleefully.

"Come on," I said, when the strollers had finally passed. "Give it to me."

"What's the magic word?"

"Now."

Instead of giving me the swimsuit, he tossed it on the beach and charged past me into the water, throwing himself into another wave. When his head broke the surface a few seconds later, he whooped and brandished his own suit in the air.

"Now we're on equal ground," he shouted, waving the navy blue square-cut suit above his head.

I glanced at the receding image of the beach strollers and paddled to deeper water. "Jamie, I don't think we should be doing this. It *is* a public beach."

He ignored me, tossing his wet suit over my head and applauding himself when it came to rest on the beach next to mine.

"Relax, Brett," he said. "We're not the first people to swim naked in the Atlantic. Just keep your dick under the surface and no one will get in trouble." With that, he dove, and I watched his pale white buttocks disappear beneath the surface.

And it was at that point that I realized that I *definitely* had to make sure to keep my genitalia out of sight, because the sight of Jamie's ass vanishing into the surf had had an effect.

But a few minutes later, something else had an effect that overpowered it.

"Uh . . . baby?" I asked, as we floated side by side in chest-deep water.

"What?"

"Are those jellyfish?"

"Shit."

It had been fun, and it had been spontaneous, and, in its own way, it had been incredibly romantic. But neither of us were particularly looking forward to being stung by jellyfish—especially on those body parts that should have legally been covered on a public beach—so we charged out of the water, squealing like schoolgirls . . .

. . . Only to discover that our swimsuits were missing.

"What the fuck?" he yelled, standing bronzed and naked at the water's edge. "They were right here."

Self-consciously, I cupped my hands over my manhood and scanned the beach. Maybe we had drifted . . . or maybe . . .

And then I saw a flash of orange, bobbing on the surface of the water some twenty feet from the beach.

"There's mine," I said, and, fearlessly taking on the jellyfish, I ran into the water to retrieve it.

"Do you see mine?" he shouted, when I reached my suit.

I struggled to keep my head above water while, under the surface,

I pulled the orange suit on and tried to look for Jamie's. And I thought, *he had to wear blue, didn't he?*

"I see it!" he hollered, as he ran toward me, fighting the surf. Following his eyes, I finally saw it drifting just below the surface of the Atlantic, a few yards from where I was treading water.

When we were both dressed and back on the beach, I said, "Well, *that* was almost a *disaster.*"

He laughed. "I can't disagree with you on that. I think it would be considered a major faux pas to walk into a cocktail party au naturel. It's not like this is Fire Island." He stopped and reconsidered for a moment. "Then again, we *are* talking about David Carlyle. . . ."

When he returned to the house, we hosed the sand and salt off of our bodies at an outdoor shower, then crossed through the backyard, where a woman in her mid-thirties lay sunning herself next to the pool. When she saw us, she half-wrapped a towel around her body.

"It's okay," said Jamie. "We're gay."

"Gay people at David Carlyle's house?" she said dryly. "What a shock."

I liked her immediately.

"I'm Jamie Brock," he said, as we approached her. "And this is Brett Revere."

She extended her hand. "Denise Hanrahan. I'm a friend of David's." She looked at me and added, "Your real name is Brett Revere?"

I shrugged. "I'm an actor."

She looked around to make sure no one was listening and said, "Well, thank God you guys are here. Usually when I come out here, I'm the only woman, the only heterosexual, and the only person under sixty."

I smiled. "Well, we've taken care of *one* of your problems."

"The big one," she said. "I've given up on men—basically, I think I'm a gay man trapped in a woman's body—so, really, the only thing I can't bridge out here is the generation gap."

We laughed, and I asked her if she worked with David.

"No," she said. "And I don't really live what you'd call a Hamptons lifestyle, except for those occasional weekends a few times each summer when David invites me out. I work for an accounting firm . . . I'm a middle-management drone."

I was trying to think of a clever response about what sounded like a dreadfully dull 9-to-5 routine when a loud woman's voice quickly filled the conversational void. I looked up to see that the author had escaped the breezeway and, cocktail in hand, was approaching.

"You!" she said, pointing at me, as her short frame closed the distance between us. "Do you know where David keeps his ashtrays?"

"I'm sorry," I said, "but this is my first time out here. I don't even know him."

She turned to face Jamie. "How about you?"

"You know he doesn't like people smoking in the yard, Margaret. What's wrong with the breezeway?"

"It's like being in an isolation chamber. The men are all in the house, Denise is back here, and I have to sit in the dark just to have a cigarette and relax. You *know* that parties in my honor make me tense."

"Actually," said Jamie, "I *don't* know that."

"Well, they do." She sighed and said, "Whatever. I'll just smoke out here without an ashtray. The lawn man can pick up whatever I miss."

Since the author had obviously already met Jamie and Denise, I took advantage of the first opportunity to introduce myself.

"Nice to meet you, Brett," she said, taking my hand. "I'm Margaret Campbell, but I suppose you already know that." She lit her cigarette. "And how do you know these miscreants?"

"I know Jamie from New York, and he invited me out."

She patted Jamie's ass, last seen unclothed and bobbing in the Atlantic Ocean.

"This one is a doll," she said. "And he's doing a wonderful job on David's house. I hope David's paying you well, Jamie, because I'd like to think the royalty money Palmer/Midkiff/Carlyle is *not* paying me is going to something worthwhile." She took a drag off her cigarette and added, "Maybe I'll have you come down to Chapel Hill and do my house one of these days. We'll talk."

"So David is your publisher?" I asked.

"Honey, if it wasn't for me there wouldn't be a Palmer/ Midkiff/

Carlyle. I don't want to sound immodest, or maybe I *do*, but I'm the only author they have who can deliver bestsellers. The rest of the crap they publish is . . . well, it's *crap*."

Denise stirred on her lawn chair. "Well . . . there's also Grant Brewster."

Margaret smiled. "How could I forget? I *did* blurb his first novel, after all."

I looked at Jamie, who simply shrugged. Denise and Margaret obviously had a history, and that history included private jokes.

I was about to follow up her comment with a question, but was interrupted by a call from the back door to the house.

"Yoo-hoo! Margaret, darling!"

We all looked up at the two men who walked out onto the lawn. I recognized Jeffrey Ryan, but not the man who had hollered, who was tall, impeccably tailored, had a ruddy complexion, and was graced with a full head of lustrous silver hair.

Margaret Campbell froze a smile on her face and, sotto voce, muttered, "Oh, dear, I guess it's time for me to start performing." She took a few steps forward to greet the new guests. "J.J., you silver fox. You get better looking with every year."

He laughed. It was deep and booming. "Darling, it is *always* a pleasure to welcome you back to the Hamptons." He turned and nodded to Jeffrey. "Have you met Jeffrey Ryan? He's the publisher of *Haute Manhattan*."

She took Jeffrey's hand. "Any man who is smart enough to print John Jacob Venezuela's social column, as well as excerpting my next novel, has impeccable taste in publishing." Seeing David enter the backyard, she added, "Maybe you could take over Palmer/Midkiff/Carlyle and turn it into a *real* publishing house."

"Here we go again . . ." said David, with a theatrical sigh. Then, looking over at Jamie and me, he said, "As much as I love to have nearly naked men posing at the side of my pool, you two should probably get dressed. The guests are arriving." To Denise, he added, "You, too, young lady."

The three of us—the under-sixty crowd—excused ourselves. Upstairs, we went to our separate bedrooms. In the room that Jamie and I shared, we peeled off our swimsuits and began rummaging through our respective bags, looking for appropriate clothes for the party. As much to divert my attention from his naked body as he strutted around the room as to gather information, I asked him:

"So who's the guy with Jeffrey Ryan?"

"That," he said, "is John Jacob Venezuela. He has a gossip column in *Haute Manhattan*, which is just about the first thing everyone reads when the magazine comes out. If there is social dirt to dish, he dishes it."

"I guess that's another reason to keep my mouth closed tonight." Despite turning my back to him, I caught a glimpse of Jamie's body and, once again, felt myself growing erect. I quickly pulled on a pair of briefs to partially hide the evidence.

Studying himself admiringly in the mirror, he didn't even notice.

"I wouldn't worry about it, Brett. No offense, but you're not in J.J.'s league. *I'm* not even in his league. *Maybe* David Carlyle is in his league. *Maybe*. Other than that, I'd guess the only person he considers worthy of his attention in this house is Margaret. You could probably set yourself on fire tonight, and he wouldn't notice unless your ashes got in her bourbon."

I took a pale blue shirt out of my bag and checked it for wrinkles. It would be acceptable . . . especially if I set myself on fire.

Jamie finally slipped on a pair of boxer shorts and said, "I like that girl . . . what was her name again?"

"Denise. Yeah, she seems nice."

He took a white shirt off a hanger and held it to his skin in front of the mirror, apparently trying to determine if it would properly accessorize his tan.

"She must be David's summer project," he said.

"I don't know about that. She seems to have known David and Margaret for quite a while."

As he pulled on the shirt, he turned to me with an uncomprehending expression on his face. "Well . . . that just doesn't make sense. I mean, she's like a . . . a shop-girl or something."

"She works for an accounting firm."

"Whatever. She's a worker bee. Unless she's running the place, she doesn't belong in David's circle." He paused for a moment as he buttoned his shirt. "I wonder if she's scamming David? Maybe *that's* why I like her."

"What?"

A crooked smile crossed his face. "Why not? Do you think we're the only two people playing the Trust Fund Boys game out here? Maybe she's got something up her sleeve."

I shook my head. "I don't believe you and the way your mind works." And with that, we dropped the conversation.

When we were dressed and properly preppy, we were about to leave the room when Jamie remembered one last accessory. He reached into his bag and produced . . . a watch.

A *Cartier* watch. Identical to the one I was wearing on my wrist.

"Where did you get that?" I asked.

"This," he said, "was my lovely parting gift from Nico Golodnya." He leaned close to me and added, "And you know what? Unlike gifts from Michael DeVries, I'm confident that *mine* is real."

Ouch.

Speaking of Michael, when we went downstairs he was the first person we came across, standing in the foyer and nursing a drink.

"Why aren't you in the backyard?" I asked.

"I just needed some quiet for a minute," he said. "And the Clampetts just arrived, so it seemed like a good time."

"The Clampetts?"

Jamie scowled. "He means Clara and Burt Matthews."

"Oh," I said. "The Lottery Hogs."

"Yes . . . *No*! Remember to call them Clara and Burt. *Please*!"

We left Michael alone and walked into the backyard.

In the short amount of time it had taken Jamie and I to dress for the party, the backyard patio had been remarkably transformed into a fully stocked bar, and a table of hors d'oeuvres had been set. The guests stood across the lawn in knots of three or four, clutching their drinks and chuckling heartily at stories they would either immediately forget or immediately appropriate as their own. It was all very civilized . . . very elegant . . . very *Hamptons*.

There were only two exceptions. I immediately picked Clara and Burt Matthews out of the crowd.

Burt covered 300 pounds oı so in a stretched, off-white golf shirt, over which he wore an ill-fitting maroon blazer. Clara wore a bright yellow sundress and cheap sunglasses. They both stood at the hors d'oeuvres table and did what could best be described as "grazing," shoveling devilled egg after miniquiche into their mouths as if the Hamptons were about to run out of food.

So that was what a Powerball fortune could buy you . . .

Jamie, of course, grabbed my arm the minute he saw them and led me in their direction.

"Hey, kids," he said, when we reached them, giving Clara a peck on the cheek. "I want you to meet my friend Brett."

"We meet at last," said Clara, offering me a sticky hand. "Jamie has told us all about you."

Burt's hand was doughy, but not sticky. "Pleased to meet you, Brett," he said, slapping my back with just enough force to momentarily take my breath away.

"I was just telling Brett that we should do something for you when you're in Manhattan next," said Jamie. *He was?* "Maybe a little reception or something, to introduce you to some of the people we know."

"That sounds like it would be a lot of fun," said Burt. "But you've got to let us pay."

"I won't hear of it," said Jamie, and I had a sudden flashback to Winston Culver-Benchley's little $300 luncheon. "Brett and I will be your hosts."

Before I started to contemplate what it would cost for two unemployed faux Trust Fund Boys to host an elaborate reception for a pair of lottery multimillionaires, I excused myself. I knew Jamie was working some sort of angle with the couple, but Michael had been working an angle, too, and it still cost me a lot of money I didn't have. I was beginning to wonder if working angles *ever* paid off.

For the next hour or so, while Jamie obsessively pandered to the Lottery Hogs and almost everyone else huddled with or around Margaret Campbell, I wandered through the party, chatting here and there with my fellow guests who had strayed from their groups, but otherwise staying somewhat disengaged. Whenever someone asked what I did for a living—which happened quite often in this status-obsessed group—I brushed off the question, and received in return the knowing winks of people who knew exactly what it meant to not work for a living.

At one point, I found myself in a corner of the yard with Jeffrey

Ryan and John Jacob Venezuela, both of whom were almost ignoring me until Michael joined the group.

"You all know Brett, right?" he asked, although I had already been standing with the men for five minutes.

"Of course," said Venezuela, placing one hand firmly on my shoulder. "Brett is thoroughly charming."

Michael said, "Stand him next to those Powerball hillbillies and he'd look like JFK, Jr."

"Now, now," said Venezuela. "The Matthews aren't *that* bad, Michael. A little crude, yes, but in time they'll smooth out those rough edges. And I sort of like their . . . their *earthiness*."

Michael shook his head with disgust. "Everyone just wants to get their hands on that money."

"Why?" asked Jeffrey Ryan. "We have our *own* money." He paused, then grinned conspiratorially at Venezuela. "Well, *most* of us have our own money, that is."

I wasn't sure if that was a shot at Michael or at me, but thought I had my answer when Michael's face reddened. Still, he didn't say a word.

"Money isn't character," I said finally, hoping to defuse the situation. "Money isn't class. I mean, money is *good* . . ."

"Amen," said Jeffrey.

". . . But it's not everything."

Venezuela again clamped his hand on my shoulder and said, "Oh, God, please stop this one before he tells us that the pursuit of money is the root of all evil."

I smiled. "I'd never be that foolish."

Leave them with a laugh, I told myself, excusing myself and heading for the bar. On the way, I again crossed paths with Denise Hanrahan. I hated myself for this, but the first thing that crossed my mind was to wonder what sort of scam she might be pulling on David Carlyle.

So by my third glass of wine, I had to ask her. In a roundabout way, of course.

"How do you know David?" I asked, cornering her near the hors d'oeuvre table.

She didn't quite make eye contact with me, which aroused my suspicions.

"I've known him for a few years. He used to be my best friend's boss."

"And your best friend is . . . ?"

"He's not with us anymore."

I felt the embarrassment immediately and muttered, "I'm sorry . . ."

"Oh, no," she said with a laugh. "He's not *dead.* He just . . . had to go away."

That opened the door to even more questions. Was he in prison? Had he been . . . *banished,* or something? *Ostracized*? But having put my foot in my mouth once, I decided to leave the topic alone.

"Well, it's nice that you and David could continue your friendship, even without your best friend."

She smiled warmly, and now looked straight at me. "David is a sweet man. Not at all pretentious . . . well, that's not exactly true. He *can* be pretentious at times, but most of the time he's down-to-earth." She paused. "And how do *you* know David?"

"I don't," I confessed. "I met him this afternoon. But I'm a friend of Jamie's." Her face betrayed no sign of recognition. "David's decorator. The guy you met at the pool."

"Oh, *him.*"

"Yeah, him."

"He seems nice enough." There was something that sounded not quite convinced in her voice.

"Uh . . . yes, he is."

We had fallen into a conversational lull, but were quickly saved by the appearance of David.

"I see you two have met," he said, and we nodded in unison. "Good. I am *such* a bad host today . . . extremely negligent in making introductions."

"Brett and I can take care of ourselves," said Denise.

"I had confidence in you, dear. I hope you don't mind me horning in on your conversation, but Margaret is on her fourth or fifth drink and she's starting to say *very* mean things to me."

Denise laughed. "David, Margaret isn't mean."

He raised an eyebrow. "Publish her, and *then* tell me that." Shaking his head, he added, "Poor Jeffrey will learn that when he runs those excerpts from *Murder in Montauk* in *Haute Manhattan.* I should warn him . . ."

I excused myself and tried to find Jamie, but when I finally spotted him on the far edge of the lawn, he was still surrounded by Burt and Clara Matthews and a cluster of other people, and there didn't seem to be any room for a newcomer. So I continued to aimlessly wander the yard until I again came across Michael, Jeffrey Ryan, and John Jacob Venezuela.

"Brett," said Venezuela, pulling me into the group. "You arrived at just the right time. I was about to share some new and juicy gossip."

"I'm all ears," I said, sure that none of the names he was about to drop would mean anything to me.

"Do you know Richard Van Veldt?"

Surprisingly that name *did* ring a bell, but Venezuela had to explain *how* I had heard it before I remembered why.

"He was the investment banker who was just sentenced to prison in that big insider-trading scandal. It was all over the news . . . and trust me on this: there's more to come once the investigators get another look at his books. I hear that the state Attorney General is all over them." He cleared his throat and ran his free hand through his thick head of silvery hair. "Anyway, Richard's wife, Johanna, was . . . how would you describe her, Jeffrey?"

"A big lush."

Venezuela laughed. "Well, I would have tried to be a bit more subtle, but, yes, I guess that would be an appropriate word. Johanna went into rehab last fall, right after the scandal broke, and she's made fantastic progress. I saw her the other night at a gala at the Whitney and she looks *fabulous*. But the poor girl had never worked a day in her life, and after Richard paid his lawyers and court-ordered fines, she was left penniless."

"They put nothing in her name?" asked Michael.

"Nothing. Johanna left all the financial dealings to Richard, and . . ." He shrugged. "What can I say? She married a thief. Richard didn't just steal from his clients, but he also stole from her. Johanna really got screwed."

"But she doesn't work?" I asked.

"She *didn't* work. She does now. She made a few calls to some people she and Richard had given campaign contributions to over the years, and she finally landed a job."

"So the story has a happy ending," I said.

"Yes and no. The good news is that she's working. The bad news is that Johanna Van Veldt, Upper East Side patron of the arts and recovering alcoholic, now has a lowly position with . . . the State Liquor Authority. You've got to love the irony."

The three men started laughing loudly. I joined in, a bit more subdued, but as I forced laughter I wondered how, if they could laugh at one of their own in her predicament, they'd ever be able to offer me the security I was looking for.

I could only hope that the bonds of sex and sexuality were stronger to them than the bonds of class.

Fortunately, I didn't have to wonder for very long.

"Ladies and gentlemen!" hollered David Carlyle from the center of the lawn. "Those of you who are going with me to the dinner party in Amagansett should leave soon! We don't want to keep Margaret's agent waiting. For the rest of you, feel free to drink my alcohol and eat my canapés . . . just make sure you lock the gate behind you!"

The guests laughed at David's attempt at humor, but quickly began obeying him, dispersing from the lawn. I looked around in the crowd for Jamie, but couldn't find him. I did, however, catch Michael DeVries as he followed the crowd, which was beginning to move en masse to the breezeway and, beyond it, the driveway.

"You're going to the dinner party?" I asked.

"I'm slipping in with Jeffrey and J.J."

"But . . . uh . . . it's a dinner party. Won't it be sort of obvious that you don't belong there?"

He shook his head. "Two things. First, they tell me it's on the casual side, so another mouth won't throw everything off. Second, Jeffrey is going to be publishing excerpts from Margaret's next book in *Haute Manhattan*, so he has a bit of pull here."

"Well . . . have fun. It looks as if Jamie and I have the run of the house tonight."

He smiled. "Don't break anything." Then, looking around, he added, "I don't see those Lottery Hogs around anywhere. Don't tell me *they've* been invited to Amagansett, too!"

I playfully punched at his shoulder and said, "You'd better get to the buffet line before Burt and Clara, or you're going hungry."

"Damn it, damn it, damn it," he muttered, skulking away toward the breezeway.

I went into the house to use the bathroom, and when I returned the yard was empty.

"Jamie!" I yelled, but I didn't see him anywhere. I was about to walk to the beach when I heard a voice from the breezeway.

"I think he left." I strained my eyes and saw Denise Hanrahan in the shadows.

"He left?" I asked. "Left for *where*?"

"The dinner party. It looks as if you and I are the only ones who didn't manage to finagle an invitation."

Huh.

Abandoned. Brought to the Hamptons as Jamie's date, then left behind.

Things could be worse, I tried to tell myself. At least I wasn't Johanna Van Veldt.

Yet.

Some time later, after the sun and a number of glasses of wine had disappeared, I walked out to the side of the pool, where Denise sat lazily sipping her own drink. I sat in the chaise next to her and let out a sigh.

"Man problems?" she asked.

"Always."

"Jamie? I'm sorry he left you behind. If I had known . . ."

I laughed. "No. Jamie is . . . I don't know what Jamie is, but he's not my man problem. Well, maybe he is in a way, but . . ."

"I almost think I understand that incoherent ramble," she said. "Let me see if this is an accurate translation: you like Jamie, but you're not in a relationship, and so despite the fact you have a crush on him, since nothing is happening it can't really be considered about him. Am I reading this right?"

"Close enough." I silently clapped my hands together. "Very good."

"I spent a few years as the best friend to the most mixed-up gay man in Manhattan, the guy I mentioned before who worked for David, so I've had a lot of experience translating half-formed thoughts."

I felt comfortable with Denise. Then again, she was a worker bee, albeit one that David Carlyle had drawn into his orbit, but even then she neither gained nor apparently *sought* financial return out of the arrangement. They were merely two people of disparate economic and social standing who, for whatever reason, enjoyed each other's company. You had to respect that.

Because of that, and because of her former status as the best friend of the most mixed-up gay man in Manhattan, I decided to open up to her.

"Jamie and I have been together," I said.

"*Been*?"

"Slept."

"Ah. Yes, that's sort of obvious. But now . . . ?"

"Now, well . . . he's staying at my apartment—temporarily, while he looks for another—but we don't do that anymore. Sleep together, that is."

"But you want to."

"Yeah."

She sighed. "Can I level with you? I know you're in love, but I think you have to get Jamie out of your apartment." She paused, and it was evident she was uncomfortable forging ahead. But she did anyway. "He seems sort of . . . I hope you don't mind me saying this, but I was watching him during the party, and he seems manipulative."

I laughed. "He's *very* manipulative. I mean, if you don't see it coming."

"But you see it coming."

"Right," I lied.

"Then why do you let him keep manipulating you?"

"Because I think I love him." The raw emotion—coupled with a number of drinks—forced tears to my eyes. "Yeah, that's it. I think I love him."

She put her arm around me, trying to comfort me.

"He lies to me," I continued. "And rejects me, and takes advantage of me, and . . . and he abandons me, like he did tonight . . . but then he's suddenly the sweetest man in the world. Take today, for instance. Ever since I got here, he's been acting . . . well, like we're boyfriends." An unexpected smile came to my face. "This afternoon we even swam naked in the ocean."

"That's been done before, Brett."

"I know . . . I know . . . but . . . not like us."

She sighed. "You can't help but like him, can you?"

"I love him."

"There, there . . ."

"And the worst part," I continued, "is that there's this perfectly great guy I like *so* much . . ."

"Jamie . . ."

I picked my head up, and thoughts swam for a moment until I had my bearings. When the earth was stabilized, I said, "No. Not Jamie. Angel."

She was appropriately confused. "Angel?"

"He's a waiter." I waited for her to give me that *ew* look, but when she didn't, I remembered that she was a worker bee and continued. "He's a waiter at the Penthouse. He's a really nice guy, and this situation—Jamie on one hand, Angel on the other—is . . . well, it's costing me sleep."

"And Angel likes you?" she asked.

"I think so. But I can't get involved with him. I mean . . . what would people *think*?"

She took her arm from me and settled in to her chaise.

"Let me tell you a quick—*very* quick—story," she said. "My mixed-up gay friend—the one I mentioned before?—well, he got involved with someone we all thought was totally inappropriate a few years ago."

"And that's why he had to go away?"

She nodded. "That's why he had to go away."

"Was it true love?"

She didn't answer for a while, and we both watched the water lap gently at the edge of the pool. When she finally spoke, her voice was distant, trapped in a remembrance of the past, "It must have been true love. It was enough to make him throw his life away . . . I mean, not literally, but, well . . . yes, sort of literally."

I had to laugh. "I'm sorry, Denise, but I'm not following you."

"That's because I don't exactly know what I can say," she said.

"I'm not following . . ."

She sighed. "I don't want to get too deep into the story, Brett, but the only way my friend Andrew could stay with his boyfriend was by running away somewhere. And so they did."

"Was the boyfriend in the Witness Protection Program?"

"Something like that. Anyway, Andrew decided that love was more important than, oh . . . working for David. He decided his boyfriend was more important than living in Manhattan, and hanging out with me . . ."

"I'm not sure I follow your point."

Again, she sighed. "Andrew met a man that he felt was worth giving everything up for. If you feel the same way about this Angel, what do *you* care about what these Hamptons people think? Follow your heart."

I was silent for a while, listening as the surf pounded the beach beyond the dunes, and concentrating on thinking with my head, instead of my heart.

Finally, I spoke.

"Nice story," I said. "But your friend had to give up his entire life for love."

She bit her lower lip, then said, "Well, yes, sort of. But . . ."

"I'm not so sure I like your story very much. I mean, can simple love ever be enough of a reason to give up everything?"

"There's more to it," she said. "There's more to every story, isn't there? But Andrew's story had a moral. At least, it has a moral the way *I* tell it."

"And his boyfriend . . . You liked him? You felt he was good for Andrew?"

"Well . . ."

"So if you're not even sure Andrew was making good choices before he made the ultimate bad choice and threw everything away for a man, why are you recommending this to me?"

"I'm just offering you an option." She was silent for a while, and it finally occurred to me that, hidden by the darkness, she was crying.

I turned, and said, "Hey . . . sorry. I didn't mean to say . . . the wrong thing."

"Don't apologize," she said, wiping her eyes as she crawled off the chaise and stood. "You didn't say anything wrong. It's just that . . . I miss him sometimes."

Without another word, she walked back to the house.

I knew I had been too hard on her, but if someone was going to offer me advice, they had damn well better make sure their *t*'s were crossed and *i*'s were dotted. Denise had recommended I follow my heart, but when her friend did that, he had to reinvent his life. I was going to reinvent my life for the last time *before* finding love. Because *that* was the plan. *That* was what Operation Hamptons was all about. And so much for the wisdom of the heart. The heart was unwise . . . stupid, really. Her friend Andrew had proven that. I had already let my goals be slowed by letting my heart overrule my head, and it wouldn't happen again.

Hours later, I felt Jamie crawl into the bed next to me.

I pretended I was still asleep.

Jamie was sleeping soundly when I awoke the next morning. I slipped out from under his arm and, after throwing on shorts and a polo shirt, crept downstairs. There was no evidence of life until I walked into the backyard.

"Good morning," said Denise, before I had even had a chance to step out of the house. "Sleep well?"

"Like a drunk," I replied.

A head peeked out from behind another deck chair and Margaret Campbell said, "Join the club. We sent David to the market for Tabasco, so try to hold yourself together until the Bloody Marys are ready."

My stomach somersaulted. "Uh . . . no, thank you." I took a seat. "So how was the dinner party?"

"Fantastically . . . dull," she said. "But now at least I can say that I've had my ass kissed by every millionaire in the Hamptons. Although if one more person introduced me as *People* magazine's grand dame of the American mystery, I would have committed my *own* murder in Montauk. Or at least *near* Montauk. Or wherever the hell we were."

At that moment, David walked around the corner of the house.

"And here he is now," said Margaret. "With the provisions."

David shook his head. "I hope you're not going to keep biting the hand that feeds you booze, Margaret, because I know a number of things I could put in your drink that would put you down for the afternoon."

"You're a doll," she said. "More mixing, less talking."

He groaned and carried his shopping bag into the house.

"You're so bad," Denise told Margaret.

"He loves it. Keeps him on his toes."

Several minutes later, David emerged from the house bearing a tray with four Blood Marys and muttering, "I feel like a servant."

"So did *you* enjoy the party?" I asked him, when he set the tray on a small table.

"I thought it was tedious," he said. "I'm really getting tired of some of those people. Michael DeVries . . ." He stopped himself.

"What did Michael do now?" I asked.

"I know he's a friend of yours, so I don't want to speak out of turn," said David. "Let's just say that Michael can rub some people the wrong way."

Margaret did not have David's degree of tact. "He got pissed off at Burt and Clara Matthews and stormed out of the party."

"Really?" I asked.

"Really. The Matthews are sort of simple folk, and a bit on the crude side, but I'd rather spend a few hours with them than *that* pretentious snob. I'm not exactly sure *what* happened—one of them said something that he took the wrong way, or some such—and the next thing I know he's stomping out the front door. I suppose he was trying to be dramatic, but it didn't have the effect he wanted, 'cause everyone cracked up."

I looked at David, who nodded in agreement.

"I'm afraid Michael's exit wasn't the best executed one I've ever seen," he said. "I just hope J.J. Venezuela doesn't write a gossip item about it." Then, more to change the subject than anything else, he asked, "Where's Jamie?"

"Still in bed."

"When he comes down remind me that he's supposed to buy theater tickets when he gets back to the city."

"Theater tickets?"

"Yes," said David. "Last night, Clara and Burt suggested we all go to see some new show called . . ."

No!

". . . *Andy*. I think it's just opened. Apparently, they've been approached to see if they're interested in investing, and a bunch of us decided to tag along."

I had to think fast.

"I hear it's terrible," I said insistently. "Poorly acted, loud, stupid, garish . . ."

"All that and more," said David, smiling pleasantly. "It has the potential to be delicious! I may invest in it myself."

I shook my head. "I really don't think you want to go."

The smile disappeared from David Carlyle's face, and I realized I was pushing too hard. "I think I *do*," he said, and that was that.

The four of us sat in silence for a while, listening to the surf and the gulls.

Finally, speaking to no one in particular, David said, "Do me another favor and remind me when Jamie comes downstairs that I need to set up a time for him to come back out and finish the job. I'm *very* happy with his work, but we wouldn't want to leave it incomplete, would we?"

"Of course not," we answered in unison.

Lying in the chaise, my eyes closed against the sun, and my head trying to get around the future group trip to *Andy*, I said, "I'm sure he'll want to schedule that as soon as possible. The sooner he's finished, the sooner he gets paid."

"Oh, he's been paid. I paid in full a few weeks ago . . ."

What? First *Andy*, and then *this*? I reached for my to-that-point-untouched Bloody Mary. Moments earlier, it had been the last thing I wanted. Now, it was the only thing.

So Jamie had already been paid . . . which meant that all those times he had insisted that he would reimburse me as soon as he received David's check had been lies.

Which meant that he had scammed me again.

"Well, I've never seen anyone drain a Bloody Mary so quickly," said David. "Can I offer you a refill?"

I opened my eyes and said, "Yes."

Brett Revere's Theory of LIfe, Part Twelve:

No Insight Can Come from Blind Items

I didn't mention knowing about the check to Jamie when he later joined us by the pool, and by the time David dropped us off to catch the Jitney and return to New York, I had decided that it was not all that important. Yes, Jamie had lied to me—repeatedly—but I had never really wanted or expected or even asked for the money. In a way, that made his lies all the more pointless and senseless. He wasn't lying to actively deceive me, or save face, or con me . . . he was simply lying for the sake of lying.

I probably should have been more troubled by the realization, but the drinks took the edge off. And, in any event, I was more concerned about keeping the Operation Hamptons/Penthouse crowd from seeing *Andy*.

"The play," I told Jamie on the Jitney, "is a bad idea."

"Why?"

"I was in it . . . well, for one day, but still. I know those people. And when Michael and I ran into a few of them the other day, he was mortified. I figure if Michael was mortified, David Carlyle and Jeffrey Ryan and J.J. Venezuela and the Lot . . . er . . . Clara and Burt Matthews will be *beyond* mortified."

He shrugged. "I'm not worried about it. If you're concerned, don't go."

"Don't worry about that," I said. "You couldn't get me to see *Andy* at gunpoint."

The rest of the trip passed largely in silence. This was one battle I was not going to win, so it was best to save my strength for the rest of the war.

There were no calls on my answering machine when we returned to Astoria. Angel had not called, which meant, I supposed, that there was a good chance he had gotten the hint.

Which made me feel more than a little sad.

But I was going to proceed with Operation Hamptons and follow my head, and that meant that Angel Maldonado could not be a consideration. I would not allow myself to end up like Denise's friend Andrew, who could only find love by giving up everything else he held dear. That was not going to happen to me.

"I'm exhausted," said Jamie, slumping to the couch.

"Me, too. This may be the earliest I've ever gone to bed on a Saturday night."

I walked into my bedroom, leaving the door slightly ajar in case Jamie . . .

I forced the thought out of my head.

I felt a twinge of guilt when I saw Angel's phone number on top of my dresser, but suppressed *that*, too, hiding the matchbook cover in the fold of my wallet. When the wallet was open, I saw Quentin's credit card, which reminded me that there was one call I felt I had to make.

I dialed the toll-free number on the back of the card, then entered the card number and my zip code when prompted. Finally, a mechanical voice was on the line, giving me the news I was dreading.

I was carrying—no, *Jamie and I* were carrying—a $10,654 balance on the card. In just over a month, we had gone through more than two-thirds of the available credit.

Which meant that the card was getting significant use while it was out of my hands. I had certainly abused it, but not to that extent.

And I was quite sure that Jamie—sitting on his income from David Carlyle and lying about it—would neither own up to overcharging nor pay up.

I sank back on the bed, deeply troubled. I wanted to blame Jamie, of course, but I couldn't. Not that he didn't deserve blame; I was still clear-headed enough to know that he did. But I had lent him the card without restriction, and . . . well, it wasn't even my credit to begin with.

Sitting in my apartment, with its rent paid through cash advances, which also provided the cash in my pocket, and which was full of electronics and clothes also purchased with the credit card, I recognized that I was no better than Jamie. If he was to blame, so was I. In fact, I was probably worse.

But beyond assigning blame, the $4,346 in available credit meant one very important thing. Operation Hamptons was now in its final weeks. Maybe I could squeeze out another month, if I kept my spending sensible, but that was doubtful. There was only a finite amount available on the card, and, in this case, money was time.

I prepared for a fitful night in bed, knowing before my head hit the pillow that I would be spending more time planning than sleeping.

When I woke to the sound of a ringing telephone, my first thought was that *that* annoying occurrence had been happening far too often in recent weeks. But then I heard Quentin King's voice on the answering machine, and the situation passed from annoying to precarious. Coming in the wake of the previous night's realization that Operation Hamptons had to be accelerated, I knew that action had to be taken quickly.

"Dude, we have to talk. I was expecting some mail that didn't make it to me. A new credit card. Call me."

I noted with irony that Quentin left a phone number with a 212 area code.

"Who was that?" asked Jamie, as I stumbled into the living room.

"Quentin King. Recognize the name?" He nodded. "Shit, we've used up more than two-thirds of the line of credit, and . . . how am I supposed to put my hands on $10,000?"

"Just deny you have the card," he said, absolutely unconcerned. "What's he going to do?"

"I suppose he could call the police." I slumped next to Jamie on the couch and buried my head in my hands. "This is not a good thing. Not at all."

I felt his arm on my shoulders, and he said, "It'll work out, baby. Everything will be all right. And remember, he cleaned you out here. Stereo . . . television . . . he really can't go to the police, can he?"

"I suppose not . . ."

"The worst thing that could happen is that he finds out you've been using it and has the account cancelled. The biggest risk to you is that you try to use it, and it gets declined. That's embarrassing, but it's not exactly jail time."

I looked at him. "It sounds like something you know something about."

He shrugged.

* * *

So there I had it. It wasn't even an arguable point anymore. The Operation Hamptons timetable had to be moved up. I had only a matter of weeks to make it pay off or concede defeat.

But Jamie was right about one thing: there was no reason to believe that Quentin knew we had been using the card. All he knew was that he mailed an application, and nothing had been received in return. That bought me just a little bit of time, because some day soon he *would* know that the card had been used, but I thought it still might be enough time.

Late in the morning, Jamie left the apartment to look at a friend's sublet on the Upper East Side, leaving me to work things out alone. But nothing came to mind. And I still hadn't developed a plan when he returned several hours later.

"Good news," said Jamie, the moment he walked through the front door. "I got the place."

"Congratulations," I said, not really meaning it.

"Upper East Side. The right address . . . the right zip code . . . East Sixty-sixth between Park and Madison." Address . . . zip code . . . prestigious neighbors . . . Everything *my* apartment did *not* have.

"How did you find it?"

"This girl I know from last summer in the Hamptons. She's moving in with her boyfriend, so I'm going to sublet from her."

"Sounds like a perfect situation."

"Not perfect, but close enough. The big drawback is that her building isn't great about sublets, so I have to pretend to be her brother." He smiled. "So . . . meet Jamie Ten Broeck."

"Nice to meet you. You have a lovely sister."

"So now I have to pack," he said.

"You're leaving *now*?"

"It's about time I got out of your hair. I might have to leave some stuff behind, but I can get it later, right?"

"Of course."

I watched him begin his usual haphazard packing job in silence, stunned and saddened that our domestic arrangement was coming to such an abrupt end.

"Are you going to give me your new address?" I asked.

"I will, but I can't remember it. I mean, I know the building when I see it, but I'll have to remember to write it down. I suppose that's one of the things I should know."

"Phone number?"

"No clue," he said. "But I still have my cell phone, so you can reach me that way." He stopped, then took my hand and squeezed tightly. "Brett, I'm not going to Europe. I'll be right across the Queensboro Bridge, right where I was when we met. This isn't goodbye, okay?"

I shrugged.

"And you deserve to have your space back. Just know how appreciative I am that you let me crash here in my hour of need."

I tried to think of a way to keep him in my apartment, for a few more minutes, if not a lifetime, but before I knew it he was gathering up luggage and asking for my help getting the bags downstairs.

"I'll give you a hand," I said. "First, though, I'd better call a car for you."

"Don't bother, baby," he said. "I'll just hail a cab."

"Uh . . . I'm not going to tell you that *never* happens in Astoria, but it's unlikely. If you're waiting for a yellow cab out there, you could be waiting for a long time."

He shook his head. "This place is positively uncivilized."

I called for a car, then helped him move the bags down the four flights of stairs. Our work accomplished—once again I decided to consider it my week's exercise—we sat on the front steps and waited for his ride.

"If things don't work out, you're always welcome back."

"Thanks," he said. "And let me know if you need a place to crash in Manhattan. Hopefully, I'll be getting that check from David Carlyle soon, and I can start paying you back."

Of course he would . . .

"Don't worry about it," I said, as the livery cab pulled to the curb. I pointed to it and said, "That's you."

The driver popped the trunk and we loaded Jamie's bags, then he opened the rear car door.

"I'll call you later," he said, kissing me on the lips and patting my shoulder. "Maybe we'll hit the Penthouse for a drink tonight, if I manage to get settled in."

"Call me."

"And thanks again."

"It was my pleasure." And as his car drove off, I realized that I meant it.

Without Jamie, the apartment felt much bigger again. It was amazing how one person could so completely envelop a room. But in a strange way, it also felt smaller, and much more isolated from the real world. It was, I realized, a throwback to the days and months and years in the recent past, when I would trudge dutifully home each night from the N train and cocoon myself in the apartment, isolated from the bustling world outside my door, trapped with nothing but basic cable and Quentin. It was a world to which I did not want to return.

I clicked the remote and the television came to life. I spent fifteen minutes rolling through the channels, looking for something—*anything*—of interest. When the closest anything came to engage me was an *I Dream of Jeannie* marathon, I turned the television off.

The Cartier watch on my wrist caught my attention in a way no television show—even *I Dream of Jeannie*—had. I had taken on face value that it was an expensive gift, but now that Jamie had warned me of its probable knock-off status, I looked at it with a new uncertainty.

Now it wasn't perfect, but it remained the perfect metaphor.

Was Michael DeVries really a disinherited Southern aristocrat? Or was that just a story?

Was Jamie Brock really a rich boy who had fallen from grace, or was that just another story?

Did either of them have any more real status than I did? Or had they simply been playing the game longer and better?

What *was* true? Was any of this true? Or was the only reality my tiny run-down apartment in Queens? Was the rest—the Penthouse, the Hamptons, the Cartier watch—merely illusory?

Were they—hell, was *everyone* at the Penthouse—acting out their own personal version of Operation Hamptons?

Alone in my apartment, I started to laugh. The thought that everyone at the Penthouse was engaged in an elaborate ruse to fake their way into society was impossible, of course, but I appreciated the irony. Hundreds of men simultaneously deceiving and scheming, playing for status like they would play chess, wearing their knock-off Cartiers and sipping their cocktails and hoping that no one would ever discover that their roots were in Trenton . . . it was too good to be true. Still, the thought gave me some comfort.

And there was always the possibility that the Cartier was real.

There was also the possibility that Michael and Jamie had at least a trace of reality to them.

But only a trace.

And who was I to talk?

In the early evening, Jamie called.

"Settled in?"

"I'm getting there. I need linens, but otherwise, it's livable."

I envisioned the jumble of clothing strewn across the floor of his new sublet and felt an almost unbearable pang of absence. He had only taken over my apartment for a week or so, but he had become a permanent fixture, and he was missed.

We agreed to meet at the Penthouse later that evening. As usual, I was the first to arrive.

I heard someone call my name and turned. There, leaning against a wall, stood John Jacob Venezuela, the gossip columnist who had been at David Carlyle's dinner party. I greeted him, noticing right away that he had obviously been drinking since whatever social engagement he had covered for lunch or, more likely, since it was Sunday, since he had left the Hamptons to return to Manhattan.

Still, he was someone I thought I should be talking to, especially now that Operation Hamptons was on a strict schedule. Michael would approve.

"Hey, J.J.," I said. "How are you this evening?"

"The important question is, how are *you*?"

"How am *I*? I'm . . . I'm . . . fine. Why is that an important question?"

"I get the impression you're not like the others," he said, staggering slightly and not really answering me.

"Which others?"

"Michael DeVries and that other kid . . . James?"

"Jamie."

"Right. You seem more . . . unrefined."

"That sounds sort of like an insult."

"It's not, though," he said. "Check out your dictionary, or a science textbook, or something like that. When something is refined, a lot of what's natural about it disappears . . . nutrients, et cetera, et cetera. What's left is purified, and while that might make it more palatable to most people, it doesn't necessarily make it better for them."

"Thanks, then. I think . . ."

"I'm not insulting you," he said. "You and I are much more alike than you think, Brett. At least, if I'm reading you correctly." He laughed. "My roots are solidly in Levittown, out on Long Island, and I've never denied that. I've found that most people respect that."

"That sounds like the opposite of what Michael would say," I noted.

"I enjoy Michael," he said, "but he's got his thing, and I've got mine." He winked. "Of course, I've got a secret weapon—my column in *Haute Manhattan*—so most people have learned by now that if they have a problem with my humble roots, it's best to keep their mouths shut."

"So you think I have humble roots?" I asked.

"I think so. But I have to admit I'm having a very hard time getting a read on you." He paused, and added, "I'll figure you out, though. I'll figure you out . . ."

"Good luck," I said, smiling.

He then leaned uncomfortably close to me, and I could smell scotch and cigar smoke on his breath. "Let me ask you a question."

"Shoot."

"Your buddy Jamie . . . You know he was involved with Nico Golodnya, right?"

I chose not to answer.

"Well, we both know that he was. Anyway, I hear things—a lot of things—but I never repeat a story unless I can be reliably sure it's true."

"I don't know what I can tell you," I said. "I've never met Golodnya, and I really don't know anything about their friendship."

"Friendship? Or relationship?"

I smiled. "You're the gossip columnist. You'd know the nature of it better than I would."

He leaned his head back and let out a throaty laugh. "Very good, very good. One correction, though, son: I am *not* a gossip columnist. I am a chronicler of society."

"My apologies."

"None needed." He took a sip of his drink, cleared his throat, and continued. "Let me try to make this a bit easier for you. How about if I call them 'Party A' and 'Party B.' Would you be able to tell me anything then?"

"No."

"The reason I ask," he said, "is because I'm running a blind item in my social column in the next edition of *Haute Manhattan*, which will be out on the newsstands next week. I don't need any more confirmation—I've already received all the backup I need for a blind item—but it never hurts if someone wants to go on the record."

"Even if I knew anything, and I'm not saying I do, it would be a non-story, wouldn't it? Who cares if any given Party A dated a Party B?"

"People care, Brett; people care. That's why I'm able to earn a living. And *of course* I can run the item. It's blind, meaning no names are used. I'm protected, the concerned parties are more or less anonymous to readers too far out of the loop to guess their identities . . . No one gets hurt. I've done it a hundred times." He leaned into my ear and whispered, "And for the record, there are a whole lot of people unhappy with your pal's sexcapades, starting with one older gentleman of considerable means and his very humiliated ex-wife, who's taking a real burn on the rumor mill because it turns out she was the last to know that her ex is now part of the Hamptons Gay Mafia."

I tried my best not to register any reaction.

"Now here's an interesting twist," he added. "Let's say the gentleman of means is 'Party A,' and his younger boy-toy is 'Party B.' From what I hear, Party A was holding some blackmail material on Party B, in the form of some very compromising photographs. Then, a few weeks ago, those photos were mysteriously stripped off Party A's computer. Most of them, that is."

Despite the air-conditioning, I felt beads of sweat pop up on my brow. "Most of them?"

"Apparently, Party A didn't quite trust the young man, and kept a few on a diskette in another room. Sure enough, when Party B erased the files, he didn't find the back-up disk."

My heart sank.

"Party A is certain that Party B erased the files, because he caught him on his computer one day when Party B was not supposed to be in his home. So that part is no mystery. The only mystery is what Party A will do now with the remaining photographs."

"How can you be sure those photos are of Jamie?" I asked.

"Did I say that? I don't think I said that. I was referring to two anonymous people." He paused. "But let's just say that I know who Party B is, because I've seen the pictures."

Shit.

Shit, shit, shit, shit, shit!

Jamie had to be warned. More important, I was expecting Jamie to walk through the door at any minute, and I didn't want to start his evening off with the news that I had not solved his X-rated picture problem after all. In fact, odds were fairly high that Nicholas Golodnya had already started sending them across the Internet out of spite.

Beyond a few photos of Naked Jamie sailing through cyberspace, though, I thought I knew him well enough at this point to know that he'd be shattered by the blind item in John Jacob Venezuela's gossip column . . . or social chronicle, or whatever he wanted to call it. People already knew about his fling with Golodnya, and the Penthouse crowd—like the rest of the population of the Upper East Side and the Hamptons—read *Haute Manhattan* and, specifically, Venezuela's column religiously. It would not be difficult for even the most simpleminded of Michael DeVries's ladies who lunch to put two and two together. Unless I did something, and did something quickly, the pictures of Jamie were days away from being public knowledge.

I looked deep into Venezuela's watery eyes and softly asked, "What could I do to convince you not to run that blind item?"

"What do you mean?"

"I mean . . ." I trailed off and let my hand roam under his blazer to his back, then whispered in his ear. "Tell me what you want me to do, J.J."

He raised an eyebrow. "Are you offering me . . . *something* . . . to kill the blind item?"

"What do you think?" Out of the corner of my eye, I saw Angel pass, tossing me a look of disgust. And, yes, I did feel suitably ashamed, but I also had to find some way to keep that story out of print.

"So, J.J. . . . what do you think?"

Venezuela smiled, but said nothing.

"So?"

Another smile. It grew broader . . . and broader . . .

Until he burst into a boisterous laugh and pulled away from me.

"*Very* impressive," he said through the laughter. "Inept, but impressive. I have to say that I was slightly tempted."

"I mean it," I said. "I'll do whatever you want if you don't put that . . . *rumor* . . . in your column."

The columnist shook his head and said, "Why are you doing this, Brett? Your loyalty to your friend is touching, but he's not worth it. You're worth more than that. I have no idea why he seems to mean so much to you, but don't let 'Party B' bring you down to his level."

"Come on," I pleaded. "Please?!"

Venezuela took a few uncertain steps away from the wall, then turned to face me.

"The very fact that I'm even considering your generous offer is a sure sign that I should go home." He offered me a smile that was almost paternal. "Again, don't lower yourself to their level. These people are sharks, and you're dead the minute they smell blood."

I was about to make one last heartfelt plea—begging, crying, whatever it might take—but, without a goodbye, he plunged into the crowded room, heading for the door.

As he squeezed through the crowd at the bar, I saw Jamie walk through the front door. They passed within inches of each other, and exchanged a short and cool greeting before Venezuela slipped out.

Jamie spotted me and pushed through the crowd in my direction.

"Hey, baby," he said when he reached me, giving me a quick kiss. "Sorry I'm late." He saw the look on my face, and immediately knew something bad had happened. "What's wrong?"

"I was just talking to J.J. Venezuela."

"What, did he make a pass at you or something?"

I shook my head. "No, but . . . we've got a problem."

"We do?"

"Actually, *you* do. It's about Nicholas Golodnya." He didn't say anything, and didn't even look especially concerned, so I continued. "Venezuela told me he's going to write something about you and Golodnya."

Now Jamie looked concerned, but he forced a shrug and said, "That's sort of an open secret. And anyway, J.J. wouldn't do that to Nico. Or, I should say, Nico wouldn't let him write that. Nico's ex-wife doesn't know anything about his gay relationships, and I'm sure he doesn't want her to find out. They still travel in a lot of the same circles, and, well . . . you know that whole 'woman scorned' thing."

"Yeah, well, I don't think Venezuela cares. He says he's running it as a blind item. You know, one of those gossipy things with no names. Just Party A and Party B."

"In that case, there's *really* no need for concern. There must be ten thousand men in the exact same position as I was with Nico. Now . . . do you want a drink?"

I grabbed his arm before he could bolt to the bar, feeling his authentic Cartier watch under his shirtsleeve.

"It's not about your relationship," I said. "Not really. It's about the pictures."

He stopped. "What pictures?"

"The ones on the computer."

"Oh, those. Well, that's just his word against mine, and . . ." Again, my face betrayed me. "It *is* his word against mine, isn't it?"

"Um . . ." My eyes fell to the floor. "Not really. Not anymore. Apparently, there were a few more . . ."

"*Fuck*!"

". . . on another disk, and . . ."

"*Fuck*!! Brett, how could you let this happen?!"

"I didn't know," I said. "And this wasn't my fault. Don't blame it on me . . ."

"But I trusted you!" He looked around and realized there was merit in lowering his voice, given the attention he was drawing. So instead of yelling, he started hissing. "I trusted you to get rid of all the pictures, Brett. And you told me you had deleted everything."

"I did. But . . ."

"You *didn't*! If you did, Nico wouldn't still have a few of them, would he?" He rubbed his face, trying to hold back panic. "*Fuck*! If J.J. Venezuela writes about them, *everyone* will know. And then everyone will be . . . they'll be . . . they'll be looking for them online and . . . *Fuck*! The *world* is going to see those pictures!"

"I tried to convince him not to run the item," I said meekly, but he dismissed my words, instead turning his anger directly at me.

"*You* did this to me, Brett. *You* told me that you had destroyed those files, and I believed you. And now . . . *Fuck*!"

"But . . . but . . ." I was torn between concern for Jamie and self-defense. "Maybe you can get Golodnya to stop it. If he wouldn't want Venezuela to write a blind item about your affair . . ."

He shook his head. "You don't get this, do you? If J.J. was just writing about Nico and me, then I could count on Nico to try to kill it. But if he's writing about those photographs, that means that Nico gave J.J. the information. Which means I'm fucked. Everyone is going to know that I posed for those pictures. And everyone is going to see them. *Everyone!* I'll be ruined."

"So what are you going to do?" I asked.

Jamie pulled out his cell phone and began dialing. "Maybe Jeffrey Ryan can stop this. He *is* the publisher of *Haute Manhattan,* after all; he must have *some* pull."

While he waited for the phone to be picked up on the other end, I asked, "What can I do?"

"I think you've done enough." His words hit me like a slap, which he followed with another slap. "Or, I should say, you *haven't* done enough."

"Jamie . . ."

He turned from me without acknowledgment, and spoke hurriedly into the phone. "Jeffrey, baby, it's Jamie Brock. Call me as soon as you get a chance." He recited his cell phone number and hung up.

"Jamie, I thought I had deleted everything."

"I don't need to hear this right now, Brett. You have no idea how devastating it will be if this gets into print. I'll be humiliated. Here I've been under the impression that those photos were a thing of the past, and . . . *Fuck!*"

"Jamie, tell me what I can do . . ."

He didn't answer me, other than fixing me with the angriest, ugliest stare I had ever seen. And then, without another word, he stormed out of the Penthouse and into the night.

Well, *that* didn't go particularly well. And for the life of me, I could not understand how Nicholas Golodnya's crusade to ruin Jamie's reputation was *my* fault. But for some reason, Jamie felt that way . . . and, because of that, I couldn't help but feel guilt.

Glass in hand, I climbed the spiral staircase to the piano bar. It was quieter up there, and I easily found a spot to lean against the bar, where I proceeded to drink and brood.

Maybe John Jacob Venezuela was right. Maybe I was too "unrefined" to live the Penthouse lifestyle. Maybe I just wasn't cut out for this world. I understood pain, and I understood vindictiveness, and I thought I even understood evil, but I couldn't understand what Golodnya was trying to do to Jamie. Jamie understood it, though; he understood it instinctively. So did Venezuela. And now Jamie was off to find Jeffrey Ryan—who no doubt *also* understood it—and, when he did, he was going to launch a counterstrike against Golodnya. What would happen after that was anyone's guess, and I was giving myself a headache just trying to keep track of the players, their motives, and their machinations.

And I needed another drink. Fortunately, Angel was just a few yards away from me, and I signaled him over.

"Drink?" he asked, as he approached.

"That's all the greeting I get?" Clearly, I was paying for the week of phone tag, and especially my lackluster effort to contact him.

"Sorry. And how are you this evening, sir?"

"Apparently, I'm unrefined."

"I see," he said stiffly. "Vodka and soda? Or are you still drinking scotch?"

I nodded, then impulsively asked, "When do you get off work?"

"Vodka and soda?"

"Can we talk?"

"I'm working. If you want to talk, you have my phone number."

"I mean tonight," I said.

"Sorry," he said, tucking his empty tray under his arm. "I'm working, sir." He began to walk away.

"Please?"

He stopped and turned. "Why are you so interested in talking to me all of a sudden? You spent a week avoiding my calls, and then . . . well, I have no idea what was going on with that gossip columnist downstairs, but you were all over the guy."

Oh, shit. "That was nothing, Angel. We were just talking."

"With your hands all over him."

"It was nothing like that. I just want to talk to *you*, okay?"

He stopped and breathed a frustrated sigh. "I have no idea why I'm doing this to myself, but I'm on break in twenty minutes. Meet me at the end of the lower-level bar, by the service area, and I'll sneak you out the back door. You can watch me smoke."

Twenty minutes later, I was waiting at the service area when Angel appeared. He set his tray down, said something to the bartender I was finally beginning to recognize as Paolo, the Brazilian, then slid under the bar to the other side where, after checking to make sure we weren't being closely observed, he motioned for me to join him. I did, and when we were both behind the bar, he led me through a small stockroom to a door. He pushed it open and I followed him onto a short metal staircase leading to a postage stamp-sized backyard.

"Elegant," I said.

"It's as close to nature as we get here." He pulled a pack of cigarettes out from under his apron and lit one, offering me the pack.

"No thanks."

We sat on the metal stairs in silence for a short time, listening to the muted sounds of traffic on the streets around us as he dragged determinedly on his cigarette.

"I don't know what I'm doing here," I said finally. "I thought I did, but . . ."

"You're drinking and socializing," he said. "Isn't that why everyone is here?"

"That's not what I mean. I . . . I'm here for a reason. I mean, I *thought* I was here for a reason, but so far . . ." I shrugged, and we both returned to silence.

Finally, he said, "So I have to ask: what reason are you here for?"

"This is going to sound stupid," I said. "But I started hanging out here to meet the type of people who could get my career back on track."

"I don't know why you're confessing to me now, after a week of avoiding my calls, but . . . whatever. Are you looking for a sugar daddy?"

"*No*!"

"Keep your voice down," he cautioned. "You're not supposed to be back here."

"Sorry. No, I'm not looking for a sugar daddy. It's just that I've been going nowhere in Manhattan for a long time now, and I wanted to jump-start my career."

"What do you do?"

"I'm an actor."

He snorted.

"Okay, okay, I know . . . Obviously, I'm not a very successful actor. So I launched this self-improvement project I call Operation Hamptons . . ."

"You're kidding."

"It made sense at the time," I protested. "Hang out here, make connections, get a job with decent pay . . . It just isn't working out the way I had hoped."

He stubbed out his cigarette and quickly lit another, explaining, "I don't have another break until midnight, so pardon my power-smoking."

"No problem. Maybe my heart isn't in Operation Hamptons. I just don't know."

He smiled. "I'm sorry. It's just that calling something Operation Hamptons makes it sound so . . . ridiculous."

"You're one of the few people who knows I even have a plan," I said. "We can keep this between us, right?"

"Right. So anyway, Operation Hamptons isn't working out the way you thought it would. What am I supposed to do about it? I'm just the waiter."

"Listen, I guess. And feel free to chime in if you have any words of wisdom."

He took another drag from his cigarette. I watched him inhale, then exhale a plume of smoke high into the cool night air. Then he spoke:

"I don't have anything to offer, because I don't understand what you're doing. Your Operation Hamptons plan is crazy, know what I'm saying?" I nodded. "You're like a . . . fish trying to be fowl. It just ain't happening."

"You're right," I agreed. "It's not happening. And if it doesn't click in a few more weeks, I'm going to have to pack it in."

"So what would you do?"

"Go back to Albany, I suppose."

Angel looked at his watch. "Let me tell you a story." He looked at his watch again. "A very quick story. The Maldonado family moved here from Ponce when I was a baby, like, twenty-five years ago. Mother, father, three babies. They didn't have nothing except the clothes on their backs."

"Sounds apocryphal."

He glowered at me. "You want to hear this, or am I wasting my time?"

"Sorry."

"They move to New York, to a two-room apartment on East 113th Street, okay? Spanish Harlem; *El Barrio*. My father gets a job as a security guard for, like . . . I dunno, maybe four dollars an hour. My mother gets a job in a sweatshop for a lot less. And me and my sisters get raised by the old lady across the hall, and when the old lady was sick we got dragged to the sweatshop until we were old enough to go to school, 'cause they both thought education was the most important thing."

"That's so true."

"No offense, but shut up," he said, taking another quick glance at his watch. "This is *my* story. Anyway, when we needed things—school clothes, a new refrigerator, whatever—they picked up second jobs. They really worked hard to provide, know what I'm saying? But in the end . . ." He trailed off into silence.

"The Great American Success Story?"

He shook his head. "One of my sisters got pregnant at sixteen and dropped out of school. Now she's bagging groceries at Gristede's. The other one is doing all right, though; she's some Wall Street dude's assistant. And my parents are still alive and kicking and living on 113th Street, still working hard."

"What about you?"

He took another drag from his cigarette. "What do you want to know? I'm a waiter, right? Isn't that all you and your friends see?"

"That's not all *I* see," I said. "I hope you know that. And, well . . . what about school?"

"Yeah, right. I go to school." I was clearly not getting any more out of him.

Behind us, a heavy door swung open and Paolo stood at the top of the stairs.

"Angel, your break is over."

"*Si.*" He flicked his cigarette to the concrete apron at the bottom of the stairs and began to rise.

"Can I ask you a question? What was the moral to your story?"

"No moral," he said. He took a step up, then turned back to me. "Okay, maybe there *is* a moral. How does this sound: work hard and most of the time you can make it." He paused. "But not always."

"Can I ask you another question?"

"Make it quick."

"Do you think I still have a soul?"

He rolled his eyes. "What kind of question is that? We all have souls, *amigo*. It's what you do with it that's the question."

"One last question?"

With another glance at his watch, he said, "Last one."

"Fine. Can I call you?"

"This again? Listen, I have to get back to work."

"I'll call you."

"You have my number." With that, he turned and climbed the stairs. And then he was gone.

Brett Revere's Theory of Life, Part Thirteen:
Every Good Fairy Tale Needs a Young Prince and an Iron Dragon

Early the next afternoon, I was back at Alan's office for my now close-to-daily routine of whining about the state of my world. The mounting debt and dwindling balance on the credit card that wasn't mine weighed heavier and heavier on my conscience—more so now that I knew that Quentin was growing suspicious—and I hoped against hope that Alan would find something—*anything*—to give me a much-needed infusion of cash. But, as usual, there was nothing out there.

And then there was the memory of Jamie, enraged, storming away from me and out of the Penthouse on the previous night. It was another unpleasant thought to dwell on.

"I'm weeks away from packing my bags and crawling back to Albany with my tail between my legs," I told Alan, after he delivered the expected news that there were no jobs.

"That would be a shame. I wish I had a solution for you, but nothing is coming to mind. Not on the acting side, at least."

"And the non-acting side?"

"Same old, same old," he said with a shrug. "Are you ready to pull the plug?"

"On?"

"On Operation Hamptons, dumbass. Because as far as I can tell, there hasn't been a payoff, and there's not gonna be a payoff. It's just a black hole where you're throwing away a ton of money—money you don't have—on lunches, drinks, clothes . . . A huge black hole."

"I don't know about *huge*."

"*Huge*! A mile-wide gaping canyon. A mile-wide gaping canyon of poverty and despair!"

"Okay, okay, I get it," I said, interrupting him. "You really like to hear yourself talk, don't you?"

He smiled. "You caught me."

I began to rise from the chair. "Well, on that note . . ."

Alan glanced at his watch. "If you don't have anything to do—and I know you don't—do you want to join me for lunch?"

"Isn't that one of those things I've been wasting money on? Throwing it into that mile-wide gaping canyon of poverty and despair?"

"Is that a no? Would you rather eat at the soup kitchen?"

I shook my head. "It's an acknowledgment that you occasionally speak some truths. And one of those truths is that I'm only carrying a few dollars in my pocket." I paused, then added, "Or are you buying?"

He thought for a moment. "Let's call it an advance on your future earnings. If any."

"Cute. Your confidence in me is overwhelming."

Alan chose an Italian restaurant a few blocks from his office, where he was apparently known, judging by the bright "Good afternoon, Mister Donovan" that greeted us as we walked through the front door.

"Afternoon, Viggio."

"Two?"

"Two."

"Right this way." We followed the well-dressed man across the crowded floor to a banquette against the rear wall, where he gestured for us to sit and handed us menus.

"So how's business?" asked Alan.

"It's good," said Viggio. "Very good . . . Last week, we had Elaine Stritch and Alan Cumming. Not together, but still, look." He nodded toward the bar area, which, even at a distance, I could see was adorned with the framed photographs of celebrities. "I got their pictures for my Wall of Fame. Up there with Tony Bennett!"

"Very nice," we said in unison.

Viggio nodded with self-contentment and said, "I will do that for your clients when you bring them in, Mr. Donovan. Maybe get them mentioned in Page Six."

"I'm one of his clients," I said.

Viggio spun, gave me a once-over, and turned back to Alan. "Enjoy your lunch, gentlemen."

I waited until he was a few steps away from the table before saying, "I think I've been dissed."

"You don't want to be stalked by *People*, anyway." He nodded a thank you as our waiter filled the water glasses, then continued. "I love this place. Viggio is a character, too. A total self-promoter. He told me once that he used to have a restaurant in Little Italy that was a mob hangout."

"So he traded organized crime for the theater crowd?"

"Have you seen Broadway ticket prices lately? It's not that big a leap. Force the Shuberts to put parsley in every Playbill, and you're just about there." He took a cursory glance at his menu. "I know this isn't one of your fancy Madison Avenue ladies-who-lunch places, but I think you'll like it. The food's fantastic. Inexpensive, too. Did you catch the part where I said 'inexpensive'?"

"*Si,*" I mumbled.

"Ah, Spanish! Are you being tutored by Angel?"

"Stop," I said, realizing that my face had suddenly reddened.

Alan noticed it, too. "Really? So I'm onto something between you and Angel . . ."

"He's a cutie, but . . . no."

"Why not? It's pretty obvious that he likes you." When I didn't answer, his expression darkened. "Because he's Puerto Rican? Or because he's a waiter? Or both?"

"Alan, it's not like that."

"I think it's exactly like that. You didn't use to be like this, Brett. That Angel is a nice guy, and he's so cute. Hard-working, too. *And* he seems to like you, for some strange reason. A few weeks ago, you would have been all over him. All. Over. Him. Happily ever after." He took a sip of water, letting his words sink in. "But now you think you're one of the Penthouse elite, and I suppose he's not good enough for someone of your station."

"Ah, jeez, here you go again. You know I'm not like that."

"No, but you're trying to be like that, which is practically the same thing. You can't give me one good reason why you shouldn't ask Angel out on a date."

I leaned over the table and said, "I've got one good reason. Jamie."

"Oh please."

I'm sure he wanted to say more, but our waiter was suddenly next to the banquette reciting the specials in something approximating English by way of Abruzzi. Since I could only understand about one of every four words coming from his mouth, I let Alan order for me. When the waiter departed, he returned to the subject of Jamie Brock.

"Someday," he said, "you'll have to explain this attraction to me, because I just don't see it."

"You're kidding, right?"

"Not at all. Here is what I'm willing to concede: Jamie is sort of attractive, in a weather-beaten way, and I suppose he's charming, if you have a high tolerance for bullshit. But I will never understand how someone with your normal degree of common sense could fall in love with him."

"Because he's a great guy, and we have this rapport . . ."

"He's manipulative. A user. And you're only going to be part of his life as long as you can do something for him."

"I think you're wrong." I punctuated my comment by snapping the menu closed. "But there's no sense in going over the same ground—over and over and over again. It's getting boring."

"I think we've finally found something we can agree on."

Our food arrived quickly, and as we dug in, Alan said, "On a more pleasant note, I was talking to Walter Pomeroy—you remember, the producer of *Andy* . . ."

"How could I forget?"

". . . and he was telling me that sales have been a lot stronger than anticipated."

"And how is that more pleasant? I'm not in the show anymore, remember?"

He twirled some linguine around a fork and said, "Yes, Brett, you'll be happy to know that I *do* remember that. The reason I'm telling you this is because Walter is willing to let bygones be bygones, if you want to get back in the show."

"No thanks."

"You could use the money."

"I'm too enamored of my dignity."

"The noble poor. How quaint. Anyway, he's holding auditions later in the week and . . ."

"Auditions? I've already auditioned for him. He cast me! I'm not going to another audition."

"Fine," said Alan, twirling again. "Just don't come crying to me when the show goes Off-Broadway."

I paused with my fork delicately balancing tortellini just inches from my mouth.

"Off-Broadway? You're kidding, right?"

"That's the buzz. If Walter can put a few threats from the *Annie* people behind him, they may take the show to a real theater. Right now, ticket sales are strong enough to justify it. And you know what that means, don't you? It means it will go Equity. They'll be entirely recasting the show. And the new cast will be seeing a significant pay increase."

"I don't know, Alan. The show is horrible."

"It's a regular paycheck. Some actors—*most* actors—would kill for that. In fact, *you* would have killed for that a month ago, before you settled on your stupid Operation Hamptons plan." He stopped, then looked me straight in the eye. "Are you the same Brett Revere who was in my office a half-hour ago begging for work?"

"But *Andy* . . ."

"Ever hear of *Cats*? Ever hear of *Mamma Mia*?"

"I didn't say everything on the stage had to be written by Arthur Miller, but . . ."

"I don't want to confuse you with Economics 101, but the theater runs on market principles. Supply and demand. If you give the public what it wants at a price it's willing to pay, you've got a hit. Pure and simple."

"And the public wants *Andy*?"

"Go figure. But apparently they've been turning people away, and the waiting list is huge. The show is practically sold out through Labor Day."

"Hmmm." I stabbed some more tortellini. "Well . . . good for Joey Takashimi, I guess. And here I thought he was bull-shitting me."

"Joey *who*?"

"The actor—and I use that term loosely—who's playing Andy. I ran into him uptown the other day. He told me the show was doing well, but I just figured he was being a bitchy queen and digging at me because I walked out."

"No," said Alan. "It's a fact. *Andy* is an unqualified hit. I've never seen anything like it." He took a bite, then asked, "So do you want an audition?"

"I'm afraid not. I suppose I wish them well, but I have another project that requires all my energy and attention."

Alan didn't say a word. He didn't have to. His downcast eyes and exasperated sigh said it all.

When we exited the restaurant, Alan turned toward his office and, after thanking him for lunch and promising to call later about social plans, I turned in the opposite direction, fighting the crowds as I made my way up Seventh Avenue. After a few blocks I decided that walking on that particular day was not appealing to me, so I pulled out my wallet to find my Metrocard. As I did, a piece of paper fell out . . . the ripped-off back of a matchbook from the Penthouse. The one with Angel's home phone number.

Well, I did tell him the night before, as we sat on the back steps, that I'd call. And I had a bad track record I needed to repair. So . . .

"*Hola.*"

"Angel?" I could barely make out his voice over the street noise surrounding me as I stood at a pay phone kiosk just off Seventh Avenue.

"Yes, this is Angel."

"It's Brett. Brett Revere."

"Yes?" He sounded wary, although I could have been misreading his tinny voice through the crackling connection and the traffic in the background.

"I hope you don't mind me calling."

"No. No, of course not . . ."

"It's just that I was . . . uh . . . I was wondering if you're working tonight?"

"Not tonight. Tomorrow. Tonight is for studying."

"Oh." I suddenly felt very nervous, like a schoolboy making his first date. My mind went blank, and I couldn't think of anything to say.

But I plunged forward anyway. "Do you . . . Do you want to get together this afternoon? Maybe hang out somewhere?"

There was a long pause. Finally, he said, "Are you sure?"

"Yes. Of course."

Another long pause, broken by, "Okay, then. Sure. I mean, I have to be home fairly early to study, but we could get together for a few hours."

"Great." I realized that a wide smile had broken out across my face, and I made an effort to control it. "It's such a nice day, I was thinking we could go to Central Park."

"Okay." Still with the not-quite-enthusiastic "okays." "Where do you want to meet? And when?"

"Let's say three o'clock on the steps of the Metropolitan Museum of Art. Does that work for you?"

"I'll see you there," he said, and hung up without a goodbye.

I cradled the phone and walked back to Seventh Avenue, with a bit of a spring now in my step.

He was waiting when I reached the museum a short time later, and flashed me an uncertain smile as I climbed the steps until I reached him and we exchanged the briefest of hugs.

"I'm glad you could join me," I said.

"Well, you called . . ." His face betrayed no more enthusiasm than his voice on the phone, and I began to think that maybe calling Angel was a mistake.

"I wanted to see you," I said, hoping for a quick save. "Or I should say, I wanted to see you outside the bar."

"And here I am."

"Here you are."

We stood there uncomfortably for a moment, until he broke the ice.

"So have you found your soul?"

I laughed. "I'm trying."

"You shouldn't have to try." He delivered the words deadpan, but I noticed the slightest of smiles creeping across his lips.

"Everything takes effort, Angel. Everything."

We walked a few blocks north along Fifth Avenue and turned left, entering Central Park across from East Eighty-fourth Street. The sky couldn't seem to make up its mind, alternating between a humid cloudiness and flashes of blue, but the thousands of people using the park didn't seem to care. It looked as if every stroller and pair of in-line skates in the New York metropolitan area was in use in Central Park that afternoon. I had an excuse, and Angel had an excuse, but didn't anyone *else* in this city work?

"So tell me a story," I said to Angel, as we stepped aside to let a bicyclist pass.

"A story? About me?"

"Yeah. I've never seen you outside the bar, so I have no idea what you do except pour drinks and carry trays."

"And all I really know about you is that you can put away vodka. That doesn't give *me* a lot to go on, either. You could be a serial killer for all I know." He smiled. "A handsome serial killer, but still. . . . Listen, I work in the bar about thirty hours a week, and when I'm not there, I'm in school. Or bed. I don't really have the free time necessary to have anything interesting happen to me." He paused. "Why don't *you* tell *me* a story first, and maybe I'll feel inspired."

"Okay," I said, as we continued slowly walking through the park. "I'm getting good at telling stories lately."

We continued our stroll and I told my story.

"Once upon a time, there was a young prince who lived far, far away, in a snowy, cold kingdom known as Albany. The young prince wished to live in the big kingdom known as Manhattan, where he could become a famous actor, so one day he packed his bags, kissed his parents goodbye, and hopped on an iron dragon, which . . ."

"Iron dragon?"

"Okay, Amtrak. I'm trying to be creative here."

"Ah!"

"So where was I? Oh yes, the iron dragon took the young prince to the big kingdom, and . . ."

"Aren't dragons supposed to be bad?"

"Not in my story. Anyway, the young prince found a tiny apartment and a tinier career in the big kingdom. Then, after many years, a magical wizard . . ."

"Redundant."

"Hush! This is my story. So the magic . . . so the *wizard* offered the young prince three wishes."

"He was treading a bit too far into genie territory, wouldn't you say?"

"Do I have to stop this story and send you straight to bed?"

He giggled. "Sorry."

"Okay. Now, the young prince had three wishes, and . . . well, do you know what he wished for?"

"Health, happiness, and world peace?"

"Close. He wished for money, success, and love." I stopped and turned to him. "The End."

"That's it? No offense, but your story sort of sucks. I mean, you never told me if the young prince found what he was after. There was no moral. There was no 'and they lived happily ever after.' "

I smiled. "Maybe that's the point. The young prince's quest continues."

"And," Angel added, "he's eternally young."

"That's my story," I said, "and I'm sticking to it." We turned onto yet another path—one with fewer people—and I gently touched his shoulder. "Now it's your turn."

"Nah. I don't have a story that could *possibly* top yours."

"Okay, then. Tell me about yourself in your own words, without the benefit of iron dragons. Although I *do* think an iron dragon adds a lot to any plot."

"What about my story last night? Won't that do?"

"No," I said. "There was no clear-cut moral, and there was no happily-ever-after. And, most important . . ." I gently poked his nose, and he grinned. "Most important, your story last night was about your family. It wasn't about you."

He sighed, but he was still grinning, so I figured I was ahead of the game. "All right, here goes. This particular young prince works too hard and studies too much when he's not working. And he likes to think he's virtuous, but . . . maybe he's lacking in a few virtues."

"Okay," I said. "Now I'm properly intrigued. Which virtues do you lack?"

"Well . . . I smoke. Is that a problem for you?"

"No. And I know better than to tell you that some day you'll quit."

"I will," he said defensively.

"Only when you're ready. Not for me, or anyone else." I paused, then ominously added, "Or when you die."

"Thanks. You're a fun time. Okay . . . moving on, I also drink."

I laughed. "That's a virtue, honey."

His eyes flashed, and the grin was most definitely gone. "Don't call me honey, okay? That was really premature."

Taken aback, I stumbled in what had been, to that point, an easy gait, and muttered, "Sorry."

"Just don't get too close too soon, Brett," he said. "That really . . . I just can't handle that, okay?"

"No problem."

He stopped. "*I* know it's no problem. It's my rule. Respect it."

"I do, I do . . ." I had no idea where this was coming from, but I wanted to get out of it with as little drama as possible.

"Okay, let's see . . . what else?" His temper had cooled as abruptly as it flared. Which was fine by me. "I also used to be a bit of a slut, but those days are part of my past."

I knew enough to keep my mouth shut on that one.

"And . . . I think your friends at the Penthouse are real assholes."

I laughed. "But they *are*!"

"True. But they pay my salary, so I shouldn't think like that. Or at least I shouldn't act like that."

"You've always been polite in the bar," I said. "Even when Michael was such an asshole after you saved him from choking . . ."

"Ugh. *That one*. He's the worst. How can you be friends with him?"

"It's trying, at times," I admitted. "But he's really not *that* bad."

"*The worst*. He's . . . well, he's your little friend, so I'll keep my mouth shut. For now."

"The point is that I've never seen you act as if you don't like the customers," I said. "So it doesn't really matter what you think of them. Unless you're spitting in their drinks, that is."

He didn't answer me, but kept walking, staring glumly ahead.

"Um . . . you're *not* spitting in their drinks, are you?"

A smile burst across his lips. "No, of course not. I wouldn't do that."

I had to ask. "So if you think my friends are assholes, what did you think of me when you first saw me?"

"I think I felt a raindrop."

I looked up, and it *was* quickly clouding over, but he hadn't answered my question. "So what did you think of me?"

"We should get out of the park. It's going to pour."

"You're not going to tell me, are you? You're going to leave me guessing until the day I die."

"Okay," he said, taking my hand and gently walking his fingers over my palm to punctuate each phrase. "Here's what I thought. I thought you were cute . . . and I thought you were very nice . . . and I thought you were exactly the type of man I could be happy with . . ." He drew his fingers away. "And now I think I've told you too much."

"No," I said softly, reaching out again for his hand. "You've only scratched the surface. You haven't told me *nearly* enough."

For the briefest of moments I was prepared to hold him in my arms and kiss him . . . but then the skies opened up and a heavy rain began to fall.

"Run for cover!" he screamed, grabbing my hand and pulling me across the grass.

Laughing, we ran for the trees, hoping that the leaves would keep us from getting drenched. From our secluded vantage point, we watched dozens of other people scurry away from the storm. Fortunately, they didn't scurry into our sanctuary, and we were still alone.

"It should pass in a few minutes," he said, taking my hand and squeezing.

"And if it doesn't?"

"Then I guess we'll have to camp out here all night."

"I could get used to that," I said, unable to suppress a giggle.

He squeezed my hand again. "And I could get used to *this* Brett."

"*This* Brett?"

"The sweet Brett. The Brett who's not the one that hangs out in the Penthouse." My expression must have conveyed dismay, because he added, "The Penthouse Brett is all right, so don't get defensive. I just like you a lot more when your guard is down . . . when you feel free to be yourself. When you're not . . . I don't know; when you're not all over Mr. Sleazy Gossip Columnist."

"I told you that was nothing."

"Okay, whatever . . . I'm just saying that I like the Brett I first laid eyes on a few weeks ago. That's all. I liked you most the way you were when I first saw you." He paused, then pointedly added, "*That* Brett would promptly return phone calls."

"So you think I've changed?"

"That's not what I meant," he said. "Like I told you, when I first saw you, you were fresh. You were nice. I liked you so much that I . . . it was like I'd get all shy around you. These days, when you're with your little friends, things feel different. You're not like them, but you're not like yourself, either. You know what I mean?"

"I think so."

"And now that it's just the two of us here, well . . . you're not Penthouse Brett. And I feel the same way about you that I felt when I first saw you."

And that was when I leaned forward and kissed him . . . a kiss he welcomed.

"Nice," he said, when our lips parted. "Yeah, I *definitely* like this Brett."

"They're the same person," I reassured him. "Penthouse Brett isn't a bad guy, and Central Park Brett isn't perfect."

"It's not about perfection, Brett. It's about being a real person."

"Okay," I said softly, positioning my lips inches from his mouth. "I'll try to make Penthouse Brett a bit more real. Will that help?"

He didn't answer me with words, but leaned up to kiss me again . . . a kiss that lingered long enough so that by the time it was over, the sound of the rain beating on the leaves had disappeared.

"So much for *that* storm," I said. "But Mother Nature had good timing."

"No," he said, wrapping his arms around me and holding me tightly. "The storm went away too soon. We were just getting started."

A thought burst through my mind and out of my lips before I had a chance to think things through, and I said, "Come home with me."

"*What?*" He pulled away from me.

"Let's go back to my apartment."

He bit his lower lip and dropped his eyes to the ground.

"I can't."

"Come on, Angel. I want to be with you."

His gaze returned to my face. "I can't, Brett. That's not me. I mean, I like you a lot, but I still don't really know you. There are still some things I have to figure out. And anyway, I'm not one of those guys who jumps right into bed on the first date. Not anymore."

I smiled. "Is that what this is? Our first date?"

He shrugged. "Whatever. That's not the point. The point is . . . the point is that I'm not like that anymore."

"Ever?"

He paused for a split second. "Don't push it, okay? Give it time. If it's meant to be, it will still be there next week, or . . . whenever it's the right time."

A resigned smile crossed my face. "Okay, then. Whenever. I guess we'll know when the time is right."

His arm wrapped around my waist again. "And besides, I still have some questions about those people you hang out with. Especially the younger one . . . the one with the brown hair . . . blue eyes . . . kind of loud . . ."

"Jamie?"

"Yeah, I think that's his name. You like him, don't you?"

I thought about that for a moment, not quite sure what the truth was, let alone if I would share that truth with Angel. Finally I said, "My relationship with Jamie is . . . uh . . . complex." All in all, that was the most truthful answer I could muster.

"You're not answering my question," he noted.

I leaned into him and planted a light kiss on his forehead. He closed his eyes and tilted his head back, offering his moist lips, and I kissed them.

"That's still not an answer," he said, with a slight smile, his eyes still closed. "But I suppose that's the best I'm gonna get this afternoon."

"Sorry, baby, but that's the best I can give."

He shrugged, then glanced at his watch.

"It's getting late," he said. "I should be getting home."

"And I suppose you're going to insist . . ."

"On going home alone?" He laughed. "Yes. We still may not know each other very well, but at least you've learned *that*. And remember that I have to study tonight. Get my education. That way, the only thing your friends can give me a hard time about is my brown skin."

"Now, now . . ."

His eyes flashed with passion. "Don't 'now, now' me, 'kay? Maybe I've spent too much time in the Penthouse, but I know the way those friends of yours are. You like them, that's good for you. But you may be even whiter than they are. When they look at me, they see nothing but brown skin and an accent. The truth."

His words sounded too much like Ty's condemnation of the bar's prevailing culture, and I felt guilty for my role as a knowing participant.

I reached for him. "Angel, I don't think . . ."

"It's not your problem," he said, pulling back from me. "It doesn't happen to you, so you don't even see it."

"So what can I do?"

He laughed dismissively. "Not much you can do, is there? What should I tell you to do? Become Puerto Rican? Oh, it'd be sort of cool if you could change the world, but that wasn't even something the young prince in your fairy tale asked from the wizard. Your young prince just wanted to change his *own* world, not mine." He turned away, and I watched his shoulders heave twice before he turned again to face me.

"Are you all right?" I asked.

He forced a smile. "Sorry. Sometimes I get carried away. Latin blood, y'know?"

"I guess I do *now*."

Without another word, Angel took my hand and led us out of the trees. Soon we were walking down a path back to Fifth Avenue.

"Hopefully this won't seem too forward," I said, offering him a shy smile. "But would you like to get together again? For dinner, or something?"

"I think I'd like that, Brett. Maybe dinner and a movie. You can't go wrong by taking me to anything with Michelle Pfeiffer or Reese Witherspoon in it."

"Is that why you like me?" I asked. "Because I'm a blond?" He laughed. "Yeah. That would be nice. I'll call you."

"Don't just *say* you'll call," he said, wagging his finger at me. "I know men, and if we don't set it up right now, you'll just end up forgetting or changing your mind, and it will never happen. And then

I'll get pissed off, 'cause I'll think you've blown me off because I wouldn't put out for you this afternoon."

I arched an eyebrow. "Latin blood again?"

He laughed. "Busted."

"You seem to have thought everything through, and too far in advance, at that." I smiled, hoping to encourage his self-deprecating mood. "But I'm not like that."

"Maybe not. But this way I'll be sure. So what night would you like to go out?"

"I don't know . . . Thursday?"

"Not this Thursday. I have an exam on Friday. But next Thursday night works for me. I don't have to work, and I don't have any early classes on Friday."

"Good. How about meeting at Bar 51 for a drink around seven-thirty? There are a lot of restaurants over there by Ninth Avenue, and we could just walk around until we see something we like."

"We could do that," he said, sounding not quite convinced. "Or maybe . . . Do you like Indian food?"

"Sure. What do you have in mind?"

"Indian food in the East Village. India Row. East Sixth Street. Very good, and exceptionally cheap. They practically give it away."

I nodded in agreement. "Sounds like a plan. Very good and exceptionally cheap both have my wholehearted endorsement."

"Good and cheap. You sure you're the same guy who hangs out at the Penthouse?"

"Maybe that's my evil twin. Asshole Revere."

We laughed, and continued up the path until we exited the park and crossed Fifth Avenue, entering a leafy side street as we walked toward Madison Avenue.

"So you're going to call, right?"

I looked at him. Okay, yes, he was a bit hot-wired. But he was young and cute and obviously intelligent and I *loved* that accent and . . . I couldn't quite figure out why he was so insecure about *me*.

"Of course I'll call," I said, pulling him into me and kissing his forehead. "You're a great guy, Angel, and I'm honored you'd want to go out with me."

To that he said "Bullshit," but his smile was so broad that I knew I had said exactly what he wanted to hear.

More important, it was exactly what I wanted to say. To confirm that, I moved to kiss him again, and this time our lips met.

After Angel caught the uptown bus to East Harlem, I took a slow stroll south along Madison Avenue, not quite ready to return to my dismal apartment in Astoria. Not quite ready to return to real life, either.

But Madison Avenue was the last place I should have been, given my state of mind. Everywhere I looked there was another example of wealth and conspicuous consumption, and I felt those dual tugs of envy and hopelessness with every upscale boutique I passed. On the rare instances when I stopped to window-shop, I realized that any given item on display would most likely cost me far more than the balance remaining on the ill-gotten credit card.

When I wasn't feeling sorry for myself—which wasn't very often—I was weighing the Jamie/Angel dilemma.

If I wasn't in love with Jamie, I was damn close. Not only did I find him attractive, but it was increasingly apparent that we were cut out of the same cloth and through that had a common bond. Beyond that, Jamie was connected to the kind of people I wanted so desperately to meet and moved comfortably in their world.

On the other hand, Jamie was a player. No doubt about that. I was fully aware that he had manipulated me on more than a few occasions. He also had an obvious propensity for self-destruction, as evidenced by those photographs on Nicholas Golodnya's hard drive. And on top of all that, there was the simple fact that he gave me such mixed signals that I never knew where I stood with him. Was he in love? Did he despise me? Was he my brother? My accomplice? I never knew, moment to moment, what he thought of me.

But *damn*, there was something about him—something I could never quite put my finger on—that I craved. In my head, I could play out Brett-and-Jamie scenarios forever: the bad boy and his devoted, indulgent lover, that good-looking couple blithely gliding through New York society. Although after he had stormed out of the Penthouse on the previous night, enraged at me, all those scenarios might have been irrelevant.

My feelings about Angel were far simpler. I could almost see us as a couple, but . . . maybe not. Angel was cute, sweet, smart, and as sincere as Jamie was cagey, but every time I tried to look into a future with him I saw a grim life of tiny apartments in unsafe neighborhoods, growing prematurely old while we carefully watched every nickel. I saw the hard-working, dead-end lives of his parents.

And then there was his *own* mercurial personality. Did I really need that in my life?

That was the unbalanced balance sheet of my life. Glibness, glamour, and excitement with the Bad Boy, or earnest poverty and dish-throwing with the Good Boy. And that was supposing that I had any say in the matter, and that either one of them would ultimately want *me.*

I passed the door of an exclusive retailer as a mother dragged her shrieking daughter to the sidewalk. Both of them were probably wearing my previous year's income on their backs.

The child's shrill cry pierced the air. "I *wanted* it!"

"Honey," said the mother, or maybe—given the fact that I was on the Upper East Side—she was the nanny, "You can't always get what you want."

I muttered an inaudible amen to that.

I had walked to the lower East Sixties, still mulling over the Jamie/Angel question, when I heard a familiar voice call my name. Looking up, I saw Michael DeVries and John Jacob Venezuela sitting at the sidewalk café of a very upscale restaurant.

"Hey, guys," I said. I approached their table warily, worrying about J.J. Venezuela's reaction to my failed seduction, but he showed no sign of holding it against me. Or maybe the memory disappeared with his hangover.

"Shopping?" asked Michael.

I patted my pockets. "*Window*-shopping."

Venezuela waved his martini glass at me. "Please come join us."

"Uh . . ." I patted again. "*Window*-shopping. Get it?"

"Got it. This one's on me." He slid a chair out for me. "Michael and I don't discriminate based on temporary poverty, do we?"

"If we did, we wouldn't know half the Europeans we do," said Michael with a laugh.

"And anyway," said Venezuela, "it looks like you got caught in the rain and . . . how does that old line go? Ah, yes . . . we've got to get you out of those wet clothes and into a dry martini!" He began laughing uncontrollably, and it occurred to me this wasn't their first round of drinks.

"We just missed getting caught in the rain ourselves," said Michael. "J.J. saw it cloud up, so we decided to duck in here."

Venezuela added, "The fates were smiling on us to give us a sudden summer shower at the exact moment we were passing our favorite restaurant. We lead charmed lives, Michael."

"Do you mind sharing some of that charm?" I asked.

Venezuela patted my hand. "I see good things happening to you, Brett. As I told you last night, you have a very natural feel to you. Solid. Trustworthy. You're going to be quite successful in this city."

Damn. He remembered . . . although he still didn't seem to be holding it against me.

"Sometimes," I said dryly, "I'm afraid of the price of success in this city."

They laughed—at least *some* people could find humor in my predicament, even if it took them a few martinis—and Venezuela waved over a waiter and ordered for me.

"So who's going to Philip Whitehead's birthday party Thursday night?" he asked, after placing the order. "I'll be seeing him later . . . if I'm able to pry myself away from the bar, that is. Bitsy McCall is hosting one of her fancy little social thingies in East Hampton tonight that I have to cover for my column, and I'm sure that Philip will be there. It's as if he and Bitsy were joined at the hip, those two."

"I'll be there," said Michael.

"Not me," I said. "Especially since I don't know Philip Whitehead."

"You know him," said Michael.

"No."

"You'd know him if you saw him," Michael insisted, adding, "He's always at the Penthouse. Anyway, you shouldn't let not knowing him stop you from going to his party. Philip will love you. He's a cute, cute man."

I looked to John Jacob Venezuela for confirmation, but he simply shrugged.

"I don't know if I'd call him 'cute,' " he said. "But he's certainly successful, and, well . . . *inoffensive*."

"Sounds fun," I said noncommittally. Actually, it sounded as if Philip Whitehead was being damned with faint praise, but I didn't want to get into that with them.

Michael continued to sing the praises of the party. "Philip is the sort of person you should get to know, Brett. And this will be his sixtieth birthday, so you just know that *everyone* on the A-list will be there."

"So I'd be . . . what? The mascot?"

"You're too hard on yourself," said Venezuela. "You fit in just fine, Brett, even if you don't feel like you do. It just takes time to get comfortable. Very few of us were birthed in a Tiffany box, you know."

"And Jamie's going," added Michael. "If he's going, you certainly shouldn't feel out of place."

I didn't exactly know how to tell Michael that Jamie was most likely not speaking to me. Fortunately, J.J. Venezuela filled that void.

"Jamie Brock," he muttered under his breath as the waiter delivered my martini. I took a sip to keep it from flowing over the rim of the glass. "Do you know what he did?"

"What now?" asked Michael, suppressing a sigh.

"He got Jeffrey Ryan to kill my blind item in *Haute Manhattan.* The one about those pictures Nico has on his computer. God knows what Jamie did for Jeffrey. I wonder if a blow job was enough."

"Now, J.J. . . ." Michael began, but Venezuela stopped him.

"You don't think Jeffrey would accept favors to spike a story? Think again. It would hardly be the first time. So much for his journalistic integrity. And *I* have to suffer . . ."

Fueled by a few tastes of the martini, I tried to make light of the situation. "Journalism? No offense, but you're not a journalist. You're a *gossip* columnist."

His response was frosty. "Liz Smith is a gossip columnist. Lloyd Grove is a gossip columnist. Gawker-dot-com is a gossip column, but I . . . *I* am a *social chronicler.*"

Michael put a hand on his forearm to silence him and said, "Now, boys, let's not get into all this silliness. Brett, I'm going to insist that you go to Philip Whitehead's party."

Even though he was still slightly put off by my comment, Venezuela nodded his agreement.

"Okay," I said. "I'll go. Can I bring a date?"

"Yes," said Michael. "Jamie can be your date."

"Um . . . can I bring a date who likes me?"

"Jamie likes you."

Venezuela hiked an eyebrow and pushed into the conversation. "*Who* do you want to bring to the party, Brett?"

I hesitated for a moment, but finally decided to bare all.

"Do you know Angel?"

They shrugged.

"Angel, from the Penthouse."

They shrugged again.

"Angel Maldonado."

Again, there were no signs of recognition.

"Angel the waiter."

Michael almost fell off his chair. To his credit, Venezuela merely reared back in shock.

"*The waiter?!*" gasped Michael. "You . . . you . . . *No,* you cannot bring a waiter! What are you thinking?"

A smile came over Venezuela's face, and he said, "Now *this* is delicious. Brett, if you were in the least bit prominent, I'd run with this item *so* fast!"

"Don't encourage him, J.J.," said Michael. "This foolishness had better get no further than this table. Brett, you cannot bring a waiter to Philip Whitehead's birthday party. I mean, that's . . . that's . . . that's just a ridiculous idea. The help does not get to dine at the master's table, Brett. The help eats in the kitchen."

"Can we *not* call Angel, 'the help'? I like him, and he likes me, and . . ."

". . . And you're going to end up in a rat-trap apartment in Washington Heights listening to malnourished little brown babies wailing all night long if you keep this up." Michael paused and shook his head, not even trying to mute his disgust. For my part, I was shocked that he had captured my own thoughts—and doubts—about a future with Angel with such accuracy, although, of course, I'd never admit that. "I hope that's not what you want for your future, Brett. That's not what *I* want for your future."

I sank back in my chair and thought carefully about what I wanted to say before continuing. But I *did* continue.

"It's *not* what I want for my future," I said. "But no one gave you a vote in this. I think I can take care of myself."

"Oh, you can?" He took advantage of Venezuela's momentary distraction by a passing Lycra-clad bicyclist to lean close to me and hiss, "We've both seen how that's been going, haven't we? Astoria . . .

pilfered credit cards . . . a useless crush on Jamie. . . . Now, are you quite sure you can take care of yourself? Or do you think maybe I have something to offer?" He stopped when J.J. Venezuela shifted his attention back to us.

"I love bicycle weather," said the social chronicler, with a sigh. "Brett, I'd bet your waiter would look good in a pair of bicycle shorts."

I forced the thinnest of smiles onto my lips. "I'm sure he would. But this is more than a physical attraction."

"Of course it is," said Venezuela. "And, as you know, I'd be the last person to stand in the way of true love. But I'd rethink the idea of bringing the waiter to Philip's party. You'd be better off going stag."

Clearly, further protest would be fruitless, so I sat sullenly and sipped my martini.

"As I said before," said Michael finally, "Jamie should be your date. You two go well together."

Venezuela leaned across the table. "And maybe you can keep him from stealing the silver."

"Now, J.J.," muttered Michael.

"Can we talk about something else?" I asked.

"Are you going to Philip's party with Jamie?" A coldness fell across Michael's eyes, and he quietly added, "Or is it Seiko for the rest of your life?"

I sighed. "I guess I am. You've already made up my mind."

"Okay, then. We can talk about something else."

"In that case . . ." J.J. Venezuela arched an eyebrow. "I've got some grade-A, high-quality gossip." He made a quick check for eavesdroppers, then continued. "Tamara Woodlawn is having an affair."

"No!" gasped Michael.

But yes, she was, and John Jacob Venezuela was off and running, gossip dripping off his tongue.

I didn't know these people. I didn't know Tamara Woodlawn, her art dealer husband, or the Argentine jockey she was seeing on the side. Weeks later, when I read about the scandal in a blind item in Venezuela's column in *Haute Manhattan*, I would barely remember hearing about it at this table.

But it was also becoming increasingly apparent that I didn't know *these* people, either. Michael DeVries and John Jacob Venezuela and all of their kind were every bit as foreign and indecipherable to me as a blind item about people I had never heard of.

And the more time that I spent in their company, the less I knew them.

So now I had two dates for Thursday night. One from each side of the unbalanced balance sheet.

There was the uber-A-list event at the home of Philip Whitehead, whom I didn't even know. But everyone who was everyone would be there, and I'd be with Jamie Brock, and I'd have one more golden opportunity to make Operation Hamptons work.

But I also had a date with Angel for cheap Indian food in the East Village, followed by a movie starring Reese or Michelle or another random blonde. It was a date that I had not only pledged not to break, but was actually looking forward to.

Haute cuisine versus cheap Indian food.

A-list snobs on Sutton Place versus the great unwashed—often, literally—of the East Village.

Upscale puffery versus downscale sincerity.

Jamie Brock versus Angel Maldonado.

The possible success of Operation Hamptons versus . . . the certain defeat of Operation Hamptons.

Shit.

I looked at the phone positioned on the end table. It was such a harmless instrument, and yet, knowing that in the upcoming minutes I was going to use it to confirm a decision I had not yet made, I couldn't think of it as anything approaching harmless. It was a bad, bad invention, and I said a silent prayer that the lines would be down when I picked up the receiver.

They weren't.

I dialed Angel's number, and soon his voice was on the line.

"Hey, baby," I said, trying to add a strained and weary tone to my voice. "I hate to do this, but I'm going to have to cancel our dinner plans for next Thursday."

He was silent for a moment, then, with obvious disappointment, said, "I knew this would happen."

"No," I protested. "It's not like that. I forgot I had another . . . thing." When there was no response, I added, "Trust me on this,

Angel. I just have a minor scheduling conflict. I . . . uh . . . I totally forgot that I have an audition."

"At night?"

"I'm afraid so. And it could go on for quite some time. I mean, you know there's nothing I'd rather do than have dinner with you, but we'll have to do it another night."

He still sounded wary. "I don't know when I'll have another night off. Thursday was supposed to be the one . . ."

"I know, I know," I said, feeling twice as much an asshole for wasting his one free night. "Go down to the Village or Chelsea or something. Go dancing. Have fun." I thought for a second, then added, "But don't see Michelle Pfeiffer or Reese Witherspoon without me, okay?"

He laughed. "As long as you remembered my girls, I promise."

I quickly got off the phone—feeling incredibly guilty and dirty and nasty—and nervously called Jamie, not knowing what to expect from him. He didn't answer, so I left a message and jumped in the shower. I was still wrapped in a towel when he called back.

"Hey, baby," he said. "Listen, before we go any further, I want to apologize about the other night."

Well *that* was a relief.

"No problem," I said. "I know that must have come as a surprise."

"It did. But I . . . *talked* to Jeffrey Ryan, and everything has been taken care of."

"Talked" as a euphemism? I tried not to think about it.

"So you're going to Philip's party," he continued. "Great. Do you want to go together?"

"Yes! Sure!" Because if we arrived at Philip Whitehead's party together, some people would assume that we were a couple, and when they reacted positively to that, Jamie couldn't help but start thinking about it, and then he'd come to the realization that we *should* be a couple, and then . . .

I slowed myself down, realizing that my mind was racing well ahead of reality. And when I did, that guilty, nasty, dirty feeling returned. I hadn't even had a real date with Angel yet, so why was I feeling so bad about this?

And why did I feel even worse when Jamie made some lame excuse to get off the phone, with a vague promise to call in a few days to firm up the details of our non-date.

I hung up and settled into my couch, trying to sort out my feelings.

It would all be so easy, I thought, if Jamie felt the same way about me as I felt about him. Or if Angel felt the same way about me as I did about *him*. Or if Jamie and Angel could simply switch personalities. Or if I could get past Operation Hamptons, humble myself by auditioning again for *Andy*, and openly date a man who was socially unacceptable by the standards of the Penthouse.

But, no . . . I had spent too much time and money on Operation Hamptons to turn back. And I was down to my last $4,000.

In the end, Michael was right. If I wanted to leave Astoria and Seiko watches behind, I was going to have to stick with the plan, and make decisions with my head, rather than my heart.

And for that moment of clarity, I hated Michael DeVries.

Brett Revere's Theory of Life, Part Fourteen:
Happy Meals Aren't Always Happy, and Rain Isn't Always Sad

Over the next few days, I left several messages for Jamie, but didn't hear back until the day of Philip Whitehead's sixtieth birthday bash. In the meantime, I made a point of avoiding the Penthouse . . . or, more to the point, avoiding Angel. I was certain that if he saw me in advance of the party, he'd see my guilt. Also, I hadn't spent nearly enough time polishing my "audition" excuse.

But early in the afternoon on the day of the party, Jamie Brock dialed his way back into my life.

"Hey, stranger," he said, when I answered the phone.

"Me? Uh . . . I seem to remember leaving a few messages for you."

"I got them, but I've been busy." And that was going to be it for his accountability. "Anyway, still on for the party tonight?"

"Yup. Are we still going together?"

"You know it, baby."

I had forgotten how much I loved to hear him call me "baby," and my mind drifted to those lazy mornings when we'd wake up in each other's . . .

I stopped myself, angry that I had again let my heart start trying to make decisions. With great determination, I forced my head to take over.

"Do you have the address?" I asked.

"I've got it. I've been to his place."

"When do you want to meet?"

"Meet me at five o'clock."

"Five? But the party doesn't start until seven."

"We need to bring a gift, baby." *Baby* . . ."I mean, we'd have to have something in hand when we show up even if it wasn't Philip's birthday, but since it's his sixtieth, there's an extra obligation."

"I suppose so. But . . . I don't even know the guy. Wine?"

"No. Better than that. Wine is . . . Hell, we might as well just stop by the Korean deli at the corner and pick up a $5 bouquet." I managed not to confess that the thought had occurred to me. "He collects Lalique crystal, so let's do this. Meet me in front of the Lalique boutique on Madison at five, and we'll take it from there."

"Um . . . isn't Lalique a bit pricey?"

"Brett!" Jamie started laughing, and it was *at* me, not *with* me. "This may be the biggest A-list party in Manhattan all summer. We'd be laughingstocks if we showed up with . . . with . . . Hummel, or something. It doesn't do to just *look* the part, Brett. Remember: you've got to *act* the part, too."

And that's how I found myself at 5:00 P.M. on a sultry Thursday in early July, pacing in front of the Lalique boutique waiting for Jamie, while a security guard kept a wary eye on me from the air-conditioned comfort inside.

Jamie arrived fifteen minutes late, greeting me with a quick kiss. "Damn, it's hot," he said. "Let's get inside."

"*Thank* you."

Once through the doors, the wide array of crystal left me completely unable to make a decision. Fortunately, Jamie had an eye for the stuff, and not only knew exactly what he wanted, but where it was.

"That," he said, directing a clerk to a reclining nude female in crystal.

Minutes later we were at the register, as the clerk wrapped the box out of our sight. That's when Jamie whispered in my ear.

"Give her the credit card."

"What?"

"You have it, don't you?"

"No," I said. "I've got a little cash, and that's it."

His face went red. "You *didn't* bring the card? You *know* I don't have any money right now, and I won't have any until I get paid by David Carlyle."

I shook my head, incredulous, but managed not to tell him that I knew all about that check. "I don't even know Philip Whitehead. Why do *I* have to spend $600 on a gift for him?"

"You've got to go get the credit card," he said insistently.

"It's in Astoria."

"Then you'd better move quickly. Take a cab."

"I don't have money for a cab." I leaned against the counter and took a few deep breaths. "Maybe if we just tell Philip that we'll bring his gift next week . . . you know, like a wedding gift, or something."

He shook his head. "No good. You've got to go home and bring back that credit card."

"I can't . . ."

"Brett," he said, and his voice grew softer as he brushed his body against mine. "We have plenty of time before the party, and the N train stops just around the corner. If you leave now, you can be back in twenty minutes."

"I doubt that . . ."

"A half-hour, then. Please, baby? We really need to do this if we're going to have any social standing. If we show up empty-handed, your Operation Hamptons thing is over. It won't look good for me, either, but I've known these people for a while, and they'll just figure I'm being scatter-brained again. I'm thinking of *you*, though. This gift could be just the thing to cement you into the A-list."

"Shit," I muttered. I didn't want to go home, and I certainly didn't want to buy a $600 crystal statuette for someone I wasn't sure I had ever seen before, but I had taken Operation Hamptons too far to stop now.

"It's the right thing to do, baby," said Jamie, gently brushing the back of my neck. "You're so close to being part of the crowd."

With a resigned sigh, I said, "Okay. Wait for me. I'll be back as soon as I can."

He smiled. "It's the right decision, Brett. This is absolutely the right decision."

I took a few steps away before he grabbed my elbow.

"One more thing," he said. "Are you carrying any cash?"

"A little bit."

"Can I borrow $20? Just to grab a drink while I'm waiting for you to get back."

I wanted to say no, but now that I was about to put another major purchase on the Magic Credit Card, I couldn't see the point anymore. I peeled two tens off the fold of bills in my pocket, leaving me with a five and a single. And as I did, I thought, *"This Philip Whitehead guy had better like me a whole damn lot."*

* * *

The round trip didn't take twenty minutes, and it didn't take a half-hour, and neither of those facts surprised me. It was almost an hour before I walked back into Lalique, slightly rumpled and overheated from the stifling subway but looking nowhere near as bad as the day Boomer stole my clothes and my temp agency recommended drug and alcohol counseling.

In that, I saw progress. Yes, things were getting better.

Jamie was waiting for me when I walked through the door and into the heaven that is an air-conditioned room on a steamy July day in Manhattan.

"Where have you been?" he snapped, when he saw me.

"Astoria. Remember?"

"You were gone forever. I ran out of money."

I had a sarcastic reply on the tip of my tongue, but left it unsaid. I was just happy to have my commute behind me, and this purchase mere moments from completion.

I handed over Quentin's card, the clerk completed the transaction, and . . . that was that. I was now the proud, if temporary, owner of a $600 crystal statuette of a reclining nude woman. Yay, me.

Jamie also calmed down after we left the store, and a light breeze made a leisurely walk down Madison Avenue, then east on East Fifty-seventh Street, not just tolerable, but pleasant.

"Thanks for doing this," he said, as we weaved expertly through the crowded sidewalks.

"Don't thank me. Thank Quentin."

"Thanks, Quentin," he called out to a passing bus. The passengers largely ignored him, although one woman seemed to think he was addressing her and pressed her ear to the window. He took a step away from the curb to avoid the bus exhaust and laughed.

"What's so funny?" I asked.

"I'll bet you never dreamed it was so hard to be a Trust Fund Boy, did you?"

I had to join in his laughter. "It's probably not so hard if you're a real Trust Fund Boy. Being a faux Trust Fund Boy, though, well . . . *that* is tough."

He put an arm around my shoulder and we walked like that for half a block.

"It's coming soon enough," he said. "We're almost there. I can sense it."

"I can't. But I'll defer to your considerable experience. You are, after all, the Artful Dodger."

"I've done a pretty good job of dodging so far, Master Twist."

"Okay, stop making me laugh. I don't want to drop the crystal."

We arrived at Philip Whitehead's Sutton Place townhouse just after 7:00 P.M. and were greeted by a doorman in a starched uniform who checked our names then ushered us into an ornate elevator, turning a key and pushing the button for the fifth floor before leaving us alone.

"Sweet," muttered Jamie. I was surprised to see him acknowledge the opulence; I was beginning to think that Jamie had trained himself never to be impressed by anything.

When we reached the fifth floor, the elevator doors opened directly into the apartment, where the party was already in full force. As the doors opened, Jamie swiftly took the gift from my hands.

"Philip!" he cried, and an appropriately white-headed man standing with his back to the elevator swiveled to face us.

"Hello, love," he said, giving Jamie the lightest peck on the cheek. When I saw Philip Whitehead's face, I vaguely recognized him as one of the Penthouse regulars, always present and always in the background.

Jamie placed the Lalique bag in the older man's hands and said, "Happy Birthday. I hope you don't mind, but I brought you a little something."

I cleared my throat.

"It's from me and Brett," he continued, placing one hand on my shoulder without taking his attention away from the birthday boy. "You remember Brett, don't you?"

"Of course," he said, nodding at me. "I see you quite often at the Penthouse."

"That would be me," I said, adding a little laugh and extending my hand to him. "Happy Birthday. Thank you for inviting us."

He clasped my hand. "And thank you for joining me to celebrate six long decades on this planet." Philip stole a glance at the gift, then said, "Thank you for the gift, Jamie. Let me put it somewhere where one of these queens won't walk off with it. And while I'm doing that, please get a drink. I have full bars set up in the library and on the terrace."

"Thanks," we said, as he departed.

Jamie looked at me. "Well . . . let's find those bars."

"He does know that the present is from *both* of us, right?"

"I'm sure he does," said Jamie, craning his neck to look for a concentration of people, which would indicate the presence of a bar.

"Good. Because, not for nothing, but *I* spent a lot of money that I don't have at Lalique . . ."

"Don't worry about it, Brett." He must have spotted his target, because he set off briskly for a far corner of the apartment. "And anyway, I'm going to pay you for my half the minute I get that check from David Carlyle."

Again, I managed to suppress my urge to comment.

We found the bar and, not surprisingly, Michael DeVries, who pulled me aside as Jamie went to order drinks.

"I see you came together," Michael said, nodding his approval.

"Of course," I replied crisply. "That's what proper gentlemen do, isn't it?"

He furrowed his brow. "Now, Brett, don't be like that. My only concern is you, and I wanted to keep you from making a mistake." He motioned at the crowd. "These people have barely met you. They don't know you. The impression you want to give them is that you are one of their crowd. And dating a Puerto Rican boy they would recognize as part of the help at the Penthouse—let alone bringing him to Philip Whitehead's birthday party—would mark you forever as someone who is *not* part of their crowd."

"Right. Because I'm a trust fund boy."

"That's the story, Brett. Stick to the story."

Jamie was suddenly pushing a Scotch and water into my hands, and insisting we see the terrace, so we ended the conversation on that note.

"You boys behave," said Michael, as we walked away.

We wandered through the sprawling apartment until we spotted the terrace. As we passed through several large rooms—any one of which, excluding furnishings, I could only dream to afford some day—I saw a number of familiar faces: John Jacob Venezuela, who smiled when he saw me, a smile that quickly vanished when he spotted Jamie at my side . . . Jeffrey Ryan, already drunk and animatedly discussing something no doubt Hamptons-related with a cluster of three younger men, all of them in matching blue blazers . . . a man I was sure was a well-known television personality, but who I had never seen at the Penthouse, and whose presence at the party didn't necessarily mean he was gay, but, well . . . everyone else seemed to be . . .

And, of course, there were a lot of familiar faces that, like Philip Whitehead himself until a few minutes earlier, I recognized without having a name to put with them.

We stepped out onto the terrace, which was remarkably uncrowded, given the pleasant evening and the presence of a bar. Only a quartet of smokers kept the bartender engaged.

"Oh, now *this* is nice," I said, surveying Philip Whitehead's view. The terrace faced the East River, offering up a dynamic view of the Queensboro Bridge. "I think I could find it in me to have breakfast out here every morning."

"When we make our first billion . . ."

I paused for a moment over Jamie's comment, but had to ask. "*We*?"

He smiled. "There's too much space here for one person. You'll need a roommate."

"Right," I said, turning to watch a ship make its lazy way down the river toward New York Harbor.

We stood in silence for several minutes, leaning against the wrought iron railing and lost in the view. The quiet was broken by a new arrival to the terrace.

"Hey, stranger," said Rick Atkins, as he bumped my hip. "Long time, no see."

"Rick!" I gave him an affectionate hug and turned to his lover, who stood behind him. "And Bill! How are you guys?"

"Never better," said Rick. "Believe it or not, this *Andy* thing isn't quite the debacle we expected."

"They're probably taking it Off-Broadway," added Bill.

"So I hear."

"That's right," said Rick. "My career might finally take off after all these years."

"Congratulations." I said, trying not to seem envious. "I have mixed emotions. I'm happy for all of you, but . . . it's *Andy*."

They laughed, and Rick said, "No arguments from me, Brett. But a job is a job. Walter's making me audition again if it goes Off-Broadway, but I've got an Equity card, so he tells me that there should be no reason I won't stay on as Sugar Daddy Warbucks. And with a lead role in an Off-Broadway show, well . . . I don't have to tell you how much visibility there could be."

"*And* a steady paycheck," added Bill.

"Damn, that's right. I'm not going to be a kept boy anymore!"

I watched their sincere, good-natured laughter and realized that they had what I wanted. They had money, they had each other's company, and, most important, they were in love. That's when my heart forced me to turn to Jamie, a broad smile on my face, and . . .

But he had disappeared from the terrace during the brief conversation. I caught a glimpse of him inside the apartment, and then even *that* vanished.

That was fitting, I supposed. My romantic thoughts dissipated, I returned my attention to Rick and Bill and *Andy*.

"Get this," I said. "I ran into Joey Takashimi and Miss Iris."

Rick laughed. "And are you and Joey playing better with each other these days?"

I waved his comment away. "I don't really care. A better question is, how are *you* able to stand him?"

"I got used to him," he said. "And he got used to me. Deep down . . ."

"Please don't tell me he's a decent guy!"

Rick smiled. "No, he's absolutely *not* a decent guy. He's as big of a flaming drama queen as he was the first day we met him. But he knows it. After people started standing up to him, 'cause there was only so much Joey we could take, his veneer started to crack, and now, well . . . let's just say that the Joey Show is almost an inside joke. And Joey is in on that joke."

"Well, good for you," I said, lightly clinking my glass against his.

"And it helps that the show is a hit," he added. "When audiences are laughing *with* you, instead of *at* you, it's a heady feeling."

I shook my head skeptically. "The thing that surprises me is that you didn't get busted for copyright infringement."

"Well . . . almost. The *Annie* people came around . . . sent some lawyer letters, et cetera, et cetera. I'm not really privy to all the details, but I heard that they were going to go after the show, until Walter agreed to do a bit of rewriting. He dropped some songs, wrote a few new ones, tweaked this, changed that . . . relied more on things in the public domain . . . It's still basically the same show, but not the same script that first drove us to suicidal despair. *And,*" he added, "even without an Off-Broadway stage, the cast is starting to make some real money. After each show, they pass a tip jar around, and we divide it up. Last weekend I brought home over a hundred dollars."

Once again, I realized that my timing was the opposite of impeccable. Ah, well . . . I was here, on a rich gay man's Sutton Place terrace, looking over a beautiful evening on the East River, and everything was working out all right for the moment.

As Rick and I enjoyed our reacquaintance, Bill wandered away, leaving us alone. Until, that is, we were interrupted by the television personality, who pushed by us on his way for a cigarette. As he passed Rick, he paused.

"I know you," he said. "But from where?"

"I don't know . . ."

"I know! You were Sugar Daddy Warbucks in *Andy*, weren't you?"

Rick blushed. "You saw that?"

"Saw it and loved it. That was the funniest thing I've seen in ages. And you guys must have a great time putting it on." He took Rick's hand. "I'm . . ."

"I know who you are," said Rick. "My name is Rick Atkins. And this," he added, pointing Television Personality in my direction, "is Brett Revere."

Television Personality took my hand for the briefest of moments, then turned his attention back to Rick. I took that as my cue to slip away and catch up with Jamie, and left them chatting on the terrace.

In the few seconds it took for my eyes to readjust to the lighting inside the apartment, the guest of honor was on me.

"I'm *delighted* you joined us," said Philip Whitehead, taking me by the elbow and guiding me a few yards away from the nearest person. "For weeks, I've been asking people about you, but 'trust fund baby' seems like such an inadequate description. I was quite confident that there was more to you than that."

"Oh, yes, Philip," I thought. *"Much, much more, and much, much less . . . but none of it palatable to* this *crowd."*

But my words were quite different from my thoughts, of course.

"I'd like to think there's a lot more to me, Philip. But tell me what people are saying, so I can judge for myself."

"You," he said, his voice hushed, "are a man of mystery. You came from nowhere, yet you seem to be everywhere these days. Some people assume you've just arrived from out of town, but, to me, you seem like such a natural New Yorker I find that unlikely. Some people have guessed that you've just come out, but . . . no. You're too comfortable in gay surroundings."

I smiled. I sort of liked the idea that I was a "man of mystery" to the gang at the Penthouse.

"So what do *you* think?" I asked him.

I couldn't read the expression on his face. It was indulgent, but dark. Philip Whitehead had turned into a grandfather with an edge.

"I keep my thoughts to myself," he said. "I learn more that way."

I flashed an uncertain smile. "That seems like a wise course of action."

"Almost always." He glanced away for a moment, and when his gaze returned to me, the trace of darkness was gone. Grandpa was no longer feeling edgy. "I'm going to get a drink. Please enjoy the party—unlike some of these gentlemen, I only intend to turn sixty *once*—but make sure to see me before you leave."

"Definitely."

He left, and I only had a split second to wonder what *that* was all about before Michael was at my side.

"I see that Philip has taken a liking to you," he said. "That's a good thing."

"I guess . . ."

"You *are* making an impression with this crowd, Brett. Now aren't you glad you came?"

"Let me ask you something," I said, noticing that my glass was almost empty, a situation that would soon have to be rectified. "What exactly are people saying about me?"

"Paranoid?"

"Not really. But our host just told me that there has been a lot of speculation about where I came from and all that, and I was just wondering . . ."

"Don't wonder about things, Brett. Just keep playing your role."

When I didn't respond, he shrugged and said, "If you must know, everyone just assumes that you're living off a trust fund, and most people have guessed that the reason they're only meeting you now is because you've just come out of a long-term relationship. Satisfied?"

"I didn't realize I have an entire back-story."

"I might have had something to do with that . . ."

Michael vanished before his words sank in. He certainly knew that I wouldn't take them well, and, when I realized that Michael DeVries had been telling everyone I was a recently divorced rich boy, I can honestly say that he was right. But by then, he had wedged himself into a safe harbor between John Jacob Venezuela, Jeffrey Ryan, and David Carlyle, where he knew I could only confront him by blowing my cover and admitting I was a fraud. He assumed I would be unwilling to do that and, once again, he was right.

Instead, I walked back out on the terrace and ordered another drink. Rick was still talking to Television Personality—Bill was apparently similarly engaged somewhere inside the apartment—and now Jamie was outside, leaning against the railing.

"Enjoying the party?" he asked.

I shook my head. "Michael just basically confessed that he's been lying about me, and telling everyone I'm . . ."

"A trust fund boy. Yes, I know."

"And you didn't tell me?"

He took my hand. "Is this a surprise to you, Brett? You know that's what people think, and you want them to think that, so what's the harm?"

"I don't mind if people *think* that," I said. "But I don't want to bury myself under a pile of lies. I want to do it like *you* do it."

He rolled his eyes. "If it makes you feel any better, Michael is the only one spreading that story. If for some reason you feel trapped, you can always deny it and blame everything on Michael."

I thought about that, and it seemed reasonable.

"And," he continued, "you can do what I do, which is never to confirm anything or deny anything."

"I suppose . . ."

He shook his head again. "Honestly, Brett, I don't know why this is such a big deal for you. Where's the harm? So what if a bunch of elderly gay drunkards are under the misimpression that you're sitting on a trust fund? You're not exactly tricking them into investing in a pyramid scheme."

"I suppose . . ."

"Sometimes I think that your heart isn't in this. And I hate to say this, but if you want to use this network to get back on your feet, you're going to have to commit to this life."

"You're starting to sound like Michael."

He laughed. "God forbid! And please keep me away from his little old ladies! I swear, I'll scream the next time I have to suffer through another three-hour, $300 lunch and listen to a bunch of those biddies babble on and on about the golden age of Bergdorf's and how distraught they were when Mortimer's closed."

"I'm with you," I said, allowing myself a smile. Maybe Jamie was right, and the situation was nowhere near as bad as I was imagining. After all, what's the worst that would happen if I was exposed? Operation Hamptons would fail and I'd either end up working at a deli in Astoria or going back to Albany to sleep on the fold-out sofa in my parents' basement. It wasn't as if the lavender Mafia in this apartment would kill me.

Well . . . no, I had looked around, and Nicholas Golodnya was not in the room.

It was time for another drink, and, as I walked by Rick and Television Personality, I heard my former cast mate say, "And Brett was in *Andy*, too. But just for one day."

"Less than one day," I said, slowing as I passed them. "Less than one rehearsal, in fact." I tossed Rick a concerned look and said, "But we really don't need to talk about that."

To his credit, Rick picked up on my hint, and dropped it.

I ordered my drink, but Jamie had disappeared by the time I returned to our corner of the terrace, so I sipped for a few minutes in silence . . . a silence broken only when Television Personality appeared next to me.

"You don't seem like the actor type," he said.

"What happened to Rick?"

"He went to look for his lover." Television Personality took one step closer, and was beginning to intrude into my personal space. "Nice guy. Too bad he's married."

"Rick? Yeah, he *is* a good guy. Very sincere."

"He seems to think the world of you."

"Really? I mean, we're friendly, but not *that* friendly."

Television Personality flashed a dazzling smile, all teeth whiter than those found in nature. "And who are you *that* friendly with? That guy you were talking to?"

I knew he was referring to Jamie.

"Not really," I said, and my heart ached just a little. "We're just friends, basically."

"I don't know . . . The way you add little qualifiers make it sound as if there's something more complicated going on."

I shook my head. "Not really. My friendship with Jamie is no more complicated than it appears."

Television Personality edged even closer.

"I don't mean to be presumptuous," he said, "but I agree with your friend Rick. You seem like a nice guy and I think you're very interesting. And if there's nothing going on between . . ."

And that's when Jamie reappeared, darting out to the terrace and squeezing into my other side, which served the purpose of crushing me between the two men.

"Brett!" he said, pointedly ignoring Television Personality. "There you are!"

"Right where I've always been . . ."

He grabbed my arm and pulled me in the direction of the apartment. "There's someone I want you to meet."

I glanced at Television Personality, who now had an icy smile fixed on his face.

"Can it wait a minute? We were just talking . . ."

Jamie looked at Television Personality and said, "You won't mind, will you? This will only take a minute, and I really think Brett should meet this guy."

Television Personality looked at me for a signal, and when he got a blank look in return, said, "I'll see you later, Brett." With that, he turned and walked to the terrace bar.

I followed Jamie into the apartment, again allowing my eyes to adjust to the interior lighting before asking, "So who's this person you want me to meet?"

He scanned the room—no, he *pretended* to scan the room—and said, "I don't see him. But he'll be back."

"Does he have a name?"

"Brett, I was doing you a favor. Trust me: you don't want to go home with that guy."

Once again, I found myself indignant. "I think I'm old enough to decide these things for myself. You are not my mother, and you are not my boyfriend. And anyway, who said anything about going home with him?"

"He was moving in for the kill," said Jamie. "Couldn't you see that?"

"What does . . . ? How . . . ? Who the hell cares what *he* was doing? I have free will. I am thirty . . . thirty-*three* years old, and I can take care of myself."

"Calm down," he said, placing his palm on my chest in what I assumed was supposed to be a soothing gesture, but only fueled my anger.

"I'm not going to calm down." I said, although I at least had the presence of mind to mute my voice and keep veins from throbbing in my forehead, so as not to disturb the propriety of the room. "*You* made me buy an expensive gift, then ripped it out of my hands the minute we walked through the door. *You* . . ."

"I told you I'll pay my half when . . ."

"Yes, yes, I know. When you get the check from David Carlyle. Whatever. If that was it, I'd be fine. But now you're compounding things by . . . by . . . well, by being a cock-blocker."

"A cock-blocker?" He looked genuinely perplexed. "Me?"

"You. What else do you call that incident on the terrace?"

"You weren't seriously thinking of hooking up with that guy, were you?"

Now, I most certainly wasn't. Being in love—or close enough to it—with both Jamie and Angel was more than enough for me to handle. But that simple fact didn't stop my mouth.

"Maybe I was."

"You're kidding."

"I'm not kidding."

"But, Brett . . ." Jamie shook his head. "I don't know what to say. I thought . . . I thought that we were sort of on a date tonight."

Now it was my turn to be perplexed.

"You did?"

"I did."

Shit.

"Um . . ." My mind reeled for a moment, and when I grounded it, everything seemed all right again. I pointed to the terrace. "Okay, then. Let's get a drink."

Michael was in our path as we walked toward the terrace, but the revelation that I was on a date with Jamie made me forget that I was mad at him. For his part, Michael acted as if nothing had happened.

"Are you boys enjoying the party?" he asked, as we passed the spot where he was chatting with David Carlyle.

I stopped and said, "And what a swell party it is."

"You know your Cole Porter," said David. "Nice touch."

Michael leaned close and whispered, "Did you remember to bring Philip a present?"

"Of course," said Jamie. "Lalique. And what did you bring?"

"A bottle of wine."

I looked at Jamie accusingly, but he simply shrugged.

After a few hours, the party began to wind down. Guests trickled out—Television Personality, rebuffed by both Rick and I, was out the door at an early hour—until there were only a handful of people left in the apartment and the bars began closing.

"I can't tell you how much I appreciate that you helped me celebrate my birthday," said Philip Whitehead, cornering me in the living room. "You're a doll."

Hmm. I had never been called a "doll" before, but since I knew he meant it as a compliment, I said, "It was my pleasure, Philip. And you have a beautiful home."

"Thank you. I like it here." And who wouldn't?

Several yards away, Jamie signaled me that it was time to leave. I nodded my agreement, then returned my attention to our host.

"Well, I think it's getting close to my bedtime."

Something resembling a leer flickered across his face, but Philip Whitehead was a gentleman, so the leer quickly vanished. What did *not* vanish, however, was the conversation.

Ignoring my comment, he asked, "And what do you do for a living, Brett?"

I had my routine down by now. "I'm taking the summer off and relaxing. Maybe I'll pick something up after Labor Day."

He nodded. "The reason I asked," he said, "is because Michael DeVries indicated that you might be looking for a position."

So Michael was meddling again. My temper suddenly burned, although I tried my best not to let it show.

"Well . . ." I couldn't think of a comeback to that.

"Yes. I happened to be asking him if he knew of anyone who was in the job market, and he suggested that you might be interested. But if you're not looking . . ."

Wait . . . wait . . . have I mentioned lately how much I love Michael DeVries?

"I . . . *might* be available earlier. For the right position."

"I'm a partner at Cooper Bauer Malnut," he continued, fishing for a business card in his pocket. "Heard of it?"

I had. In fact, I had temped there for two weeks a year or so earlier. But, of course, it wouldn't do to confess that.

"It's a law firm on Park Avenue," he said, taking my non-answer for a lack of recognition. "If you'd like, we can set up an appointment."

I managed to suppress a smile, instead soberly saying, "I'll give you a call."

"Saturday would be best," he said. "I'm out of the office tomorrow, but I'm afraid I have to work on the weekend. Don't believe a word that they say; it's not always wonderful being a Park Avenue lawyer."

He finally found a business card, and we shook hands. Minutes later, after proper goodbyes and another promise to call, Jamie and I were walking to the elevator.

"What are you so happy about?" he asked.

"Me? What do you mean?"

"You've got this shit-eating grin plastered on your face, and you look like you're about to start dancing."

"I'll tell you downstairs."

While we waited for the elevator, Jamie asked, "Are you hungry?"

"Starving," I said. "But we spent all our money at Lalique, so . . ."

His mouth was practically in my ear as he whispered, "McDonald's."

"Are you kidding?"

"Shhh." The elevator doors opened in front of us, and two other departing guests were suddenly behind us.

In the descending elevator, I felt through my pockets. All that was there were a few bills—all small bills, I was certain—and some change.

"I've only got a few dollars on me," I said, my voice muted. "We'll have to split a Happy Meal or something."

The men in the elevator with us snickered. Jamie's face reddened, but he didn't say a word . . .

. . . until we were standing on the sidewalk outside Philip Whitehead's Sutton Place townhouse. Then he had a lot of words to say.

"What the fuck was that? How could you say something like that in front of those people?"

"Do you even know who they were?" I asked.

"No. And it doesn't matter. If they were at Philip's party, they were A-listers. And you had to let them know that we're broke . . . sharing a fucking Happy Meal at McDonald's! What the fuck, Brett! What the fuck!"

"Calm down," I said, for once feeling composed and serene in the face of one of his tirades. "It's not that bad, and yelling at me isn't going to change anything."

He shook his head, still simmering. "You still don't get it, do you?"

"What I don't get is why you're blowing this out of proportion. If it was a faux pas—and I'm not ready to concede that it was . . ."

"It was."

"Whatever. We'll both survive it."

He looked at me, a scowl still on his face. "What are you so happy about?"

"Am I grinning again?"

"Yes."

"Come on," I said, turning toward East Fifty-seventh Street. "I'll tell you on the walk to McDonald's."

And as we walked, I explained the source of my sheer joy. It was, of course, because my plan had worked. When Philip Whitehead made me that all-but-formal job offer, Operation Hamptons—my much-maligned effort to get ahead in the world, and do it on the fast track—had been proven a success. Once, the Alan Donovans of the world could scoff, but no more. In days, I would officially be an up-and-comer at the Park Avenue law firm Cooper Bauer Malnut. In days, I would have a respectable income. I would be on my way to an apartment in Manhattan. I would no longer wonder where I was going to get money for food. No more auditions. No more acting. No more poverty.

No more resentment and envy, either.

My happiness must have been contagious, because by the time we reached the McDonald's on Second Avenue, Jamie had sufficiently recovered from the Happy Meal faux pas to take my hand as we walked down the street.

We were back on our date.

And Operation Hamptons had worked.

And life was good.

And Brett Revere was a happy, happy man.

Our Happy Meal shared and disposed of, Jamie and I ended our date and went our separate ways. I was so happy about the turn of events that even the train ride back to Queens didn't depress me.

It occurred to me that I was actually surprised that Operation Hamptons had worked. Despite my optimism and what I hoped was flat-out pragmatism, or cynicism, or whatever you wanted to call it, there was nothing about the plan that should have worked. These people—the Penthouse crowd—had spent their lives in and around the upper crust. Decades had gone into cultivating and polishing their tastes, their friendships, their styles . . .

If I knew at the onset what I was getting into, I thought, with the benefit of hindsight, I never would have dared to pursue Operation Hamptons. When I had walked into the Penthouse weeks earlier, nothing but an unsuccessful actor and a soon-to-be-unemployed temp, there was no reason to believe that I would be invited into their world. And yet, in my naivety, I adopted their ways and mannerisms and, in an acting triumph far outstripping my modest career, I managed to fit in. If my real acting career had been anywhere near as successful, I would have been coming home to a house full of Oscars and Tonys, instead of . . . well, *Astoria*.

Fortunately, by the time I knew enough to see the folly of my plan, I was already beating the odds. There was something to be said for ignorance. Sometimes, it truly *was* bliss.

My telephone rang shortly after four o'clock in the morning. I knew that, whoever was calling, it couldn't possibly be good news, so I let the machine answer. After the fourth ring, I heard my distant voice informing the caller that I was unavailable to take the call, then another voice left a message as I drifted back to sleep.

The next morning, as I was having a third cup of coffee in an as-yet unsuccessful effort to clear the cobwebs from my brain, still awash in euphoria over the success of Operation Hamptons, I remembered the late night phone call. Warily, I tapped the answering machine's playback button.

"It's Angel." His voice was low and flat. "Some of your little friends were at the Penthouse last night, and they told me you were with them at a party earlier. A party, huh? Funny; I could have sworn you told me you had an audition." He paused, then added the kicker: "I expected better from you. I guess I was wrong." With that, he hung up.

Fuck. I sat back on the couch, angry with myself for not having foreseen that this would happen. Why had I been so confident that the Penthouse regulars—people who ordinarily looked right through Angel—wouldn't think to tell him I was at Philip Whitehead's party? Well, yes . . . there was the fact that the regulars *never* talked to Angel, and it was a logical assumption that they weren't going to start including him in their conversations. But conversations between them could easily be overheard by the wait staff. I just hadn't thought things through.

Another thought occurred to me: Michael DeVries. Michael, after all, was adamant that I not become friendly with Angel, which gave him the motive. As for the opportunity, well . . . if Michael wasn't at the Penthouse post-party, I would have been very surprised.

But it really didn't matter whether it had happened by accident or through Michael's machinations. The fact was that Angel knew I had cancelled our date to go to a party, and—worse yet—he knew I had lied to him.

Which meant that I was in deep trouble with him.

I sank back into the couch and tried to think of a way to win back his good graces, but nothing came to mind. I had lied, and I had made it clear that the A-listers were more important to me than he was, and there was no way I was going to be able to rewrite that history.

And deep down, I still wasn't certain *what*, exactly, Angel meant to me.

He was nice, sincere, honest . . . or so he appeared. And he seemed to legitimately like me, which was a plus. Given a choice between Angel and, say, Michael DeVries, there would be no contest. But my heart wasn't torn between Angel and Michael.

Because the previous night I had had a date with Jamie Brock.

I picked up the telephone and pecked out the number to Jamie's cell. He answered immediately.

"Hey, baby," he said, when he answered. "You're up early."

"I thought you might want to grab breakfast at McDonald's."

He laughed. "For breakfast, I prefer Burger King."

"Don't tempt me. Okay, the *real* reason I called is to see what you're up to today."

"No plans. I was thinking about jumping on the Jitney, but I don't know if I'm up to the possibility of running into Nico."

"Want to see a movie or something?"

"That sounds like a plan."

There I had it: another date with Jamie.

Or was it just a plan?

No matter. Plans had been treating me well that week.

I met Jamie outside the theater, and we spent the next two hours in air-conditioned comfort. I did feel vaguely as if I was cheating on Angel, but only because the movie starred Michelle Pfeiffer, not because I was on a date—or a *plan*—with Jamie.

When the movie ended and we walked outside a heavy rain was falling, cooling the late afternoon air.

"I wasn't expecting *this*," I said, as we stood beneath the marquee.

Jamie pointed at a bodega across the street. "Five-dollar umbrellas. Want to make a run for it?"

We waited out of the rain until traffic broke, then sprinted across the street. We were both drenched and laughing when we reached the store.

"One of us is going to have to start watching the Weather Channel before we go out again," he said, as we carefully maneuvered past baskets of fresh fruit and vegetables displayed under the store's canopy, narrowing the path through its front door.

"I don't know about that," I said. "It's sort of nice to get caught in the rain every now and then."

He smiled. "Yeah. Yeah . . . it is." Then, sliding his wallet out of his front pocket, he added, "But once was enough for this afternoon. So . . . two five-dollar umbrellas. And these are on me."

"You're buying?"

"I sort of owe you, don't I? As soon as that check from David Carlyle arrives . . ."

"Yeah, yeah, yeah. I know."

Jamie bought the umbrellas and soon we were walking side by side down the sidewalk, avoiding puddles as we strolled nowhere in particular.

"So what do you want to do now?" I asked.

"I don't know." He thought for a minute. "Want to catch a drink at the Penthouse?"

I shook my head, remembering Angel's voice on my answering machine. "Not the Penthouse. Somewhere else."

"Here." He stopped abruptly, and I took a half-dozen steps before I realized he was no longer by my side, but instead stood next to the door to a Mexican restaurant. Large signs posted by the door advertised a special on frozen margaritas.

"Margaritas," I said, as I doubled back. "I could do that."

Since it was before five o'clock on a Friday afternoon—when the rest of Manhattan was either working or on their way out of town for the weekend—we had our choice of tables. Jamie pointed to one on the far side of the restaurant, away from the handful of other customers, and the hostess seated us. No sooner had she left when a waiter appeared, and we both ordered the special, no salt.

"I like afternoons like this," he said, when we were alone again. "Lazy. No rushing around . . . nothing to do. Getting caught in the rain . . ."

"And then having a frozen margarita to unwind from all that nothing," I added, with a smile.

He smiled back. "Exactly." The smile flickered, then disappeared. "Do you ever wonder if it's all worth it?"

"What do you mean?"

"Life," he said. "No, not 'life,' but *this* life. All the keeping up with the Joneses at the Penthouse."

The waiter set our margaritas on the table, and I waited until he was gone to reply.

"It works, though, doesn't it? You get decorating jobs, and now it looks like I'm getting a job with Philip Whitehead." I leaned back in my chair and added, "Maybe it shouldn't have to work that way, but it does."

"I guess . . . It's just that sometimes I think I'd be a lot happier if I was poor."

"That's the romanticized notion of someone who isn't poor. If you were poor, you wouldn't feel that way." I paused. "Trust me on that."

"You're not poor," he noted. "And I'm not rich. We're just . . . in-between."

"Like most people."

"Exactly."

The conversation trailed off and we sipped through straws at our margaritas in silence for a while, punctuated only occasionally by pointless observations about the handful of other people in the restaurant. But it didn't take long for the bite of the tequila to loosen our tongues.

"Tell me about Philip Whitehead," I said.

"What about him? He's okay. A bit of a lecher, but quiet."

"A lecher?"

"Yeah, but I don't think you have anything to worry about. Philip is the type of man who might put his hand somewhere it doesn't belong after a few too many cocktails, but he's very protective of his reputation. If you end up working for him, I'm sure you'll have nothing to worry about."

"That's good to hear." Jamie's words were both reassuring and troubling. I made a mental note to be on the lookout for inappropriate behavior.

Jamie reached across the table and patted my hand. It was a peculiar gesture coming from him, comforting but almost maternal.

"It'll be all right, Brett," he said. "You've made it."

Delicately, I pulled my hand out from under his, and we both returned to our drinks. When they were gone, he ordered another round.

"You made it," he said again, a trace of wistfulness in his voice. "As for me, though, well . . . I'm thinking of giving up the game."

"Giving up the game?" I looked at him expectantly, waiting for a self-mocking smile to break across his face. But none came. "What do you mean, you're thinking of giving up the game? You're all about the game."

He looked to the floor. "Is that what you think of me?"

"Jamie, you know exactly what I think of you. You mean . . . *your friendship* means a lot to me. But I can't imagine you just giving up, just . . . just working for a living, serving people margaritas forty hours a week."

When he looked back at me, I wondered for the slightest moment if his eyes were damp, before deciding that the restaurant lighting was creating an illusion.

"This isn't what I'm all about," he said. "I work . . . I design. I create the beautiful homes that people like David Carlyle entertain in. I'm not like Michael. I contribute something productive to society."

"I didn't mean . . ."

"The reason you don't think I work is because you *somehow* got this idea in your head that I'm just riding the Penthouse crowd—the A-list—for all they're worth. But I know how to work, and I work hard."

"Jamie, I'm . . ."

"That's not what I'm about, Brett. Put whatever preconceived notions you have behind you. That's not what I'm about."

"I'm sorry," I said, and we both fell into silence.

Minutes passed. I know, because I counted them on my Cartier watch, which may or may not have actually been a Cartier. Finally, though, he spoke.

"Why is it that every time we have a date, you have to say something that becomes an issue? Last night you had to mention splitting a meal at McDonald's, and now . . ."

"A date?" I asked. "Is that what this is?"

"Well . . . sort of. I mean, we went to a movie, we're having drinks . . . *I* think it counts as a date."

Much as my heart thrilled to hear those words, I fought the emotions bubbling to the surface. I *had* to let my head do the thinking.

I pushed my chair back a bit from the table and said, "I never know what to think about you."

"What do you mean?"

"Why is it that last night constituted a date, and *this* is apparently a date, but none of the other times were considered dates?"

He thought for a moment, then shrugged. "I don't know. I guess it's a feeling I have about them."

"What about *my* feelings?"

He shrugged again. "I don't know what to say. You're right, but . . . I don't know what to say." After a pause, he added, "I have to sort out my feelings, Brett. We're at such different points in our lives that, well . . ." Another pause. "You're right, though. I know how I can be, thinking that it's always all about me."

He was getting no argument from me on *that* point. And in any event, I had a bigger question.

"So . . . are we *dating*?"

He looked at me warily, and answered carefully. "We're on a date."

And I knew that was the best and only answer I was going to get.

There are many people in the world much smarter than me, but even *I* knew there was no point in pursuing that discussion. Jamie knew it, too. Smoothly and seamlessly, as if by a mutual and unspoken agreement, we steered the conversation onto topics distant from the minefield. Routine gossip, banal observations . . . the subjects under discussion didn't matter, as long as they had nothing to do with the nature of our relationship.

After several more margaritas, Jamie suggested we pay a visit to Michael.

"He's not in the Hamptons?" I asked, as we walked under dark, threatening skies in the general direction of his apartment, clutching our five-dollar umbrellas under our arms.

"I don't think so."

We reached Michael's building at the exact moment the rain began to fall, accompanied by a loud rumble of thunder. At the lobby desk, Jamie greeted the doorman warmly.

"Hey, Freddy," he said, clapping him on the shoulder.

"Good to see you, Mr. Brock. You just beat the rain."

Jamie smiled. "I planned it that way. It makes for a more dramatic entrance. Is Mr. DeVries in?"

Freddy the doorman looked uncertain. "Would you like me to call up?"

"That's all right." Jamie flashed his keys. "I have a key. We'll surprise him."

I followed Jamie a few steps into the lobby before he stopped and turned back to the doorman. His voice fell to a whisper.

"Mr. Culver-Benchley isn't here, is he?"

"No, sir."

"Thanks." With that, we were once again crossing the lobby to the bank of elevators.

"Blake?" I asked. "Why . . . ?"

"In the elevator."

Once the elevator doors were closed and we were ascending to the nineteenth floor, my curiosity was satisfied.

"Blake pays for Michael's apartment," said Jamie, who was observing the elevator custom of facing forward and avoiding eye contact, even though I was the only other person in the car.

"But . . . Michael told me that Mina Pfeffer gave it to him."

Jamie shook his head. "That's just a cover story. This is Blake's place."

"I don't understand. Why would Blake pay for it and let Michael stay here?"

"Don't breathe a word of this to anyone," he said. "And *especially* don't let Michael know that I told you this. Blake pays because he has an arrangement with Michael. This is where Blake brings his mistress while . . ."

"He has a mistress? But he's, like, ninety years old!"

"He's worth . . . well, it's closer to a billion dollars than not. That kind of money can buy a lot of mistresses."

"But how does he get away with it?" I asked. "Winston doesn't catch on?"

He shrugged. "Maybe she knows. That's none of my business. But I *do* know that Blake has Michael distract her. You know those long, expensive luncheons?"

"Yeah."

"While Michael is entertaining Winston, Blake is up here, entertaining his mistress."

"No shit."

"No shit. In return, Blake pays for the apartment and reimburses Michael for the cost of lunch."

"Wait . . . Blake reimburses Michael for those luncheons?"

He smiled. "Michael made you pay half, didn't he?"

I nodded.

"In that case, you got scammed by him."

I sighed. "I guess I did . . ."

We reached the nineteenth floor and walked the short hall to Michael's apartment. Jamie pushed the doorbell and, when there was no answer, used his key to let us in.

"Can I ask another question?" I said as we entered the dark apartment. "Why do you have a key?"

"When he's out of town—like when he takes his ladies to Palm Beach, or when *they* take *him* on a cruise—I'm in charge of watering the plants and bringing up the mail. It's a pain in the ass being Michael's houseboy, but I get the side benefit of having a place to crash every now and then."

He flipped on some lights, then quietly walked to the bedroom door and looked in.

"Nope," he said finally. "He's not here. Now let's figure out where he is . . ."

While he dialed a number on his cell phone, I looked out on Michael's view. The clouds were low, but not so low that they obscured the view over the East River. The rain lashed the window in waves, distorting the shimmering lights nineteen stories below the apartment. It was beautiful.

Jamie was suddenly next to me. "Found him," he said. "I tracked him down at David Carlyle's place. Some dinner party that I wasn't invited to." He sounded annoyed.

"In that case," I said, "we'll have to make our own dinner party."

We never did eat dinner. Instead, we sat together in the window, watching the dance of those shimmering lights in the rain, in near silence, sharing a bottle of wine from Michael's pantry. I figured the wine was the least he owed me, and worth nowhere near my $300 portion of Winston Culver-Benchley's lunch tab.

At some point, as the rain continued to beat down, I realized that I would not be going home to Queens that night.

Sure enough, Jamie did not intend for me to go. Wordlessly, he led me by the hand to Michael's bedroom.

"Nap time," he said.

"Nap as a euphemism?" I asked.

"A what?"

"A euph- . . . I mean, do you want to nap, or . . . *you know* . . ."

He smiled, but shook his head. "Not tonight, baby. I'm *really* tired. Let's just get some sleep."

That was as good as it was going to get, but I felt no regret. We stripped down to our underwear then climbed into the bed, his back to me. I curled one arm around his body and pulled myself close, feeling my flesh against his, and every doubt I had ever had about Jamie and my life seemed to ease with every soft breath he took.

Brett Revere's Theory of Life, Part Fifteen:

Some Men Aren't the Marrying Type . . . No Matter How Hard You Try and Beg and Cry

"Are you awake?"

I wasn't, really, but still I stirred at the sound of Jamie's voice, licking my lips to clear away the stickiness before answering. I still tasted the saltiness of his back.

"I'm awake," I said finally.

"I've never told you what you mean to me, have I?"

My eyes fluttered open, and I was staring at the back of his head.

"You mean a lot to me, Brett." He rolled over, and I was staring at his face. "I'm not the kind of person who usually admits things like that, but . . . well . . . I think you deserve to know that."

Despite my better judgment, I found myself moving my face just a little closer to his.

"So . . . so what do you mean?"

Confusion crossed his face. "What do you mean, what do I mean?"

"I mean . . . Wait. Why are you telling me this? Why now? Why not when I was trying to tell you how much *I* liked *you*." I paused. "And why am I saying this out loud?"

He laughed, stretching one arm out from beneath the sheets and placing it gently on my naked chest.

"Brett," he said, "you mean a lot to me. You've been a friend when I needed one, and if . . . if it wasn't for you, I don't know what would have happened to me."

"You would have become one of the hottest downloads on the Internet."

"Shit," he playfully moaned, and his head briefly vanished under the sheet. When it reappeared, his smile was gone. "Doubt it. Doubt it. But I probably would have stayed with Nico, which would have been worse." He shrugged. "Comfortable, but worse."

"Can I say something? I know it's no secret, Jamie, but I've lo- . . . I've really liked you since the night we met."

"No. It's no secret." With a laugh, he added, "Remember when I went to the Hamptons the day after we first slept together?" I nodded my head against the pillow. "Well, I called Michael that weekend and— Did he tell you?"

"He told me you called."

"Did he tell you what I said?"

"No. He said that gentlemen don't discuss personal conversations."

He shook his head and muttered, "What a hypocrite. Selective mortality."

"*Morality*."

"Right. Anyway, I told Michael that you and I were getting married as soon as I returned to Manhattan."

I lifted myself up on one elbow. "Really?"

"Really."

"So . . ."

"But then Nico hauled out those pictures, and, well . . . that was that. I was sort of stuck with him."

With a heavy sigh, I settled back into the bed. "Sure. Of course."

He brightened. "But *you* were still there for me, Brett Revere. You were there for me when I needed someone to hold my hand, and . . . well . . . you were there to take care of business for me. You've really helped to straighten out my life." He paused. "And I love you, baby."

"Jamie, I . . ." Wait. Did Jamie Brock just tell me that he loved me? "Huh?"

"I said I love you."

I couldn't think of anything to say. Nothing at all. The only thing I could think to do was kiss him, and so I did, with the passion and intensity of someone who has spent two decades looking for Mister Right and finally found him.

"Brett!" Jamie squirmed out from under me and bolted upright in the bed.

I was confused. "But . . ."

"That's not where I was going, baby."

I shook my head, trying to erase the past few seconds. "Oh, yeah," I mumbled. "I, uh . . . Jamie, I was just . . . uh . . ."

But he wasn't listening. Jamie had slid out of the bed and was moving far too quickly toward the bathroom.

"I'm sorry," I whispered, too low for him to hear, and I sunk down into the pillow and muttered, "Shit."

The sound of running water provides an excellent backdrop for introspection. Especially when you're sitting in an unmade bed, suffering from multiple levels of deep regret.

Or, in the vernacular, when you realized that you had managed to majorly fuck up everything in your love life in less than thirty-six hours.

Jamie was in the shower—had been in the shower for far too long, as a matter of fact, obviously hoping I'd leave before he got out. He had finally said he loved me, and, because I had wanted to hear those words for so long, I completely overreacted. *Damn*, I overreacted. *Fuck*, I overreacted. And now Jamie Brock's main goal in life was to shower and get away from me as soon as possible. His love was brotherly, I now realized, and realized far too late.

And Angel . . . well, I fucked that one up, too. Angel was as guileless as Jamie was manipulative, and I had destroyed our budding relationship through some of the most inept lies ever before uttered by man. No, my lies were not merely inept. Looking at them through Angel's eyes, I can see how he would feel that my lies were designed to insult his intelligence.

Despite everything I knew, I still loved Jamie. And while my feeling for Angel had not grown quite so intense, I felt those familiar first longings.

And both options were now gone.

Fuck.

When the shower was finally turned off, my heavy mood hadn't lifted. But I tried to hide it from Jamie when, with a towel wrapped around his waist, he walked out of the bathroom a few minutes later.

"I'm sort of embarrassed," I confessed.

"Don't be." He smiled, but it seemed forced. "We're just at different points in our lives."

"Right."

"Not that far apart, really. Just a bit."

"Right."

His towel dropped to the floor, and I had the briefest thought that maybe . . .

But no. He quickly slipped on a pair of boxer-briefs.

"The thing is this," he said, looking away from me to check his dark hair in the mirror. "There are times, and there are *times*. Do you know what I mean?"

"I think so . . ."

"When we first met, well, that was the *time* for us. Since then . . . I think it's passed us by."

"But we've slept together since then," I said, finding my voice.

"Yeah." I caught him smiling in the mirror, but he had suppressed it by the time he turned again to face me. "And those times were great, Brett. But they weren't . . ."

"I know. They weren't the *time*."

"Right."

"Okay." I pushed my head deep into the pillow. "Sorry."

"No, Brett. *I'm* sorry. What I said before—that I love you—is true. You've been great to me. I just wish that things could be different . . ."

"But they're not."

"No. Not anymore. You . . ."

"Let me help you," I said, having a moment of clarity. "When you met me, you thought you might be in love. But then you realized that you weren't."

"It wasn't quite . . ."

"And *then* . . ." I stopped, realizing that despite my disappointment and embarrassment, it was actually something approaching anger that now drove my words. After faltering for a few seconds, I decided to let those words flow, and damn the repercussions. "And *then* you realized that you couldn't be in love, because you had complications. Nicholas Golodnya, for example."

"Nico wasn't . . . well, yes, he was a complication. But that wasn't love."

I watched him dress in silence for a few minutes, sorting things out in my head. I felt as if I had won the war—the success of Operation Hamptons—but nevertheless lost all the important battles. Falling in love with Jamie was starting to feel like the most self-destructive thing I had ever done in my life.

"Let me ask you something," I said, as he buttoned his shirt. He didn't reply, but I continued. "Do you ever feel love?"

"I just told you I love you, baby. Just not . . ."

"I mean *romantic* love. Not brotherly love. Not love like . . . like . . . like people have for kittens. Do you feel romance?"

He looked confused. "You mean, like meeting someone and falling in love and wanting to be with them forever?"

"Yeah."

He shrugged. "Of course I feel it. I felt it when I first met you. But . . . I don't know, Brett. Maybe I'm just not the marrying type."

The bedroom again fell into silence.

I looked around at all the beautiful things Michael had collected from his ladies, and at the apartment he was handed in exchange for his complicity in Blake Culver-Benchley's trysts, and I saw Jamie's future clearly for the first time. No, Jamie wouldn't grow up to *be* Michael, exactly. But he would grow up to be *like* Michael. He was going to be a collector, and there was nothing I could do about it. All the creatures in this exotic world—the Michaels and Jamies and John Jacob Venezuelas and Jeffrey Ryans and maybe even the Lottery Hogs—were different, but similar enough to be classified in the same genus. They could be venal, like Michael, or slippery, like Jamie, or display any other set of individual characteristics, but, in the end, they belonged to the same world.

It was a world in which pooling change for a Happy Meal was a terrible social blunder. A world in which $600 birthday gifts were thrown at strangers to buy social standing. A world in which you were mocked for wearing a sensible watch. A world in which the hearts and minds of men like Angel *were* judged by their jobs, their accents, and the colors of their skin.

I could visit their world, and I would, now that Operation Hamptons was about to pay off. But unless I sold my soul, I couldn't establish residency. Jamie, though . . . Jamie was one of its naturalized citizens.

And that realization led me to my next insight: there had never been any hope for a future with Jamie Brock.

Even on the night we first met—the night that led him to later tell Michael that we were "going to get married"—his feelings for me were certainly based, in part, on his belief that I was really Brett

Revere, Trust Fund Baby. I now *finally* understood that he could not allow himself to fall in love with Brett Revere, Regular Guy. He was able to shake that emotion off. And occasional sex and professed brotherly love was now all he was capable of.

I had received all I would ever get from him, and more than I ever should have expected. That knowledge—suddenly clear after all the weeks of wondering—came as both a knife through my heart and soothing relief.

"Baby?" I broke my staring contest with an antique chess set—a gift from Flora Howell, of Palm Beach—and turned my attention to Jamie, who was now fully dressed. "I'm going to get out of here, okay?"

"Sure," I said. "I'll shower and pick the place up, so that Michael doesn't kill us when he gets home."

"Remember to wipe down the bathtub."

"I will."

He dropped his gaze to the floor and asked, "Are you all right?"

I shrugged. "I'm fine. Get out of here."

Smiling, he jabbed a finger in my direction and left the bedroom. I lay back down on the unmade bed and listened to his footsteps echo off the hall floor. Moments later, when I heard the front door slam shut and knew he was gone, I buried my face in the pillow, willing tears to break down the numbing pressure in my head. But none would come.

After a short while, I found a robe, and padded to Michael's kitchen, where I started to brew a pot of coffee. Then I picked up the cordless phone and dialed.

"Cooper Bauer Malnut."

"Philip Whitehead, please."

"And who may I say is calling?"

"Brett Revere."

There was silence for a moment, and then another receptionist was on the line.

"Philip Whitehead's office."

"Yes, hi, my name is Brett Revere. Mr. Whitehead asked . . ."

"Oh, Mr. Revere. Yes. Mr. Whitehead is expecting your call. One moment, please."

Expecting my call? Nice.

"Philip Whitehead."

Ah! The birthday boy at last! I softened the tone of my voice, made it a bit more playful, and said, "Philip! This is Brett. How *are* you?"

"Quite well, thank you." Like the other Penthouse regulars, there was always more than a trace of formality, even in the most informal conversations. "And you?"

"Hanging in there." No one was going to confuse me with one of the formal-speaking crowd. "I wanted to follow up on our conversation at the party."

"Of course. I might have something to offer you. It seems I'm in need of a personal assistant. This isn't a secretarial position, really, and don't worry about technicalitics. The firm has three floors of paralegals and research assistants. No, Brett, because I'm such a . . . well, a *dinosaur* who's been around forever"—he laughed—"I have a number of civic responsibilities and social engagements and the like. I need someone to help coordinate them."

"The firm pays for an assistant for your personal life?"

He laughed again. "Cooper Bauer Malnut sees the value in my high profile. So, does this sound like something that might interest you?"

Bingo. That was it. I made mental plans to toss Alan Donovan to the ground and do a celebratory dance on his stomach to punish him for his skepticism about Operation Hamptons.

"Although I'm a bit embarrassed that I can't pay you quite the salary you probably ordinarily command . . ."

The dance ended.

"Well . . . uh . . . what were you proposing, Philip?"

"I can pay ninety."

"Ninety?" Ninety *what*? Ninety a *week*? Mentally, I picked Alan Donovan off the ground and brushed footprints off his shirt.

"I'm afraid that's as high as I can go, at this point. Of course, there are benefits, and retirement. . . . But I'll understand if you can't afford to work for that salary."

Although I didn't care about retirement—I had no plans to buy a Winnebago and see the world after decades of hard labor—I perked up when I heard the word "benefits." Maybe, just maybe, I could afford to work for ninety *whatever* if benefits were in the mix. For a while, at least.

Maybe. But I really needed to clarify this "ninety."

"The salary again was . . . ?"

"Ninety thousand. And, again, I apologize."

The Alan Donovan Stomach Dance resumed.

Playing it as cool as possible, I said, "I think I can do that, Philip. Yes, I think I can."

"Perhaps next year, when the economy picks up . . ."

"We can discuss that next year. For now, though, I accept your gen- . . ." *Watch it, Brett! Don't call that "generous."* "For now, I accept your offer."

"Wonderful," he said. "Can you start next Wednesday? Is that too soon?"

"Let me check my calendar." I put the phone down and leafed through a week-old copy of the *Times* before getting back on the line. "Yes, Philip. I'm available to start Wednesday."

"What good news! We should meet for dinner to seal the deal."

And dinner would surely be harmless, wouldn't it? After all, I was about to become Philip Whitehead's personal assistant, so there would be many dinners in the future, while we discussed . . . law firm things, or whatever lawyers discussed with their personal assistants over meals at the Four Seasons.

"Dinner sounds like an excellent idea," I said.

"How about Monday? I'd recommend this evening, but I want to get out to the Hamptons this afternoon."

"Monday works for me."

"Shall we meet at the Penthouse at . . . is seven o'clock too early?"

"No. Seven will be fine."

We said our goodbyes, and I did a dance—a real dance, not a mental dance on Alan Donovan's body—as I celebrated the success of Operation Hamptons and my new job as personal assistant to Philip Whitehead, attorney at law.

My happiness—which was considerable—was tempered by the knowledge that it would have been much, much sweeter if Jamie Brock hadn't just walked out my door . . . if Angel Maldonado was still speaking to me . . . if I hadn't accrued a laundry list of regrets on my path to success.

But I was determined not to let those regrets haunt me. Life was full of them, and we move on. The important thing was that I *had* succeeded . . . I had triumphed, and Operation Hamptons had proven itself.

I would miss Jamie. I was certain of that. There was something about him—from that initial electricity to the way he called me "baby"—that would have completed my life. But Jamie had made it clear that our feelings weren't in sync, and I would have to live with that. And I would.

Similarly, I would always wonder what might have happened if I had met Angel at a different point in my life. I had met Angel—like Jamie—at the wrong moment. If it had been two months earlier, I had little doubt we could have had a wonderful relationship. Now, though . . .

No.

Some day, I would have the opportunity to love again. Maybe that would be later, rather than sooner, but still the day would come. Then, I would be complete.

In the meantime, Operation Hamptons had offered me a once-in-a-lifetime opportunity to resolve most of the other issues in my life.

The next man to love me would love me as Philip Whitehead's personal assistant.

And if that wasn't complete consolation for an aching heart, it would do for now.

Since I had done an imaginary dance upon his body, and since he had been such a skeptic about Operation Hamptons, the first person I called when I arrived back at my apartment was Alan Donovan. Since it was Saturday, I wasn't surprised when he didn't answer the phone at his office. I left a message, saying that I had to talk to him urgently, and hung up.

He called me back twenty minutes later.

"What's the emergency? Do you need cash?"

"Those days," I said, "are fast becoming my past. I want to let you be the first to know that I landed a job."

"You're going back into the cast of *Andy*?"

"As if. No, Alan, I'm going to become the new personal assistant to a prominent lawyer."

"Who?"

"Philip Whitehead."

"Never heard of him."

"Once I'm working for him, you'll be hearing a lot about him."

"Do I get a vote on this? Because I think you might be overestimating my interest."

I ignored him. "We're meeting on Monday for dinner to discuss the details, but there's one important detail that's already been discussed."

"Which sexual favors you'll be required to perform?"

"Ha. Ha. We discussed salary. How does ninety thou sound to your ears?"

He let out a low whistle. "It sounds sweet. Congratulations. How did you hear about it?"

"That's the best part," I said. "I got the job as a result of . . ."

The realization hit him. "Don't say it!"

"Operation Hamptons!"

"You had to go and say it." He paused, then added, "Well, congratulations are still in order. I've got to hand it to you, Brett. You knew what you wanted, and went for it."

"Thanks." I was nothing if not gracious. "I feel like celebrating. Do you and Ty feel up for an evening at the Penthouse?"

"Another night listening to him whine about the Penthouse attitude?" He sighed. "Okay. But only for you. Uh . . . are your friends going to be there?"

"No," I said, trying very hard not to mourn the passing of Jamie's feelings. "Most of them are in the Hamptons, and Jamie's . . . sort of out of the picture."

He was uncharacteristically quiet, then said, "I'm sorry to hear that. For you, I mean. But it's probably for the best."

"I guess . . ." I said noncommittally.

After we made arrangements to meet at nine o'clock, I hung up, and slumped on the couch. I knew I had put myself in a position that could prove to be uncomfortable that evening, but there was no way to avoid it.

I hadn't called Angel back on Friday, and I couldn't bring myself to phone him on this Saturday, but I knew I couldn't avoid the Penthouse forever. I was, after all, meeting Philip Whitehead there on Monday night.

I would have to apologize to Angel in person that evening . . . and it was best to do it while the Penthouse regulars were all out of town, replaced by the unfamiliar faces of the Saturday Bridge-and-Tunnel crowd, and when I had the moral support of Alan and Ty.

It wasn't going to be pretty, but it would *never* be pretty, and it *did* have to happen. It would not be good to have an angry Angel confront me in front of the regulars . . . or, worse, in front of Philip Whitehead on Monday night.

Which didn't make the thought of it any easier.

Alan and Ty were waiting at the downstairs bar when I arrived. I looked warily around the room, but saw neither Angel nor any stray regular who hadn't made it out to the Hamptons that weekend. We exchanged greetings and I ordered a drink. When I returned, Ty was already in a dark mood.

"Is something wrong?" I asked Alan, when Ty's attention was diverted.

"Apparently, everyone who crosses that threshold—with the exception of him and *possibly* me, in my good moments—has a slave-owner's mentality."

"Sorry." I thought for a moment, then asked, "He thinks that about *me*, too?"

"You could probably redeem yourself by dating Angel. But don't even begin to ask me what his problem is with *me*. I'm proudly dating a gay black man, breaking two social taboos at the same time, and you'd think . . ." He shrugged. "I don't know. Just date Angel and save yourself from the wrath of Ty."

I sighed. "Yeah, well, I sort of screwed up the Angel thing."

"No Jamie . . . no Angel . . . suddenly, you're all alone in the world. Just like old times!" He laughed at his own joke, but when he noticed that I was distinctly *not* laughing, he asked what had happened.

So I told him.

By now, Ty's attention had returned back to our conversation, and he was the first to react.

"You really fucked up," he said.

"Yeah," I agreed. "I mean, it paid off, because I got the job, but . . ."

"Did you ever think about *his* feelings?" asked Ty.

"Not nearly enough."

"That's for sure."

Alan jumped in, as much to reduce the intensity as to offer his opinion.

"Let's go upstairs," he said. "Maybe he's up there, and you can apologize to him, and . . . well, maybe he'll understand."

I shrugged. "Maybe."

The walk up the circular staircase to the piano bar felt like a walk to the electric chair. I knew I had to speak to Angel, and it had to be this evening, but it was the absolute opposite of anything I looked forward to.

And, of course, he was standing at the top of the stairs. Our eyes met—his, steely; mine, full of remorse—and he started to walk away.

"Angel," I said, breaking away from Alan and Ty. "Hold on for a second. I want to talk to you."

He paused for a split second, but then continued to walk away, forcing me to run a few steps to catch him. My opportunity came when he reached an impassable spot in the crowd, and I maneuvered in front of him.

"I'm sorry," I said, hoping I was loud enough to be heard, but not loud enough to be broadcasting to the rest of the bar. "I shouldn't have lied to you. I should have called . . ."

He feinted to the left, but when I tried to follow him he reversed course and disappeared into a group of people. My eyes darted across the bar patrons until I spotted his head bobbing through the crowd toward the rear of the bar.

That's where I finally trapped him several minutes later, as he waited for Paolo to complete his drink order.

"Can I talk to you for a second?" I asked.

He looked around for an escape route, but finally shrugged. His jaw was firmly set in place as he said, "So, talk."

I didn't know how much time I had—not nearly enough, I suspected—so I rushed out my words, sprinkling a few fresh lies in with the truth in an effort that I hoped would mitigate the damage.

"I am *so sorry* about everything. It's just that after we made our date, I heard about this party, and there was this opportunity to land a job, so I wanted to go. But I never should have lied and told you I had an audition. That was just stupid. I thought you'd be mad that I was going to a party, instead of on our date. I know I should have just been up-front and told you about this job opportunity, but I . . . I . . . I'm sorry."

The steeliness remained in his eyes. He turned to Paolo, who had been pretending not to listen, and said, "Do you believe him?"

Paolo smiled. Busted.

"Do you?" he asked.

"I'm not sure." They were conversing as if I wasn't there. "Brett here doesn't have the best track record."

Paolo thought about that for a moment, then said, "Maybe you should give him another chance to take you out on a date. And if he screws up again . . . well, that's it."

"I don't know . . ." Angel paused while Paolo loaded his tray with drinks, then continued. "I mean, if he did it again, I'd be so angry . . ."

"Yeah," said Paolo, "but maybe he was telling the truth. Maybe he's just stupid, not mean."

When the tray was loaded, Angel hoisted it up on a shoulder and, turning, finally addressed me.

"I'm still not sure," he said. "I don't know if I want a date with you." He smiled, but it looked forced. Still, it was an evident good-will gesture. "Thank you for your apology, though. I'll think about the date thing—if you're even offering, that is—but I'm not angry anymore."

"Thanks," I said, sidling out of the way to let him—and his tray—pass. "And I really *am* sorry."

"I told you I believe you. So stop apologizing."

With that comment, he and his tray of drinks melted into the crowd.

I turned to catch Paolo smiling in my direction.

"You've got to watch that one," he said. "Beautiful, and so nice. But that temper . . ."

I smiled. "I guess I owe you one, Paolo."

"Don't worry about it. Just remember: with Angel, you only get *one* second chance."

I dropped a twenty on the bar for Paolo and went to find Alan. When I did, it appeared that whatever issues had come up between him and Ty had been resolved, given the proximity of their lips.

"Ahem," I said, rather dramatically.

"Find your own man," said Alan.

"Yeah, well, that's another problem . . ."

Alan broke his clinch with Ty and turned his attention to me. "So how did it go with Angel?"

"Better than I had any reason to expect."

And that was the truth. One hundred percent the truth.

On Monday evening, I arrived at the Penthouse precisely at seven. Philip Whitehead had not yet arrived, so I went to the upstairs piano bar, waved Paolo over, and ordered a drink. While Paolo mixed, I scanned the sparse crowd for evidence of Angel.

"He's around," said Paolo, reading my mind as he handed me the drink. "If I see him first, I'll tell him you're here."

"That's okay," I said. "I'm just having a quick one before dinner."

"Dinner? Where?"

"That's up to my new boss," I said.

"Ah! The guy who had the party the night you were supposed . . ."

I stopped him, preferring not to take another verbal trip to the minefield. "That's him. Let's not go there, though. Okay?"

"Gotcha."

The piano player began singing *Love for Sale*. Paolo smiled at no one in particular and said, "This is the perfect place for that song."

I laughed, but—as someone who was beginning to think of the Penthouse as home—I wasn't quite sure I appreciated his remark.

In any event, I really didn't have time to dwell on the point, because I was quickly—and rudely—interrupted.

"How are you?" blasted in my ear, and I no longer had to turn to know that the Evil Mime was on the prowl.

"Hello, George," I said.

"You know my name?" Despite my better judgment, I turned. His face, caked with make-up, was inches from mine, forcing me to lean back.

"You've introduced yourself to me a few times," I said. He looked confused, so I added, "It's been a while, though, so don't worry about not remembering me."

I lost any distance I had gained by tilting my head back when he continued to move forward. Although we weren't actually touching, I wasn't quite sure if a sheet of paper could fit between us.

"Let me buy you a drink."

"No, thanks." I held up my untouched glass. "I just got one."

"Come on, now. I want to buy you a drink."

"Thanks, but . . ."

"It would be my pleasure." He backed away just slightly, then drunkenly faced the bar and signaled for Paolo. "One for me—my usual—and one for my friend."

I shook a "no" at Paolo, who silently acknowledged my distress.

His order accomplished, the Evil Mime again stuck his head in my personal space. "So what's your name?"

I sighed. "Brett."

"I'm George." I think he was trying to shake my hand, but he was so close he ended up jabbing his fingers into my ribcage. "You'll never guess what I used to do."

"I suspect you're correct."

"Come on, guess."

Another sigh. This was sad.

"Okay," I said. "If I had to guess, I'd say you were . . . a mime."

He furrowed his brow. "You can tell just by looking at me?"

"Yeah. You have a mime body-type."

"Hmm." He thought about that for a bit, then apparently decided that my nonsense made sense. "I did some acting, too. I studied with Jayne Mansfield."

"Really."

"She had this huge crush on me"—he spit on the word "crush"—"but I had to break her heart and tell her I liked men, not women."

"She must have been devastated."

"Poor thing." He reached for the drink the bartender had placed on the bar, and I couldn't help but notice that he left far too little money in return. "She died, you know."

"I heard."

"You're probably too young to remember . . ." For a moment, his mind wandered, lost in tragedies of several decades past. I used that opportunity to desperately search the room for Philip, who still wasn't there, or Angel, who was . . . somewhere else. It was only when the Evil Mime stumbled backward a few steps—in a manner unbefitting the normal gracefulness of a mime, at that—that I was able to take advantage of his distraction and slip away.

"Hey! Where are you going?"

"I'm meeting someone," I said. "And I think he might be at the downstairs bar."

"But I bought you a drink," he said, and I realized he was getting angry.

I was going to correct him on that, but thought it would be easier to say, "Thank you" and move quickly to the circular staircase. Mercifully, he chose not to follow me.

I was halfway down the stairs when another familiar voice whispered in my ear from behind.

"Smooth exit," said Angel, who was following me down the stairs.

I stopped and turned. Standing two steps below him, he was actually taller than me.

"Thanks," I said. "Or were you being sarcastic?"

"Sincere. Avoiding George is an art form."

He gave me a tiny smile, which I took as encouragement.

"What brings you out tonight?"

"I'm meeting up with the new boss."

"Congratulations. So . . . we didn't get into this the other day. Your new boss is gay?"

"Yeah. He hangs out here."

He frowned. "What kind of job is this? Kept boy?"

"Oh, come on . . . You know I'm not like that." My peripheral vision caught a glimpse of Philip Whitehead making his way through the bar. "And the guy is a gentleman. In fact, that's him right there, in the gray suit."

"With glasses?"

"Next to the guy with glasses. Red tie."

Angel picked him out of the crowd, then shook his head with disgust. "That one . . ." He sighed. "Whatever, Brett. I just hope you're happy doing this with your life."

He quickly slipped past me and down the stairs before I had a chance to respond, most of which would have been an astonished, "*What?!*" But the moment passed, and it was time to greet the new boss.

"Hello, Brett," said Philip as we approached each other. "I hope you're hungry."

"Starving. Where are we going?"

"Eleven Madison Park. I love that place. But first, a drink." He glanced at the glass in my hand. "Back-up?"

"Sure."

Philip went to the bar, leaving me standing near the wall. I caught a glimpse—but only a glimpse—of Angel as he darted through the crowd and back upstairs to the piano bar, leaving me wondering what exactly he knew about Philip Whitehead.

It was probably nothing, I told myself. By his own admission, Angel wasn't fond of the clientele at the Penthouse. Therefore, as a regular, Philip would be an object of his scorn, and his vague comments to me would have been just more of the same. After all, Jamie had given him a *relatively* clean character reference, drunken lechery aside.

No, it was nothing. Nothing at all.

Philip returned with our drinks, which were quickly drained amid amiable, if perfunctory, conversation. Soon we were in a cab heading south on Second Avenue, and no more than twenty minutes after that, we were being shown to our table at Eleven Madison Park.

"So, Brett," he said, after we placed our drink order, "I know so little about you. Why don't you run down your background for me?"

Which were exactly the words I had hoped not to hear.

But after a few hems and haws, I began to string together enough of a series of lies—cobbled from Michael DeVries's made-up biography of me, among other sources—to make for a consistent and interesting personal history.

And because I didn't feel I had quite enough material, I went with the assumption that Philip had underestimated my age and shaved eight years off my imaginary life story.

I was, of course, a trust fund baby, with family in . . . *Chicago*—that sounded safe—and . . . *Dallas*, where I implied there might be some oil money. I graduated from . . . not Harvard or Yale or anywhere Philip might know people . . . I graduated from *Union College in Schenectady*, a vaguely remembered vestige from my early days in Albany, which fit my mutual needs of being prestigious, yet small enough to be under his radar.

Immediately after graduation, I had met . . . *George*! No, that was the name of the Evil Mime . . . *Maxwell*! Maxwell . . . *Robinson*. Whose family was in textiles. And he was a few years older . . . no, no, I didn't want to give Philip the idea I was into older men. He was . . . he was born exactly one month after me. And Maxwell—never "Max"—and I spent ten glorious years together.

By the time I got to our breakup, midway through the appetizer, I had spun such a compelling tale that I was afraid I was going to burst into tears. *Oh, Maxwell, how could you have done that to me after all those years together?*

Between the success of Operation Hamptons and my ad libbed life story, I wondered if it wasn't time to give acting another chance.

If I dominated the time period from cocktails through appetizers, the entrée belonged exclusively to Philip. Over the next hour, he told me—in excruciatingly minute detail—about each of his many accomplishments. For my part, I listened with what to him must have looked like rapt attention. In reality, I was doing math in my head, trying to calculate the biweekly take-home pay of a $90,000 salary divided by twenty-six pay periods minus a thirty percent tax rate.

"So then I told Rudy that while the divorce was turning into a fiasco, by moving in with a gay couple he was doing a great service to softening his image. And do you know what he said?"

"What?" It was not only the *only* answer I could give, it was the safest.

"He told me that he wished he could serve another term, just to appoint me Corporation Counsel." Philip leaned into the table and cackled. "I told him I couldn't afford the pay cut." With that, he let out a loud roar of laughter. I joined in, to the best of my abilities.

During dessert, he said, "I think we're going to get along just fine, Brett."

"I agree, Philip. Or should I call you 'Mr. Whitehead' now?"

He smiled. "Just in the office, Brett. Over drinks at the Penthouse, or out at dinner, we're simply Philip and Brett."

Oh, Christ, was I really supposed to call him "Mr. Whitehead" in the office? Well . . . he *was* the one dangling the $90,000 paycheck.

"So can you start Wednesday?"

I nodded firmly. "I can think of nothing I'd like more, Philip."

Brett Revere's Theory of Life, Part Sixteen:

Bad Things Always Happen in Threes . . . or Fours . . . or Seventeens . . .

On Wednesday morning, I arrived at the law firm of Cooper Bauer Malnut, in a building fronting on Park Avenue in the upper east forties, promptly at 8:30 A.M. I spent most of the morning filling out paperwork—pleased and relieved to see no familiar faces from my long-ago temp assignment—before being ushered upstairs to a clubby suite of offices occupied by the senior partners. At this level, each partner had his or her own assistant, and each assistant had his or her own office, and beyond their assistant's office, each partner had an expensively appointed private office large enough to land an airplane in, with sweeping southern exposures.

Janelle Banks was Philip Whitehead's executive assistant, and it was to her I was passed off by the clerk from Human Resources. Janelle was a compact black woman in her mid-30s who gave off a friendly aura, tinged with just enough "don't fuck with me" sassiness to not only give her some street cred, but to keep the old boys at the firm on their toes. The minute I met her I knew we were going to get along famously.

"Let me show you to your office," she said, after introductions were completed. She marched me a short distance down a hall, then ushered me into an office. No, not *an* office . . . *my* new office.

My new office. Probably 400 square feet of prime Manhattan real estate, with a southerly view of the MetLife Building and Grand Central Terminal.

My new office. With plush carpeting and the finest furnishings and drapes and a sofa and a refrigerator and . . .

"Are you sure this is the right office?" I asked.

"Honey, this is the best we've got." She laughed. "You want something better?"

Now it was my turn to laugh. "No . . . I mean, it's just so . . . *big*."

"Everything's big on the forty-seventh floor, Brett. Especially the egos. But, hey, you must deserve it, or else you wouldn't have it. Just keep telling yourself that."

"Uh . . . okay."

When she was gone, I grabbed the phone and dialed Alan's number, spinning in the desk chair while the line rang until I faced my unobstructed view south over the buildings on the east side of Park Avenue.

"You would not believe this," I said, when he answered. I described my physical surroundings, finishing with, "I'm in heaven. Between the pay and the office and the view. . . . This is better than I ever expected."

"Want to trade?"

"No thanks," I said. "Plus, your building's weekend staff has seen me in my underwear. I wouldn't feel comfortable."

"Yeah, well try not to run around in your skivvies in your new office. On Park Avenue, people will talk."

My first few days at Cooper Bauer Malnut were even smoother than I had hoped. Philip was demanding without being an asshole about it, and I found that I took naturally to keeping the details of his life organized. Janelle was great, too, filling me in on firm gossip and particulars it would have taken me months to learn on my own.

Those long lunches at the Four Seasons I had anticipated did not come to pass—in his business dealings, Philip was scrupulously professional—but that was all right. The point of Operation Hamptons, after all, was not to idle away my days. The point was to work for a decent income. And that was exactly what I was doing, up there in the forty-seventh-floor offices of Cooper Bauer Malnut.

Yes, my life was good . . . so good that even a few more calls from Quentin didn't faze me. Much. Soon, I would have a substantial paycheck. And every two weeks thereafter, another would follow. Debts would be erased, rent would be paid, and, if I was feeling especially benevolent, I might even pay off part of Quentin's credit card balance.

The first dark cloud came literally in the form of dark clouds, and crossed overhead the following Wednesday, one week into my employment, and in such an indirect way that it seemed impossible it could begin the chain of events that followed.

But it did.

It had been raining for several days when I reached the building housing Cooper Bauer Malnut that morning, after dodging umbrellas for several blocks down Park Avenue. I shook off my own umbrella and pushed through the revolving doors, my wet leather soles sliding slightly on the polished floors as I walked to the bank of elevators.

"Brett, hold the elevator!"

I turned and saw Janelle Banks, rushing through the lobby . . . and then watched helplessly as she slipped on the smooth, wet floor and her legs flew out from under her.

I left the elevator—and let me add here that I was the *only* person who left the elevator—and raced to her side.

"Are you okay?" I asked.

"I don't know. My leg hurts . . ."

As it should have, because a short time later we learned that Janelle had suffered a compound fracture.

"Such a shame," said Philip, when he heard the news. "She'll be out for weeks. Brett, would you see to it that flowers are sent?"

"I've already taken care of that, Philip," I said.

He smiled. "I knew I was right to hire you." Philip Whitehead looked around the office and said, "Maybe you should call down to HR and have a fill-in sent up. I don't have anything *too* pressing, but in case anything comes up, I don't want to have to burden *you*."

No, of course not. We wouldn't want to burden *me* with mundane matters, would we? I told Philip I'd take care of arranging a replacement for Janelle right away.

In turn, Human Resources told me that while the pool of available assistants was strained due to the traditional New York in August vacation schedule, in which everyone flees the city because all their psychiatrists have taken the month off, they would take care of the problem as soon as possible.

And that, I thought, was that. Another task well done.

While HR dealt with the Janelle problem, my phone rang.

"Brett Revere," I said, answering it.

"Jamie Brock."

My heart fluttered.

"Hey!" I shouted, when I regained my composure. "I was wondering what ever happened to you." And, in fact, I had been. I had not heard from Jamie since the morning he professed his love—his *brotherly* love—and I wondered if enough time had passed to call him without creating an awkward situation.

Apparently, it had.

"How is it working for Philip?" he asked.

"It's great. You should see this office."

"I'm happy for you, baby." *Baby* . . . "I'm glad things worked out."

"Me, too. *Believe me*. So what's going on with you?"

"Same old, same old. I finished the job for David Carlyle, and I'm in the middle of my next job . . . and I think I might be picking up another one. And when I get some money . . ."

"I know . . . I know . . ."

"In the meantime," he said, "I was hoping to speak to your employer."

Oh. So Jamie wasn't really calling to speak with *me*.

I didn't know why that surprised me.

"Let me see if Mr. Whitehead is free," I said. I quickly put Jamie on hold and dialed Philip's extension. "Jamie Brock is on the line," I announced, when he picked up. "Do you want to speak to him?"

"I'll take it."

I patched Jamie through and hung up. A few minutes later, my phone rang. Philip was calling me back.

"Brett," he said, "I need you to put something on my schedule for Friday night."

"*This* Friday?"

"Yes. Eight o'clock. I'm going to see that show *Andy*."

Shit.

I wanted to talk Philip out of it, but realized that would only raise a red flag. And in any event, I was *not* going, so I had nothing to worry about. Nothing. Nothing at all.

Or at least that's what I kept telling myself.

And then I called Jamie back.

"What are you doing?" I whispered, when he answered.

"I had an extra ticket and thought Philip might want to go."

"But you know I have connections to that show," I said. "Don't you think that inviting Philip is striking too close to home?"

"What do you care, Brett? You're not in the show anymore."

"I know, but . . . it's just wrong."

"Don't worry about it." With that, he broke the connection.

So I tried not to worry about it. Again.

Around noon, my phone rang again. This time, it was Human Resources, advising me that two women were on their way to the forty-seventh floor to discuss filling in for Janelle while she was on the mend. I stopped by his office and personally delivered the news to Philip.

"Wonderful," he said, putting on his suit coat to meet his new assistant.

Philip waited in the quiet reception area, while I went back to my office to retrieve his schedule. The temporary assistant would need to be up-to-date, after all. In the few seconds I was gone, the two women arrived . . . as did the beginning of the end.

"Don't I know you?" asked one woman—the taller and older of the two—as I returned to the reception area. And indeed she did. It was none other than Mary Devlin—a.k.a. Cruella DeVil—the owner of MetroTemp, my former employer.

I prayed that the past few months had erased her memory of our last meeting, when she had referred me to AA and NA. In one sense they did, because she clearly couldn't remember my name. But her face indicated that she remembered our last encounter.

"This is my personal assistant, Brett Revere," said Philip, trying to be helpful. "Brett tends to my personal schedule and the like, and you . . ." He indicated the younger woman, obviously a MetroTemp temp " . . .will see to my matters related directly to the firm."

"I *know* Mr. Revere," said Cruella, no doubt grateful to have her memory refreshed of my name, as she took my hand. "He used to work for us." Turning to me, she said, "And I'm so glad to see that things have worked out for you, Brett."

Confused, Philip said, "Brett worked for MetroTemp?"

"I . . . uh . . . I . . ."

"You were a *temporary worker*? I thought . . ."

I know what you thought, Philip. Because I told you what to think. The trust fund . . . the Dallas oil money . . . the ten-year relationship with "Maxwell Robinson" . . . And now you knew that every word out of my mouth had been a lie.

I tried to salvage those lies.

"I tried it out for a while," I told him, as I shot Cruella a look that said "save me." To her credit, her eyes responded sympathetically.

Unfortunately, not having been briefed on the new, improved biography of Brett Revere, she only made things worse while trying to make them better.

"Yes, Brett was with us briefly," she said. "He's *really* an actor."

Philip nodded, and—after the minutes of confusion—there was a new clarity in his eyes.

"Quite a good one, it seems," he said softly.

And with those words, I knew that my employment with the law firm of Cooper Bauer Malnut was quickly coming to an end.

Some time later, after Cruella had departed and I had the temp up and running, Philip phoned and asked me to come to his office.

"I'm afraid this isn't working," he said when I walked through the door, looking up for a brief moment before returning his gaze to the computer monitor on the side of his desk.

"Philip, I'm sorry. I don't know what to say."

He returned his eyes to me.

"I don't really care that you used to be a temp, Brett. What I care about is the lies. I have to be able to trust my personal assistant, and . . . well, I'm afraid that level of trust has been shattered."

"But I was just . . . shading the truth a bit. I'm still competent to handle your affairs."

"You are unable to assist me, Brett." Philip sighed, wiping a hand across his weary eyes. "I'm very sorry about this, but that's the long and short of it. When I hired you, I thought I was hiring someone who understood the lifestyle of the people I deal with . . . not to mention my own. That's the way you presented yourself, after all. But then you backed up your presentation with all this nonsense, none of which appears to be true, and compounded the error." He leaned forward and said, "Let me ask you a question. There isn't any trust fund, is there?"

"No."

"And that ten-year relationship . . . that never existed, did it?"

"No."

He shook his head. "I may be older, Brett, but I'm only sixty, and my mind is sharper than it was when I graduated law school. So let me see if I can put together the case here. You were a temporary worker and an actor, and at some point a few months ago—when you first broke onto the scene—you decided to use your acting skills to con me and my friends into accepting you, with the goal of securing money which would otherwise be unobtainable. Am I correct?"

Looking at the floor, I said, "Basically, that's the story."

"I'm very disappointed, Brett. I don't like to be conned." He paused, then added the words that would sting and shame me for months to come.

"At least when you deal with a hustler, you get a degree of honesty about the terms of the transaction and something in return."

"But Philip . . ." I didn't want to say it, but I had to, so I lifted my eyes from the floor. "I *need* this job, Philip."

He leaned back in his chair. "Maybe you should look around for something you're better suited at. Maybe . . . temping."

Philip looked away from me, attempting to make our break as impersonal as possible.

"That will be all," he said. "Stop in HR on your way out. They will be expecting you."

"Okay," I said, as, head lowered, I made my exit from his office. In the doorway I turned and said, "Keep the Lalique."

"I intend to."

Since I had logged a paltry six working days at Cooper Bauer Malnut—the woman in Human Resources said I'd be paid for them in seven to ten days, and the check would be mailed—I hadn't accumulated anything of significance, which made the clearing-off-the-desk ritual unnecessary. I was out the door in less than three minutes, after one last, sad glance at my forty-seventh-story view.

As I walked up Lexington Avenue to the subway station, I tried to calculate what the pay would be for six days. Something slightly more than two percent of $90,000, which, after taxes, would come to maybe a thousand dollars. Enough to stave off the wolves for a few more days, but not quite the big payoff Operation Hamptons was supposed to bring.

Worse yet, I was now going to have to tell Alan that he had been right all along. But *that,* I decided, could wait.

On the train ride back to Astoria, I wondered if I should make a final plea to Philip Whitehead. Maybe when his anger and disappointment cooled, he could be convinced to take me back . . . or at least not tell anyone of the nature of my dismissal. Maybe I could still salvage Operation Hamptons.

On the other hand, when he said that my actions and honesty were worse than those of a hustler, he didn't leave a lot of leeway.

I didn't bother opening my umbrella in the light rain as I walked through the quiet streets from the station to my apartment. It was as if I hoped I could wash away my sins.

But, no.

Apres Philip Whitehead, *le deluge.*

I was reaching to unlock the front door of my apartment building when I heard a car door slam behind me, followed moments later by another slam. I turned to see Quentin King crossing the street toward me, steps in front of another man who looked like I had always imagined . . .

But wait. No, that couldn't be right.

I squinted, and was shocked to have my first impression confirmed. Because there, parked at the opposite curb, was a Lexus bearing the license plate NYSNICO1.

Quentin was indeed headed toward me, and following him was a bear-like figure with a bad toupee that could only be Nicholas Golodnya.

"Dude, we need to talk," said Quentin, as he reached the bottom of the stoop.

"Uh . . . uh . . ." I looked down at the two men on the sidewalk below me. This was very confusing, but there was no way anything good was going to come out of it. "Uh . . . What do we need to talk about?"

"A credit card."

Of course. But I had already known that the credit card was about to come back to haunt me. What I didn't understand was why Golodnya was there.

Still, I did my best to keep a straight face.

"Credit card?"

"You know what I'm talking about," he said. "You've been using a credit card that's in my name, and I want it back. And you're gonna pay me every dollar you've charged against it, too."

"I have no idea what you're talking . . ."

"Give him the credit card, Mr. Revere," commanded Golodnya. "And then tell me where I can find Jamie Brock."

I decided to play dumb, which was surprisingly easy, given the numbness in my brain.

"I don't think we've met," I said.

He sneered. "It is not important you should know my name."

"If you're looking for Jamie, *I* think it's important."

"I do not," he said with finality.

I shook my head. "I don't have any credit card. And I don't know where Jamie is."

He took one menacing step forward, placing one foot on the bottom step.

"Mr. Revere, I am not kidding. Would it help your memory to know that my name is Nicholas Golodnya?"

I struggled to keep my composure. "Sorry, the name doesn't ring . . ."

"The credit card, Brett," said Quentin, interrupting. "I mean it."

Golodnya added, "Give it to him." He paused, letting a thought gel, then asked, "Or does Jamie Brock still have possession of the credit card?"

Think fast, Brett. Think fast.

"Mr. Revere? We are waiting."

"Dude, listen to the dude. Give me the card and cover the charges, or we're gonna have to go to the cops."

"No police," hissed Golodnya, a statement in which I took some relief until he added, "If Mr. Revere or Mr. Brock will not return what is ours, I will take care of things myself."

I took a deep breath, then bravely descended one step closer to them.

"Honestly, Quentin, I have no idea what you're talking about. You have to believe me." I nodded toward Golodnya, standing with his arms folded at the base of the stoop. "And what is *he* doing here?"

"Dude, I've been stopping by to pick up my mail, and I found a statement."

"You've been stealing mail?"

He shook his head. "I can't believe this shit. You've been using a credit card in my name, and you're pissed off that I found the statement? Unreal." He looked away to collect himself, then continued. "So I see there's, like, a bunch of charges at Barneys and places like that, where nobody remembers who used it. And I check out these charges at La Goulue, but they aren't telling me anything . . . like I'm scamming or something. So finally I check out this place in the Hamptons, and—surprise—this waiter dude remembers the card."

"Well, there you go," I said, taking on an expression of innocence. "I've never eaten at a restaurant in the Hamptons, so it couldn't have been me."

"You know the Hamptons," snarled Golodnya.

"I didn't say I've never been out there," I said. "But I've never . . ."

"Dude," said Quentin, "that's not where I'm going with this, okay? Anyway, I hop a train out there and the waiter tells me that your buddy used the card to take Nick here to lunch."

"Which buddy?" I asked, hoping that Quentin's research wasn't as thorough as it seemed.

Quentin was about to reply when Golodnya roared. "You know we are talking about Jamie Brock, Mr. Revere, so stop playing games. Jamie took me to lunch, to reconcile, on the same day that someone broke into my computer and erased . . . uh . . . valuable files. I do not believe in coincidence, Mr. Revere. I think Jamie took me to lunch as a ruse, leaving you behind to erase those files and get out of my house before we returned. I think you are guilty of breaking and entering, and industrial sabotage, and . . . many other crimes."

I swallowed hard. "So why don't you go to the police?"

His nostrils flared. "I don't believe in the police. I am my own police."

Okay. I stepped back to the top of the stoop.

Quentin tossed Golodnya a much more dismissive glance than I would have dared, and took over. "The waiter in the Hamptons led me to Nicholas, which has led us to this point. So let's not drag this out, okay? The card, the cash, and we're out of here."

"The card, the cash, and the place where I can find Mr. Brock," said Golodnya. "*Then* we will leave you alone."

"Again," I said, spreading my arms in a peaceful, honest gesture that did not seem to fool either one of them. "I don't have the credit card. And Jamie just moved, so I don't know where he is or how to contact him."

Golodnya said, "He is your close friend, but you don't know how to reach him?"

"He just moved. *He* reaches *me*. And, anyway, we're not that close."

"This is a waste of time," said Golodnya abruptly. "We will go find Jamie Brock. If Mr. Revere will not assist us, I know other ways to find him." With that, he turned and launched his burly frame toward the car, navigating puddles as he crossed the street.

Quentin descended the stairs to the sidewalk, then turned to address me a final time.

"Your buddy had better have that credit card, Brett. This is serious business, man."

Yeah, I thought, as I watched them drive off. This was so definitely serious business.

Let's see: I had just lost my job because my boss learned I was passing myself off as someone I was not, and I had now been threatened by Creepy Quentin and Crazy Nicholas Golodnya. This had been quite a day.

I lumbered up the four flights to my apartment and got the key in the lock just in time to hear the phone ring.

It was Jamie.

"I hope your day is going better than mine," I said.

"What happened with Philip?" he asked. "I just called for you, and they said you were no longer with the firm."

"I don't really want to talk about it," I said. "Let's just say that Philip was very adamant that I leave Cooper Bauer Malnut." I paused and added, "And anyway, we've got bigger problems, effective five minutes ago."

I filled Jamie in on my encounter with Quentin and Golodnya.

"Fuck," he muttered, when I had finished. "He doesn't know where I am, does he?"

"No. I don't even know the address myself. So what are we going to do?"

"Do they know you have the credit card?"

"No. And it's pretty well hidden."

"And did Nico . . ." Jamie's voice trailed off, and I was afraid we had lost our connection before he cryptically asked, "Did Nico ask about anything else?"

"Well . . . I told you that he knows about our scam with the computer files . . . and they mentioned the credit card, of course. But, other than that, nothing."

"Nothing about a watch?"

"No, not— Wait a minute. What about a watch? Your *new* watch? The Cartier? The watch you said he gave you as a goodbye present when your relationship ended?"

"Um . . . yeah. The thing is, it was sort of a one-sided goodbye present."

"You *stole* his watch?"

Jamie grew defensive. "I *deserved* that watch, Brett. Look what he put me through. It was . . . it was psychological abuse."

"Jamie, I can't believe . . ."

"I deserved this watch for the same reasons you deserved to use that credit card to replace the things that Quentin stole from you."

I rubbed a hand across my face, and realized I was dripping with sweat.

"I don't think there's an equivalence there," I said.

"I see it," he said. "Can't you? Quentin stole, so you stole to get your things back. Nico was an asshole, so I stole to get properly compensated. Same thing."

"Thanks," I said. "This is the first time I've truly felt like a thief since you first talked me into using that credit card." There was a gap in the conversation as we contemplated our situation, until I filled it with, "So what are you going to do?"

"About what?"

I shook my head. Was Jamie really that oblivious to the serious business at hand? "About Nicholas Golodnya, and the fact that he's out to get us."

He thought for a moment. "Well . . . first off, I guess I'll have to avoid the Penthouse for a while."

"That would be advisable."

"And . . . I don't know . . . I'll avoid Ben Grover, and that crowd. La Goulue. Places I'm known."

"Again, advisable. But what will you do? Hole up in your apartment for a few years, until he goes away or dies?"

"I'll . . . I'll start hanging out in Chelsea and the Village. Places he wouldn't think to look for me."

"Maybe you should just give him back the watch."

"No way." That was it. His mind was made up and the case was closed. "The watch is mine. I worked for that watch. Look, this apartment's a sublet, the phone isn't in my name, and if I change my routine, well . . . this is a big city, and he'll never find me."

"But if you gave up the watch," I explained, "then he'd go away. I think I can handle Quentin alone, but if he's got Golodnya with him, well, that's not good. If Golodnya is out of the picture, I can and will deny ever seeing that credit card . . . at least until I can afford to pay Quentin."

"But there's a principle involved . . ."

I was losing my patience with him. "There's no *principle* here, Jamie. You stole the guy's watch! Give it back and let's move on."

"No." And with that, he hung up.

Yes, it had been one great fucking day.

When I saw him later at the Penthouse—where I went for once to drown my troubles, rather than to social-climb—the first words out of Michael's mouth were, "What the hell happened with Philip Whitehead? The phone lines have been buzzing all afternoon."

I had pretty much had it with Michael DeVries and didn't even try to hide the contempt in my voice.

"Philip discovered the real Brett Revere, and he didn't like what he saw."

"Oh, Brett," he muttered. "How could you let that happen? Haven't I tried to teach you the proper way to act around these people?"

"Shut up, Michael," I said, turning from him.

"Get back here!"

I ignored him and walked up the staircase to the piano bar. When

I reached the top of the stairs I turned and saw that Michael had followed me.

"I was doing my job and doing it well," I said, before he had a chance to speak. "But Philip discovered that I had been telling some lies—that I used to be an actor and a temp, instead of a trust fund baby—and he decided that I could no longer work for him. And that's the story."

"Maybe if you came up with a new story to explain away . . ."

I shook my head. "No more lies, Michael. I can't even keep them all straight anymore. And the payoff has not been worth it. This project has cost me money and love, and I can't do it anymore."

He leaned against the staircase railing. "You *can* do it and you *will* do it. This thing with Philip . . . here's how you explain it away. Your parents held back on your money because you had this crazy dream of being an actor, and . . . and you got your back up and decided to temp for a while, to show your independence. But after a while you gave up the acting and temping, and the parents let you access the trust fund again, and . . ."

"No more," I said.

"You're a fool."

I looked around the bar, finally spotting Angel at the far end, where Paolo was filling his tray with drinks, and said, "You know what else I've been a fool about?"

Michael followed my gaze, then groaned. "That little Puerto Rican boy? Not *that* again, Brett."

"Watch me."

Angel approached, carrying the tray, and smiled when he saw me. "Need a drink?" he asked. "I'll be with you in one minute."

"No," I said. "Now."

He looked at me with confusion . . . and with even more confusion when I took the tray from his hands and handed it to the patron he was trying to serve, as I told the man, "This will only take a second."

And then I took Angel Maldonado in my arms and gave him the slowest, deepest, most longing kiss I had ever given another man.

When we broke for a split second, he whispered, "You're going to get me fired."

So I kissed him again.

When it was over, Michael muttered, "That was the most disgusting display. . . . Next you'll be kissing the blacks like your bald friend . . ."

"Pardon me," I said to the tray-laden patron, as I grabbed a glass of red wine off the tray and casually tossed it in the face of Michael DeVries.

Fagin had been vanquished.

Michael roared and sputtered and, most important, stormed away. I turned as Angel retrieved his tray and said, "I think I owe someone a drink."

"That would be me," said the man who had held the tray. He was smiling, and I noticed for the first time that his skin was darker than the Penthouse norm. "And on the contrary. I have never seen a glass of cabernet sauvignon put to such good use."

"My hero," said Angel, beaming and balancing the tray as he kissed my cheek. "I don't know what got into you, but I like it. Even if it gets me fired."

"If you get fired, we'll have more time to go on dates," I said.

He arched an eyebrow. "We'll talk."

My first thought the next morning was, *I really did that?*

I *really* tossed a glass of red wine in Michael's face? And I wasn't even drunk?

Well, good for me.

"That was pretty stupid," said Jamie, when I got him on the line and recapped the night. "Michael is not going to just forget that."

"I don't care. Michael is a pain in the ass, and he had it coming."

His tone grew quiet. "And what's this about kissing the waiter?"

"I *like* the waiter. I want to *date* the waiter."

"Oh."

Was Jamie Brock expressing regret? Jealousy?

If he was, it was soon forgotten.

"I'm going to see most of that crowd tomorrow night at *Andy*," he said moments later, markedly more chipper. "And I'll do what I can to smooth things over."

"Jamie," I said, "I really don't know if I *want* things to be smoothed over. Maybe it's a good thing to break out of the pattern of lies."

"I'll try to take care of things." It was almost as if he didn't hear me. Maybe Jamie had a hearing impairment that filtered out the words of those who had grown tired of social climbing.

Alan, on the other hand, had the opposite reaction when I updated him on my days of drama. While he expressed regret that I had lost the job with Philip Whitehead, he was delighted to hear that I had doused Michael.

"I never liked that bastard," he said.

"I know . . . I know . . ."

"I'm just glad that you finally saw through him. So does this mean you won't be going to the Penthouse anymore?"

"I don't know. There *is* Angel . . ."

"True. Maybe you can get him fired yet."

"Good point. It's probably considered bad form for the waiters to make out with the patrons."

"The reason I asked," he said, "is because Ty wants to go and sing tomorrow night."

"Is he going to get into one of his moods?" I asked.

"Probably. But he's worth it, even when he's sulking. Don't tell anyone, but I think I may be in love."

"Why, Alan Donovan! I never thought I'd hear those words come out of your mouth."

"You're sworn to secrecy," he said. "Especially in front of Ty."

"He doesn't know?"

"He knows . . . he knows . . . But I want to keep him on his toes. Otherwise, he'll get comfortable and realize that his boyfriend is a middle-aged bald guy."

My final call of the morning was to Angel.

"It's your hero," I said, when he answered the phone.

He laughed. "So . . . I see that you're getting better at using the telephone."

"I've been practicing. Anyway, I was wondering if you'd like to go out on a real date some time."

He was silent for a short while, then said, "Maybe. I just don't know what my schedule looks like, and . . . and . . . and frankly, Brett, I'm still not sure about you."

"But . . . why not?"

Silence again, then, "You have a mixed track record."

"I know," I conceded. "But I'm trying to change."

"We'll see. Let me think about things."

I hung up and hoped that Operation Hamptons hadn't done even more damage than I knew it had.

And then I went out to buy a newspaper. For the Help Wanted ads.

"You're *not* going to sing that," said Alan.

"What's the matter?" asked Ty. "You don't like 'The Trolley Song'? I can *channel* Judy!"

"Baby, I'll need rabbit ears to bring that channel in."

Ty was on deck to sing, and it was Friday night at the Penthouse, and for once I was grateful not to see a single familiar face, with the exceptions of Alan and Ty, although Angel's face would have been welcome. But Paolo had told me that Angel phoned in that he wouldn't be to work until eleven that night, so I'd just have to wait another half-hour or so.

Still, there was no Michael DeVries, sulking and plotting revenge . . . no Philip Whitehead, gossiping about my lies and phony trust fund . . . no John Jacob Venezuela to capture it all in print . . . and, especially, no Jamie Brock, to distract me and make me forget that we weren't in love.

"You realize," I said to Alan, as Ty walked to the piano to wait his turn, "that now that I'm broke and out of work again, I'll be in your office every day, bothering you."

"That's all right. I'm very good at saying 'no.' " Looking over my shoulder at the top of the staircase, he muttered, "Oh, shit."

I tensed. "Who is it? Michael?"

"No. It's Quentin."

I resisted the urge to turn around. "What's *he* doing here? He's *straight*!"

"At least we hope so. But he's here, and I'm sure that's because he's looking for you. And there's some other guy with him."

"Big guy?" I asked. "Older? Sort of burly? Bad toupee?"

"Yeah."

I shook my head. "*Very* not good. That's Nicholas Golodnya."

"The one who's looking for Jamie?"

"That's the one. Jamie swiped his watch."

"Your former friends never cease to amaze . . . Hold on. I think they've spotted you."

"Okay," I said. "Act casual." But it was too late. Alan had already scurried away to the safety of Ty's side, near the piano.

Which meant I was on my own.

"Brett?"

I plastered a smile on my face and turned around to face Quentin and Golodnya.

"Quentin! What are *you* doing here? I didn't know you came out of the closet!"

"Not funny, dude. We're here to see you . . ."

"And Jamie Brock," added Golodnya.

"Jamie's not here tonight," I said. "He went down to the Village to see some show."

"Oh, man," said Quentin enthusiastically, temporarily forgetting the purpose of his mission. "He went to see *Andy*, right? I have *got* to see that show!"

Of course he did. How could I forget?

"Yes," I said. "That's where he is. And I don't expect to see him tonight."

Golodnya was unmoved. "We will have a drink and wait. Maybe he will show up after all."

I could only hope that Jamie and his crew weren't planning on a post-theater drink at the Penthouse, although, knowing them, that was *exactly* what they were planning. In the meantime, Golodnya and Quentin found a spot near the bar where they could watch the new arrivals, and I walked to the piano, seeking refuge with Alan and Ty.

And Angel, who was now making his way through the crowd toward us.

"Sleep in?" I asked, when he was near.

"I wish. More studying. I'm way behind. Can I get you anything?"

"How about a date?"

He smiled. "We'll see. How about a drink?"

I ordered and he returned to the bar.

A short time later, I excused myself to go to the bathroom. Out of my peripheral vision, I saw Golodnya and Quentin watch me and begin to follow, only to stop when it was apparent that I wasn't making a break for it.

I stood for a few minutes at the top of the stairs, waiting for the bathroom to be free. Just as the person inside unlocked the door and prepared to exit, a raucous group began making its way up the spiral staircase to the piano bar. I glanced down and saw . . .

Everyone.

Joey Takashimi, still in costume in an orange fright wig, blousy blue shirt—open to midchest—and strategically ripped jeans, led the way, followed by several orphans, Miss Iris Whiskey, a few other stragglers, and several people out of the Penthouse/Hamptons vector. I spotted Burt and Clara Matthews, David Carlyle, J.J. Venezuela, and, regrettably, Philip Whitehead among them . . . and trailing the group was Jamie Brock.

Ducking behind the crowd of newcomers, brushing off their greetings, I grabbed Jamie's arm and pulled him into the bathroom before Golodnya could notice, locking the door firmly behind us.

"Good to see you, too, baby," he said, smiling. "You missed a great show."

"They're here," I said, ignoring him and double-checking the door.

"Who?"

"Nicholas Golodnya. And Quentin King."

He stared into the mirror for a long time, then said, "Nico and . . . that credit card guy?"

"I *told* you they were looking for us!" I said. "So what are we going to do?"

"We are going to get out of this . . ." He stopped, then looked under the bottom of the stall before continuing. "Everything is all right."

"Jamie, are you delusional? I just told you that Golodnya is out there . . ."

"I can take care of Nico."

"How? By sleeping with him again?"

He pulled a few paper towels from the dispenser. "If I have to."

I shook my head. "No, Jamie, that's not the way to do it."

He fixed me with a look that was almost completely vacant. "If that's what has to happen, that's what has to happen."

"I don't think you understand how angry he is."

"I don't think you understand . . . *anything*, Brett." Without warning, Jamie leaned against the basin and sobbed, his façade shattered. "This is *not* how I want to live my life, but I'm going to make it, no matter what it takes."

I wrapped an arm around his shoulder. "Jamie, Jamie . . . calm down. Let's try to work this out."

When he looked up at me, tears were streaming from his eyes.

"How?" he asked harshly, despite the tears. "How are you going to work this out? This entire situation is fucked, Brett, and there's only one way out."

I thought quickly. Maybe too quickly.

"Let me see if I can negotiate this with Golodnya."

"Negotiate? He'll crucify you. Nico doesn't negotiate with . . . with . . . with the Brett Reveres of the world."

I suppose there was an insult in there, but I chose to ignore it.

"Listen," I said. "If we just give him the watch . . ."

"No." His right hand instinctively covered the watch on his left wrist. "The watch is mine. I've explained that already."

I leaned against the wall, feeling the cool tiles at the back of my head. On the other side of the door, I heard voices, then a knock.

"Occupied!" I yelled. Let him use the bathroom at the ground floor bar.

More tears from Jamie. "Brett . . . what am I going to do?"

A thought, not fully formed, popped into my head. It wasn't the same as having a well-developed plan, but it was as good as it was going to get on such short notice.

"Wait here," I told him, unlocking the door.

"Where are you going?" Jamie asked.

"One of us is going to have to talk to Golodnya, and I got the job. Lock the door behind me."

I left the bathroom and heard the lock *click* behind me, which had to have pissed off the three men waiting to relieve themselves. I really didn't care, though. Confronting Nicholas Golodnya was a lot scarier than confronting three gay men that had to take a leak. Sort of.

The Russian-born Pentagon contractor was standing at the bar with his back to me when I approached, Quentin at his side.

"I need to talk to you," I said

"Talk."

"Alone."

Golodnya turned to Quentin and said, "Please give me a private moment with Mr. Revere. Once we have talked, he is all yours." Reluctantly, Quentin walked a dozen paces away, and Golodnya said, "Do you know where Jamie is?"

"Maybe."

Golodnya snorted. "Maybe? That is not very helpful. I do not like to have my time wasted."

"Let me ask you a question," I said. "If you have the watch back, will you leave him alone?"

"Nothing would give me greater pleasure. I no longer have use for Mr. Brock. You can assure him of that."

"Okay," I said. "Wait here one minute."

I raced back to the bathroom, my pace broken by Miss Iris Whiskey, who was suddenly in my way.

"Brent, darling," she said. "Give mama a big hug!"

I pushed past, mumbling a quick, "Later, Iris. Gotta use the bathroom."

"That's *Miss* Iris," she called after me.

The line outside the bathroom was now four-deep, but I pushed to the front and knocked, saying, "Jamie, it's Brett."

"There's a *line* here," whined one of the waiting men.

"I'm sorry," I said, "but he's really sick. Throwing up all over the place. You really don't want to use this bathroom . . ." I heard the lock click open and pushed through the door, looking back at four men with disappointed, slightly disgusted looks on their faces.

"It's all about the watch," I said, when I was locked back inside the small room. "Give him the watch and he'll go away."

"No."

"Jamie, why are the two of you going to war over a stupid fucking watch? What, is there microfilm hidden inside? This is insane."

"It's the principle."

"It's the principle for *him*, too."

He crossed his arms and turned back to the mirror, signaling that the discussion was over.

I sighed. He was trying in his bullheadedness, but there was still something about him . . .

I moved behind him, facing his image in the mirror, and wrapped my arms around him.

"You're not giving in, are you?" I asked.

"No."

"Okay . . . Well, then, I guess I'll have to hang in there with you. Because if Golodnya and Quentin are going to work as a team, we'd better . . ." I looked at the two of us reflected in the mirror a bit more closely. "Baby, does Golodnya's watch have an inscription on it?"

"No, it doesn't. It's just a plain old, exquisite watch."

"Good. I'm going back outside to talk with him. Wait a while before you leave the bathroom . . . and, to be safe, put your watch in your pants pocket where he can't see it."

"Why?"

"Let's not make him any angrier than he is, okay?"

I left Jamie, passed three *new* men who were grumbling because they couldn't get into the bathroom, and found Golodnya still standing at the bar.

"Here," I said to him, placing a Cartier watch in his hand. "Jamie says that he's sorry."

He looked at the watch carefully, then, apparently satisfied, slipped it on his wrist.

"You are a good friend to him," he said, nodding slightly. "You may have saved Mr. Brock quite a bit of grief."

"It's what I live for." I looked around the bar. "Now, for my next act, where's Quentin?"

"I last saw him talking to the huge drag queen."

Which figured.

"I am taking my leave, Mr. Revere," said Golodnya. "I trust our paths will seldom, if ever, cross in the future."

"I'll do my best, and you do yours."

I watched him leave, shoving people in his path aside, and thought how strange it was for me—a man who generally tried to please everyone—to have made so many enemies in just a few days. Michael, Philip, and now Golodnya . . . and who knew who else? The room was full of potential candidates.

First, though, there was the issue of Quentin to resolve. As I scanned the room for him and Miss Iris, I heard the opening chords to "It's a Hard-Knock Life," which I could only hope was being performed with its original lyrics intact.

It was not to be.

"What's going on?" asked Angel, suddenly at my side as I cringed at Walter Pomeroy's lyrics. "Some guys have complained that you've been hogging the bathroom."

"There's a lot of drama going on," I said. "And I'm trying to clean it all up."

"Well, keep it out of the bathroom, 'kay?"

"Okay."

I finally found Quentin and Miss Iris Whiskey sitting on a low, plush couch tucked in the corner, where they were almost invisible through the crowd.

"I've been looking for you," I told him, after I managed to push through the patrons.

"Brent," said Miss Iris.

"Brett."

"Are you sure? I thought it was 'Brent.' " She shrugged her padded shoulders. "Anyway, Quentin here tells me that the two of you have some . . . financial disagreements."

I nodded. "That's the only reason I'm here to talk to him." She didn't move. "Uh . . . in *private*?"

"Will there be nasty words and drama?"

"Maybe."

"And I can't stay?" I shook my head and, with a sulk and some readjusting of her dress, she left us, leaving Quentin looking on in her wake.

"So, Quentin," I said. "You want that credit card?"

"The card, and money for what you charged on it."

I pulled out my wallet and said, "Here's what we're going to do, Quentin." Taking the card out, I said, "You know that there's no way in hell you deserve a $15,000 line of credit, and that means you had to commit fraud when you applied. Right?" He didn't answer me, which did not come as a surprise. "So here's what I'm going to do . . ."

And with that, I bent the plastic card until it snapped.

"*Dude!* Uncool . . ."

"That's the bad news," I said. "Here's some more bad news. It cost me a few thousand dollars to replace all the things you stole from my apartment. I'm not going to pay that portion of the balance on the card . . . and I'm also not paying for the dinner I had at La Goulue the night you robbed me. Let's call that 'interest.' The good news, though, is that after I tally everything up, I'm going to reimburse you for the entire balance I ran up on the card, minus what you owe me. It will take me some time, but I'll do it."

"But my credit . . ."

I sighed. "Quentin, you know as well as I do that you're going to report the card stolen, or lost in the mail, or whatever, and that every dollar I reimburse you is going straight into your pocket. That'll be on *your* conscience, okay? I'm going to clear *my* conscience by paying you for my charges and cash advances. So don't give me any more 'dudes' or bitching about what this will do to your credit record."

"*Du* . . . uh . . . Okay."

"One more thing."

"Yeah?"

"Get out of my bar."

Nicholas Golodnya was gone, and Quentin King was gone, and Michael DeVries, well . . . he seemed to be out of my life, too. And as for Jamie, he was still locked in the bathroom, but that was *his* problem.

I did not intend to tell him that, after I saw our images reflected together in the mirror, I had remembered that *my* Cartier watch looked exactly the same as *his* Cartier watch, and now Nicholas Golodnya was wearing a gift from Brett Revere via Michael DeVries via some old woman or another. It may have been the best-traveled watch in Cartier history.

Jamie could keep his ill-gotten watch, just as Creepy Quentin could keep my payments against the credit card balance. I would be poor and wearing a Seiko, but at least I'd have my soul.

I looked around the bar and realized that I was witnessing the most remarkable blending of otherwise disparate groups I had ever seen, as people socialized easily and amicably across the divisions of race, class, age, gender, and sexuality. The Penthouse and Hamptons regulars and the *Andy* cast apparently found more in common than not. That, or they found each other so exotic that they had to learn more.

Burt and Clara Matthews were talking with Joey Takashimi . . . J.J. Venezuela and David Carlyle were apparently enchanted by Miss Iris Whiskey . . . Ty chatted with Rick Atkins and his doctor husband, while Alan was similarly engaged with . . . Philip Whitehead.

And I realized that there was one more person with whom I had to set things right.

"Mind if I interrupt?" I asked Alan, who smiled slightly and moved away to give us privacy. When I was alone with Philip, I said, "I owe you an apology."

He shook his head sadly. "Brett, if this is about the job, I'm sorry, but . . . once my confidence is shaken, I'm afraid that's that."

"It's not that," I said. "You did what you had to do, and I'm not going to beg. I just wanted to tell you that I understand. I mean, it was a *great* job, and I wouldn't turn it down if you offered, but I *did* lie to you. I lied to everyone. I just want to ask for your forgiveness, and for no hard feelings."

He took my hand. "No hard feelings."

I left Philip and again stood alone, scanning the room and realizing that I had largely underestimated the people in it over the past few months . . . or, at least, many of them. I had tried to play to their basest instincts for weeks as I willingly let Michael and Jamie make me over into someone who was no longer Brett Revere, when all along Brett Revere—the *real* Brett Revere—would have been just fine.

Poor, perhaps, but just fine.

Of course, I ended up poor anyway . . .

"About that date . . ." I said, as Angel walked by.

"I'm working!" He was also smiling.

"Michelle Pfeiffer and Indian food, right?"

He shook his head. "You're crazy. You've got to woo me some more. Candy . . . flowers . . ."

"Walks through Central Park in the rain?"

"That works, too." He smiled again, and added, "I've got customers."

"Go get 'em. But keep an ear open for the piano. I'm going to sing."

He laughed, and went back to work.

When I returned from placing my name on the pianist's list, Alan said to me, "Guess what! Those Matthews people have promised to invest five hundred thousand dollars in *Andy*."

"You're kidding."

"Brett, listen to me and listen carefully. Get. Back. In. That. Show."

"Will you make the calls?" I asked.

"Yes," he said, and would probably have said more but suddenly J.J. Venezuela was upon us.

"Where's Michael tonight?" he asked.

I looked at him warily. "Why are you asking me?"

"Because I wanted to see that expression on your face." Venezuela laughed and brushed a hand through his hair. "Good lord, Brett, that's the funniest story I've heard in ages. You really threw a full glass of red wine in his face?"

"I did."

"Not that he didn't deserve it, but what did he do to provoke you?"

"I did something, and he made a crude racial comment."

"What did you do?"

I spotted Angel about to pass and stopped him. Taking his tray and handing it to Alan, I repeated the kiss.

"Brett," said Angel, squirming out of my arms. "I really can't keep doing that while I'm on the clock."

"Beautiful," said Venezuela, as Angel took his tray back from Alan.

"Isn't it?" I said.

A few minutes later I was summoned to the piano, where I picked up the mic and faced the crowd.

"I think that many of you will recognize the meaning of this song in my life," I said.

And as the first notes rang out, and as the patrons realized that I was about to sing "I Got Plenty O' Nothing," the laughter began. First, only a few people got the joke . . . then a few others . . . and soon the laughter became infectious. Even people who didn't know me were caught up in it.

And no one was laughing harder than me.

Brett Revere's Theory of Life, Part Seventeen: All Theories of Life Are Bullshit, So Live Life and Hope for the Best

There was a knock on the bathroom door and he asked me, "Are you ready, honey?"

"Just freshening up," I said, as I let cool tap water refresh me. It had been a hot summer, and I had spent the past three weeks feeling less than fresh. I hated this decrepit apartment, and I hated the shower with the mildew that wouldn't go away, no matter how hard you scrubbed, and I hated the nasty super and the summer grayouts and the pigeon shit on the stoop and . . . well . . . maybe I was just in a bad mood because of the excessive heat and humidity, but, still, I hated it all. And being sweaty and feeling gross wasn't helping things.

"David Carlyle and J.J. Venezuela are here," he said, from the other side of the door. "I think you should make an effort here . . ."

I sighed.

And opened the door.

"Sorry, baby," I said, spotting David and J.J. over his shoulder. "I didn't mean to hog the bathroom."

"No problem. You okay?"

"Yeah," I said. "Maybe I'm stressing a bit, because this is our first dinner party. You know, dinner parties aren't exactly my forte."

"You'll be fine." He kissed me. "*We'll* be fine."

David Carlyle exaggerated a harrumph from the foyer.

"Break!" I said, and broke, walking to greet him with the full attention he deserved.

"We brought a bottle of wine," David said, presenting the bottle. I thanked him profusely.

"Sorry it took me so long to get out of the bathroom," I said, as Angel took the bottle of wine and walked to the refrigerator. "The heat is . . ."

"Oppressive," he said. "Horrid. Ghastly. Inhuman. Inhum*ane*. But we'll survive it. Especially because I was promised a deck."

"We *do* have a deck," I said with a smile, taking his hand and leading them through the small apartment to the deck . . . which overlooked a concrete courtyard.

David and J.J. settled onto twin utilitarian chairs made tolerable by thin cushions. Making sure that Angel was out of range, J.J. asked, "And you're happy here?"

I shrugged. "Happy *here*? As opposed to what?"

"Good point." He paused, looking out over the buildings surrounding us, and said, "So this is East Harlem! I live so close, but never thought to visit. And now I know why."

I smiled, a trace of conspiracy in my face, even though I no longer had anything to conspire about. "It isn't my dream life, but it's cool. It really is. Angel is great, and, well . . . I'm getting my act together."

"*More* than getting your act together," said Angel, suddenly behind me. "You're in a Tony-nominated show." After he handed David and J.J. glasses of wine, he wrapped an arm around my waist. "*And* . . ."

"And *what*?" I asked.

"And you understudy for the lead. That's cool, too, right?"

I laughed. "Well, first Joey Takashimi has to *literally* break a leg . . ."

Angel shushed me as the intercom rang.

"That's probably him now," he said, as he left to answer the door.

"Good for you, Brett," said David, when Angel was out of earshot. "You've found love . . . you're in a hit show . . . you understudy for a Tony nominee, which counts for something . . . I suppose . . ."

"Just Joey," I said. "And he's a bit *trying* as a friend."

David raised an eyebrow. "He's an actor. Of course he's 'trying.' And trust me; you haven't dealt with 'trying' until you've worked with writers." He sighed, then took a large gulp from his glass of wine. "You are all cut from the same cloth. Egos run amok— No offense, J.J."

"None taken. My ego *does* run amok."

"As long as you're self-aware. You see, Brett? This is why J.J. and I have such a beautiful friendship." David stopped, looked over my shoulder, and beamed. "You must be Joey Takashimi!" Lifting himself off the thin cushion, he extended his hand and said, "If you ever want to write your autobiography, I *insist* you call me."

People rolled in, and soon Joey Takashimi wasn't the only Tony nominee in our upper-upper-Upper East Side apartment. Rick Atkins, nominee for Best Supporting Actor, soon arrived, along with his competition, Miss Iris Whiskey, even though she kept insisting that she really deserved a Best Supporting *Actress* nod.

Yes, as you have probably figured out, *Andy* was a runaway hit. Coupled with one of the most miserable years in theater history, the hideous play that was supposed to open and close in the back room of a Christopher Street bar had swiftly moved Off-Broadway, then made the huge leap to a legitimate Broadway theater, where the *Times* hailed it as one of the most insightful pieces of satire on the stage in the past decade.

I know, I know . . . I don't get it, either.

As David Carlyle and John Jacob Venezuela soaked up theater gossip on the deck, Angel sidled up to me in the kitchen and kissed me.

"What was that for?" I asked.

"For being the best boyfriend ever." He smiled. "Well . . . maybe not ever, but you know I didn't have high hopes for you way back when, and *now* look at us."

"Thirteen months and counting," I said. "And you'd better be careful, because one of these days I'm going to make an honest man out of you."

"And then we can have babies!"

I shook my head, smiling. "Babies? I don't think so."

"We'll adopt! A boy for you, a girl for me. What are you going to name your boy?"

I laughed. "Angel, Junior."

"Okay. My girl will be Cher."

Mercifully, we were interrupted by the intercom, because there was a good chance that I was about to say the wrong thing. When Angel went to buzz in the new guests, I walked out on the deck, where Joey was holding court.

"So if I win the Tony," I heard him saying, "there's a good chance I'll be offered the role of the Emcee in *Cabaret* in the national tour."

I left the deck.

"It's Alan and Ty and, well . . . it sounded like a bunch of other people," said Angel, walking away from the intercom.

"Who'd ever think we'd be so popular?" I said, kissing him gently on the cheek. "And you promise to be a good boy?"

He fluttered his eyelids innocently. "What*ever* do you mean, Mr. Revere?"

I laughed and took him in my arms. "You know what I mean. I don't want you and Ty to start bashing the Penthouse in front of David and J.J."

"No promises." He lifted his head and quickly kissed me. "And anyway, those guys are the good guys. Well . . . at least I think they're the good guys *now*. If I had to rate assholes on a scale of one to ten, I'd put them at the bottom of . . . of . . . assholedness."

"Is that a Spanish word?"

"Kiss me . . . Wait! No time!" He turned away from me—giving my thigh the slightest squeeze—as the apartment door opened.

"Someone is going to die in that elevator one day," said Alan, leading the pack through the door and bearing a bottle of wine. "Has it ever even been inspected?"

"Sure," I said. "By the same guy who inspected the deck."

"Hello. My name is Alan Donovan, and I'll be partying in the kitchen tonight."

"Hey, kids," said Ty, all smiles as he kissed Angel, then me. "Hear the good news?"

"Brett doesn't talk to me anymore," said Alan. "For months it was yap-yap-yap about Operation Hamptons, but once I got him back in *Andy*, he went mute."

I ignored Alan and asked Ty, "*What* good news?"

He smiled. "*Cabaret*. I'll be playing the Emcee in the national tour as soon as Ricky Martin's contract expires."

I burst into laughter.

"What?" he asked.

"I think you should go out on the deck and tell that to Joey Takashimi."

Ty headed for the deck, and Angel leaned over to whisper: "You can be an evil bitch, can't you?"

"I try."

"And what if Joey flings himself off the deck to the concrete seven blocks below?"

I smiled, then he smiled as I said, "I'm an understudy. These sorts of things are to be expected. Now be quiet for a second."

We waited a three-count until Joey's enraged shriek was heard from the deck.

"What was that?" asked Paolo, whom I hadn't seen enter the apartment.

"The sound of an actor in heat," said Angel, who kissed his co-worker and added, "There's a lot of that going on tonight."

Paolo grabbed a beer out of the refrigerator and went to the deck, leaving Angel and me alone again.

"You know," he said, "we should be mingling."

"I know. But they're all doing such a good job of entertaining themselves . . ." The intercom rang once again. "Plus, we have more guests."

This group—the last, as it turned out—included Rick's lover, Bill, as well as two special guests.

"I love this apartment," said Clara Matthews, the moment she walked in the door.

"Great neighborhood," said Burt, on her heels. "*Real* people live up here."

I wasn't sure if he meant the neighborhood or our seventh-floor apartment, but he was right.

Real people lived up here. And *real* people were our guests.

And I silently congratulated myself on learning the difference between the real and artifice.

Not to mention saving my soul. That was important, too.

I poured Burt and Clara drinks and led them to the deck.

Hours later, after we had cleared out our guests, Angel and I lay in bed, eyes closed, ignoring the mess in every other room of the house and taking comfort in each other's arms.

"Do you ever miss it?" he asked, sleepily.

"Miss what?"

"The Penthouse? That life?"

"Do *you* miss it?"

He laughed. "You kidding? The night I quit was the highlight of my life." He rolled over, snuggling next to me. "One more year, I have my J.D. Then . . . then I can get a job with a law firm and take care of you in the style in which you had become accustomed, once upon a time."

My eyes still closed, I said, "Not Cooper Bauer Malnut, though, right? It's a great firm, but I don't know if I could stand the humiliation."

"Hmm . . . No promises." He nestled just a bit closer to me and said, "And then, one day, when we have money, I'll buy us tickets on an iron dragon and we'll go on an exciting adventure."

He smiled. I smiled. We drifted off to sleep.

I woke up at 4:42 A.M. to go to the bathroom. But maybe more than that, too. Most nights were like this, after all; interrupted by . . . the darkness of the night.

After I finished relieving myself, I walked to the foyer closet and rifled through topcoats until I found what I wanted.

It was a postcard, forwarded from my Astoria apartment, dated six weeks earlier.

Hey baby. Greetings from Ibiza. You'll never believe this, but I've met the greatest guy and fallen into the greatest situation. I miss you and wish you were here . . . We would have been fantastic forever.

Love,
Jamie

I knew he meant to write "fantastic *together*," not "fantastic *forever*," but still . . .

In a remarkable moment of clarity, I started ripping the postcard in half.

And then, well . . .

I put the postcard back in my winter coat and navigated through the darkness until I was back in my bed, lying next to the man I loved.

Some things just aren't meant to be, and it does no good to regret what never was.

And other things may have been meant to be, but didn't happen. Those are the things you regret in the dark of night, taking a small measure of comfort in the knowledge that the flights of fancy your mind takes—the *what-ifs* and the *if-onlys*—would certainly not work out the same way in real life.

And then you drift off to sleep, where they can. . . .

ACKNOWLEDGMENTS

I need to thank a few people. Indulge me.

Once again, my editor—John Scognamiglio—is the best, the reason you're reading this in book form, rather than from discarded sheets of paper scattered on the street after trash day. Nods, too, to Doug Mendini and Michael Vernon of Kensington Publishing.

My agent, Katherine Faussett of the Watkins/Loomis Agency, is awesome. Especially since looks like she's maybe twenty-one years old. But she's a zealous advocate for me and takes me for drinks to the Harvard Club, so it's all good.

Since I'm needy, I'm proud to have a circle of friends that keep me grounded and entertained. My posse (in alphabetical order, lest I be accused of playing favorites): Patrick Byer, Matthew Crawford, Lynette Kelly, Bob Liberio, Denise Murphy McGraw, Pam Paulding, Brian Scribner, Chris Shoolis, Lisa Stocker, Mark Zeller, and especially, Mark Siemens, who is out of alphabetical order because he sold me his computer in time to finish my manuscript and didn't even lean on me for payments. Special mention to Paul Donelan, who gave me insight into the world of . . . well, talent management, and Troy Cavaliere, who has been there for me when I've needed a graphic artist. I should also thank my long-suffering family: Dad and Trudy, Mom and Dave, Marje and John, Tim and Cheryl. You guys rock!

My day job is demanding, but with Mark Valenta, Bob Iovino, and Candace Taylor to watch my back, I have time to write after hours without having an ulcer eat me alive . . . usually. And I owe a retroactive nod to Matt Bauer, John Hunt, Lisa Maluf, and Danny Bernstein.

Thanks to the owners and staff at Posh (especially), the Townhouse, O.W., and xl in Manhattan; JR's in Washington, D.C.; Freddie's in Arlington, Virginia; and Nasty D's and the Avenue Pub in Rochester, New York. They've not only kept me well nourished over the years but given me ample opportunity to eavesdrop on conversations, many of which have found their way into print. Thanks, too, to Michael Holland and Karen Mack for being my friends, creating great cabaret, and providing my writing background music.

As always, the kids in the CompuServe Literary Forum are the best resources and better cheerleaders. Thanks especially to Margaret Campbell, John L. Myers, Mick LaMarca, Cady Santineau, Janet McConnaughey, Elise Skidmore, and Diana Gabaldon. And thanks forever to one of our CompuServe alumni, Rabih Alameddine, for more than I can say.

Finally, if you took all the love, support, and inspiration I've received from everyone else in these acknowledgments and wrapped it into one package, you'd have Brady Allen. It might be wrong to dedicate a book about cynical, deceitful people to Brady because that's not what he's about. But that's the way it is.